Michael Pytkiewicz is a South African author from the small town of Secunda, Mpumalanga, and is an advocate for mental health awareness and suicide. Having faced many ordeals of his own, he tries to raise awareness around such topics and engages in various events for these causes. Michael uses this novel to showcase how people can change through hard work, how important the relationships with others are and how people with mental illnesses suffer under the surface. Michael works in the financial services sector and is an active rugby player for Newbridge Rugby Club.

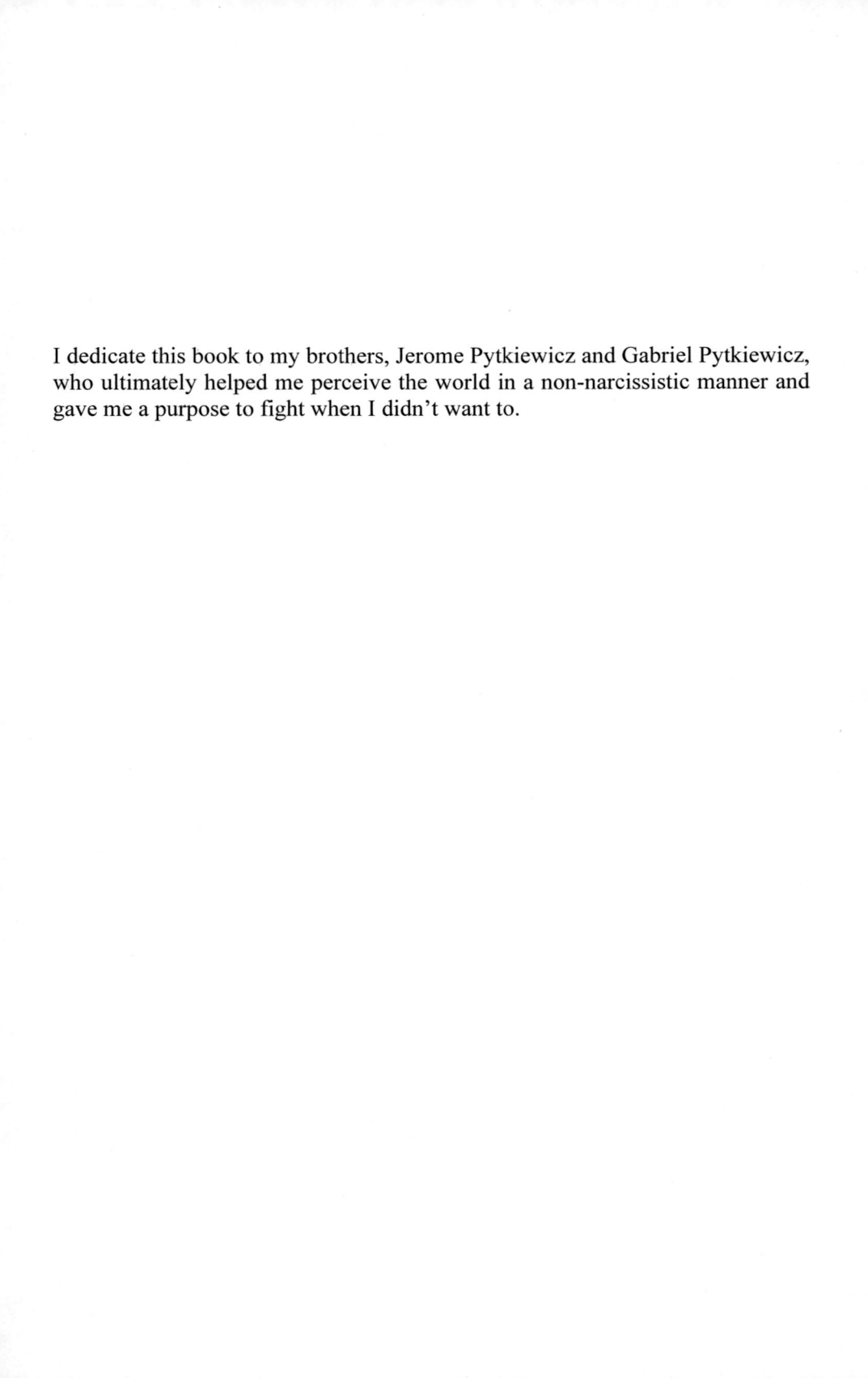

I dedicate this book to my brothers, Jerome Pytkiewicz and Gabriel Pytkiewicz, who ultimately helped me perceive the world in a non-narcissistic manner and gave me a purpose to fight when I didn't want to.

Michael Pytkiewicz

I AM ELLIOT

AUSTIN MACAULEY PUBLISHERS™
LONDON • CAMBRIDGE • NEW YORK • SHARJAH

Copyright © Michael Pytkiewicz (2020)

The right of Michael Pytkiewicz to be identified as author of this work has been asserted by the author in accordance with section 77 and 78 of the Copyright, Designs and Patents Act 1988.

All rights reserved. No part of this publication may be reproduced, stored in a retrieval system, or transmitted in any form or by any means, electronic, mechanical, photocopying, recording, or otherwise, without the prior permission of the publishers.

Any person who commits any unauthorised act in relation to this publication may be liable to criminal prosecution and civil claims for damages.

This is a work of fiction. Names, characters, businesses, places, events, locales, and incidents are either the products of the author's imagination or used in a fictitious manner. Any resemblance to actual persons, living or dead, or actual events is purely coincidental.

A CIP catalogue record for this title is available from the British Library.

ISBN 9781528938617 (Paperback)
ISBN 9781528969611 (ePub e-book)

www.austinmacauley.com

First Published (2020)
Austin Macauley Publishers Ltd
25 Canada Square
Canary Wharf
London
E14 5LQ

Chapter 1
Take a Hard Look

Hidden, about five kilometres away from civilisation, in a dark forest, shrouded by peerless pines and opulent oaks lies a large mahogany coloured, cottage styled home. With support pillars on the porch, holding the upstairs terrace in place and a fancy black SUV out front. There's the pleasant sight of a small lake some 75 m from the front door, where both the sun and the moon place their reflections. This isolated dwelling is a prison for most but a palace for one...one of obscure nature and a haunting past...one Elliot Smith. This abode; a purchase made five years prior with no debt or credit, just smart investments and extraordinary savings, is a dream come true, a goal reached for this peculiar man.

A matte-red tie, half undone, but still knotted...an overdue five o'clock shadow and the lingering scent of hard liquor shapes the 'successful' image Elliot created for himself. He walks over to his open planned lounging area, places his hands behind his head and lets out a slimy, crackling sigh as he throws himself onto this dark brown three-seater sofa piece in front of the fire he lit an hour prior. He seems on edge, slightly under pressure, but not family life pressure, not work pressure, it's something deeper, something he tried burying a long time ago, hoping it wouldn't come back to haunt him, something he knows he wants to get off his chest.

The mood is deep and persistent; a thunderstorm slowly brews up outside, thick, white smoke rises from the chimney, and an unclosed window creates the stereotypical howling sound from a 90s horror movie. Staring at the almost burnt-out flames, Elliot reaches for his just-about-empty tumbler, filled with his favourite Scotch whiskey on the rocks. He sips it slowly while the reflections of the flames dance loudly in his glassy eyes, feeding his unsteady soul. He snaps out of it and puts the empty glass down on the table beside him. With a drunken swoop forward, he gets his intoxicated self up, almost planting his face into the freshly polished flooring. Elliot walks over to the slightly dusty, vintage record player in the corner of the room; a prize he acquired after outbidding a classic collector from Sweden. He reaches for his favourite record, a classic, Beethoven, blows the dust from it and places it in position. Elliot rotates the crank three times and lowers the arm so that the diamond point stylus lies on the very start of the record. An empty, soft, crackling sound fills the room, inflating the drunk with anxiety, but the tune starts playing harmoniously a few seconds later. Elliot's eyes close and a tiny smug smile is let out in acceptance of the musical masterpiece. The classicals have always calmed him down, even when he was a mere lad, but the photos of a long-forgotten home and the haunting memories unpleasantly mix with the seven glasses of whiskey frothing in his belly, making it harder for him to relax, to find this inner peace he fought so hard trying to discover. Tonight, will be harder than most. Elliot finds himself lost in the sounds of an era long gone, humming to the tune coming from the old music box, but before his background vocals can assist the perfect melody, he feels a tingle in his urethra. He backs away from the sounds and makes his way to the bathroom. *Down the hall, third door on the right*, something he mentions to most of his one-night stands that prefer sex in front of naked flames opposed to the traditional bedroom. After stumbling and nearly falling over a few times, he finds himself on his feet, hovering over the toilet, going about his business; his aim isn't on par tonight, the whiskey clearly beating him like a red-headed stepchild. He starts criticising his actions, *how did you pull all those ladies? You clearly don't know how to use it. I'm actually surprised your dick hasn't fallen off because of your slutty ways.* The feel-sorry-for-myself argument goes on, getting louder and more intense, it shifts from the porcelain bowl to the huge 1.5m x 1m rectangular mirror he installed on his own a while back. This is a common occurrence in this lonely household, he just wants someone to be there, to argue back, to never leave while he's talking or making valid points, and he knows that the man in the mirror is stubborn, and that he won't leave a fight that easy. The reflection starts bringing up the past, telling him how he could have changed things, how he could have made them better for himself and the ones around him, but Elliot's only replies are excuses. It becomes more severe as profanity starts flying back and forth, both getting agitated with one another, the pure look of hate shines bright in Elliot's eyes. He grinds his teeth as the reflection continues to insult him, pillorying his existence. "Enough!" he cries out in front of an audience of hand sanitizers, fresh towels and a French vanilla-scented candle positioned at the edge of the counter. Elliot punches the reflection square in the nose, ending the conversation right there. The impact leaves his hand lacerated and the mirror, shattered, with sharp pieces dispersed all over the counter top, in the sink and on the floor; luckily none stuck in his knuckles. The pain and sight of blood help him snap out of this argumentative state, allowing him to realise what he's done. He falls down, nearly kneeling into the reflective shards, upset with his own self and the embarrassing situation. Elliot gets emotional and starts to whimper, the words that the reflection shared were true, and were starting to engrave themselves in his mind. He stands up from the cold, tiled floor and reaches into the medicine cabinet, scratching around for an anti-septic liquid bottle and a bandage. Elliot leans over the basin, still in a drunken state, and starts pouring the fiery-orange liquid over his wound, "Ah fuck!" he cries out as the stinging begins. He wraps the bandage tightly around his right hand, hoping that the bleeding doesn't persist into the night. Elliot makes his way back to the lounge; a bit steadier compared to his previous trip, and fills his tumbler up to the halfway mark with The Devil's Mouthwash. He knows that he has had too much and should probably sleep it off, but he's angry with himself, the world, his past, his actions, and the lack of time machines in this day and age. Elliot switches the TV on and starts flicking through the Dutch channels that are available to him. After about 14 channels, something catches his attention; it's a man, presumably in his 40s, speaking to a teenage girl, the caption at the bottom reads 'Self-mutilation as a scapegoat', interested, Elliot starts paying close attention. The presenter, more than likely a psychologist, says something special, "Every time you want to cut or burn yourself, write down on a sheet why you want to do it. The thing that most people get wrong…is not understanding that they control their own feelings, that they choose their happiness. When we are faced with tough situations, it can affect how we think, and limit our perceptions on how to get out of it. Writing down feelings and thoughts is a good way to track progress out of a certain situation, a good way to express feelings without conforming to the notion that you need to respect the people around you, you just write what you feel, and keep it to yourself. Once you have the black and white in front of you, it makes it much easier to decide on how to approach the issue."

He sips his whiskey and comes up with an idea; "I can do the same, write down all the things that affected me in life, and then see whether I approached them correctly or not. Hopefully, it will help me cope with thoughts." *It's a great idea,* Elliot thinks to himself, and possibly the only solution to his issues, seeing that he's already wasted thousands on psychologists, hunting, fishing, extreme sports, smoking, yoga, meditation, the works. Maybe instead of running to other people with tons of money and participating in meaningless activities, he should have been there for himself. Writing isn't a hard task for him, he used to excel at it in his younger years, a top student in high school. People admired his poetry, essays and short stories, but he gave up on it a long time ago, after writing a beautiful, innocent poem to a girl that showed no interest towards him or his sweet words. Elliot downs the rest of his glass and starts looking around for a notepad and a pen. He finds nothing but financial reads, WW2 books, coins and phone numbers written on pieces of paper from women he met in bars. After searching almost everywhere, he finally finds 2 blank pages in the back of an old notepad that he uses in meetings. Elliot briefly reads through some notes he took, "Productivity is key, we need to inspire those around us and under us, with enthusiasm… lead by example." It's not that he was a slacker or didn't care about things being said in those meetings, Elliot was more of a listener and a thinker, being able to visualise the words being said and placing them in proper scenarios, besides he led by example and would never let anyone feel left out or alone. Excited to begin this chapter of 'self-help', he starts spinning and flicking a black, ballpoint pen in his left hand, eager to write, contemplating his beginning. He walks over to his six-seater dining room table, anxious to get the shit off his chest. He sits down at the head of the table; where the man of the house should sit, just as his father taught him when he was a young boy asking too many questions.

Elliot presses down the top button of his pen and starts…

"In order to know where we are going, we need to know where we have been." He rewrites a famous quote by David McCullogh, but with a twist of his own. Elliot always loved inspiring quotes and phrases that were passed on by positive, determined people through the ages, often using them to inspire the people he worked with; keeping their spirits up and the atmosphere pleasant. Maybe it's so that people view him as a positive, emotionally stable person who has all the answers; a slight manipulative play from behind the disfigured mask. Maybe deep down they actually mean something to him and he really cares about the people around him too.

"I've not always been a man of feedback, but I took all the criticism over the years, and tried to shape myself into a flawless gem," he continues to write, "Sadly I know now, that I can never be, nor can anyone else…there will always be a crack or a scratch, ruining the integrity of the stone," he openly admits to the thin blue lines on the sheet.

"However, the only person that can possibly know me for who I am and understand my way of thinking is me…therefore I am writing this…to allow myself to criticise myself and get feedback from myself. To see what I've done, and where I'm going, to document my existence before I leave this planet for the next chapter of life." He pitifully portrays before standing up to get the rest of the booze. Elliot places his right hand on the neck of the bottle, taking a huge swig of whiskey, before gasping loudly as his throat turns into a furnace. The bandage on his hand gets doubled as a cloth to wipe the droplets of alcohol from his wet lips. He was never much of a drinker, maybe the occasional drink at the bar in town to meet someone; to quench his sexually deprived thirst, or at home to ease the pain, but it has gotten out of hand recently. Elliot sits back down at the large oak table, ready to conquer his demons with a pen, but his eyes are getting heavy, consciousness starting to disappear due to the booze overload. Mr Smith's neck weakens, even with his head resting on his right hand. He puts the pen down, allowing both hands to hold his head up while he closes his eyes just for a minute. *'Ding Dong...'* the long case clock atop the fireplace sounds, echoing through the house like a church bell at a funeral. Elliot jumps up with a fright, like a child getting caught doing something naughty by his mother. He looks at the expensive gold analogue watch on his right wrist; the traditional left wrist for a man doesn't work so well for a left-handed person; the writing hand should always be free from obstruction and weight, he notices that it's midnight. He lets out a few moans and groans, like a child who wants to stay up to watch a bit more TV, but Elliot knows that bed would be the best thing now. He stands up, slowly making his way to his bedroom, swaying from side to side before falling against a wall and sliding down to the cold floor. He crawls for about a metre and gets up; focused on reaching that bed, if it's the last he does tonight. Success! He reaches his chamber of nightmares. He takes three drunken steps and lands on his 'pristine' white-covered bed, face first, straight into a pillow, no tucking himself in, no getting under the covers, passing out instantly. The big, lonely, king-sized bed eats him up, consuming him like a sandwich in the hands of a bricklayer. This bed, a shrine of memories…bitter-sweet memories; with the one he used to love every night, and ones that used to love him most nights. This non-virgin furnishing is a place of comfort, 'a fortress of solitude' for him and his painful past.

The hours of drunken slumber pass by restlessly, Elliot is already sweating buckets and his breathing grows heavier. The repulsive stench of stale liquor fills the room rapidly due to his respiratory pattern and the fact that there are no open windows to evict the odour. It's the same re-occurring nightmare, accompanied by visions of his puckish reflection… "No!" he cries out loudly before regaining consciousness and coming back to his senses. He's seated up right, panting like an old dog, staring into the darkness of the room, the sickening taste of booze still on his tongue. After a few minutes of trying to calm down and finding his bearings, he hears a bird tweeting beautifully outside, indicating that it may already be morning. Elliot stretches out, reaching for the bedside lamp, the time is needed; not that it matters because it's a Saturday. 05:47…too early for him, but the booze is still settling down and the hangover is arising from deep within the bowels. "Never…again," he manages to push out a dry, sore throat, as he coughs up a bit of slime. He gets up and removes his clothing; still the same outfit as yesterday, surprised that the tie didn't choke him to death in his sleep for his atrocities. He starts undoing the buttons on his dress shirt and notices the bandage, questioning his belief to it all being a nightmare. Elliot takes his shirt off and rushes over to the bathroom to investigate. There's dry blood all over the counter top, in the basin and on the floor, glass pieces scattered in every direction, orange residue from the anti-septic liquid dried up inside the right-hand side of the basin and a huge hole in the centre of his fancy mirror. He quickly realises that his actions weren't dream bound and that this was a sad, disturbing reality. Elliot becomes hesitant in his decision-making for the situation in front of him, listing the pros and cons mentally, its either clean the place up, which he has to do either way, or clean the wound and wait till it's healed before straining it with labour. Elliot realises how childish he is being and heads over to the kitchen, wearing nothing but the slacks he wore the previous day. He finds a broom, a dust pan and a mop in his utility closet, and proceeds to clean the bathroom like a responsible adult, watching where he steps with his bare feet. Elliot cautiously picks the sharp particles out of the basin and places them into the dust pan, turning the cold water on and allowing the smaller fragments to be flushed down the sink. Once the shards clear up, he wipes the blood and anti-septic stains from the sides of the basin, and proceeds to clean the rest of the bathroom. The entire floor gets swept and mopped back to a decent state, despite the huge displeasing sight of a broken mirror and the reminder of seven years of bad luck. Elliot starts removing the bandage from his hand; "Fuck!" he exclaims as he separates the material that seemed to have merged with his skin in the few hours it had been on. He grabs the last of the cotton balls from the cabinet, and pours the disinfectant over them, ready to clean his wounds, expecting a little sting due to the wounds still being slightly open. Elliot hops into the shower and starts scrubbing himself clean, an uneasy task with his right hand stretched out to avoid the water from contaminating his efforts. Twenty-five minutes pass, and he has waxed his hair with one hand, brushed his teeth and applied a few squirts of his favourite €125 cologne. He heads to his room to get dressed, pulls out a black polo, with dark blue jeans and begins contemplating whether writing this therapeutic book is worth it. He has to head out into town for a few groceries anyways, so he might as well just get a new notepad and continue once he's back, *no harm in trying*, he convinces himself. Once dressed, with fallow coloured Chelsea boots on, and his SUV's keys in hand, he proceeds out towards the front door. A fresh morning smell hits his nose, the sunrise, softly glistening on the lake's undisturbed water and the sight of two rabbits chasing one another in the far treeline sets in motion a positive tone for the day ahead. Elliot gets into the vehicle and starts it, leaving it to idle as he searches for his aviators; the sunny morning is going to play with his eyes. He opens the glove compartment and starts digging around, finding a collection of strange items; lighters, half a cigarette, playing cards, toilet paper, mouthwash and even a black bra with pink polka dots, amidst the mess…he finds what he was looking for. He puts his 'noble steed' into first gear and follows the gravel pathway that later joins a proper tarred road, which then leads to a small town called Aalst, located between the great city of Eindhoven and Waalre. Elliot isn't originally from the Netherlands, not even from Europe for that matter, but this is what he chose when he was 20 years of age; a decision he doesn't regret one bit, even though it cost him a lot. He checks the time on his watch and realises that the shop won't be open for another 47 minutes, so he takes a little detour, a more scenic route, along the outskirts of Eindhoven. There are a few kids playing football on this sunny, Saturday morning, trying to be the next Pele, Messi or even Van Persie. There's a couple of elderly people walking around, some reminiscing and others walking pets. Elliot leisurely drives under a canopy of green trees, greeting someone every so often, watching the kids dribble to their friends. He does this because he is lonely, all he has other than his above average wealth, are the people at work and a house filled with emptiness. This route is a few extra cents toward the gas bill and a few extra kilometres on the dial, but it's worth it, to see a bit of fun and civilisation. It's a confusing way of life for most to understand, because despite the loneliness and sense of solidarity which he clearly enjoys and chose, he also misses human interaction and company. The only conversations he is blessed with are those at work or at the shop when Margaret asks him if he would like a bag for an extra 75 cents.

Elliot takes a left onto some random street, waving at the few people that know him; he isn't exactly renowned but a few people do recognise his face and they wave back. He used to captain the Eindhoven Rugby Team, even though it wasn't as big as the London Wasps or Munster. He also ran a few marathons for causes such as suicide awareness and fund raisers for local orphanages. Among his generous acts were little get-togethers with colleagues to maximise clothing donations for the homeless every winter. Secretly, he does these things to allow other people to accept and acknowledge him because he has had a very hard time accepting himself.

This slow-moving adventure grows boring and Elliot starts heading towards the local super market. He parks his SUV in the second designated spot closest to the store, just in case someone has plans of getting a lot of groceries; this would save them walking another two metres. There are about six cars parked there already, three of which probably belong to employees, indicating that the store is rather quiet. The sensors of the automatic sliding doors pick up on Elliot as he approaches the store, provisioning him an entry. Elliot walks in, '*Stationary…stationary,*' he mumbles to himself whilst anxiously looking up at all the Dutch signs hanging from the ceiling. He isn't a native Dutch speaker, but has been living there long enough to secure confidence in the language, besides it's very similar to Afrikaans; which he does know. The signs don't resemble anything close to what he's in search of, so he starts rushing through the aisles, scanning for either notepads or empty books that he can use. Elliot leaves the third aisle and rushes into the next one; the frozen section, making a sharp left turn, proceeding into what he knows won't be the correct aisle either. On his turn, Elliot bumps into a woman, knocking her and the items she had in her basket all over the cold floor. "I'm so sorry, miss," he manages to politely mention, trying to avoid any conflict or a scene, offering his hand to help her up.

"It's fine, don't worry about it," she says as she moves her fringe, which was hovering over her right eye, to behind her ear. She looks up at Elliot as she grabs his hand, he is astonished, he hasn't seen such a beautiful creature around these parts before; bright blue eyes, medium-length brown hair, luscious natural pink lips and a voice dipped in honey, either it's the whiskey really fucking with his stomach or he's got butterflies. Elliot hesitates a tad and starts picking up her groceries; a pack of frozen peas, a box of green tea, an energy drink (that's well shook by now), a few cuts of meat that are part of a *Three items for €12* deal, and a pack of tampons. The embarrassment sinks in and she starts shying away from the awkwardness.

"Sorry, I don't mean to intrude, I'm just trying to help," Elliot quietly whispers as he understands the situation she is faced with. He was always a sucker for blue eyes, those shy types, that petite girl figure. He starts thinking to himself, '*What are the chances of crashing into the perfect woman here?*' He's a bit too quick to judge, but he always fell for 'em fast. "I am Elliot by the way," he politely states as he raises his left hand to greet her; he is no coward when it comes to chatting to women, but the scenario he is faced with this time is different, there's something else at play here. She kindly stretches out her left hand to greet him, knowing that this isn't the traditional hand but taking note of the bandage on his right.

"I'm Katrien," she sheepishly informs him as she gives a soft, delicate handshake.

"I'm really sorry for knocking you over Katrien, I was just looking for a notepad and wasn't paying attention," he apologetically informs her as she lets go of his hand to dust herself off.

"It's okay, Mr Elliot, we all make mistakes from time to time," she tells him with a cute, warm smile, either being sarcastic or flirtatiously playful. She seems very independent, mentally strong, but there's definitely something holding her back, something weighing her confidence down, perhaps just a bad day? Perhaps a former lover that broke her down? Perhaps something else…

Elliot knows that the conversation is still at pleasantries and doesn't want it to die out, she'll go home and they'll never see each other again, he can't let that happen, he wants that face in his life; he needs to know where this will go. "I haven't seen you around here before, are you new to the area?" he expeditiously asks before she can even hint at the idea of leaving his presence.

"Oh no, I'm from Luyksgestel, near the Belgian border. I just came to visit a friend in the area and needed some stuff," she innocently avows.

"Oh, that's nice, is it a nice area?" Elliot asks, trying to keep the conversation going. "Yeah, it's quiet and beautiful," Katrien states, trying to kill the awkward interrogation.

"Well, have a good day, miss, and again I am so sorry about bumping into you," Elliot sadly says, knowing that the conversation has died.

"Thank you very much; you have a good day too!" Katrien says as she turns and starts walking around the corner. Elliot kind of knew that he couldn't push it anymore, it would seem too desperate, he doesn't want to seem like a creep, but he blew it nonetheless.

"Notepads are two aisles up, Mr Elliot," Katrien mentions as she quickly pops back around the corner to get a final glimpse of the 5'11", tanned man that seemed well-mannered and polite.

"Thank you so much," Elliot gratefully says as he starts walking in the opposite direction in search of them. She likes him, or so he thinks, but it's clear that he likes her, and at least he's gathered some information so there may be a chance.

Elliot skips the next aisle and walks into the second one, as Katrien suggested, trusting her blindly. He finds a variety of pads, takes two and heads through the other sections, acquiring the groceries he initially intended on getting. He proceeds to the checkouts, for his daily chat with Margaret, pays for his goods and walks out like a man on a mission. Elliot puts the goods in the back seat of his car, takes a glance around the parking lot, hoping to see if Katrien is still around. Unsuccessful in his search he gets on the driver's side of his car and heads home. On his way home, he tries planning on how he'll go about writing; will he just write down everything according to a timeline, mapping life changing events, giving feedback in the end, or will he just write and add feedback as he progresses? Does he even need to write the feedback? What's wrong with a mental note? The ideas swarm his mind, but in the background of these constructive thoughts, all he can see is Katrien's perfect face, smiling back at him. Elliot parks his car in its designated spot; under a tree, in the shade because the car is black and it's a warm day. The front door of this mad man's Manor opens with a creek, and he steps in, removing one shoe with the other and the other with his foot; trying to avoid traipsing dirt all over his glossy brown flooring. With hands full of groceries, he walks over to the kitchen area and places the goods down on the counter; where he prepares his meals. He takes the notepads from the pile and puts them on the table where he will be working, pours himself a glass of water from the tap and takes his seat.

Chapter 2
Baby Steps

Elliot rewrites what he had written down the previous night in the new pad and continues with what he has in mind.
So here goes... He writes down before skipping two lines.

18:10, September the 8th, 1994, a fresh spring evening in the small town of Trichardt, Transvaal, South Africa. The cries of what appears to be a healthy baby boy...me. In a big room of a private hospital, I begin with this thing called life, with an eye for an eye concept, my rebellion begins; the doctor smacks my bottom and I piss on him, simple as that. The first born of two interesting, yet crucial individuals; Sylvain, a simple, modest and humble man, intelligent beyond his appearance, kind, yet hard, and Audrey, an ambitious, self-inspired, tea loving girl...not yet a woman. This awkwardly put together couple, married for two years at the time, tried for a baby from Day 1; doctors, drugs, tests, priests, positions, foods, but to no avail, but then one day my mom took a pregnancy test and it ended up being positive. What influenced the fertilisation is beyond me, and I can't bare another story...

Audrey was 18 at the time of my birth and Sylvain was 38...a huge age gap and what some may refer to as 'cradle snatching'. But age is just a number, as they say.

My existence started proving difficult for the inexperienced folks. The issues were far greater than the normal crying in the middle of the night, the constant need to be picked up every five minutes and the shitting all over the place. My inability to see; indicating blindness, inability to hear; indicating I'd be a deaf, and an epileptic fit that completely shattered my father's hopes and dreams for me, as well as the refusal of sucking on a nipple for food, which saw my mother cry a lot, thinking I'd die of starvation. Sylvain's patience grew thin, to a point where he started verbally abusing Audrey and started locking me up in a dark room, forcing me to man up. Audrey on the other hand, grew despondent with life, slowly wanting to quit. Franky, my mother's mother, that once had my father arrested on suspicions of rape, came by every so often to lift Audrey's spirits and teach her some parenting tricks...but in life we are all prone to human error eventually.

As time went on, they became more acquainted and more experienced with parenthood, instead of growing apart, they grew together, as lovers and as parents, the way it should be. Sylvain's violent outbursts calmed down completely, I wasn't isolated in darkness anymore and Audrey's face dried up from the regular waterworks. The poor neighbours... They had all made bets on how long this couple could go on, before complete failure and the termination of their relationship... Take that ye fuckers!

For the first time, life started looking good for the Nowak household, despite the disabilities which the doctors were still trying to figure out. The man of the house, working in a local mine; a prestigious position in the 90s, and bringing home a decent salary, started enjoying time with his first-born son, cuddling me and letting me fall asleep on his chest while he ran his fingers through my dark brown curly hair. I may not have had a conscience or memory at the time, but I know it was one of my favourite memories. The very inexperienced Audrey went from a terrified mother and amateur cook, who on one occasion put concentrated raspberry juice in a pot of boiling rice in order to change the colour so that she could dine Sylvain in fancy cuisine, to a great, confident nurturer, who became her family's favourite chef. As for me, I was driven back and forth, to and fro doctors, undergoing tests for my eyesight and hearing abilities, only to find that I was completely fine. I just showed no interest in listening or interacting with stuff placed in front of me, except the teddy my father bought me to comfort me throughout these tests.

What really influenced the great change in my parents and their parenting skills, in my opinion, were my grandparent's presence and their ability to help. They may not have been the greatest parents for my mother, but they made up for it by being there to better my circumstances. John, Audrey's stepfather, probably of Scottish descent, and Frankie, Rhodesian by nationality, but from German routes; both heavy drinkers and a messy couple, went from top of the food chain, to the bottom of the barrel and all the way back again, a never-ending cycle throughout their lives. Their drinking habits mainly fluctuated with John's inability to keep a job or stay in the same career for longer than a month, and this ultimately led to the abuse, sexual harassment and total negligence of Audrey and her half-sister Sonja, who is the definition of 'the apple didn't fall far from the tree'. How the universe brought the Rhodesian Audrey and French-born Sylvain together under a South African flag is a mystery. From my knowledge, they met in a super market, my mother playing the role of 14-year old cashier and my father the role of 34-year old customer. She rejected him and his romantic interest for a bit, but gave in and fell for him, she stayed over at his place one time and that's where the rape rumour came in, tests came back indicating that she was still a virgin, he was set free and my grandparents agreed to the marriage when she was 16, and the rest is history.

Despite the rest of that time frame being a blur to me due to my inability to grasp reality, there were several perks in this 'era'. I was a born free, meaning that I, based on my Caucasian ethnicity, didn't need to conform to the regulations undermining the black community, I was able to befriend anyone I wanted too, and due to me being of foreign descent there would be an opportunity for me in the future. I was living the life, and had no concept of the English language yet, all I understood was 'mamam', my word for food. It was not till November of the following year where another chapter of my life would begin, one of the most crucial pieces in shaping me into the man I am today...

Elliot puts the pen down and stares out across the room, at the half-empty whiskey bottle. "Not today, Satan," he mumbles, initially contemplating drowning him and his sorrows in booze once again. He finishes the water left in the glass and gets up, heading towards the front door. Standing on the porch, in the middle of Strabrecht, overlooking the Wasven Lake, Elliot ponders whether he should go for a walk through the woods before it gets dark, or try and find some popsy scapegoat to ease the infatuated longing for Katrien. How do you possibly long for someone you don't know? Was it the pleasant smile that lasted like 19 seconds? The solicitous chemistry they may share? The random butterfly feeling he felt when he looked down at her for the first time? It's strange for him, to find one voluptuous woman, who took his breath away like a first crush, in a city of over 250,000 people. Elliot starts walking in the direction of the woods, trying to plan his writings, to walk off the image of her. This boscage in the southeast part of The Netherlands is a tranquil, undisturbed yet perilous place; due to some bodies being uncovered there and the occasional wild boar encounter. This maritime climate is home to many types of animal life; the endangered European Mink, and of course, the Beech Marten that is native to the country.

Elliot inhales the fresh air, pacing himself slowly on this outing, he is a real fan of the outdoors and is receiving all the perks nature has to offer on this walk; purple herons flying about, here for the summer, a rare arcane, a goshawk sitting on the branch of a tree, hares and weasels alike, and all of this under a warm Dutch sun. He thinks to himself, *How does God create something so magnificent and abandon it?* Families and couples pass by him, seems like they had the same idea on this overall congenial day.

Elliot finds himself at home, *hungry like a wolf*, but too lazy to cook anything. He looks at his watch, 17:23, pondering driving down to the town of Luyksgestel, to grab something to nibble on, hoping to test the possibility of bumping into Katrien (pun intended). Back into the SUV the desperate man goes, charging towards the Belgian Border via the N-69, luckily there is no congestion or traffic on this clear-skied evening. Upon arrival, Elliot discovers that the town isn't as big as Aalst, and not even a quarter the size of Eindhoven, but it isn't small either, finding Katrien will still prove to be difficult, especially on a Saturday evening. Besides, what if she's still at her friend's house? *You're stupid, Elliot*, he becomes disheartened and tells himself as he gives up on the possibilities, parking his car next to what seems to be an old man's pub, ready to grab some grub, and head back home. He opens the door to this placid place and discreetly makes his way inside, unaccustomed to the folk of this community. It's a typical bar scene; a few old men watching some sport on the overhead TVs, freshly-watered plants in almost every corner of the room, and traditional rock faintly playing over the speakers. Elliot saunters up to the bar, grabbing a food menu that lay on the counter, left behind by some patron after their order was placed.

After scanning through the list of available cuisine, the head chef appears; apron smudged with grease and ketchup; hopefully. "Welcome, have you been served yet?" the chef exhorts, annoyed at something, maybe it's been a long day.

"No, not yet," Elliot politely informs the bulky man on the other side of the counter. The chef turns to his side; facing what appears to be the kitchen, shouting out in Dutch, "Kat! Come and do your job!"

A soft, almost inaudible, "Yes, sir!" is yelled back at him, undoubtedly from this Kat character. Elliot turns his back on the bar and takes no notice of the situation behind him, admiring the relaxed atmosphere associated with this place. The chef walks away as the barmaid comes over to get Elliot's order.

"Hi, sorry for the wait, sir, what can I get you?" she courteously asks in Dutch. Elliot's back is still turned, but the voice seems familiar, so he turns to face the person addressing him, it's Katrien, what are the chances? "Mr Elliot... What are you doing here?" she enthusiastically asks before he even attempts to greet her. "Are you stalking me?" she quips as the surprise dies down.

"Hey–hey," he stutters at her, flustered with hesitation, "I didn't expect to see you here…or…ever again," Elliot pessimistically responds, but he knows that this is exactly what he wanted. "No, not stalking you at all," he retaliates with a fatuous chuckle. Elliot realises that he can't order a huge meal now, because; (i) he doesn't want to eat on his own, especially not in front of her. (ii) he can't enjoy his food while she slaves away for what seems to be minimum wage and (iii) barmaids don't usually engage in conversation while patrons are eating.

"So, can I get you anything?" Katrien politely offers, noticing the chef diligently watching her from the kitchen.

"Uhm…yeah, just a pint of stout to start with please," Elliot quickly responds, trying to adhere to his previous thoughts. She walks over to the tap and starts filling the freshly polished glass with a famous Irish dry stout, making the biggest mistake in any Irishman's eyes; not leaving it to settle for a few minutes before filling it to the brim. He forgives her and takes a sip, letting out that sigh of acceptance most beer-drinkers tend to have. A conversation sets off, and seems to hold, despite the frequent interruptions by other clients looking to get their fix. Elliot orders a large plate of chips with some goujons, trying to ease his exposure to an inevitable famine, but decides to share the platter with Katrien; who steals a chip here and there when the head chef isn't looking. He notices that her English isn't perfect, it's slightly broken, backed with a genuine Dutch accent, but it's cute to him. His favourite feature is her nose, the celestial type; the sky bound tip, but it's hard to pick a favourite feature when everything looks like heaven to him. The bar starts filling up fast, reaching a tad over half the maximum capacity, it seems that this is where all the young ones go to pre-drink before heading to a club. Katrien is getting busier with the rapid increase of customers, even the chef has closed the kitchen and put on a regular shirt, to stand in as a bartender; easing the customer-to-server ratio. Elliot sees no point in staying any longer, she is too busy to hold a proper conversation and staying there will only look desperate, so he finishes his second pint and stands up, ready to leave; at least now he knows where she works and where to find her. Elliot turns around, ready to leave the packed establishment after leaving his due and a tip on the counter, but before he can take a step towards the exit, Katrien calls out his name over augmenting ambience. She tells him to wait a second while she quickly turns around, grabbing a napkin, along with a pen, hastily jotting something down. She timidly hands him the unorthodox writing apparatus, nervously saying

"Call me sometime."

"Sure," he responds, smiling at her before turning towards the exit.

Elliot gets into his car, but before starting her up he opens the note and reads the additional comment that she added along with her phone number: 'Katrien x'. He doesn't understand why she's written her name, obviously he knows that it's her, but maybe she doesn't want to be forgotten, assuming that he's just a player and she's just one of many. With the biggest smile on his face he places the key in the ignition of the car and starts the engine, second-guessing himself; operating machinery whilst under the influence. He doesn't feel drunk, and will probably make it home safe, but the law is the law, and Dutch Police don't take shit. The devil on his shoulder swings around his neck, kicking the angel on the other side off, leaving the *it's only 2 beers* tune playing in his mind. Elliot avoids highways and main roads, using nothing but back routes that are more time consuming, but safer. He drives carefully, trying to keep a low profile, but it's parlous, especially in a vehicle that's popular amongst mafia and gangsters. Murphy's Law reaches out to greet Elliot, and a police siren is heard. He looks in the review mirror, hopeful that they're just rushing past for something else, but the two headlight flashes eradicate all optimistic thoughts.

"Fuck!" Elliot exclaims as he lowers his speed and starts pulling over; the devil makes a run for it, leaving the angel just shaking her head in disappointment.

He awaits the officers, who approach towards the vehicle, but remembers a trick he learnt as a devious adolescent who had a tendency to always be in trouble, and quickly reaches for the glove compartment, grabbing the mouthwash he noticed earlier. Elliot takes a swig, swirls it around in his mouth for a few seconds before spitting it back into the container, and throwing the bottle into the cubbyhole. The officer approaches the window and starts off in Dutch, but he's quickly corrected by a firm voice demanding English.

"Ahh…sorry! How are things tonight, sir?" the officer continues.

"All good thanks and yourself, officer?" Elliot responds politely.

"Good… Any drinking tonight?" the law enforcer asks him.

"No, ha-ha…not yet, I have a date at this lady's house, so I may have a glass of wine there," Elliot feigns, hoping for the best. His charm works on most people, but he has never tried it on a cop before, luckily the strong, minty smell of mouthwash is masking the barley and hops pretty well.

The officer looks uninterested with his statement of possible coitus, and asks for his licence and registration before walking to his car to check the validity. All the papers check out and the officer returns to the SUV, but before he sends Elliot on his merry way, the second officer comes out, interrupting the dismissal of this innocent citizen, with horrible broken English.

"Sorry, sir, you fail to indicate when turning on this road, so I am asking if you have drink tonight?"

"No, as I informed your partner here, I am still on my way to get drunk, with a female, hence the strong smell of mint," Elliot sarcastically answers. The annoying brat of a cop, with less than a year of experience on the force blindsides his claim and asks.

"So you would not have problem doing breathalyser test?"

Who the fuck is this annoying piece of shit? He's going to expose me, Elliot thinks to himself before agreeing to the test. The initial officer apologises for the continuation of this traffic stop, while his partner runs to the squad car to acquire the dreaded device. The inexperienced officer returns, asking

"Would you blow this?" Elliot and the older officer let out a little chuckle. The baby-faced policeman doesn't realise what he has said, but he's too focused on protecting and serving.

"Yeah, sure," Elliot says as he grabs the device. *This is going to be a tough one to get out of,* Elliot thinks to himself as he blows into the device. It surpasses the legal limit by a bit.

"Please step out of the car," the brat commands.

"I can explain!" Elliot states, hoping that they will spare him another minute to hear him out.

The younger officer isn't interested in excuses, but before he can place the handcuffs on Elliot's tattooed wrists, the older officer asks Elliot to proceed.

"Thanks, I honestly didn't drink, I can do a blood test, walk in a straight line and anything you want. The reason I am over the limit is because I am going to this lady's house and I really want to impress her, so I used mouthwash. Everyone knows that the alcohol inside it kills bacteria," Elliot pleads out, being well-read, cunning and sticking to the liars code of following through with the fib.

"How do we believe you?" the young officer asks, annoyed at the fact that he can't just take this drunk off the street and get credit from the chief.

"The mouthwash is in the glove compartment…take a sip, spit it out and then test yourself, you will see you are over the limit," Elliot states, knowing that he is totally in control of this situation now.

The older officer isn't very interested in what's happening, Elliot wasn't severely over the limit and the mouthwash theory makes sense. He orders the other officer back to the car as he apologises to Elliot and asks him to be careful with his methods of freshening up, suggesting mints or even waiting until he arrives at her house, and sends Elliot on his way. Elliot starts the car and proceeds home, still in shock as to how he managed that escape, *That shouldn't have happened*, he thinks to himself. Upon arriving home, after what seemed to be a very eventful day, Elliot contemplates going on with his writing, but every ounce of him just wants to sleep; he has been operating with only five hours of sleep to his name.

Chapter 3
Toddle Tale

Elliot is having a reasonably good sleep, despite having gone to bed anxious a few hours earlier; the ambitious feeling of beginning something so profound clashes a lot with the regretful pain associated with those writings. On top of the internal battle, the desire for Katrien burns like a thousand suns, but he knows that he has to be patient, something he is not.

4 A.M strikes, Elliot gives up on sleep, he's been half-awake and half-asleep, running through memories since 3:30, there's no point in trying to sleep anymore. He gets out of bed and makes his way to the kitchen, eager to get a coffee, eager to continue his composition of confusion. He pours the hot water into the two sugars, no milk, and walks over to his desk, hovering over the already opened notepad, reading the final sentence he had jotted down the night before. Elliot sips on his coffee, enticed to continue his work, just slow to figure out where he wants to begin...

November 1995, the scantiness of offspring saw an increase in my parent's venereal adventures, to a point where another pregnancy indicated the reality of a sibling. This time, it was easier to conceive, whether it was my mother's body now accustomed to fertility and birth, or my parents' preference to use previous triumphant methods, is beyond my curiosity. There I was...inadequately and innocently grasping at the concept of another infant in the household, but not yet understanding the concept of a brother... As the months progressed, I was introduced to my first aeroplane; a flight to France, to visit the not-yet-met grandparents; Henri and Angel. I found my unsophisticated self in the north of France, right next to the German Border, between the town of Sarreguemines and Metz, in the small village of Henriville (ironic isn't it?), stupefied with the mixture of French and English. My presence on Earth pleased my grandparents; their first son had a first son, the family name can go on, despite my father's siblings' sons. My grandfather, Henri, a WW2 survivor, a hard, honest and disciplined person that ensured his children were brought up in a similar manner, was pleased that my parents decided to use his name as my second name. He deserved that much, especially after almost being starved to death and shown first-hand; the eradication of fellow humans during his unpleasant stay at the infamous Auschwitz. Angel, his wife; a sweet and innocent woman, kind and thoughtful, who had raised five children and ensured that they performed well in every aspect of life, was happy to have another grandchild to stuff with baked goods. Together, the two formed a beautifully inspiring yet prude couple, sleeping in separate beds at night-time, adhering to the Laws of God or privacy and decency. This was also their first time meeting Audrey, even though she was about to pop out child number two. Audrey tried her best at impressing them, but neither they nor Sylvain's siblings were impressed, according to my understanding, but accepted her due to her status in my father's life. I picked up French quickly and couldn't speak English anymore, not that I could before anyway; being a one-year old. I was fed incredibly well and spoilt rotten by everyone, and met my amazing cousins who loved to play and have fun. It was good, until a few weeks later when my father, my bulging-by-the-belly mother and I found ourselves on a flight back home. The days flew by quick, up until the 3rd of August 1996, the date that marked the birth of someone special, Jerome Angel Nowak, my little brother. I visited Mom in the hospital and got to meet the little fella, I was happy. Mom came home and I was enlivened by the idea that we could keep him. I followed Audrey around like an adopted stray dog; she had Jerome in her arms...but as time went on, I realised that I was getting ignored and this infant was taking my family from me, and this is where my first trait was acquired; Jealousy... I wasn't yet able to understand why they treated him better than me, I hated it...along with him, but I suppose this is where the contradiction was born, because I loved him dearly. Confused by this evil characteristic I became wicked, patronising and taunting the innocent infant, and then pretentiously being affectionate whenever my parents were around. I may not have had any remorse or care for my actions back then, but if I could go back in time, I would give myself the biggest beating. There were moments where cute little me, did cute little things, for my cute little brother; sing him to sleep, tell him stories while I caressed his head, like my father had done for me, let him firmly hold onto my finger, making him feel that his big brother was there, looking after him, I really deserved that hiding right about now. Luckily some of those moments were captured by my parents in the form of photos and placed on the wall.

Days became weeks, weeks became months, and months became an entire year, nothing really interesting happened in the time it took Jerome to complete his first lap around the sun, other than my parents' confidence and authority gains; they seemed to have more experience with this child opposed to the first one. Experience didn't really count as much here because Jerome was always delightfully quiet, never whining or crying, never needing attention or love from anyone, ridiculing my jaundicing exploits. My early conscience started shaping and my mentality concerning fellow human beings improved, the envious nature became dormant and I was a pleasant child, but the Richter scale was often tested when my parents went about demonstrating favouritism. In my perspective the 'love' in this household was unevenly divided, the inequality was based mostly on one concept, the fact that we both resembled a parent in one way or another; Jerome took on Sylvain's appearance; hair and chin, also traits such as quietness and determination, and I resembled Audrey; dark curly hair and a stubborn attitude, but stubborn and stubborn never go well together, placing Audrey in Jerome's corner too.

I kept my patience with him because I loved him with all my heart.

The growth of my brother saw us old enough to leave the nest, in search of education and friendship in this infant-based institution called 'crèche', which was funded by my father, opposed to the European state-funded method. This was a good and a bad phase for me; good in the sense that I got to learn things, meet new people, get off my brother's case and get out of the house to experience the outside world, essential parts of growing up, but the bad. This is where I learnt trait number two;

Competitiveness. I thrived on individual attention, especially from the lone authority figure hired to teach us. I knew that in a class of thirty of the cutest kids, I had to go big or go home. I built the biggest houses with the blocks provided, ate all my vegetables at lunchtime; despite my hatred for them, first to fall asleep at naptime, and the first to wake. Those gold stars we received for things we had done drove me to intense levels. Jerome on the other hand was calm, making friends fast and taking things slow, on one occasion we clashed, it was his 3rd birthday, Mother sent him to school dressed as his favourite television hero. Everyone was in awe with the costume, saying how cute and cool he looked, I was so angry that I started believing that even family could be out to get you. Was it stupid? Yes, extremely, but so was I. My envious nature came back full swing, and I started acting up a lot, to a point where my father held me down and 'corrected' me with a belt, rectifying my attitude before I got more rebelliously out of hand, but little did he know the level of my stubbornness.

    A bit more time passed and my parents…with their relationship getting boring or too routine…took up gambling at the local casino. The routine was simple…my father would find a slot machine he thought was 'warm', give my mother money to fetch him a beer and get herself something; most of the time it was a soft drink due to her hatred for alcohol, and the rest would normally cover the expenses of the child care centre they had. They would sit there blowing hundreds, maybe thousands of Rands, not yet accustomed to the phrase 'the house always wins'. An hour or three would pass before my mom came to collect us; it mostly depended on their profits or losses, or my dad's drunken state. The beginning stages to this habit were fun; we always met new friends and had tons of toys to play with. Jerome always had his head leaned against a glass door, looking at the rabbits jumping around outside, eating grass, doing rabbit things while I enjoyed the loud-roaring engines of the go-karts on the track beside the facility, sometimes taking toy cars and pushing them around, trying to match the sounds I was hearing. Leaving the newly made friends part was easy, because we knew that Sylvain was a generous drunk, and would insist on stopping outside a fast food joint where we were treated to fried chicken and Cola. In the midst of all this fun, something happened that I never told anyone…

    After a few months of this so called 'new found passion', we were yet again thrown into this kids' den, but on this occasion there was a new employee; a young, tall, light-complexioned girl with long blonde hair that reeked of cheap shampoo. In the corner of this huge space was a little play house, which Jerome and I considered our fort, it held the best toys, and only people with the password could enter; Jerome and I were the only ones who knew the password. My mother paid and left us in the care of this woman, who told us to go play, which we did; going into the fort and acquiring the toys we needed for the evening. This child-minder came up to us; playing so innocently, and intrigued us with a little challenge, telling us that the winner would get a prize. Jerome was told to build the biggest, most beautiful building that he could, and I was asked to show her the fort, give her the grand tour, but that password was the only authority I had in the world, so I refused, but she somehow managed to work her way inside, to which I followed.

    She closed the plastic door behind us, locking it with the plastic latch that swung from the wall, and proceeded to close the plastic window, taking note of Jerome's construction; making sure that he'd be busy for a while. Without hesitation she turned to me, took off her shirt and bra, and grabbed my hands, placing them on her firm, round breasts. She squeezed my hands, squeezing her boobs, asking me to rub and play with them. I had no fucking idea what was going on, I thought that she had aches and needed my help in making them go away. She then asked me to kiss and suck on her nipples, I was pretty sure that I had already finished breastfeeding, but I did as she asked, while she rubbed her pants. A minute or so passed before she took my right hand and slid it into her trousers, under what I now know as knickers, against a funny feeling, slightly wet body part, shaped way differently to mine. She asked me to rub hard, while she leaned back, tilting her head up at the plastic ceiling in enjoyment. Her mind changed and she took her pants off, she wore a pink thong, which she moved to the side, I was then asked to put as many fingers as I could fit inside the part she pointed at, to move them in and out as fast as possible; maybe she had pains in there too. She lay wide open against the wall of my fort, permitting the pleasure I provided. After thrusting for a bit, my arm got sore, and she allowed me to take my wet fingers out, licking the entirety of my hand. I thought my work was done and I was ready to receive my doctorates after helping my first patient, but she had other plans, and so my pants came off. She started playing with my gentleman bits; I was pretty sure I wasn't in any pain, until my manhood rose; for the first time. She placed it in her mouth, and started sucking...or what felt like sucking. About three minutes passed before she stopped and took her undies off, placing me against the wall, getting on her knees and bending in front of me, hunching her back, allowing her upper body to rest on the floor. She commanded me to lick the wet part I had played with. I got grossed out by the situation and started whining, but she quickly hushed me with talks of compensation; curse the addiction to sugary treats. She asked me for one more favour before we left; to do what I did with my fingers again, but for longer than the previous time, so I went about pleasing her, going as fast as I possibly could; I knew the faster I got this done the faster I could get my candy. After a few minutes she let out a little sigh and mentioned that it was finished, so we got dressed and preceded to the bathroom, where she helped me wash my hands and made some funny jokes to ease my suffering. She grabbed a chocolate bar from the vending machine and began handing it over, but before it was placed in my sinful hands, she asked me to promise her that I'd never tell anyone, that this was our secret; for a chocolate bar that size...I'd do it again, so I promised. We stood admiring Jerome's palace which was fit for a queen, but before he received anything for his efforts, the sound of go-karts starting up drew our attention. The child-minder noticed the smile on my face, unlocked the glass door that Jerome was so fond of staring out of, and gave me the option to stand outside, under a pavilion, to see the go-karts. I walked out the door as she took Jerome towards the fort. For the first time in my life, I felt a rush of responsibility flow through my body, I had to stop Jerome from going through that; because if I didn't like it, he probably wouldn't either, but then the demonic sounds of screeching tyres won the fight and off I went...in search of the speed machines. A few laps had passed before I realised that watching amateurs go round and round on a circuit was boring, so I headed back like the mature five-and-a-half-year-old I was, only to walk into the building to see Jerome's face covered in chocolate. Half an hour passed before the doorbell of the kid's centre rang, we knew it could only be our mother since there were no other kids there that night. "Did they behave themselves?" my mother jokingly asked the minder as they walked over towards us.

"Perfect angels, miss," she responded as she gave Jerome and I the purest look of intimidation; frightening me into silence for the next how many years.

"Are you two ready for fried chicken?" my mother asked...a question that made me realise that there were bigger things in life than child molestation. Looking back at it now, it never really negatively affected me in life, except the fact that I should have been there for my little brother, to protect him against these kind of events.

Elliot puts the pen down and massages his left hand, releasing the strain from the burdens put to paper. He gets up from the chair, back and neck in bits, legs slightly dead, but the pins and needles feeling reassures him that the blood is flowing again. Elliot makes himself some food, eats it up and heads to bed, passing out almost instantly due to the lack of sleep over the past two days.

Chapter 4
It's Unfolding

The sun rises in harmony with the tweeting of birds nesting in nearby trees, a magnificent morning in the south of the Brabant province. Elliot's eyes gently open; he is surprised to have slept decently, as it seemed like an eternity of booze and night terrors. The fresh Monday morning sees Elliot make his way to the bathroom for a relaxingly, peaceful shower, where he gets his hair washed, face scrubbed, toe nails clipped, the works. With a towel tightened around his waist and fluffy slippers on his damp feet, Elliot heads to the kitchen, straight for the fridge, to get the medium-sized, free-range eggs out, along with milk and bread. He works away scrambling the mix; eggs, milk, garlic salt, black pepper and oregano, in a pan over a gas stove, whilst keeping an eye on the bread he put in the toaster; the spring activation is no longer in sync with the heating elements, so manual intervention is required. After devouring the hearty breakfast, Elliot heads to his wardrobe, to get dressed for his day off. Once fully clothed, Elliot leaves his house and heads into Eindhoven, to comply with his appointment at the GP, bringing along his notepad; just in case the waiting room is filled and the magazine's hogged. Elliot walks into the clean lobby, notifying the receptionist of his arrival, sits down on the cushioned bench and observes fellow patients; a plump man reading a car magazine, a mother getting agitated with her child who keeps coughing and an elderly woman smiling back at him. He begins thinking of ways to pick up where he left off, but there are too many thoughts running through his mind, so he just stares at the blank space his pen intended on marking.

"Mr Smith," the snobbish receptionist calls out.

"Yep!" Elliot replies as he closes the notepad and starts making his way towards the consultation room.

It's nothing but a mere check-up, and all seems to be okay, other than the scabs on his hand, which were cleaned to the doctor's satisfaction. Pleased with his well-being, Elliot finds himself driving deeper into the city, in search of a well-recommended kitchen and bathroom store; to replace the mirror he had demolished. Elliot stops outside the store that may as well have their own television channel with the amount of ads they spam online. He walks in, and heads directly for the mirror aisle; he knows exactly what he wants, so he doesn't bother asking a floor boy for help. He pays and leaves with the huge mirror in hand. On the drive home, Elliot questions his happiness, and feels content with the answer; financial and health aspects are good, he has a roof over his head and is still filled from breakfast, the only negative is the isolative state he has forced upon himself; the loneliness affects him most days. He decides to keep the good feeling rolling and copies Katrien's phone number from the napkin he had left on the passenger seat, into his phone. After 45-seconds of ringing, her voice mail answers.

"Hey… This is Katrien! I'm not available at the moment, leave a message and I'll get back to you as soon as I can, Thanks!"

The happy mood slightly declines, and Elliot frantically scrapes together some words to respond after the beep.

"Uhm, Hey, Katrien! This is Elliot, Uhm…from the supermarket and the bar, I was just calling to say thanks for the company the other night…I really enjoyed it. We should do it again sometime if you're up for it."

Elliot is slightly overconfident at times, with an impatient attitude, expecting results and replies immediately, but upon his arrival home and putting his notepad down on the dinner table, he realises that there's a huge possibility that she was only being pleasant to make some tips. Standing on the porch, Elliot starts feeling the disappointment sink in, questioning why the universe would build up this amazing feeling, only to knock it down again, but he knows that his impatience is to blame and not the great beyond. As his depressed eyes stare at the hard wood beneath his shoes, he is reminded of a lesson his father taught him when he was younger; 'Just because there are plenty of fish in the sea, doesn't mean you will catch one immediately, patience is what makes a happy and successful fisherman.' Dumbstruck with the memory from his childhood, Elliot's sight elevates from the wooden deck, to the lake right in front of him. In a flash he makes his way to the shed out back, passing the padlock-shut garage on the side, in search of his fishing rod. The cleaning of the shed was on the to-do list last summer, but so was finding a suitable companion. In the middle of pushing and throwing things around the shed, he finds the dismantled rod; a tad dusty, and places it on the grass, heads back into the shed to find his father's old lure box, hopefully the extra reel he had is still in there. After acquiring all the pieces, Elliot goes about assembling it; shafts, reel, hook and lure, stabbing his thumb several times in the process of tying a knot in the wire to the hook, and heads toward his regular spot. It is illegal to fish there, and if caught he may face a fine of around €2000, but if he has learnt anything from his adventures, it's that fear is our greatest enemy, limiting us from achieving what we want, stopping us from becoming the person we are destined to be; sentences he no longer recites in the mirror every morning, it became a way of life for him, something imprinted in his mind. With a fold up chair in his left hand, a fishing rod in the right, two cans of beer; one in each pocket and an old khaki cap on his head, Elliot ambles towards the lake like a dog with a bone. He finds his usual spot; in the sun but right next to the shadow of a tree in case the situation gets heated, he makes sure the lure is still attached properly and casts the line far out, as if he was still playing cricket for his high school. He plants himself onto the stool, takes a beer out and places it in-between his knees while trying to manage the reel; if he doesn't reel quick enough, he'll lose yet another lure to the algae and too fast will scare the fish. Elliot opens the beverage, spilling a bit on his leg, but takes a sip regardless, quenching his alcoholic thirst.

Elliot sits there for four warm, long hours, twiddling his thumbs, catching the common Allis shad, but tossing them back, and waiting for the device to notify him of a decent catch; either his cell phone with a call from Katrien or a huge tug on the line from a beast. While the reeling-in and casting-out process takes place again and again, he starts arguing with himself, *I'm not good enough, I'm not Dutch. Did she talk to me because I'm a nice guy or was it part of her contract and politeness?* Drowning in a river of ambivalence, confused between anguished lust and miserable depression, he starts chewing his muddy, wet from the water, nail on his index finger. The empty, stray look on his face accompanies the confusion within. He snaps out of the disorientated gaze and looks at his watch; 15:32…the fishing hasn't been as successful as he had hoped, and he missed lunch hoping that he would have caught something worth starving for. Before making the choice of ditching this fishing gig, there's a huge pull on the line, almost dragging him in the water with it. The fight begins…something similar to October 1, 1975, when Ali took on Frazier in the Philippine Coliseum; an exchange for the ages. After a solid ten-minute battle between the earthbound anthropoid and the aquatic demon, the fish decides to give up, accepting his/her fate; the termination of his/her existence, like the ancestors before him. Elliot reels him in and admires the fight the fish gave him, but decides to unhook the beast and casts him back into the water before it drowns; Elliot doesn't believe in killing unless really needed. The confused barbel just rests in the water, half submerged, experiencing trauma; from being dragged across the grainy sand and nearly drowning in the abundance of oxygen. The big fish thanks the gods for the second chance, and hastily swims off, leaving a muddy cloud behind it. Elliot decides to reel the rest of the line in and hook the 4th guide to the camping chair, securing it from falling over, and runs up to the house. He grabs charcoal from the shed and the barbecue from the side of the garage, placing both in front of the house, in order to overlook the lovely body of water. Back into the house he goes, this time filling his hands with a packet of two defrosted cod fillets, and a blue-gazed earthenware plate, which holds some other necessities crucial to this barbecue. He grabs a few final pieces; the stool from beside the lake, bringing the rod and lure box with him, a small, portable table from the porch, firelighters from above the fire place, a lighter from the kitchen table and a half-cut lemon to sprinkle over the cooked fish to add some acidity to the dish. Before lighting the fire and getting his party for one underway, Elliot adores the vista; more than a handful of evergreen trees surrounding the venue, a bright-blue sky with the slightest amount of harmless, white clouds in the distance, a placid blue-ish green lake, dark brown, sandy soil, untouched by the water, the sound of a calm breeze grazing the trees, birds accompanying the visuals with an orchestra of tunes. As Elliot admires Mother Nature's handiwork, the hexamine smell from the fire lighter in his hands reaches his nose, and that infamous, destructive humanity feeling kicks in. He lights the firelighter and places it in the barbecue, including human intervention in this picturesque setting. The charcoal takes a while to heat up, which gives him enough time to run back inside to grab a beer and his trusty acoustic guitar, gifted to him by an old friend in Dublin. He cracks open the beer, takes a sip of the ice-cold, canned lager and places it down on the table before seating himself down on the stool, placing the musical patrimony on his lap. Elliot's left hand hovers over the G note, the right ready to finger the strings; he is no musician, but does remember a few cords from his younger years. A bluesy tune begins to emerge from the sound hole, his eyes close and the notes keep coming, regularly losing hand placements and distorting the 19th century slave genre. He changes between a variety of genres after each missed strum; from blues to indie, all the way to Irish traditional and Latin contemporary. After the multi-cultural concert for an audience of bushes, he puts the guitar down, standing up right against the table, and prepares the grilling apparatus for the fish. He places the two fillets on the fire, examining the sizzling sound the fish gives of as it is placed in the open flames. Elliot allows the fish to sear a few minutes on each side before he plates it and drizzles it with some fresh lemon juice. He devours the dish, takes the cutlery and plates back inside, along with the guitar and the equipment he used, throws the fishing rod back in the shed and extinguishes the still roasting coals with some water. Elliot has about three hours to kill before bedtime, so he decides to replace the old mirror with the new one, using tools from the garage, leaving the old mirror lying sideways next to the glass recycling-bin beside the house. He thinks about jotting down a few lines but decides there's no point in getting into it this late at night, so he plants himself onto the couch and flicks through a few TV channels, not looking for anything in specific. Elliot dozes off like a child after a long day of playing in the yard; no pillows or blankets required.

Tuesday morning, the second gloomiest day of the week for most, a day where Elliot can leave his dejected shell and isolative nature in his sequestered utopia and head towards the norm; according to the rest of mankind. He only has three days of work this week, due to the annual three-week holiday he takes every year in a week's time. In the beginning, these holidays saw him travel to unseen destinations, but for the last two years it's just been lengthy summer hibernations, accompanied by miasmatic flatus every so often. Elliot dresses up in one of his many formal shirts; white with blue stripes, accompanied by the infamous asshole collar and cuffs, along with his dark-blue slacks, dark-tanned formal shoes and the same red tie he wore the day he got promoted from a regular analyst to a business consultant. He has been promoted three more times since then, taking up more responsibility and leading greater groups of people worldwide, just another goal he set for himself and smashed. The three days are filled with client meetings, video conferences, quality brainstorming exercises with younger prodigies, looking at visual representations of growth, talking about expansion and personally saying 'Happy Birthday' to Linda, the receptionist, who has been with the company for about eight years now. Elliot is an all-rounder, being able to focus on many different things at once, whether it is the hardest decisive decision or the easiest walk-by greeting, he can operate on all levels. The notepad and its confessions are ignored in this space of time, there are more important things happening and 100% focus is needed; the smallest detail missed can cause the biggest damage. The staff gossip, wondering what happened to Elliot's hand, whether the loneliness became too much and it was self-inflicted or whether the ever-so-calm attitude came to an end and he finally snapped, injuring a bystander in the process, he confesses to no one and the building is left with only their assumptions.

Friday morning arrives with a fresh summer rain. Dark grey clouds hover over the terra firma, blocking out the sunlight, but not the humidity. A slight westerly wind sweeps in. Elliot is woken by the sound of rain hitting the regent type roof tiles, mouth dry as bone, creases all over his skin from the where he became one with the sheets. He listens but hears no tweets, no chirps, just the continuous sound of water crashing into the house accompanied by the shrieking of wind. Eager to quench his thirst, he launches himself from the bed into those bachelor maroon slippers most lonely people seem to own, and heads towards the kitchen. Gulping away at the freshest glass of water, his eyes take note of the weather outside, without hesitation his eyes switch to the notepad, he decides he has no other choice but to write a bit today. Elliot's recently dusted off passion takes control and steers him in the direction of the pen.

It was almost time to leave this block stacking institution, for bigger and better things, finally out of this child-infested hellhole, on to big boy school. I wouldn't see any of these Afrikaans competitors ever again, my parents decided to put me in an English school, it was a good choice seeing as the world seemed to have shifted from its cultural uniqueness to a universal style of living, and English was the language of this new movement. Before I could go anywhere, life had to give me a lesson, to take with me, something I needed to be aware of, death... The owner of this fine toddler academy passed away, I have no idea why, leaving behind a mischief of mice and concerned staff members. I recall being told 'She's staying with the angels' by my parents. I had the slightest idea of heaven and hell, angels and demons, from the little time I paid attention in church, but I wasn't sure how it all mashed together. I was dressed up in a suit, nonetheless, and brought to the funeral of someone I admired but didn't quite know. I mistook the graveyard for hell, due to her being lowered into the ground, and thought she was a bad person because if she was good, she would go to heaven, and the people lowering her would be raising her. I thought the wooden box matched the same criteria people look at when buying a product in store; non-boxed, left open for air contamination would be seen as inferior, and this is how we offered people to Satan, the imagination of children... The tears of friends and family wet the fresh, green grass; teachers looked completely lost, "my condolences" and "I'm sorry" out played the windy South African breeze. I didn't weep or spend much time thinking about the Grim Reaper's gift to this sweet, old lady, I was almost six, I didn't know much about anything to be honest.

Time flew by and I was suited up for my graduation ceremony in an extra small, super long black robe and the fascinating academic square cap. The turnout was an estimated thirty people, including my proud parents and a few teachers that taught other classes. "Malcolm No... Whack?" The announcer called out, unfamiliar with Polish surnames, a round of applause began and my face lit up as my teacher slightly nudged me on stage, I liked this feeling; fame, glory, power, YES! "Marcus Van Der Merwe," the man with the mic continued, more confident with this name, the claps got louder and even a whistle was heard, my smile turned into a jealous frown, why was the kid I competed against and beat in everything getting more than me? Do they not know of his unsuccessful time at this academy? I quickly came to my senses and realised this was a send-off, congratulating the kids that were moving on with their lives. I awaited the third name but it never came, it was only the two of us that were of age and ready to leave. After the ceremony and some small talk with other parents later, my father took us for fried chicken to celebrate the occasion, he was happy. I was one step closer to leaving the nest, and he could finally have the ever so famous 'peace and quiet' he so desperately wished for. For Audrey, it was a sad realisation that her cute, rebellious little boy, who danced in his underwear to George Michael, was slowly growing up, and will eventually leave home in pursuit of bigger and better things, replacing her with another woman. Jerome never showed any emotion towards the evening, maybe my intimidation scared him from interfering in my life, and maybe he realised how pathetic congratulating a five-year old going to primary school was...perhaps a three-year old couldn't comprehend such things at the time. The last few weeks in this kindergarten took long, perhaps the excitement and constant over thinking led to the discovery of my third trait; Impatience, and my parents didn't really assist in declining the anxiety because they wanted to be three steps ahead at all times, so they purchased all my school related gear long before we really needed to, adding to the impatience. A week or two before school started, my mother dragged me along with her to visit her friend, Amelia Watson, who lived across the road; to get guidance and help on various school related concerns; clothing measurements and adjustments, how to handle a child with school work and all the extra activities, how to ensure that I would take in all the education. What made Amelia the perfect person to ask fell on two main reasons; firstly she lived right across the road which made it handier for her to come to us or us to go to her, and secondly because she was the mother of a bright, little girl called Sarah, who seemed to be excelling in life. Sarah followed her mother around like a shadow, a person I took no notice of, but because she was a year older than me, it made Amelia the ideal role model for my mother, that one-year extra experience played to my mother's advantage, or so she thought.

Holding my mother's hand, we walked out of our yard, looked left and right before crossing good ol' Piet Retief Street, taking note of the strategically placed trees. We approached this medium-sized, cadmium green painted gate locked with a chain and a brass padlock. "Amelia!" my mom shouted in her high-pitched voice, a trick she had learnt from Amelia's neighbours. Since they didn't have a doorbell, shouting was the only method to get her attention. Out came a short, medium-built woman, bob cut on top and pink slippers down low, followed by a little girl; innocent, cute, brunette, freckles, brown eyes and an upward pointing nose, along with a big, black Rottweiler. As they walked up to unlock the gate, time stood still and that cute smile the six-year old gave me, sent butterflies swarming through my intestines. The space and time continuum went back to normal and I found myself hiding behind my mother's backside for the first time...shy and awkward. Amelia unlocked the gate and allowed us in, chasing the big mutt to the back of the yard with her authoritative voice. We took what seemed to be a thousand steps to reach the front door, my mother and Amelia chatted away, leaving me and Sarah staring at each other behind them. The fresh smile she displayed and the sparkle in her eyes left an imprint in my mind forever. Upon entering the house, our parents sat down in the lounge and engaged in those long, women conversations, her mother suggested we play in the next room; probably to avoid me listening in to the details of my demise. Sarah and I went to the next room and awkwardly looked at each other for a while, she didn't know English all too well and I didn't know a word of Afrikaans. "My name is Sarah," she said in a sweet voice, turning away with a giggle, trying to hide the sight of her blushing.

"I'm Malcolm," I responded, trembling with fear but smiling from the childish pleasure.

We took crayons from what seemed to be her play box, opened a colouring book and began shading the black and white images in front of us in the loud silence caused by the language barricade. Due to the hands we wrote with, she sat on the right, me on the left, going about our childish masterpieces. Every few minutes we lifted our heads, looked at each other's efforts and laughed, cordially judging one another's colour choices and inability to stay in the lines, but she was better than me; putting that extra year experience to good use, but I felt no urge to compete with her, she felt like a friend. Our parents walked in the room with smiles an hour or so later, whether those were evil smiles after plotting against me or if they were genuinely happy with the outcome of their conversation, is beyond me, I just needed to spend more time with Sarah.

The remaining days were filled with my mother sewing and stitching my school clothes, getting me ready for the pedagogical adventure nearly upon us. Jerome and I played in the yard; running, kicking a ball around, laughing, growing as brothers, we were often interrupted by Mother's cry.

'Mikki Moo' her pet name for me...well, when I was a good boy, to be an exact, scaled to size mannequin for her, to see whether her hours of efforts were successful or not, or if more work needed to be done. The six o' clock, Monday morning alarm went off and my eager soul was out of bed before anyone could rush to wake me for my big day. Dressed in a white, short sleeve dress shirt, grey shorts, grey, knee-height socks and pristinely polished black formal shoes, I made my way to the kitchen, ready for breakfast. I walked into the kitchen but before I could pour myself some cereal, I saw my dad staring out of the kitchen window, posed in the traditional dad stance, contemplating something, his coffee standing on the green counter top in front of him, which was attached to the wall. Normally he would be at work, leaving at five A.M, but there he was, dressed in a cerise-coloured polo shirt and regular fit blue jeans. Most mornings I'd be woken by his bedroom door opening, his heavy footsteps that lead towards the front of the house, the creaking passage door he would have to open; we closed the door believing it would act as a barrier between us and any intruders; South Africa's crime rate started rising in 2001. Awake with the knowledge that he had left, I would normally rush to his room to snuggle in next to my mother, to put my head on his pillow and smell the scented conflict between his sweat and the after shave he took a liking too, it was a memorable aroma; a safe smell. He booked off this day, to witness my first of many academic days, to support me in case I got cold feet and wanted to go back to crèche. It was strange because he never really cared for such small things, up till now he wasn't really interested in our lives, financially he would back us in anything, Mother was the emotionally involved parent, but I was happy that he considered me and the memory of him I'd have forever. After breakfast and getting things together, all four of us got in my dad's little, 1986, light-blue, Ford hatchback, ready for the 2-kilometre drive to the new institution. We parked in the sandy parking lot the school provided, in front of the reception entrance and walked through the busy lobby; parents and kids, smiling and crying alike, after the pushing and shoving we finally got out and arrived at my class, 1A, ; grade 1, class A, which was for the more English based kids. Not that the school was divided by race or other differences, it was 2001, five-and-a-half years after Mandela freed us, the country should already be building bridges to eliminate the divide, but that dream seemed to die with him. Come to think of it some of the teachers attended university during the apartheid era, maybe there were teachers that preferred teaching classes with similar colour, but one could never tell. I stood in front of a bricked wall, posing in front of my parent's camera, with a huge smile on my face, and my grumpy father beside me, with his arms folded and a frown on his face. Whether he was upset with the amount of people around; he wasn't a fan of crowds, or if it was his perceptive forecast that my time and money wasting capabilities would kick in and that school was a bad idea, wasn't too clear, I was in heaven. My mother snapped the photo, securing the unacceptable memory in digital format.

This short, fat lady opened the classroom door and told us to find our names on the desks provided, and take a seat at our tables. I entered and searched the tables for my name, after about 10 desks, my father pointed out that the surnames were arranged alphabetically, "Ah," I exclaimed, no idea what that meant, but I found my place; first table in the 3rd row from the door, right in front of the tutor's table. The tables were 1.2 metres in width and seated two people, meaning I'd have a table friend. In a class of about 40 very diverse children, I found myself secretly hoping that I wouldn't be placed next to a girl, I wasn't worried about race or religion, I wasn't brought up in the typical Afrikaans ways, and at the time wasn't able to discriminate against skin colour. I took my seat and placed my brand-new pencil case at the top of the desk, ready, willing, waiting for the start. Parents started leaving the room, blowing kisses and winking at their kids, my parents were long gone, eager to leave I guess, it didn't matter to me, everything I ever needed was in front of me. In the midst of the loving chaos, I hovered over the name of the person that would be seated on my left; Unathi Phiri, a strange name for me, being used to Afrikaans/Dutch names, this seemed African, but I was new to the diversity, as my pre-school only had white Afrikaans people. I looked around the room, targeting potential academic threats and getting excited to make new friends with all the kids behind me. The chair beside me was pulled out, scratching the floor, I turned to look and saw this boy, same height as me, wearing long grey pants and a red jersey.

"Hi! I'm Malcolm," I enthusiastically announced.

"I'm Unathi," he calmly responded.

He copied my pencil case placement idea. I felt excited, my first African friend. We chatted a bit about our excitement towards school, but the conversation was interrupted by the hard closing of a smooth surfaced wooden door, it was the teacher, pushing the narrow frame eyeglasses she wore up with her chubby index finger.

"I am Mrs Basson," she stated, "I will be your teacher for the year. You can refer to me and all other female teachers as Ma'am, Miss or Mrs, and Sir or Mister for the male teachers. You are all part of class 1A, please remember that. The school welcomes you and hopes you all achieve what you set out to achieve. In this box is a diary, this is how I'll communicate with your parents, and how you will remember homework or activities. All of you get in a line and come and get one."

We all got up and formed a slow-moving line, collecting the first collectable the school had to offer. She didn't walk around the class handing them out, I suppose it was due to her being bigger than the gaps between the desks that formed pathways for us. Upon taking our seats, Mrs Basson allowed us to introduce ourselves, one by one, starting with the girl in row 1, table 1, all the way on the left-hand side of the class, right next to the door, continuing with the boy beside her, and so on. The class focused their attention to the speaker, and collectively moved their heads to the next person, I was more focused on the basic human anatomy and numerical posters stuck to the walls around us, but distantly listening to the bunch of African names being called-out, with a few English and Indian names thrown into the mix.

"Nicole," I heard in the shyest voice; my concentration shifted from essential classroom surroundings to this pale, freckled girl with long, brown, curly hair, deep brown eyes shielded by a pair of glasses, thin, powder pink lips and a warm smile.

Like my concentration, my thoughts of Sarah vanished and someone new held the spotlight in my childish mind. After the introductions, we were told to play *outside, the area we were given to play in laid in front of the double story building we were in; bottom floor grade 1 and second floor grade 2, behind the pavilion's that rested on a steep, sloped hill; which was difficult to climb as a five-year old, and in front of the main gates; overlooking the small shopping centre across the road, on the left. The playground was covered in sand and unplanned patches of dry grass, three jungle gyms and loads of bushes and trees. I immediately fell in love with the large, open area, but there was one rule, we weren't allowed around the back, that area was for grade 3 to 7. I ran around the playground, playing on all the structures with Unathi and our newly made friends, verbally pushed away from the group due to them all speaking in an African tongue. I moved my focus to Nicole, staring at her like a fat kid staring at an ice cream truck, she was befriending this Indian girl, Advika, she was unique all right, innocent, honest and very religious; but most Indian people back then were. I planned and planned on getting Nicole's attention, but before I could execute my perfect plan of 'accidentally' falling from the jungle gym, the teachers from all the classes came together and called us toward them. They stood on the corridor, in front of the classes. They needed to teach us how to line up in a decently structured queue; girls from class A on the left, boys from A on the right, a huge gap, and then Class B girls and so on.*

Elliot feels a shiver up his spine, not from fear, but because the cold wind was slowly creeping in through the cracks. He stands up and heads toward the fireplace, where he strategically places the logs diagonally, and a fire lighter under the formation, lighting it once satisfied. Above the fireplace, a wooden shelf that holds the things dearest to him; photos, certificates, a glass snow globe someone gave him for Christmas, and obviously the clock. The shrine of heartbreak catches his eye, he stands up from the kneeling position he was in, knees cracking in the process. He picks up the first photo frame, a professional photo of him, his brothers and parents, a family portrait, he smiles at himself dressed in a snow camo military shirt, earphones hanging down his shirt, serious face, everyone happy and youthful. He places it down and picks up the second photo, a proud father standing beside his eldest son; that has many badges on his blazer for things accomplished in school. He puts the photo down and heads to the wine rack in the kitchen. Elliot pulls out a French produced Rose wine and spins it around; looking for a date, 2003, not too old but no longer young either. Drama queen Elliot pours the wine in a crystal clear, crystal shaped glass and slowly paces back to the fireplace, picking up the 3rd photo frame. Elliot takes a huge sip as his eyes gaze at the image, a happy memory of him and Jerome standing in front of an aqua-coloured car, smiling and rather unaware of the camera man, he lets out a painful smile and his eyes tear up, he slowly touches the photo with his index finger, and places it back down on the shelf. Elliot takes another sip from the glass, face folding from the bitterness, as he takes a step to the right and picks up the snow globe, shaking the non-soluble soap flakes around the place before the gloomy reminiscing can continue, the message tone of his phone laying on the table sounds. Soaked in regret and remorse from the book and the shrine of sadness, he walks over to the slim, black smart phone, unlocking it with a slide of the thumb. He taps on the messages icon in the menu and takes a nervous breath in the few split seconds it takes the phones processor to process the request, he open the message, 'Hey, Elliot… Sorry for only getting back to you now, I've been busy… How have you been? Regards, Katrien.'

Elliot immediately fills up with rejection and paranoia, guessing the reasons behind her long-awaited response; whoring around? In a relationship and wanting to cheat? Just not interested? Most guys would play it cool and either messaged her back already or just ignored her, but Elliot is desperate for companionship on an emotional and mental level, sex comes way too easy for him. Elliot takes a sip of wine and puts the glass down, primed to text her back, 'Hey, Katrien, no worries, I've been good thanks, how about you,' he places the phone down on the notepad, not locking it, leaving the phone's screen shining bright, and walks over to the bottle of wine, refilling his glass. He looks over at his phone across the open plane lounge, dining room and kitchen design; no walls to partition off his rewards, to see it lock itself automatically. He stands at the black, marble counter top, sipping the wine; his throat getting more acquainted with the burn. Elliot awaits a text but nothing yet, so he decides to poke the fire a bit, continuously refilling his glass, opening a new bottle in the process, mixing rose and white, playing memories in his mind. Elliot grows bored with the flames dying down and six glasses of wine back his eagerness to find another activity. He extinguishes the burning pieces of wood with the remaining booze in his glass, letting off a sweet burning aroma. He makes his way back to the table to continue the much-needed therapy, but lifts the pen and watches the words dancing around on the paper, and passes out, head first on the un-summoned script.

Chapter 5
The Good, the Bad and the Hook-Up

Elliot's Saturday begins with a slimy cough and a wet face; he lifts his head from the notepad it rested on, neck in pain from the lack of movement during his slumber. He wipes his face, quickly realising that it's saliva and looks down to see a few words submerged in a puddle of drool, "Never…again," he mutters his famous last words. He picks himself up and tears the infested sheet out; luckily it's only a quarter of a paragraph affected. Elliot drifts past the TV, towards the kitchen, throwing the sheet in the bin and switching on the kettle, hoping a hot cup of coffee would make him feel more human. He realises the kettle will take a while, so he heads to the shower to clean himself up. A shit, shower and shampoo passes before he returns to the now lukewarm water, it will suffice this time, despite his hatred for cold coffee. Elliot takes two Paracetamol pills with his black coffee, and stares out the window, at nothing in particular. He remembers the text from Katrien and responding, so he rushes over to the phone, to see if there's any update on their situation, there is.

'I'm good thanks, just some issues but all is okay now, are you doing anything this weekend?'

Elliot quickly responds.

'Hopefully, nothing too serious, nah I'm having a quiet weekend, how about you?' rethinking the assumptions he had the previous night. The phone and the half-finished coffee get placed on the table as Elliot sits down to continue his writing, but Katrien was quick to respond this time.

'I asked for the weekend off, needed to get away from the 10-hour shifts, six days a week, planning on staying in and watching some TV.'

Here's a chance, Elliot thinks to himself, and words back, 'In that case would you like to go out for a dinner tonight? On me of course.' Putting a smiley emoji at the end of the sentence. The anxious suspense begins, like a twelve-year old that just asked his crush to the home coming dance via a folded love letter. A minute passes before she replies. Elliot opens the message before the beeping sound even stops.

'Yeah, dinner sounds good, where did you have in mind?' He smiles and raises a clenched fist, a gesture he uses to symbolise victory, prematurely proud. He texts back.

'That's great; I'm thinking the Italian 'La Casa del Amici', on Dillenburgerstraat in Eindhoven? So 6 P.M. side?' He puts the phone down, no longer desirous for an answer; he knows he's already won. He sips the remaining caffeine and places the cup in the dishwasher. The phone goes off again; Katrien.

'Perfect…x,' he doesn't respond, trying to avoid a common forlorn attempt at love. He books a seat via some dining app on his phone, and is notified shortly after that the reservation for him and his romantic interest has been successful, leaving him six hours to kill before actually needing to get ready.

I was upset, but education and filing children on the quad had to commence. The rest of the day was filled with numbers and fun. The final school bell rang, indicating home time, and the teachers let us leave. Flocks of kids aged five to thirteen swarmed the gates like the Bactrian horse archers swarmed the Macedonian phalanxes at the siege of Samarkand. There my mother was, in her black hatchback; exact same car as my dad, puffing away on a cigarette, covering 35% of the filter with the red lipstick she always wore and Jerome in the back, in his little car seat, intrigued by the hordes of children. I got in and put the oversized bag my parents insisted on getting on the floor under the almost broken glove compartment.

"*How was your first day my angel face?*" *my mom asked as she turned the key in the ignition.*

"*It was great, I made a chocolate friend,*" *I was never able to say colours of people.*

"*His name is Unathi,*" *I excitedly blurted out as the car was reversing.*

"*That's very good,*" *she replied as we left the school.*

The days passed and Audrey noticed the amount of kids passing our house, she recognised them from the days she spent collecting me, among the children was my new friend Unathi. They were walking home it seemed, meaning they lived near us, we stayed in the last street before the short drive to the next town, Trichardt, so there was nowhere else they could be going. I was excited at the fact that I now had friends close to me other than just Sarah. Audrey however was more focused on capitalising on these circumstances, and schemed up a business idea to cover the expenses of collecting her children from school every day. She wanted to be there properly as a mother after school but also earn a profit on the side, as working was not yet an option for her. So Audrey spoke to Sylvain, got his opinion, worked out a strategy to find clients, and tried understanding the legality behind it all. Over the course of two days, she spoke to other parents, mapped her routes and figured out prices to maximise profit without greatly affecting the client pool, and thus 'Rainbow Kids Afterschool Care' was created. Essentially what this business entailed was dropping a few kids off at school, collecting them when they were finished, drop a few off at home, and the left-over bunch would stay at our house playing board games and doing homework until their parents collected them at 5 P.M. The first few days were simple, it was Unathi and another boy that would walk to our house at around 6:30, we all got in the car and followed the business protocol as mother intended. As days went on Audrey obtained more and more clients, I got more friends, and profits showed growth, meaning more sweets and toys for me and Jerome. However, Audrey forgot one crucial detail to her scheme, the foundation that this business was built on, the core of operations, the car, and the space in it. This Ford was meant to seat five people at max; one driver, one front seat passenger, and three back seat passengers, the client pool was on six; the three of us and six other kids. Audrey faced her first big business decision, either drop four clients and avoid a fine and any other negative outcomes, or, squeeze them all in like sardines and hope for the best, Audrey chose option two... fuck the legality. So there we were, Audrey driving, Jerome in the front with no car seat, the brother and sister; our most recent clients, in the back along with Unathi, me on Unathi's lap; sometimes we would switch, my newly found friend Pule Morafo, on one or both of the siblings, another newly made friend called Brennan King, in the boot with another kid whose name I couldn't pronounce. Luckily, the boot canopy was removable. It was very funny for us all, my mother was always on edge every time a police vehicle was in the vicinity, and whenever she called out 'Quack', we would duck as the law would be around, the only people remaining up were the two kids sitting on laps, that always seemed too tall for their age. Even the routes we took were to avoid suspicions, we drove through residential areas; steering clear of other drivers and their concerns, all the way to school where she parked a distance away from the parking lot. She would then easily drive up the main road to the other school which almost always had a traffic officer, drop the siblings off and then proceed to Jerome's' crèche, which happened to have the social welfare office, along with a charity shop behind it, where she met her social worker friend, Antoinette Melcher. On one occasion, my mother had a bingo day at our house, for the kids that remained with us after school, it was a great idea and there were prizes for first, second and third, everyone got involved. The only problem was that no one ever taught me how to lose, so when I placed fifth out of six people, I was pissed. I recall shouting, "This is unfair! Everyone is cheating," and running to take refuge in my room, while everyone laughed at me and ate their mouse shaped marshmallows my mother had provided. Audrey tried comforting me, telling me not to be a sore loser, to allow friends to win sometimes. Friends? I wanted victory, not playmates. I never really changed.

In the last week of January, my father got very ill, the shivers as they called it. Private doctors; that the medical aid covered, couldn't even figure out what it was, perhaps it was because he quit smoking cold turkey the week before, after many years of feeding his body that shit. My grandparents came over to support us mentally, at one point Frankie turned to Audrey and told her that she didn't think Sylvain was going to pull through; hinting at certain death. Jerome and I weren't aware of the magnitude of the crisis; Audrey didn't want to scare us so she asked Gugu to keep us busy. Gugu was our hired help, living in South Africa it was more affordable to have someone clean your house and look after the kids opposed to anywhere else in the world. She made sure we had things to do and avoided our bed-bound father. Gugu was a Zulu woman who worked and lived in our house for about a year at the time, she was someone we trusted and grew on, despite the white neighbours that had an issue with colours. Sylvain was booked off work, allowing him to recover from whatever this was, and Audrey continued with the shopping, stocking the house up, doing her rounds with the kids and looking after him as soon as she got back. It was good that they had this we're a team mentality. Something I wish I had understood earlier.

In nearly no time, Sylvain recovered, got back to work and led the household the way he did before. It all seemed to return to normal, less signs of stress on Mother's face; she wouldn't be a young widow, and the kids were all right. Doctors still couldn't find out what had caused the constant shivers throughout his body.

A few days later, Audrey received a call…

Elliot puts the pen down, it's 4 P.M., time to shower and get ready for his 'hot date'. The Paracetamol worked wonders as he is able to move without the skull-pounding feeling keeping him down. After a relaxing 15-minute shower, Elliot finds himself in front of his collection of clothes in nothing but a towel hugging his waist, trying to figure out which dress shirt would work best with beige slacks, black wing tips and a gold watch. He settles for a light-blue shirt and a navy blazer; it is a bit nippy outside, but the purpose is to please her aesthetically. 16:27, Elliot has enough time to wax his hair and brush his teeth before needing to leave to beat possible traffic.

Elliot anxiously drives down to the venue, fearfully questioning his intentions. He knows he'd sleep with her if the chance arose, but he wasn't looking for a quick, meaningless one-night stand. The road isn't too busy and he arrives at 17:45. Elliot gets out of the car, tucks his shoulders in, adjusting his blazer and resurfaces his wristwatch, smiling at two women passing by. The sun reflects off of Elliot's aviators, he lets out a smile from a face covered in short stubble. The ladies looked impressed by his stereotypical Greek, playboy attitude, but said nothing, and continued to walk on. One of them turns around and looks at his ass in the tight pants he's got on, she lets out a whistle as the other giggles and slaps her friend's shoulder. Elliot feels confident now. The teenage girls' actions reassure that he is dressed just fine, besides if Katrien doesn't like him he can always try catch up with the girl that uses her lips that well. He walks into the establishment, takes his glasses off, placing them in the pocket of his blazer and politely greets the waiter standing in the entrance.

"Hey, good evening, I have reservations, Mr Smith…table for two."

She smiles, looking down at the logbook, finding his name, and asking him to follow her. It's not the poshest place in Eindhoven, but it definitely is a good start. She seats him down at a well-decorated table near a window, hands him a menu and asks him if he'd like anything to drink while he waits for the second person.

"Just a glass of sparkling water please, miss," he kindly requests.

He places the menu down on the table and waits for Katrien before making any decisions. Elliot sees a taxi pass by with what appears to be one woman seated inside, but he doesn't get a clear view of the lady, his reaction was a bit slow. A minute or so later, the friendly waiter walks into the section of the restaurant where he is seated, smiling at him, before turning 90° to the right. Left side facing Elliot, and right facing someone else. She lifts her hand with an open palm gesture, indicating towards Elliot's table. Time stood still as Katrien appeared, walking past the waiter, towards the suggested table. She looks amazing, dressed in an azure-blue, V-neck, pencil dress that hugs those hips tighter than he could, showing enough cleavage but not too much, matte-red lipstick; that brought out her perfect blue eyes, hair curled at the ends, bit of make-up to finish up the work of art. Elliot stands up abruptly, knocking over his chair in the process, exuberant to greet her. He bends over to pick the chair up, before turning to her now standing beside the table. The timid man shakes her hand gently.

"You look beautiful," he admits while making the most meaningful eye contact.

"Thank you very much, Mr Elliot," she says, showing her shy side once again.

Elliot enthusiastically pulls out her chair and asks her to have a seat, taking note of her perfectly rounded ass; not too big and not too small, just the way he likes it, and gets back to his seat. They open the menus and start going through the various Italian dishes on offer together. In between deciding on meals, they raise their eyes, looking at each other's features, and then quickly ducking behind the menu before the other notices. The childish game persists until the waiter returns with a jug of water, filling their glasses just a bit over half. The server asks if they were ready to order, Elliot responds with, "Ladies first," exhibiting his chivalry in front of the two women at his table. The waiter is forced to focus on Katrien, readying her pen and booklet, awaiting the order.

"Can I have the mushroom risotto to start with, a seafood linguine as a main and a tiramisu for dessert please?"

Elliot loves a girl that can eat, and she doesn't seem to be shy in the art of consuming it seems. The waiter turns to Elliot.

"And yourself, sir?"

"Uhm…Yeah can I have chicken risotto to start with, the chicken scaloppini for the main dish please and uhm…" He starts hesitating, not being a dessert person. After scanning through the sugary list, he points out the Affo Gato dessert, asking for that as it seems to be the least sweet dessert.

The waiter finishes up taking the orders and turns to go place the order, but before she can walk off Elliot apologises and asks.

"Could we possibly get a bottle of your finest Malbec please?"

"Certainly, sir," the waiter replies. Smiling ever so proudly, knowing the cheapest bottle of Malbec was €179.99.

The two start talking, about work, life in The Netherlands, how she seems to be over worked for minimum wage.

"What about your boss? Is he okay? Or is that guy the chef?" Elliot questions.

"He is the boss. Poor guy," she starts off, "about two years ago, his wife divorced him for a regular, and since then he let the bar consume him. He is a great guy most days, but very strict when he needs to be, but I guess it's because he is over worked too, as he manages the entire place and then acts as a chef or server for the most part. I haven't seen him take a day off in months," she gets out, it seems to be something that affects her.

"I understand completely, but is he a good guy to you?" Elliot tries to approach the question differently.

"Ah yes he is, he is like a father to us, he tries his best to look after everyone, but you know how it goes, sometimes maybe good, sometimes maybe shit," she jokingly tells the interested man opposite to her.

Katrien takes a sip of her water before exclaiming her happiness for the much-needed break, the first one away from a TV and paying bills in a while, playing on Elliot's soft spots pretty well. He knows he gets a decent salary, is always free to fly wherever he wants, and can afford to do anything he feels like doing. The waiter brings over the first course, serving the woman and then the man, the way Elliot wants it to be, despite the hordes of feminist groups running around the place; he believes in women being equal to men, and has interviewed and employed many females for high paying jobs, but he knows women have taken it to a new level, killing off chivalry worldwide, something he will never stand for. The meals are pleasant and delicious, the wine tastes good and is slowly making its way to their heads. The conversation continues, she becomes more and more flirty with every sip she takes, and Elliot notices it, he suggests moving to water to avoid regrettable mistakes, subliminally hinting at the possibility of sex, but she politely refuses anything other than wine, she deserves a break to let her hair down, and tells him that she won't regret anything. Half of his hormones are exuberant with the knowledge that he'll score with this petit woman tonight, but the other half stand strong, side by side, supporting the decent man Elliot is, but the internal conflict only leads to him ordering more wine for the both of them. Katrien excuses herself from the table, making her way to the restrooms, and Elliot takes advantage of the alone time to pay the bill; €648. The dessert plates were cleared an hour ago, but they remained seated, the sparks flew as the room emptied. She returns to the table with her white purse in hand, one can see she is no longer sober, but she is having fun, and Elliot isn't stopping it. The waiter approaches them, informing them that the section needed to be closed off for the evening – bad news for them – but Elliot schemes up a great plan and asks the waiter for a bottle of wine before they go. Despite her policy to not let anyone leave the building with any forms of alcohol, she hands him the bottle; she clearly believes in love and knows that it's going somewhere, but Elliot doesn't leave her empty handed, handing her €50 as well as the price of the bottle, a win-win some may say. They leave the building, to their surprise it's a bit windy and Katrien didn't plan on such weather, but Elliot comes to her rescue and places his blazer over her frail shoulders, she smiles; innocent and honest, and they start walking down the road, Elliot on the outside, closer to the road, as he was taught by his father. The two lovebirds come across a kid's playground, and decide to head inside. Sitting on the swings, Elliot does the honours of opening the wine with his trusty Swiss pocketknife, which has 20 plus attachments. He didn't bank on it coming to this and has no glasses with him, so he hands her the bottle, to sip from first, like scruffs, before taking a swig himself. They sit on the wooden swings, chatting and discovering things about each other; Elliot is very work-oriented and Katrien used to be engaged once, but she left the jealous drunk because he started gambling and cheating on her. He lives near her, so contact is unavoidable. The conversation starts getting one sided as Elliot notices that she's falling asleep against the rope holding the wooden plank up, and decides to ring a taxi. He has no idea where she lives exactly, and can't just leave her at the bar, so he makes an attempt to wake her, but she's sleepy, telling him he's cute and she just wants to nap for a bit. Her unresponsive state leaves Elliot with a serious problem. A little while later, Elliot's phone sounds, it's the taxi driver, waiting at the entrance for him. He tells the driver to wait a few minutes and picks Katrien up, carrying her like a sack of potatoes over his shoulder towards the taxi. Elliot reaches the entrance, only to find the driver puffing on a cigarette, enjoying the ability to stand on what is most probably a busy night. The driver doesn't seem happy with the idea that a grown man came out of the park with a woman on his back and needs a ride to a forest, but Elliot reassures him that they're married and were only reliving their younger years with some wine. The driver isn't fully convinced, but it's obvious that he needs the money, and this will be a pricey drive, so he agrees to drive them home. Whilst in the cab, Katrien wakes up and kisses Elliot on the cheek before resting her head on his lap, he is unsure as to what to do now, it's been so long since he touched a woman with good intentions, so he strokes her hair over her ear. The driver makes his way up to the house, where the porch light is burning brightly; Elliot always leaves it on when he's out, and awaits his payment, to which Elliot replies with four €50 notes. The driver drives off, leaving Elliot with Katrien in his arms; thoughts of taking advantage of her don't even cross his mind as he opens the front door and switches the light on with his elbow. He carefully makes his way to his bedroom, walking sideways through the hallway, ensuring her head doesn't bounce off the walls. Elliot lays her down in his bed, under the blanket, tucking her in and contemplating waking her up for a night of passionate, drunken sex, but kisses her forehead lightly instead and switches off the light as he closes the door behind him. He retires to the lounge, lighting a fire to heat up the room and opening another wine after sobering up trying to look after this vulnerable young lass. Elliot takes his notepad and glass of wine to the couch, lying across the width of it, head on the leather armrest. He takes a sip of the wine and places it on the little table behind him, and picks up where he left off.

"I'm not sure who phoned her, but they told her to drive to Kempton Park, in the Gauteng province; something to do with Frankie. She decided to take me and Jerome out of school for the day, and let her clients know that she wouldn't be able to operate the next day. We woke up as usual the next morning, got dressed and had our breakfast which had been prepared by Gugu, before setting out on the long road ahead, picking Sonja up on our way. Gauteng is a chaotic place to drive, and we got lost a few times, all Audrey had to find her mother with was an address she scribbled down on a piece of paper. This was before the invention of GPS, and none of us had a clue of how a map worked, so that saw us stopping at nearly every petrol station, asking the petrol jockeys for directions. After our detours and near collision experiences, we arrived at the correct address, it was a torn down, mess of a place, and it seemed to have been abandoned for some time. Audrey made sure we stayed in the car and locked us in, telling me to press the hooter for as long as possible if anything was to happen, after which she and her half-sister bravely proceeded into the house that housed many squatters. Jerome and I kept ourselves busy with a simple game of I Spy, but we were distracted by the horrific sight of our grandmother; old, dirty clothes on her body, struggling to walk; holding on to Audrey and John for support, swollen cheeks, mouth ulcers, and her once long, beautiful blonde hair now knotted from lack of washing. The smell of vomit and urine seemed to pursue her. Apparently, she had been sleeping on an old, torn to pieces, double-bed mattress with my step-grandfather, drinking cheap wine mixed with certain drugs to drown out the regret. Frankie had been begging for money at the traffic lights in town, making very little to support John's alcohol cravings and to sustain her own life. When the gastro and vomit kicked in, John took her to public hospitals but they refused to admit her, probably perceiving her as a washed-up druggie. The three adults stood outside, smoking, deciding whether bringing her to our house would be the best option, they could see her into a hospital and she could get cared for, but Audrey knew that Sylvain has to be asked and informed about any decisions, mostly because he was a very emotionally stable person, and knew how to solve problems quickly. On this occasion she didn't consult with father and decided to bring her home, leaving John there, he mentioned he would make his way there via hitchhiking. We found ourselves in Evander two hours later; a town close to us, at a public hospital, but the lack of equipment and shortages of rooms; due to high concentrations of patients, mostly AIDS and Tuberculosis, saw them refuse her admission. Audrey broke down, not having any answers, but Sonja fought hard, she was always one to pick fights and argue her way through things, but once again to no avail. Audrey ended up giving into the not so feminist idea of phoning her husband, asking him for advice and a solution to this issue, and he; as the brainy problem solver he was, came up with the idea to bring her home, giving her Jerome's bed to sleep in for the night. This gave Audrey the option to sleep in the same room but on my bed; Jerome and I slept in the same room at the time, but we would sleep by our father this night, away from the sights and sounds. With a Band-Aid solution deployed, we all got in the car, and drove home in the heavy rain. Upon arriving at our house, Sonja phoned her hired help to assist them this evening, in the bathing and caring of Frankie, but everything hurt, even water burnt her mouth. Sylvain took Audrey aside and told her that they would consult with their own GP in the morning, and if the public hospital didn't take her in after that, that he would pay for private health care, despite the rape case he faced and how keen they were on giving up on him a week prior. The next morning arrived faster than expected and stressed out Audrey went to our private doctor, he knew that her organs were failing, but also knew Sylvain's' medical aid wouldn't be able to cover her and he would be wasting money trying to help her; reversing liver failure is a tough one, so he wrote a note, demanding that the public hospital admit her, to which they did. They were grateful for his help, but the doc refused Sylvain's money for the check up, he knew that tough times were coming. Audrey and Sonja got her pyjamas and things for her time in hospital, being hopeful, seeing her through the x-rays, blood tests and urine tests, before returning home for the night. Audrey struggled to sleep that night, but was driven by fear the whole of the next day. We returned to school and things felt bleak. Frankie seemed to be in better condition when Audrey went to check up on her, she just couldn't speak due to the ulcers, Audrey felt a bit of relief, after hours of praying and putting positive energy on the situation. She collected us from school and took a nap, but half an hour into the nap the hospital phoned her, informing her that dear old grandmother went into a hepatic coma. Audrey grabbed Sonja from her house and went to the hospital in tears, and once there, the doctors confirmed cirrhosis of the liver, caused by heavy drinking, stress related circumstances, tranquilisers she acquired over the counter and neglect of healthy foods. Later that evening, Sylvain got Jerome and me to go to the hospital, to say our goodbyes because the doctor felt that we wouldn't have another time to do so. We were urged to kiss her goodbye but we couldn't, the smells were just too strong and we as kids had no understanding of goodbyes forever, despite my earlier lesson. They moved Frankie into a private room and we were asked to leave. 11:05 A.M. the next day she was pronounced dead, Audrey and Sonja were by her side when it happened, Sonja held on to her mother's arm, screaming at the top of her lungs 'come back', but nothing would change it, Audrey broke down as the vulture-like nurses took the body away. In the midst of it all, John was nowhere to be seen, and there was no way of contacting him, but police later informed him about the passing of his wife. The funeral arrangements were made, but they had no money to pay for it, so good old Sylvain, who recently became a smoker again, coughed up R10, 000 for her cause. The family from Botswana and Gauteng came to our house the day before of the funeral, and so did John, smelling of booze, having drank with 'friends' prior, he ended up staying with Sonja due to lack of space in our place, but I think my parents were a bit mad at him too, I think everyone was. The funeral commenced and I watched how it destroyed my mother, I also saw my father step up to the plate and pay for everything, comfort my mother and keep us on track with school."

Elliot's eyes become heavy and he dozes off, notepad on his chest and pen still in hand, hanging a few inches above the floor.

Hours pass as the two enjoy their divided slumber, Katrien wakes up, thirsty, but fearful, not knowing where she is, still in her dress. She quietly gets up and switches the light on, seeing a half messy room; it's a man's room, and a photo frame, upon investigation she realises that it's Elliot and she may be at his house. She panics and checks herself, making sure nothing happened, but she is relieved when she feels her underwear still soft opposed to semi wet or hard dry. He respected her integrity while she was intoxicated, the way men should. She takes her dress off, followed by the bra, leaving her knickers on and scratches in Elliot's wardrobe, where she finds a dress shirt to sleep in. She looks over at the alarm clock; 4:21, and wonders how she'll acquire water, she still doesn't know where Elliot is either.

She slowly and inaudibly treads down the hallway, towards what she assumes is the kitchen, noticing a lamp still burning bright, and Elliot passed out on the couch. She tippy toes past him, and randomly opens cupboards, looking for a glass. She finds a mug and fills it with tap water, before downing it, upon putting it down it slips off the edge of the basin and falls in, smacking into the aluminium base, waking Elliot. Elliot jumps up, fists at the ready; living in South Africa for a while you tend to be more aware of things and have to jump into action faster than normal people.

"Oh, good morning," Elliot mumbles after realising it was only Katrien.

He takes notice of her wearing his white work shirt draping above her black undies, walking around barefoot, the light flickering off her freshly shaved legs. She feels embarrassed and invasive.

"I'm sorry; I was just thirsty so I got some water."

He smiles and says, "You're all right, don't worry."

Elliot lies back down, staring at the ceiling while she walks back to the room.

"Thanks for taking care of me," she stutters out in appreciation.

"You're welcome. I didn't know what to do, so I brought you here," Elliot replies.

"How did we get home?" Katrien asks as she makes her way to the single-seater beside the couch Elliot is laying on.

"Oh, we got a taxi," he replies, abruptly sitting up in respect to her initiating a conversation.

"How much was it? I'll pay you back," she says after noticing her purse on the table.

"You're fine, I don't need money," he gets out with a slight laugh. Elliot took his shirt off during the night and realises how awkward it is sitting in front of her.

"Oh my God! Your hand looks bad," she calls out with concern, rushing to him, grabbing his hand. "What happened?" she asks as she hovers her fingertips over the scabs, as if she didn't notice it in the restaurant.

"I got a bit angry with myself and didn't handle it in the best way possible," Elliot convincingly states, as she sits up next to him. Their eyes meet, the blanket that once covered Elliot's naked torso, slides off. She hesitates; fighting herself from looking at his bulky, cut chest and ripped abdomen; he obviously spends a great deal of time in the gym. The room is dull, only a single, warm-white glow fills half the room, the lights reflection meet the awkward, teenage-like silence, and in a swift movement, Elliot's right hand is placed half on her cheek and half at the back of her head, she knows exactly what's happening and leans in for the kiss, resting her hand on his unclothed shoulder. They make out, wildly, the sexual frustrations they've held back from one another starts showing. Elliot starts moving his passionate kisses from her lips, to her left cheek, then jaw, then neck, before reaching the soft spot under her ear, provocatively sucking on her earlobe, trying to secure the deal. His other hand grips her thigh tightly, indicating how badly he wants her. She doesn't stop him, letting out soft murmurs as he progresses his mouth around, letting go of his shoulder and sliding it on to his chest. Things start getting fervent as Elliot begins unbuttoning the shirt she's wearing, but only the first three buttons, leaving the cleavage in the open but not exposing her breasts. He bites her shoulders lightly, turning her on, she lies back, opening her legs at the same time Elliot presses his body on hers, and she imperceptibly scratches his chest, enjoying the way he does things. He stops kissing her and sits up, asking her.

"Is this the alcohol or your intentions?"

She grabs the back of his head and pulls his head beside hers, and whispers.

"I'm sober…"

His stomach churns with excitement and passion; he knows where this will end up. Elliot undoes the remaining buttons on the shirt, firmly grasping her boobs, gently squeezing them, before leaning in to give a soft suck on her nipple, her body spazzes a few times from the seductive actions being carried out on her Dutch body. Katrien grabs his lower back, pulling him closer, encouraging him to rub his parts against hers, despite the clothing still being on. Elliot hovers his fingertips lightly across her belly, she feels the mild tingles. She wants him bad but she waits for him to make the moves. His hand loses its' innocence as it makes its way to her flower, it hovers over her lacy lingerie, fingers dangling and randomly teasing spots near the wet area, like a puppet on a string. She reaches for his belt and loosens it, leaving the ends dangling from the front two loops, and makes her way to the button above the fly. Elliot starts getting hard, itching, as she lingers around his manhood. She teases him, rubbing her hand over his semi-erect penis. He reaches down, knowing that it's up to him, and places his index, middle and ring fingers beside one another on her labia, feeling the dampness of her under garments, initiating a soft, circular rubbing motion. Katrien unzips his pants, seeing Elliot's underwear struggling to contain the firm erection, and places her index finger and thumb on the head, docilely squeezing it. Elliot gives up on the pleasantries and starts kissing her belly, moving back in order to take her panties off, and makes his way down, kissing and biting the inside of her upper legs. Katrien gently drives her nails into his shoulders, wrapping her legs around his neck as he starts muffing her, licking her moist, salty vagina. Elliot isn't a fan of going down on a girl because most taste bad, but Katrien is as enjoyable as a roast dinner to a homeless man. His tongue wags over her clit like a dog guzzling fresh water. He sucks it and starts rubbing his finger near the hole. After a while of licking and fingering her, he gets up and she throws him down, taking her shirt completely off, her boobs, a perfect C cup, firm with very little sag, she pulls his pants off. She slowly takes his underwear off, grabs the hard penis, and starts stroking it vigorously. She goes on her knees to match the height at which he's seated, and starts licking the tip, circling the circumference of the head and shaft alike. She slides the thick tip in her mouth, slowly sucking and working the shaft. She seems more experienced than what Elliot thought, but he isn't complaining. As the blowjob continues, she raises her head, Elliot notices her not so innocent blue, bedroom eyes, and wants her now, so he asks her to stop the act, suggesting she should lie back down. She feels his authority and does as she's told. He gets back on her, both naked now, kissing, touching, biting…but Elliot reaches down and feels her pussy dripping, so he grabs the shaft, and rubs the head slowly; up and down against the moist slits, before slipping it in gently. She is tight, and the slight painful expression on her face shows him he is big enough for her, but he sticks to his benign approach, leaving only the head to explore her, adding a few millimetres with every soft thrust. Her vagina loosens up after a few jabs, and she can handle all of him inside her, so she wraps her legs around his waist, excavating his back from the enjoyment. He normally wears condoms, but he wants the bond with her, and wouldn't mind a child at this age. He starts going faster, but decides he wants her to remember him, so he reaches down and starts rubbing her clit at the same pace he is going in and out, in and out. The gouging of his back continues and moans join the sound of skin pounding against skin, like a child running in flip-flops. He pulls out, wanting to change position, to make things more passionate, and sits down, grabbing her, lifting her onto him, making her face the same way he is facing, wanting her from behind. She opens her legs and slides it in, closing her legs after the insertion. He places his warm, strong hands on her; right around her waist, left on her right boob, they lean back, and she starts riding, matching his attempts to thrust from the no room he has to move in. While she bounces on him, taking what he has to offer, he kisses her neck, bites her shoulder and squeezes her boobs. She arches her back, accepting everything he's giving her. It's been 43-minutes and he starts wondering why she hasn't cum yet, so he roughly opens her legs; acting dominant, she likes it; she wants to be a slave to him, and starts rubbing her clit again, applying more pressure, going faster. Before his forearm starts going numb, she almost cries out, "I'm cumming!"

Elliot's second wind kicks in and he responds to her seductive plea by not giving up, by going faster. She squirts all over his legs, couch and a bit on the floor, letting out moans as she does. She thinks the act is finished, but Elliot has other ideas, he lifts her up and carries her to the bedroom. Elliot throws her on the bed, bending her over, and rubs his penis against her soaking vagina, teasing her with a round two. He puts it in and starts thrusting hard, smacking her right ass cheek once, and trying to be kinky about it. Her toes curl from the pleasure she's feeling, she grips the blanket and sheets together, squeezing hard. Elliot is close to finishing but is unsure where to release. He tries to pull out, but ejaculates before he can, releasing a lot inside her, but some still dripping out. She turns around and starts kissing him, happy with his efforts towards her. They climb in under the sheets and cuddle, an act he hasn't done for a while. Normally he hides in the bathroom, waiting for the lady to fall asleep, but this time he wants to be there, and she wants him there too. Katrien fearfully asks.

"Are you still going to be here in the morning?" confused Elliot laughs out and asks.

"I live here, of course I will be, what do you mean?"

"Well, I don't want to be left after this. I'd like something a bit more meaningful with you…" she states, placing the ball in his court.

Elliot gets nervous, he wants her, more than she knows, but he's struggling to identify whether the feelings are lust, convenience or something real, he quickly responds.

"I do want more than this."

Katrien leaves it on a silent note and lays her head on his muscly chest, content with the answer. Elliot strokes the hair over her ear, dragging his fingers up and down her arm; signs of affection he never shows. He thinks he found the answer he was looking for. An hour of thought passes before Katrien rolls over, facing the window; he is stuck between holding her and getting up for a shower. He chooses to get up, the sun slightly shining on his naked bottom through the divide curtains create when they can't reach one another, and heads to the bathroom. While scrubbing the bodily fluids off his skin, he hears a phone ringing, he pauses scrubbing for a second, but it doesn't match any device he owns, it must be Katrien's, so he continues washing up. A few seconds pass and Elliot hears her voice, confirming it was her phone, she sounds upset, so he turns the water off; to have a better listen, but she hangs up the phone before he can recognise any of the Dutch. Elliot wraps a towel around him, ready to investigate, but she knocks on the door, "Can I come in?" she asks.

"Yeah, you can," he quickly responds, anxious to see what's going on.

"Is it okay if I showered? I really need to go," she mentions.

He moves towards the taps and says, "Yeah you can, this is hot and this is cold, I have this body wash here and some shampoo, I'll grab you a towel. Is everything okay?"

"It's nothing, I just have to go." She mysteriously mentions. He grabs a towel from under the basin, places it on the counter and lets her shower in peace. Elliot gets dressed and angrily makes coffee for the both of them. Katrien gets out of the shower, gets dressed, and from the room calls a taxi, but doesn't know where she is. She hangs up and walks over to Elliot, sipping his coffee in the kitchen, and asks.

"Would it be possible to ring a taxi?"

"Yeah sure, I'll get one for as soon as possible," he responds. He is curious, but does what she wants before anything else. He pulls out his half-charged phone, calls a friend that happens to be a taxi driver; they became friends because Elliot always had clients visiting his company, and they needed a way around, but the taxi driver doesn't answer his phone, most probably still sleeping. She starts panicking, but he comes up with a risky solution, he has a four-wheeler round back, and they can drive that to the closest bus stop. Katrien has no other option, the weight of whatever's making her leave is heavier than the risk of being a passenger on an unlicensed, non-road worthy ATV, and so she impetuously agrees to his suggestion. Elliot doesn't even know if it has petrol but he wants to help, so he grabs the one helmet he has from the utility room, heads out the door; placing the helmet on the table out front and goes around back, pushing the ATV round front. He gets on and initiates the kick start, but the first four attempts fail, eventually it starts up and Elliot grabs the helmet, places it on Katrien's head, telling her to hold tight. The 500cc ATV is powerful, so he proceeds carefully, making sure not to open the throttle, slowing down near shorter bends. After a few kilometres, they come across a bus stop, there's a single lady standing there, probably doing the walk of shame home too. Elliot decides that this is far enough and that the gods have been kind, it's time to go home and not over stay his due. Katrien gets off the quad, struggles to get the helmet off; still an amateur to these things, and hands it back to its rightful owner. Elliot leans in for a hug goodbye, but she doesn't seem so enthusiastic about it, but embraces him anyway. He feels rejected; hurt beyond anything, *'Did she only use me for sex?'* Is all that crosses his mind. Elliot places the helmet on his head, locks in the first gear, looks in front and behind him, makes the U-turn, opens the throttle, and speeds off, triggering the power band in 2nd, forcing the bike to lift.

Upon arriving at home, Elliot parks the ATV round back; where he found it, and heads inside, contemplating whether he should go back to bed or continue writing. Despite the sun being out and the sexual burdens being lifted, he calls it a night, heads to the bedroom and crashes into the pillows. He turns a bit to his side, sniffing her pillow; the rose, candy smell she left behind, fuelling his doubts and queries as to why she acted the way she did. Elliot lays there in thought, before passing out for the day.

Chapter 6
War Never Changes

After a long, decent sleep, Elliot awakes, remembering the resentful display from Katrien. He stretches as he gets out of bed, yelling awkwardly, embracing the tingling feeling. Elliot looks at his phone, seeing a text from Katrien, sent three hours prior, he opens it.

'Hey, I'm sorry for how I acted; I know it's unusual but I have a few things going on at the moment, so please forgive me.'

Elliot tries being understanding, but he won't allow himself to be used for sex – ironic – and walked all over, and struggles between hitting the reply and back button.

'Sorry, I was asleep, yeah it's okay, I understand. If there's anything I can help with let me know.' He unwillingly replies, before putting the phone down to head to the kitchen.

With breakfast consumed and a filled tummy, Elliot has nothing else to do, other than continue writing and retrieving his car from the city. He already misses work, but still has a good bit of holiday left, so may as well try getting these things off his chest.

The entire family blamed John for Frankie's death, his instability, his mood swings, eagerness to beat women, inability to hold down a job, creating all the stress, alcoholic influences, which evidentially lead to Frankie's death, were among the factors the family brought up. I don't think anyone ever told him how they felt, mainly due to how he'd take it, having PTSD from the border war in Rhodesia; being stabbed, hit by a mortar, watching his friends die next to him, and on one occasion the military vehicle he was transported in drove over a land mine, and any bit of conflict would push him over the edge, resulting in what everyone thought would be prison. I suppose he was aware of what he did and he had no coping mechanisms other than drinking every day, but most of the family were upset at Frankie for not leaving him after the first beating, but she had to stay, how else would she raise two daughters and get them ready for the big bad world? A few days after the funeral, things seemed to go back to normal, well it seemed that way, Audrey finally became a woman, the pain tore the childish, little girl heart apart, and from the broken pieces emerged a strong, independent woman; she disbanded her business. The stress hit Sylvain too, this saw an increase in the violent outbursts, not towards Audrey however, but towards me. He knew Audrey suffered a loss that he hadn't yet felt, and didn't want to hurt her any further, and I was the closest emotional punching bag, so I was beaten. The beginnings of these beatings weren't so bad, it was mainly done with a belt on the butt, but they soon became more physical, involving hands, fists and safety boots. Nothing can justify beating a kid, but I deserved them most of the time. Gugu stood in front of my father's flying punches a few times, trying to save me, allowing me to run to her room; the back room we called it, bless her soul. Around this time three things happened, that seemed to affect the rest of my life, influencing me, the first was my fondness for the military and war, I always felt that there were men out there, fighting for the rights of their people and because of what my father was doing to me, I would one day grow up to be one of them, fighting for kids that were beaten like I was. The second was my love for geography and history; after finding an old atlas in my parents book shelf, I just wanted to leave, and go far away, but I wasn't sure as to where I would go, so I started learning about all these places from the encyclopaedias we had; I could read well for my age. The third was the start of psychological evaluations, I think my parents; mostly my mother, understood that I had witnessed two deaths already, got arguably justified beatings from my father, and the pressures of school would end up being too much for me, and I would crack, so I was booked to see Dr Christo Van Zyl once a week to find ways to help me overcome these emotions that were ready to boil over. I wasn't sure as to why I had to see this guy every Tuesday, I thought everyone in the school saw him, but it went past the drawings of trees and IQ tests, he spoke to me and actually listened, which felt good, because when I tried that at home I would be met with the famous 'children speak when spoken too' comment passed down from generation to generation. He seemed like a father figure to me, so I always enjoyed sessions with him. Christo showed me that I could do anything I wanted in the world, and told me the only thing I really needed was to invest time in learning things, advice that I took immediately, so after school every day, I went more in depth with military, history and geography. Trying to grasp the concepts of continents and countries, the evolution of their military, from knights and kings, to commandos and presidents, to their participation in wars, the equipment they used such as guns and tanks. Among my educational adventures, I found myself drawing the flags to every country in the world; which I completed to everyone's amazement, reading different books on WW2, asking about Henri's time in the war, and drowning in French patriotism whenever reading about Napoleon Bonaparte and his conquests. The year quickly came to an end, with no other significant events taking place, other than the tears I cried after understanding that I had to leave for second grade, leaving Mrs Basson behind, not that I was a fan of hers, I was just scared of growing up I guess, the unknown scares most, but I got a fancy silver certificate. South Africans always awarded children with certificates based on their grades at the end of the year, the criteria varied from school to school, but they were difficult to acquire nonetheless. I found myself in Grade 2A, in a classroom directly above my previous class, with Mrs Van Dyk, a tall, skinnier teacher, she was a lovely woman, strict but fun. Nicole and Unathi moved with me luckily. Advika unfortunately moved to another school, but that didn't affect me much as there was a cute German girl that moved to our class that seemed to grab my attention, Mila Muller was her name; a tad chubby, with blonde hair, blue eyes, a button nose and a drawl accent. I suppose this is where I learnt trait number four; amorous, due to my awkward social skills and poor boundaries, a variety of poor examples set by my parents on dealing with conflict in unhealthy methods, maybe even a lack of love. I befriended her quickly with my knowledge of Germany thus far, and being from neighbouring countries; skipping the history between the two, we got well acquainted. Her family went to the same church we went too, and our mothers got speaking. Audrey decided to put us in the catechism classes provided by the church. Religious education was something not yet completely introduced to the South African school system, and essentially we would have to pass this class to be legible to do our communion, and being from a Roman Catholic background, this was mandatory, so we were 'enrolled', along with other kids such as Mila, Brennan and Pule.

My father was into peaceful activities, such as putting puzzles together, cooking and growing his own crops, and on our 950 square m property; bigger than most European properties, but in the low-medium bracket in Southern Africa property sizes, we had a small patch, in the far back corner, which my father dedicated to growing his own fruits and vegetables. Scattered around the yard we had peach, apple and orange trees, with a grape vine wrapped around metal framework; my father tried building a canopy for his car to hide under whenever hailstorms came around, but never finished. My father utilised Jerome and my unworked backs, and still flexible legs to his advantage by getting us to help him out in this garden. All three of us set out to work as Audrey made dinner; something Gugu normally covered, but Audrey needed to manage when Gugu was on holidays. Sylvain would give us both buckets and sections of the garden to work in, and we would have to finger pick each and every weed out of the bed; beds were 3 metres in length and 1.2 metres in width, there were 12 of them. My father would be in a middle bed, next to a radio blaring the radio station's music, a can of beer beside him, and a cigarette in his mouth, picking out his fair share. All three of us would sit in the hot African sun, shirtless, clearing this plantation so father could sow seeds, and when harvest came around we would save a bit of money on food shopping, having the freshest produce available, only problem was I hated fruits and vegetables with a passion, I considered myself a carnivore, sometimes acting like a dinosaur at the dinner table; an inside joke Jerome and I had going for many years. I have no idea how Jerome felt with the child labour, I on the other hand dreaded it, sometimes it was a fun pass-time, but it's a happy memory now, where the three of us sat there doing something constructive together, bonding the way father and sons should.

Near the end of the year, Audrey came out, announcing a third pregnancy, hoping for a girl this time.

2003 swooped in and took the calendar by surprise, this was going to be a tough year for my parents, so many things were bound to take place this year, and my rebellious ways weren't helping them out, which inevitably ended in more beatings. The year started off good, Jerome fit right into primary school, he was a pleasant, quiet kid, smarter than most of the children in his class. If you ever made a complaint against him you were either jealous or a liar, he was too perfect and could do no wrong. The way they depicted Jerome annoyed me and this caused me to smack him around, which got me more hidings because this time round he could speak English and notify my parents on my behaviour. I quickly started noticing that my social skills weren't up to par, compared to the other students, and I started being treated as an outcast, from time to time I resorted to making a fool of myself in front of people for attention. Audrey was made aware of my strange behaviour on parent-teacher meetings, but had no way to justify it. It wasn't so much the way you spoke to people that mattered at that age, it was more what you brought to the table and I wasn't the smartest in the class, I wasn't cool, not so great at sports; despite playing for the soccer team in first grade, and my family wasn't as financially well off as opposed to other parents, so either way I looked at it, I would never live up to the *paradigm set out by the ten-year olds around me. I had this love-hate friendship with a boy called Shaun, a little, chubby, freckled face prick. He was a bit bigger than me. There was Justin; the boy all the girls wanted, Brennan; the spontaneous, quirky friend Audrey sometimes gave lifts too, then the usual suspects, Nicole, Mila and Unathi. Pule had followed Advika and enrolled at another primary school. One wintery morning, on our way to school I spotted what I thought was a stray dog, picked her up and gave it a name, Beauty. Sarah used to watch me sit outside, talking with a dog, supposedly feeling sorry for me as Audrey mentioned to Amelia that I had problems at school; at least she started greeting more frequently. I thought to myself that this was where my loyalty should have been, instead of trying to impress people in my school; despite her being in another school, I should have tried to impress her, but that idea disappeared as soon as Audrey yelled 'food's on the table'; the quickest way to my heart. Months went by before Mila and I considered each other as boyfriend and girlfriend, not yet fully accustomed to what it meant, but we would always walk with one another on Friday's to church, which was like 300 metres from the school. Her mother was one of the teachers there, which made things even more awkward when her mother found out we had a thing for each other. One particular, warm Friday afternoon, Mila and I walked down to the church. Jerome always walked in front of us, by himself, not that he was a loner, but because he was a very inquisitive nuisance, so I had pushed him away to spend time with my woman. I forgot to use the bathroom prior to leaving the school; the bathrooms were normally locked earlier as the janitors and facility staff always wanted to go home sooner, so I held it in. I assumed that I would be able to go at the church, but on this occasion Mrs Muller was very impatient, and wanted us in class immediately, so I followed orders, because if reading WW2 books taught me anything, it was that one should never get on the wrong side of an angry German. We sat in the class, I remember this lesson, as it either haunted me or inspired me for a long time after, we were asked to find a solution to change the world in a positive manner, and how we would approach doing so. The answers varied among the class, Brennan, who occasionally placed his genitalia on the corner of table and bounced, unaware of how it looked for others, mentioned something about saving water, Mila, who probably got given the question the night before, suggested introducing religious studies and all-round peace practices into school; keeping in mind the school had Indian, Muslim and African religions, but the school only adhered to the Christian way of things. I; at this point ready to explode, came out with an innocent, childish suggestion; which the teacher felt, in theory, would be great if the world worked together on it, of doing a good deed for someone, and that person went out and did a good deed for the next person, and so on until the world was a better place. However, thinking of it now we don't always have good days. As the question went across the rest of the room, my threshold broke, and I wet myself, pulling myself toward the table, trying to hide the accident, it was more than just a wet patch in the front of my shorts, as we were seated in dipped chairs, so the urine gathered at the lowest point of the dip, unfortunately where my ass was. The colour of my shorts resembled the colours of an old WW2 Tiger 2 tank, dark grey on the tracks, light grey on the sides and turret, and nearly black on the cupola. I sat there, almost submerged in urine for 25-minutes, the air around me got contaminated by the stale smell of piss, but no one noticed, thank God for windows. Mrs Muller's lesson finished up and everyone was allowed to leave, and they did, but I remained in my* seat, embarrassed with the situation. Mila's mother noticed that I hadn't even attempted to get up from my seat; I was usually the first to leave, and asked me what was wrong, I tried to avoid the topic by talking about my infatuated feeling for her daughter, which was debunked by Mrs Muller as 'puppy love', an awkward conversation that I grind my teeth at still, but the stench reached her nostrils and she understood the reasons behind my actions. My mother collected me half an hour later and luckily no one ever found out about the mess. Shaun and I started growing closer as friends, but also had rough patches where we hated each other, and due to our mutual interest in wrestling, we would run up to one another and perform moves; spear tackles and RKOs, that we were urged not to try at home or at school, putting ourselves at risk of back and neck injuries. We did it out of spite and attention seeking, as he also struggled making friends, despite being smarter than 60% of the class, he was a gold mine for bullies; chubby-build, freckles, vulnerable, easily pissed off. What really stood in our way of friendship was the idea I had that he was after Mila, and she was mine, but I was unsure about his intentions. We were both friends with Justin; who was arguably the coolest guy in the school, along with Brennan's bigger brother; who could fight really well and was an expert on a stunt bike, but it was all about who was closer to Justin that mattered, as that person would be in the cool circle, and thought highly of, which we both wanted. One sunny Friday evening, we finished catechism classes earlier than normal, and we had to drive home with the Mullers, as my mother was busy, and Pule came with us; as he lived seven houses away from us. While sitting in the red hatchback they drove, Mila turned to me, and planted a kiss on my small, awkward-shaped lips. I was hesitantly happy at the act, but as I saw the 9th cloud, Mila turned to Pule and kissed him too, what the fuck? I felt sick, this was my girlfriend and she just cheated on me in front of me, those brave Germans...any other group of white people would have seen this as a huge mistake, but none of us were brought up in a racist manner, so we didn't see it as that. Pule and I remained friends over the years, and always shared a laugh when this story was brought up. I sat through the drive to Mila's huge house, in hatred for my friend and girlfriend. We arrived and everyone got dressed to swim in the Mullers' swimming pool; Jerome and I never learnt how to swim, but I sat there, angered by the event, as they all had fun in the water. I always watched over Jerome whenever we were near water, as a year prior we had gone down to Roodeport, so that John could visit his sister, and Sonja; being a neglectful mother; having given her first son up for adoption, and basically giving her second born away too, brought her third and fourth sons; Jacob and Steven, with. The two decided to play near the pool, unmonitored. It was all fun and games, until Steven, the youngest of us all fell in the water, and started drowning, Jacob; the cocky, wannabe tough bastard, started crying, leaving Jerome and I to jump into action. I stretched myself over the water while Jerome sat on my legs; holding me down, ensuring my safety. I reached out for the five-year old and grabbed his arm, putting all my power into keeping his head above water, Jerome realised that he wasn't heavy enough to hold me and Steven down, so he shouted out at the cry baby to sit on my legs too. I finally got Steven into my arms, and grabbed him around the chest, as Jerome and Jacob dragged me away from the water. We sat there for about a minute breathing heavily, asking Steven if he was okay, while Jacob ran inside to notify our parents; taking credit for saving his brother, the little fucking snake. Mrs Muller came outside to keep an eye on everyone in the pool, so I headed inside to Mila's brother; Harold, *who was playing computer games, something I had not yet experienced as my father hogged the computer.*

Elliot's phone starts ringing, he puts the pen down and reaches for the mobile, it's Katrien. He solicitously answers.
"Hello?"
"Hey Elliot, I just wanted to personally say sorry about this morning, a message is not respectful enough. Would you like to come over to my friend's house tonight and I'll explain things to you?"
She lays the cards on the table. Elliot realises it's late; 22:13, but he isn't tired, having had a good nap earlier.
"Yeah, sure, in Aalst right?" he asks.
"Yes in Aalst," she confirms.
"Give me ten minutes to get ready and I'll get a taxi down to the city, grab my car and head to the sports park, then just meet me there or give me directions to yours."
She agrees to meet him there and he closes the notepad, rushing to the room to get dressed and call a taxi. He isn't sure as to why she needs him at this time of night, he feels like a booty call, and he's allowing her to walk over him again. He closes the front door behind him as he walks into the darkness of night, headed for the taxi idling outside. The porch light is left off on this occasion; he doesn't forecast himself coming home soon. Elliot hops into the vehicle and greets the driver; that seems eager to call it a night. After a lengthy, expensive drive down to the big city, Elliot gets in his car and heads towards Aalst. His journey down Eindhovensweg is accompanied by the sounds of a young rapper on the radio, aggressively rhyming about a woman he fell for, perhaps a sign from the universe? He decides to take a left at the intersection, getting on to Voorbeeklaan and soon after taking a right on to Arembergstraat; that leads to the stadium. Elliot pulls out his phone after parking at the entrance, and starts ringing Katrien.
"Hey, I'm here at the entrance of the stadium," he mentions before she could even greet.
"Who the fuck is this?" a male voice asks.
Baffled, Elliot pulls the phone away from his ear and looks at the caller name, it says 'Katrien'. *'Who is this clown?'* he thinks to himself.
"I'm looking for Katrien," he says in his professional voice.
"This is her boyfriend, who is this?" the man replies.
Elliot's heart shatters, and the fragments fall like raindrops in his belly, the man still needs an answer, but Elliot slowly pulls the phone away from his ear, hearing several curious *hello's* as his thumb reaches for the red button, ending the call and all his good intentions in her boyfriend's ear. The car is started and Elliot spins the back wheels in anger as he drives off. *'Why would she lie? Did she just use me for one decent night away from life? For the fine dining and long grinding? Why did I allow this to happen?'* he thinks to himself as his car begins to exceed the speed limit to the hard rock music playing through his phones Bluetooth. "It's fucking funny how you ask me whether I'd be there in the morning, expecting more than just sex, and you go against what you made me believe!" he loudly confronts the image of her in his mind. After a fairly quick drive, he arrives at his asylum, heads inside, straight to the whiskey bottle. "I should have focused on my writings and wellbeing

instead of another Dutch pussy," he blurts out to himself as he turns the golden cap of the bottle anti-clockwise. Elliot takes a huge swig of alcohol, places the open bottle on the counter and heads to the bathroom to drain the lizard. He walks past the mirror, "Back to square one," he mentions after seeing his reflection, he doesn't want to meet the monster again, he doesn't want to buy another mirror or follow his grandfather's drinking habits. Before he can shake it; no more than twice, he hears his phone ringing, but he ignores it, guessing it would be Katrien with an excuse or her boyfriend demanding answers. Elliot heads back to the front of the house, switching off lights and locking doors; not that anyone would ever find him or break in; psychologically he is trying to shut the world out again, after being hurt. In the midst of his lock up, the phone rings again, he hovers over the flashing LED screen and ringing sound, to see Katrien's name as the caller. He really isn't interested anymore, continues locking up, and heads to bed. As Elliot tries to comfort himself in the white, after-sex stenched linen, he continuously hears the plangent tune, upsetting him further. He gets up and slams his bedroom door, shutting out her cries, and gets back under the covers, envisioning Katrien's naked body crawling on the covers in front of him. Things get quiet, finally he can just retire his broken heart for the night, but he lets out a soft sigh as he hears the phone ringing again, this time it's softer and duller.

Chapter 7
Troublesome

Elliot wakes up earlier than normal and makes his way to the front of the house, checking up on his phone in the process; 35 missed calls, all from Katrien's phone. Either Katrien really liked him and wanted to apologise or this guy really is crazy and wants to know who was calling his girlfriend. He really doesn't care anymore, the look of his straight face expresses it all too well, he fell for someone again and as the elders say, "History repeats itself."

Fed up with where his loyalty laid, Elliot opens the notepad to right his wrongs...

Education continued in this primary school, and being in the third grade we were given a time table of our class schedules, something we all dreamt about in our previous years. It was hard to choose a favourite teacher, as Mr Sanders taught history, and that gave him a direct line to my heart; I'm sure he noticed my love of WW2, and then there was Mrs Fisher, who taught us life orientation, and allowed us to have a lot of fun in class. Justin and I seemed to bond over the deployment of American troops in Iraq, rap music and cars. This meant that I was ahead of Shaun in brownie points. Near the middle of the year we were introduced to another student that moved from an opposing school, Sean. Sean seemed like a nice guy, being the only child of a single mother; who taught at our school, and we thought that he would be respectful and not affect his mother's occupation in a negative manner. Oh, boy...were we fucking mistaken. Sean was taller than most of us, cocky, smart and witty beyond expectation, and having a mother in a high position meant he would get away with murder. Sean immediately gained the love of majority of the girls in the class due to his British surname and accent. Girls like Jenny; who bullied me by kicking me in the privates a lot, and Samantha; who was a straight up bitch, fell for him fast. He realised he had the class wrapped around his finger. Shaun and I tried making friends with him, we succeeded but he had bipolar manner of treating companions. In front of girls he would be a dick, and with no audience he would be a sound lad, which outraged us. A few weeks went by and July the 14th had come, Sylvain collected us from school and took us to the hospital where Audrey had given birth. Upon arriving I could see the twinkle in Jerome's eyes, finally another brother, someone he could actually enjoy. Jerome and I started hating one another, my jealousy towards him and his hatred for my exhibition of brotherhood drove us to fight and argue a lot. He would purposely hurt himself, run to my father and blame me, ensuring the unavoidable battering. Revenge for how I treated him when we were infants I suppose. He was right to do so I deserved more hidings than what I received. We walked into the ward behind our father, seeing so many new mommies and daddies, hearing the screams of mothers still trying. We prowled into this magnolia-coloured room, with clean white curtains and linen, and found Audrey under the covers, holding onto the infant.

"What's his name?" Jerome's sweet, innocent voice questioned.

"Gabriel," Audrey's nearly lost voice stated.

My dad's facial expression seemed to read out fucking hell, here we go again. I walked over to this Gabriel character, and looked him in his blue eyes, but before my hatred and jealousy could manifest, he grabbed my pinky, and squeezed on it, the most reassuring feeling in the world. Audrey got up to sit down on the chair the room provided, holding Gabriel in her hands, Jerome on her left with his red vest and me on the right with my blue football jacket, ready for the first of many photos with her boys. I didn't learn from my mistakes, and tormented Gabriel when no one was around, saying things like, "This is my family, and you won't steal my parents from me. I'll beat you up if you try," and devilishly enjoying the tears he cried, just another memory I grind my teeth to whenever it pops up. There are certain things in life you shouldn't do, and this was one of them. Despite Secunda being a rather quiet town at the time, Piet Retief Street was always filled with kids playing soccer on a tar road after school and on weekends, among these football prospects were Unathi, Pule, Brennan, Myself and Jerome. We divided ourselves into teams and placed two bricks in the middle of the road, with a 50 m distance between them; giving enough space for cars to pass, and play for hours. Sometimes Audrey would try live up to that stereotypical, white suburban mom that made lunch for everyone, which gained us a bit better reputation, but all that was knocked down when Sylvain came home and asked us all to clean the garden.

"There is a time to work and a time to play," he would always utter out.

Jerome and I had no choice, we had to clean the yard, but everyone jumped in and helped, making it go by faster. One Tuesday morning, at school, Mila told me that Shaun had held her hand, and that he tried to kiss her, but she didn't want too. I overreacted and in the heat of the moment I told him.

"First break. You and me. On the field." I was so pumped for my first fight.

First break eventually came; I was filled with anxiety and anger, ready to engage in this mano-a-mano showdown. Shaun showed up to everyone's surprise, looking as cool as a cucumber. It started off with simple words.

"Why you going near my girl, bro?"

"She's not yours, she wants me," then escalating to pushing and shoving.

There were hordes of kids around us, all chanting 'Scooroo', which I believed meant 'fight' in some African dialect. He threw the first punch, it landed on my cheek, ding-ding-ding.

"Game on, fatso," I cried out as I stormed towards him, fists at the ready.

We stood there boxing it out; left hooks, right jabs, upper cuts and cheap gut shots. It went on for several minutes before two prefects and Mr Sanders intervened, scorning us for the fight. We were sent to the principal's office, where we received detention and an incriminating note in our personal file. It was worth it, I stood up for my belongings, although women aren't possessions. The fight blew over as the days went by, and things returned to normal, Mila and I broke up, due to her wanting friendship with Jenny and Samantha, they didn't like me, and that seemed to be the prerequisite to joining the posse. From that point forward, my movement towards an outcast in this primary educational institution seemed irreversible. Unathi and Brennan had their own friend circle, and the only time I could interact with them was on weekends when we played soccer. Sonja came over one evening, bringing some strange friends with her, who just had to meet Audrey. Sonja may have been my mother's half-sister, but we never trusted her, especially after giving up on two kids, involving herself with the scummiest people and finding herself under the influence of either drugs or alcohol. There were times where Jerome and I were entrusted with the task of watching her around the house, as she had been caught stealing my mother's jewellery before. Sonja had no real form of income and relied solely on the men she was with. This saw her pawn almost all the goods in her house so that she could get high or drunk with John, who always seemed to travel wherever she went. Sonja was in and out of our lives like a whack-a-mole machine in an arcade, only coming around when money was up for grabs. There was a guy, with tattoos, that gave me a gift. It was a CD of Linkin Park. This disc, filled with early 2000s metal quickly replaced my rap CD's that I had lent from Justin, and rap meant a lot to me, as I hand-wrote the lyrics down to most Eminem songs on sheets of paper which I hid from my parents. My parents gave me my own room, and along with it a boom box to play my CDs in, but in a reasonable volume as they didn't want to hear my shit taste in music.

One Saturday, after breakfast and early morning cartoons, Unathi appeared outside with a soccer ball. I got dressed and we headed off, in search of our friends; luckily we all lived within 500 metres of each other. After acquiring the gang, we set up our bricks and proceeded as normal. To our discomfort, down the road came JonJon, Doug and Sid; Racist, Afrikaans bullies, that were trouble in their schools and almost neglected by their parents, Unathi and Pule were all too familiar with their work as they lived closer to them. Jerome and I heard the rumours, but were yet to meet them. Doug was our age, while Sid; his brother, along with JonJon, were three years old than us, but they all smoked and drank, real bad influences. They got to where we were playing, and asked Jerome to pass the ball, one could see by the way they trapped the ball, they weren't skilled at all, and the evil look in their eyes proved their intentions were horrid. JonJon picked the ball up and kicked it up in the dense air, far from where we were. The ball landed in someone else's yard, out of our retrieval reach, due to the gates and electric fences they had; we normally climbed over walls and gates to acquire our ball if there were no dogs. I tried standing up for our group, but my good intentions were smothered with a "What are you going to do about it?" They laughed at us and walked away. We were lucky that Unathi's big brother would stand up to them; being twice their size, but he wasn't always there for us. The timing of these bullies was bad, as I was already committed to a two-faced asshole, that dissed me in front of fellow classmates. Gabriel was the centre of attention at home, Jerome was learning how to cook with Sylvain; playing on his weak spots, I was doing rather shitty at school. The only thing I had going for me was weekend soccer and a metal CD. For the first time in my nine-year long life I went into a shell, unable to fix things, or talk my way out of it. I figured out how alone I was on my ninth birthday party, when I had no one but family around me, that seemed forced to be there. Just before I thought things couldn't any get worse, 19 days after my birthday, Henri was on the phone to Sylvain, speaking French as usual. We understood a few words, but could never make out what was going on, so we always waited till after the phone call, when Father explained it to us. This phone call was different though, Sylvain's voice wasn't as jolly as normal; there was no enthusiasm in his sentences. After several paragraphs we picked up on a few words, such as "I love you, Father", "Goodbye", and having the experience of two previous deaths in the family, my theory of my favourite WW2 hero passing was confirmed. I watched this brave, sometimes cruel man, that I secretly admired and looked up to, sit on his computer chair, right leg folded over the left, with his favourite red polo and blue jeans on, become sad. He had one arm resting on the counter of the computer stand, which held a cigarette hovering over a green ashtray, and the other struggling to hold the phone to his ear. He hung his head over his lap, as his voice became softer and the words slowed down drastically. I watched this hard man shed tears, something I never saw before, something we thought we would never see in this lifetime. Audrey walked over to him as she understood more French than Jerome and I had, and started massaging his shoulders, cuddling him from behind. The actions before my eyes started proving my theory correct. On most phone calls to the French family, we would be asked to say hello and try speak with them, but that was not the case here. The house seemed three times larger than what it was, placing everyone at further distances away from one another. I stole my dad's Mozart CD from the cabinet and retired to my room. I remembered my father telling me that among Henri's favourite music was a composer known as Mozart. I took out my metal CD from the boom box, and put my Grandfather's artist in, pressing play on the first song. Tears began to leak out of my eyes as the harmonic symphony filled the room in a regulated volume. I heard my father's loud footsteps walk towards the master bedroom; which was beside mine, and the door closed behind him. I awaited the second set of footsteps, but my mother's comfort couldn't change the outcome, and sometimes a man needs to be alone. The rest of the night was quiet, Sylvain passed on dinner, and we sat there in silence, Jerome wasn't yet informed of the situation. I broke the silence by asking my mother if my father would be flying to France; for the funeral of course, but she wasn't sure what he wanted to do, as tickets would be expensive and he couldn't book days off with such little notice; being a very important person in his sector. Henri passed away the next day, the 28th of September.

We approached the last day of the year, and went on our regular walk around the neighbourhood. My parents would be holding hands as the fireworks shot out into the night sky. Jerome and I would be well ahead of our parents, trying to find where the loud bangs came from, but due to trespassing legalities we never found them. Gabriel was in a pram, being pushed along by Audrey. The joke that people were celebrating my father's birthday came out once again.

2004 finally arrived, and Jerome and I found ourselves promoted to a higher grade and in new classes. I realised that I was shit out of luck when they told me Mrs Barns would be my register teacher. I really hated her, she was by far the grumpiest woman I ever had the displeasure of meeting. Anyone else in the school's limited amount of employees would have been better, hell I would have settled for the elderly janitor that drove a lawnmower instead. She believed in favouritism, and having experienced this idiosyncrasy at home on day-to-day bases, I knew that I wasn't going to win. Nicole; who had established her name through hard work, was on top of the class in everything, followed by Samantha and Jenny, preceded by others such as Shaun, Sean and Unathi. My stupidity and inability to grasp basic concepts of enlightenment saw me place in the bottom three. She had a meticulous way of tutoring, and her modus operandi was too far advanced for the likes of the suffering simpletons, contributing to the hypothesis; the rich get richer and the poor, poorer.

Being in her presence really upset me to great extents, but I had to bite the bullet and finish, and when I graduated to be a lawyer one day; the realistic occupation for disputation against unfair practices, I would sue her for the emotional trauma, bankrupting her in the process. This primary institution was proving to maintain the diversity and cultural differences pretty well, compared to other schools in the vicinity, in spite of the ten-year Anniversary of Mandela's freedom. Afrikaans institutions seemed to still perceive Africans as an inferior race, and Black schools were significantly vindictive to whites. This factor, among many more, contributed to the school's flourishing eminence. As a bit of time passed, I realised that my performance at school was affecting my fellowship circle, meaning my friends would spend little to no time with me, only associating with me where no one could see. I found myself befriending the infamous Doug, why I ever thought that this would be a good idea I have no clue. The verbal abuse from Mrs Barns, along with the jokes kids made behind my back, and how Sean treated me in front of girls I thought I had a shot with, forced me to steer my ship against the winds. So there I was, next to the little cottage we had beside the house, with a fag, that Doug had sponsored, in-between my index finger and thumb. I piss-potted the filter and nearly died from a coughing fit, this clearly wasn't a hobby I was keen on taking up anytime soon. Doug stood there laughing at me, calling me a pussy as he puffed away so professionally. He pulled out a bottle of beer; that he more than likely stole from his dad, from his bag, and offered me the dirty second sip. I declined as I knew this was going too far, but I was afraid I would lose possibly the last chance at a friend I would ever have, so I recalled my cancellation and took a sample, it tasted bitter and horrible, but I swallowed it like a determined teenage girl. He scoped out my pad and how I could be beneficial to him, and probably realised I was a sucker for attention, so he started taking advantage of me. He would get back from school – this was his second or third school, as he was expelled due to fighting – and ask me for smokes, obviously using the knowledge he acquired after seeing my parents smoking. I was trapped in this conflict of interest, but tried to do the right thing, and said.

"No, they are my parents and I can't steal from them."

He wasn't too happy with my answer, so he intimidatingly punched me on the right arm, and asked again. I stood strong for a second time, declining pilfering from my folks, but a second punch came, this time harder. He started threatening to beat me up if I didn't get him a smoke. I walked inside and suspiciously looked at my mother, who asked me if I was having fun, to which I responded.

"Yep," and felt so guilty for what I was about to do. I went to their not so secret stash of cigarettes and stole a carton, from the pile they had, went to my room and cached it in my pants drawer. I opened the box, took a packet out, hid it in my underwear; my pants had no pockets, and proceeded to go outside. I stood under the grape vine; which was still in its early years, and handed the smokes over.

"You're a great guy, you know that?" came from his mouth.

I was pleased, finally someone gave me a compliment, other than the regular; "You're a spitting image of your mother." I was stuck in a situation that would affect me badly, I was aware of Doug's bad intentions, that he was using me, and his defiant attitude was brushing off on me. I also knew that I was able to identify the mistakes I was making, and rectifying them by getting rid of him should have been prioritised, but it was a tough decision, because if he left, I would have no one, only my dog, as the soccer gang ditched me for my affiliation to the racist bigot. I had one opportunity to fix this, but I chose against it, silly me. My parents started asking questions such as why smokes and beer went missing, why I was always around Doug, meeting outside in secret, long after hours. I never drank or smoked, it was all purloined for him and his deplorable habits. My family grew suspicious of the situation, Jerome didn't like Doug at all, as he would oppress him too, aware of my inability to arbitrate. The guilt was too much and I began heinously swearing at my mother, maliciously attacking Jerome for the smallest thing, I even allowed my below average marks to plummet even further, it became reckless, in spite of my father's violent attempts to amend the situation. In the midst of all these emotions and outbursts, Gugu was diagnosed with tuberculosis and my parents were unsure as to how it would affect us, especially with a new-born in the house, so she was let go until she was cured. Unfortunately, she never recovered and passed away, and once again I was exposed to a close death. Who was going to protect me from my daddy now? Who was going to cook me the best tasting porridge in the mornings? Who was going to sit there teaching me how to knot a tie or some Zulu vocabulary? We attended the big, black funeral in Embalenhle; a squatter district on the edge of our town; inhabited by mostly African people, which was the norm; white people were urged to stay away from the area, due to the still healing wounds from the apartheid era. We were three white people surrounded by hundreds of black people, on sandy grounds, in front of a preacher, who asked my mother to get up and say a few words, awkward, but she managed it with tears in her eyes. Audrey and Gugu grew close as friends, so it was easier for her to cry, I feel had she not shown any remorse or emotions at the funeral, things would have ended very differently. We went to the memorial after the church service and I was introduced to her son, who liked me and my soccer talents, apparently his mother told him all about me playing soccer in the streets for hours.

As the saying goes 'when it rains, it pours', and Audrey once again received a phone call… Who this time? It was relatives in Zimbabwe, in need of help. They were related to John, who wasn't directly related to us. I never grasped the concept as to why this was our responsibility? Apparently, Liam, the father of the household suffered a mental breakdown, and lost his job. Liam's wife, Caitlin, was unable to work due to her disability, being wheelchair bound for the rest of her life. They had two daughters, Fabian and Xena, as well as two boys, Benny and Leonard. Fabian was engaged to a Lebanese man, who stood as a pillar for the family, supporting them financially and emotionally, Xena was enthralled by cigarettes and Jamaican music. Benny, had long hair and was a bit too flamboyant for a lad and Leonard was still a mere tot. Audrey drove north, to the border, and collected them, along with Amir who used his car to take the few that remained. They were in search of a better life, and the proper facility to treat Liam, so that he could go about supporting his family once again. Sleeping arrangements were made once they arrived at our house, which was onerous as we were five in the house already, and we needed to magically find space for another six. Amir was in the middle of negotiating a housing solution for himself and Fabian. A resolution developed, Audrey and Sylvain stayed in their room, along with Gabriel who was still in a cot. Liam, Caitlin, Benny and Leonard got Jerome's room. Fabian and Xena shared with me and Jerome in my room, but most nights I was subliminally forced to sleep on the couch as they too found me vexatious. Jerome and I were displeased with the situation and kept our distance. Amir was the only one of the bunch I had liked, he was cool, and had a cool car. Leonard was still a toddler and thought hosting a crying competition with Gabriel in the middle of the night was a great initiative, meaning none of us had any sleep. A few days of complete chaos and little sleep went by before I found myself in class, once again in trouble, but unaware of what I did this time. Apparently, someone tipped the school off with the fib that I had brought a condom to school and was preparing to rape Samantha once the final school bell went. So, Mrs Barns' class was interrupted by a senior male teacher, who escorted me out of the classroom along with my possessions, an embarrassing event. We stood on the soft primrose coloured corridor of the third floor, unpacking my green bag, looking for the rubber contraceptive. During the search I was dynamically questioned on my intentions with Samantha, but he only found my purest romantic aspirations towards her. It became obvious that the tip off was fake and that I was being framed after they asked me to describe what a condom looked like, and I provided a description resembling a tampon. Rape was a serious accusation in an ever-increasing crime crammed country, and I was scared. I was exhorted to go to the principal's office after the search, so I stood up and looked at my class looking back at me. Everyone had this concerned look on their face, except one person, Sean, who was smiling ever so gleefully at me. Upon arriving at the office and receiving horrendous looks from the administrative staff working there, my parents were called, along with Samantha's parents. Samantha's mother was a huge lady, and was the leader of the boy scouts group I had attended the previous year. Her father was smaller than the mother, which was always a funny sight to see. Samantha's parents suggested letting us get on with our schoolwork, and invited us to their house to speak about the matter in private after hours, to which my dishonoured mother had no choice but to accept. During second break, I was questioned by various members of my class as to what had been going on, but Sean filled them in before I could, it seemed like he knew a bit too much, so I asked him if he had tried to frame me, to which he smiled and whispered in my ear.

"No one would believe you anyway."

I felt the rueful hatred consume my perplexed soul in an instant. We drove down to Samantha's house once my father got back from work, sat down in their lounge, and spoke about the iniquitous situation at hand. Samantha was well aware of what Sean had done, but her childish lust for him outweighed her decency. Despite my tenacious claims of innocence and relentless pleas, I was blamed and called a liar, my father assured her parents that I would be punished for the act, and once we got home, I was. My parents blindly sided with the enemy that day, erasing the quote 'Blood is thicker than water' from my mind. No one could be trusted. People started treating me differently at school, as if I was some sort of criminal or animal. All I knew was that I was going to hurt Sean so bad, I just needed to grow a bit more to match his stature. My behaviour purposely got out of hand, I viewed everyone as an adversary, and I wasn't going to stop until the people guilty admitted to their mendacities. It got so bad that Sonja had to involve her neighbour, who happened to be the captain of the town's police force. He came over to our house a few times, trying to persuade me into changing my ways, but never once hinted at the notion of listening to what I had to say. Fucking moron adult, I thought to myself.

Mrs Barns got fed up with me, not being able to do long division, so she sent me to the principal, who took it upon himself to teach me. I felt humiliated every time I walked into mathematics and she said, "Your class isn't here, Mr Nowak." After two weeks of tutoring with the principal, I was allowed back into her class, where her witticism persisted. Until one day I snapped. I stood up and called her a jerk, it wasn't harsh at all, and my legs shook with fear as I said it, but I challenged her authority in front of 30 something other kids who turned their heads in awe. She couldn't allow me to get away with it, so she messaged the principal on her phone, and two minutes later I heard my name being called over the intercom. I stood up to leave the class as she spitefully held the door open for me, accidentally bumping her on my way out, which was seen as a serious attempted assault, and added more petrol on the fire. I sat in the reception area that seemed to be growing on me now, until my mother arrived. She didn't look happy when she got there; this was the second time in a month. I overheard her and the principal talking about me, that I was a problem child, that my parents have to find a solution to fix my attitude or I'm going to have a problematic life, the threat of expulsion was on the table too. Enough was enough and Audrey grabbed me by the arm, dragging my school bag and me with her towards the car. She drove in the opposite direction of our house, as I sat fearfully beside her and her grumpy face. The car stopped and we got out, I realised that we were at the police station, but before I could run for it my mother grabbed me, and on this occasion, I couldn't fight my way out because there were police officers all around. I submitted to what was to come and allowed her to drag me inside. She asked for the captain, calling him by name and demanded me to sit far away from the door. He came out with one of his colleagues; both were six-feet something, heavy build guys with guns strapped to their sides. Audrey explained the situation and switched to Afrikaans so I wouldn't understand. After four minutes I was escorted down to the cells, where other inmates awaiting trial were screaming 'Fresh meat' and 'Sleep by me, little boy'. They opened up an empty cell, made entirely of concrete, with a zinc toilet in the corner, an open barred window at the very top of what appeared to be a 20-foot wall. They declared this cell to be mine and proceeded to lock me up, but before they did, I pitifully requested a blanket and pillow. They informed my ten-year old ears that they would return at 5 P.M., to hand out the much-needed necessities, and that I should be patient as it was six hours away. I kept quiet during my time and never shed a tear. I sat there, harvesting hatred, acquiring anger, further feeding my scorching rage, I wanted revenge, but it all included murdering my teachers, parents and police officers. I knew I was capable of doing it, but what was the point? They would unarm me faster than I could kill. So, I sat there, listing out everyone's name that I hated, it was a long list... After two hours of isolated detainment, the captain returned with my mother, talking to me through the cold metal bars.

"Mikki Moo, this isn't where I want to see you end up. You have to learn from your mistakes and listen to people older than you."

Her words fell upon deaf ears, the eerie whispers of retribution is all that I could apprehend. We headed upstairs, to the offices, where I was seated on a wooden bench almost as cold as my soul was becoming. The captain asked me what music I listened too, what activities I engaged in after school, what friends I hung around. I refused to answer, and looked at the floor, waiting for Audrey to rat me out.

"Oh, he listens to some metal and rap music, and he is really into this card game that has dragons or dinosaurs as characters, and he hangs out with a child called Doug a lot," she mentioned, right on schedule you fucking snake.

"Ah, Doug is a troublesome child, try to keep him away from your son. We've been called to his house several times for violent outbursts towards his family and neighbours. Other than that, break the CDs and burn the cards, they are satanic, this is probably the source of his anger," the captain informatively replied.

Dr C Van Zyl was informed about the incidents and we had another fifty sessions, but I was very withdrawn, my words muffled by hatred, I didn't want to talk to anyone, despite him being the only person willing to listen. I was pushed way over board, hearing how fellow students spoke to me, how teachers spoke about me behind my back, how Sean got away with everything; pulling off a similar thing with Shaun, how my parents just seemed to give up on me and focused more on Jerome and Gabriel, Doug with the continuous bullying me for things, having no real friends to enjoy life with. This was the end I thought to myself, I was ten years old and treated like shit, where was my love and happiness? Where was this youth elders encouraged me to enjoy? So, one day after school, I went into the garage, to where my dad kept all his tools and equipment, and picked up a chain, along with a padlock, and proceeded to the built on back area of our house. I looped the chain around the support beams that held the metallic roof up, measured a perfect hole for my head to fit through, and locked the padlock on the tightest possible mark. The books I read gave me an outstanding understanding of suicide, and just like Hitler, before the great city was swarmed, I didn't want to wrongfully be held accountable for misinterpretations made by imbecilic moppets. So, I decided to end it, like he did. I stood there, heart racing as I kicked the chair out from underneath me. The chair made a loud bang as it hit the concrete floor, and out came our newly hired help, Precious, from the room we provided her.

"Audrey! Madam!" she cried out, trying to notify my mother as I hung there.

In a swoop, Precious came to my aid, lifting me up by the legs, elevating my throat over the chain, allowing me to breathe. My mother came rushing out with a piece of hosepipe my father had cut off for her; she used things to hit us with. Audrey proceeded beating me with the hosepipe as Precious held me up in the air. She connected Precious a few times but it didn't matter, she was more focused on keeping me alive. My father was never notified of the incident, and no one ever spoke to me about it afterwards, besides everyone was too concerned with Liam getting admitted into a mental hospital and how the family would survive if things went to shit.

Chapter 8
I Admit

Elliot jumps up with a fright as his phone rings again, Katrien still trying to get in touch. He was in the zone, feeling the weights being lifted off his shoulders as he wrote down each unfeigned word. He decides to answer the phone.
"Hello!"
"Hi, I'm sorry for everything, Elliot, it's not what it seems like," she mentions in an apologetic tone.
"Explain then," Elliot says in a nasty voice, being really done with her shit.
"Can you come over to mine and I'll explain?" she asks so innocently.
"No, I'm not driving down to Aalst, just to get my heart broken again?" he firmly states.
"Can I come to you then?" she suggests, being upset that he won't try again, but she understands his frustrations.
"Fine, come here then," he rudely says in agreement with her suggestion, Elliot really wants this to work, so he has no other option but to concede.
He hangs up the phone and opens a few windows, allowing the smell of sex, still hanging in the air, to vacate. He switches on the TV and makes a cup of coffee while he waits for Katrien to come over. Meanwhile Katrien drove up to the bus stop where Elliot abandoned her, working on the words she would say to make him understand her situation. After arriving at the bus stop, she slowly starts making her way up the wet, narrow roads, retracing the path Elliot took on the ATV hours prior. It's hard to see as she heads further into darkness, with no streetlights lighting up path. Her headlights are switched on bright, looking for the luminescent traffic cone Elliot has placed outside the big, wooden gate. He placed it there so that taxi drivers had something to look out for, because he would often need a ride home after a night on the town, and due to how he slurred words and their inability to comprehend drunken English, he had to find a solution. Katrien's car doesn't leave third gear, as she's determined to find it, the rain falling down heavily, trying to stop her from getting that second chance. She sees the cone and turns right; parking her decade old vehicle in the muddy gravel the path consists of. The car is left idling, with her brights still on and the windscreen wipers waving at the clouds in the sky, as she gets out of the car, obstinate to open the heavy gate. She lifts a first time but to no avail, it's too heavy for her, but the power of desperation and penitence impels her, so she tries a second time, this time more successful. Katrien spots a huge stone right next to her, possibly left there by Elliot for a similar situation. She places her leg in front of the gate, securing it from swinging back as she leans over and rolls the wet rock through the mud to where she needs it. The messy task is complete and she gets back into the car, proceeding down the path to Elliot's house. After about a three-minute drive she

spots a light, shining bright from the house. A now nervous Katrien pulls up to the house, noticing Elliot standing on the porch with arms folded and a disgusted look on his face, he probably heard the engines high revs as she tried to conquer the mud, and came out to add tension to the situation. She gets out of the car and makes her way towards Elliot, despite the awkward atmosphere in the air.

"Hi, Elliot," she greets him in a depressing manner.

Elliot feels bad for her, a woman chased after him in the rain, not the way it should be, *'But she fucking deserves it,'* he thinks to himself. His kind instincts kick in and he puts his anger aside.

"Hey, come inside, you look cold." Elliot runs to the bedroom and grabs a fresh towel along with a blanket, doing what he believes to be right, whether she's messed him around or not. He asks her if she would like a cup of coffee or hot chocolate to warm up with, but she refuses, she's more interested in getting her name clear and trying to work on propinquity. It may have only been a night together but she felt the connection, he is charismatic, smart, kind, good looking and she would be stupid to let an opportunity like this slip away. Elliot wants her just as much, conversation with her just flows, it's not forced, he never feels awkward or 'out' around her.

"So, look, the reason I left in such a rush yesterday and the reason I was off…" she begins to explain as Elliot sits on his seat at the head of the table, looking at her warming up on the couch a few feet away "…is because my father was diagnosed with cancer two years ago, and my mother passed away in a traffic collision with a drunk driver, so I've had to look after him ever since. I use to live in Luyksgestel, but had to move into my father's apartment in Aalst, I wasn't visiting a friend like I stated when you bumped into me. The beginning was easier, as he still had savings in his bank account and I could afford to help with everything, but it came to an end and I needed to work extra to afford things, so I worked two jobs, and had no time for anything. I got into a relationship with Henrick, worst decision of my life. I met him in college and we had a one-night thing, but he came back while all this was happening. I felt vulnerable and alone, so I said yes to the relationship. It was fine in the beginning; he helped so much with bills and looking after my dad. We dated for about eight months before he asked me to marry him, I said yes as he was decent, but two months later I found out by my friend that he had cheated on me with his ex. My best friend is a friend of his ex, and she snooped on her phone one drunk evening, saw all the naked selfies they had sent to one another, she confronted her friend about it, who came clean about the entire thing. They sat down with me and showed me the chats and pictures. I later confronted Henrick about it, and he lied to my face about it, so I left him." As Katrien opens up and confesses to Elliot, she starts tearing up, but Elliot is cold and wants to know why he was messed around before any comfort can be given. Katrien takes a breather and goes on, "my father is still a heavy smoker, smoking about two packs a day, and he suffered a stroke Thursday while I was at work. I booked the weekend off to attend to him. When I texted you saying that I would be watching TV, I was actually at the hospital and doctors said that he would be fine, so I took it as a positive and agreed to the dinner. During the two years, Henrick came back and left several times, trying to work things out, but I was focused on my father and my wellbeing, so I refused him each time. The hospital phoned yesterday while you were in the shower, they mentioned my father's condition was becoming critical, so I had to leave. I didn't want to mention anything because I didn't want to lose you or any possibility with you due to my baggage. I got home to collect some clothes for my father, and invited you so I could explain before I went to the hospital because I felt bad for what I did. The door opened and Henrick came in with a key he had cut without me knowing. I threatened him with police, but he tried showing his intentions were good, and that he had heard from a friend in the hospital about my father. I didn't care; he made a cup of tea as I continued packing. I left my phone in the kitchen on charge, and that's when you called. He questioned me and accused me of cheating on him, grabbing me by the arm threatening to beat us both if he found out I was cheating. I told him that it was a wrong number and that we aren't together anymore. So that's the story and I'm sorry for how it looked and if I hurt you, you are a real nice guy and you make me feel special, I don't want to lose you." Elliot pensively sits there, processing each dolorous sentence. Katrien harrowingly asks him if he's okay, but before she can get up to stand beside him, he answers.

"I understand. I am sorry for being clingy and demanding. This situation has happened to me before and I was afraid of it happening again. You won't lose me as long as you're honest, you're a great person and I respect you, along with your actions towards your father. Is there anything that I can do to help you or your father?" Katrien seems puzzled at his answer. No one has ever been understanding or cared so much for her. She smiles at him and says.

"You're a great guy." They stand up simultaneously and give each other a lengthy, warm hug. The embrace slowly becomes intimate as they start kissing. Elliot places his hands on her ass, squeezing tightly before lowering them to her hamstrings. He lifts her up as her legs fold around his waist. Elliot takes a few steps with Katrien's body attached to him and places her on the hard, cold dinner table. Elliot's fist is clenched on her shirt as he un-tucks it from her tight black jeans. His hand is placed in between her boobs, delicately guiding her body down on the table, but her lower back starts crushing the notepad. Elliot's kisses pause and he reaches around her to remove the pad, but she is curious.

"What's that?" she asks.

"Oh, it's nothing," he quickly responds, turning it over, shyly trying to hide it.

"C'mon let me see," she says as she grabs it from his dubious hands. Katrien flips through about fourteen pages before realising he's writing what appears to be a book. "Are you an author?" she asks as her face starts lighting up.

"No," he declares, trying to laugh it off, "I'm just writing a simple thing," he mentions, trying to avoid the topic, but she is too interested to let it slide.

"Tell me what it's about please," she persistently continues.

"I'm just writing down my thoughts of how my life went, and trying to see where I went wrong. In case I ever come across similar situations in the future," he tells her, trying to hide the therapeutic motive.

Katrien cockblocks Elliot and starts asking more questions.

"Are you going to publish it?", "Am I in it?", "Can I read it when you're done?", Elliot smiles and calmly answers each question.

"I don't think that it's publish worthy, it's just my little story of how I got to where I am. Well I'm still at a young age in the book but if you affect my life greatly then you'll probably be in it and yeah you can but I'm far from finishing it." Elliot walks over to the kitchen and places the captivating manuscript down on the counter, trying to conceal it from her prying eyes. Elliot returns to Katrien's open legs, slipping in to continue their make out session. A minute of intense tongue locking goes by before Katrien's phone rings. She pulls the mobile out of her jackets' pocket, to see the name Henrick as the caller ID. Elliot looks at her in a disapproving manner, hoping she won't make the same mistakes, but she reduces tension by answering and leaving it on speakerphone. He sounds angry and it's hard to understand his thick Dutch accent, but Elliot is pretty sure he heard him ask where she was, why she isn't at home or the hospital, as he checked both places. That he's on his way to her work to find her. Katrien tries telling him that she's with a friend but he is dead set on his definition of 'adultery'. She tries correcting him by telling him that they aren't together anymore and haven't been for a while. That he should move on, but it all just aggravates him further, making him believe that she is only saying that because she's trying to move on. Elliot feels the urge to intervene as Henrick starts swearing and calling her names, but he knows from past experiences that it could only lead to her being abused or even worse. Elliot walks over to the kettle in order to make coffee for the two of them, but he lets out a cough. Henrick hears the deep croak and mentions that he's going to find the person and beat him up. Elliot walks over to Katrien; who is seated on the table still, holding the phone in her right hand which is laid across her lap, and presses the red button, hanging up in his ear again.

"You don't need that kind of shit in your life," Elliot mentions, justifying his action. He switches her phone completely off and starts making coffee. They forget about the intimacy and start engaging in conversation over her ex. Sitting on the couch chatting about it all, in front of a warm fire that crackles as the flames invade the virgin logs. She seems to have a great deal that she wants to get off her shoulders, but never had anyone to confide in, until now. Elliot; being well trained in identifying emotions and having the ability to help when told things in confidence, listens carefully to each detail, trying to find solutions to her problem, mostly displaying his much-needed affection, comforting her through the harsh stories. She rants and raves for about an hour over how abusive he was towards her, his drinking problems, the drug and gambling addiction he had when he was in college. She opens up to him, admitting that she never thought she was good enough for more, and settled for Henrick based on her surmise, but she feels as if Elliot is her reward for all she's endured. Elliot isn't sure how to take it as he feels special being valued as a trophy but he doesn't want to be seen as a piece of meat that one earns. Some more time passes and Katrien suggests that it's getting late and she should retire to her own home for the evening, but Elliot expeditiously puts that thought to rest, suggesting it would be safer if she stayed the night, because they don't know what her ex will try. Before they turn in for the night, Katrien hops into the shower, cleaning up just in case Elliot wants a midnight snack. Elliot on the other hand is crouched in front of the fire, stoking the flames, no longer feeling the carnal ambience. They jump into bed, its awkward being sober and next to one another for the first time. In the space of 3 years, no woman has laid her head on his pillows with the intention of falling asleep without any sexual activity. Elliot lays with his hands behind his head, staring at the dark black ceiling above him, wondering what the circumstances would be if Henrick found out, how he can protect her, but his thoughts fall short as she places her head on his semi hairy chest once again. Elliot runs his fingers through her soft, freshly shampooed hair, hoping that the comforting feeling along with the dead quiet room will help her fall asleep easier, despite the hundreds of things on her mind.

Chapter 9
It's Dark out Here

Morning arrives and the sound of the birds tweeting penetrates the timber walls of the room. Elliot wakes with a hard morning wood; being restrained from going to the bathroom by a heavy head and the thoughts of early morning intercourse with Katrien swarm his mind. He leans over and kisses her lips softly; she reacts from her unconscious state and kisses back. Elliot decides to make the thoughts a reality and places his hand under her pale pink shirt, reaching for her soft breasts. She is fast asleep but her body reacts with each lingering touch. Elliot leans over her and starts kissing her belly, making his way up towards his hands. Katrien's hand steadily slides up the inside of his leg, until it reaches his hard erection. Her actions start off nearly lifeless, as she fondles with it through the pants, but each touch sees her grip get tighter and strokes more passionate. Elliot let's his hand slither from her bristles down to her beaver. She's still dry but he wants to change that. Katrien regains consciousness and quickly comes to her senses, feeling Elliot rubbing her in a circular motion and him in her tight grip.

"Good morning," she manages to get out with heavy breathing, but Elliot is busy and doesn't want words to interrupt this. She starts pulling off his underwear, but they hook to the boner. She manages to overcome the obstacle and notices his hard dick standing tall in front of her face, with his balls just dangling down. Katrien leaves the underwear around his thighs; ten fingers above his knees, and tenderly begins stroking it back and forth. Elliot starts rubbing faster, inconveniently bent in front of her to reach. They speed up and slowdown in sync with one another, as if the other controlled the speed to their own pleasure. Elliot takes Katrien's shirt off, and starts canoodling as the playing continues. The over-sized pyjama pants she lent by him start getting pulled down in an attempt to have breakfast. Elliot places his head on the pillow beside her and tells her to get up, guiding her onto him. She remains open minded despite the anomalous shifts. She sits on his face and bends over, legs wide open so Elliot has no excuse for not eating everything on his plate. She grabs his penis and starts sucking it as he licks her. Her perfect curves and smooth, dripping pussy make him hungrier, and she's giving him an all-inclusive today. A few minutes pass and his cum quickly surges through his pipes, through his dick and he ejaculates in Katrien's mouth. He lies there wondering what's going through her mind but she swallows it and starts licking the shaft in a kinky manner, trying to get every drop, putting her own twist on the ever so famous 'Please, sir, may I have some more'. Elliot shimmers his way up, keeping her ass facing him. He rubs her wet clit a bit before sitting her down on his erection. She starts moving back and forward, pleasuring herself at her own pace. Katrien's French manicure sinks deeper into Elliot's upper legs as her speed increases. The trembling sensations rush through her body, allowing her to verbalise her pleasure in the form of soft moans and groans. A little time passes and Elliot decides to turn her around. He remains seated with his legs open, and she is seated on him, legs wrapped around his lower back. Her perfect boobs are pressed up against his muscular chest as she starts initiating the forward-backward movement, slow and steady. It's an awkward position to work from, but Elliot doesn't rush her. Her riding gets faster and the kisses get sloppier. From her hips she controls the pace but she starts cumming and moves faster, trying to get it out. Elliot isn't far behind her with ejaculation and in attempt to please both of them he swiftly gets up with her still on him and crashes into the bed. He lifts her lower back, angling her vagina upwards, allowing him to bury his penis deep inside of her and starts thrusting as if his life depended on it. It pains her a bit but she opens up, allowing him more room to fuck the brains out of her. "I'm cumming," is moaned in a shaky voice. It motivates him to go faster; he doesn't want to let her down. A few seconds pass and she squirts all over his upper legs and abdomen. He doesn't care, he wants to finish too, but he's once again uncertain whether he should pull out and cum on her or just do it inside. Before Elliot can make a decision on where he's going to drop his load, Katrien softly moans.

"In me, please."

Elliot does as he's told and lets it loose inside her. Elliot gets off of Katrien, crashing back into his pillow, breathing heavy, feeling his heart beat in his eyeballs. Katrien starts pecking his chest, announcing her satisfaction in his rigorous performance. He smiles, feeling profoundly hubristic, but doesn't say a word.

Elliot lays there cuddling her, allowing his heart rate to return to normal, making the joke, "Who needs cardio day after that?" She laughs as she used to be a gym enthusiast back in college. They lay there in silence for about half an hour before Elliot asks her.

"So what's the plan for the day?"

She isn't sure herself yet, or whether this is Elliot telling her to go home now.

"Well, I'm going to try see my dad today, and then see from there whether I can return to work or not, how about yours?" she openly reveals.

"I have nothing to do, I'm still off work, so I can come with you if you want?" he offers, but her response heads in the opposite direction of Elliot's plans.

"Well I wouldn't mind the company, but I'd prefer to see my dad alone, it's just a weird situation having someone else there." Elliot understands completely, intruding on one's family in such situations should be avoided.

"That's not a problem at all, you can always call or text me if you need something." He politely says.

They enjoy the last few minutes of each other's bare company, before Katrien gets up to shower. Elliot has a bad feeling in his gut, but he leaves things in the universe's hands, hoping all will be well. Katrien makes her way to the shower and Elliot gets out of bed, walks butt-naked down to the kitchen and starts making his favourite warm beverage. The caffeine addiction is something he's had since the age of 23. He yells out to Katrien, asking her if she wants a cup too, but she declines as she doesn't have time to drink it. So, he only takes out a single mug from the cupboard and proceeds to make his coffee. Elliot picks the notepad up from the kitchen counter and puts it back on the table, hovering over it, whilst sipping his coffee. He can't write now, as Katrien is still in the vicinity, and he'd prefer her not to shadow him. Katrien makes her way through the hallway, looking fresh and ever so cute, placing a smile on Elliot's face, they aren't exactly official, but they both seem to want it.

"Shoes!" he calls out.

"Excuse me?" she confusingly asks him.

"I like your shoes," Elliot admits to her, taking notice of the zipper boots she had on, but the initial comment was an inside joke he had running with friends for a while before they all got married. She walks up to Elliot, gives him a sincere kiss, along with a warm embrace.

"Well, let me head off, I'll phone you later to let you know what's happening," she tells Elliot. Elliot rushes to the bedroom to get some shorts before they proceed to the front door, where Elliot walks out with her, into the fresh morning sun. He stands arms folded, leaning on the porch's support pillar with his shoulder, watching that fine ass walk away. She turns around and smiles at him, and he smiles right back. Katrien drives off, and Elliot once again finds himself in the sound of silence. Elliot lands in the treasured seat, trying to rid himself of the bad feeling in his gut by writing.

2004 proved to be far harder than what we had anticipated. Sylvain grew impatient with the situation at hand, every day he would be swarmed by complaints from me and Jerome about how Xena treated us; she hogged the TV, blasting her rubbish reggae music from my boom box and ate all the cheese. Sylvain too had little to no sleep due to the two babies crying all night long, and faced working overtime nearly every day to feed the 10+ mouths. No one seemed to appreciate Sylvain or his efforts, always thanking Audrey for how she helped everyone, it still disgusts me to this day. He offered Xena some money to assist us in the garden, but she would sit in the shade, chain-smoking cigarettes, watching me and Jerome do all the work. Father would see the progress and bestow riches upon the 15-year old girl, omitting his own blood. The influence of reggae music showered Xena with various commentaries regarding marijuana, allowing me to perceive her as a junkie, and having a junkie Aunt that always found herself in Xena's presence only confirmed my perceptions. The thing about Sonja was that no matter how hard the people around her tried positively influencing her; she would do the exact opposite and cut her nose, spiting her own face. This ultimately saw her face some of the shittiest thing a woman can face. Sonja found herself physically and emotionally abused, cheated on and neglected by her husband, which led to yet another divorce, and due to her financial and mental instability, she had to leave Jacob and Steven in his custody, abandoning more offspring. This slowly became the norm for her, and we got used to it. One Saturday afternoon, Audrey needed sleep; from attending to Gabriel most nights, and Jerome and I were told to go for a walk with Sonja and Xena. Initially it was to view a house that Xena's family decided to rent; they didn't want to go back to Zimbabwe, between the nearly dead economy and white genocide going on, they felt that South Africa would be more prosperous from them, but they were a month away from moving into the place. It was a fairly large property, consisting of a main house, which the landlord lived in, and a flat on the side, where a young paramedic lived. According to Sonja's stories, Xena was secretly seeing this paramedic lad, and this whole 'view the house' story Sonja placed out there for my mother was baloney. She told me at a later stage that Xena wanted to lose her virginity to this man, and needed help; not exactly something you mention to a 10-year-old, whether she was truthful or not I couldn't care less. Sonja devised a plan;

she would chat to the tenants that lived in the house with the landlord and Xena would go to his little flat to carry out the nasty deed. It made sense to me as Sonja craved Audrey's attention, and this whole taking us for a walk thing would ensure just that. Jerome and I were told to walk a good few steps ahead of Sonja and Xena, as they had private matters to discuss over a smoke, but I was on to them, I could smell bad intentions a mile away. I had my own childish guesses as to why we were really here, but kept quiet, as I was taught two things my whole life; (i) You look smarter with your mouth closed, and (ii) speak when spoken too. The other tenants were good friends of Sonja, so they invited us into the house, offered us drinks and put on loud music. They challenged us to see who had the best dance moves, so Jerome and I danced like never before. An hour or so passed before we saw Xena again, we asked her where she had gone, but she was secretive and mentioned she went to the shops; which were six-minute walks away from the house. The more I tried to tell Audrey that Sonja and Xena were into bad things, the more she shoved me off, telling me that I was paranoid.

The day finally came where Xena and her judgemental, uncanny family moved out of our home and into their new house. I was excited to have my room and sleep back. Audrey went out of her way to help Xena get back into school, and raise money to aid the family, via donations, church events; which I found extremely blasphemous as they were Jehovah witnesses and would always mock our religion as inferior. Despite her lack of support and inspiration, she succeeded. I spent most of my school year sitting on the corridor, leaned up against a wall, right outside the class, because some teachers didn't want to be associated with me, and with accusations like rape still lingering, who could blame them? The safety of the majority of their students is what mattered most. Christmas came, Jerome and I were once again faced with the kind act of getting our parents gifts, but we lacked money, as always, so we sat down on my bed, devising a plan to show our warm heartedness. To our benefit Audrey purchased something for Sylvain, and signed our names on it, so that was one gift done, only Audrey left. We brainstormed for hours, but the only solution we could come up with was theft. So, we crept into our parent's bedroom, went into Audrey's jewellery box, took her silver necklace, wrapped it up and presented her with it when the time came. She quickly figured out what we did, and our efforts were nullified. The end of the year was upon was, thank God, I couldn't bear another minute in 2004. It was absolutely mind-wrecking. We took our lengthy walk around the neighbourhood once again, this time with less enthusiasm.

To everyone's surprise I just barely passed 4th grade, and I saw myself moving to a new teacher's class; thank The Lord up above, along with the gang that followed me from grade 1. Standing in the far-left corner, Mrs Fisher, five-feet nothing, weighing in at a 100 kg easy, she was appointed as our new register teacher. She was a fun, straightforward person, who was familiar with my behaviour, and was on high alert whenever I was around. I was much calmer than the previous year, despite the sad atmosphere that followed me around like a fly. I was still subjected to Sean's bullying and limited friendship. The only interaction I had with other students was when we had group projects, but they tried their best to exclude me from visiting their homes and sitting near them. One project in particular, was a dance we had to perform. We were split into groups of three, I drew the unlucky stick and was placed with Sean and Shaun, but that didn't matter much on the day of presentation as Sean had a leg injury from playing cricket, and Shaun called in sick. We never practiced anything, we never communicated on music or the type of dance we would be doing, so I had no other option, I had to improvise. Fortunately, Xena left behind a rave CD which I quickly used to my advantage, remembering moves I had seen on TV. Jenny, Nicole and Samantha finished their dance, which the class thoroughly enjoyed and I was up next, I was scared, having only ever danced in front of family whenever we were on good terms. I placed the CD in the radio that Mrs Fisher brought to the class, chose track 3 as it was my favourite, turned around, and made an absolute mockery of myself. The class laughed, along with the authority who vowed to protect the mental wellbeing of the children in her class. The song never even saw its ending; I just took my CD out and sat back down at my desk, ashamed. I kept quiet, like I did with everything else that ever happened, let it bottle up, keep it deep inside until one day... As children we develop certain skills that subliminally imply which direction we would go into, and for Jerome it was easy to see that he was headed for greatness, as he was a very meticulous child, paying extreme attention to details and was willing to learn no matter how difficult the task at hand. He would take apart old computers, keyboards, TV's, and put them back together, trying to understand how they functioned. To everyone's amazement, once they were put back together, they worked perfectly, which essentially played on Sylvain's' heart strings as he was the exact same in his practices. Jerome was an extremely quick learner, and shadowed my father whenever he cooked or worked on the car. Jerome absorbed so much information from watching him, occasionally helping out as the sous chef. Sylvain and Audrey never had a doubt in Jerome, or what his future would hold, he would come out on top for sure, and I on the other hand, had no talents, apart from eating and the ability to find myself in trouble. It drove me to a point where I would constantly wish death upon Jerome. I later found myself befriending a brother and sister duo that lived three houses away from Unathi; Cathy and Brock. They were two very outgoing people, fun and kind, just like their mother, who was a real estate agent. They knew about my situation at school, but it never stopped them from interacting with me. I had a thing for Cathy, she was cute and feisty, a little tomboy. I suppose I was desperate and this was the only female in my life that was my age; well one year older, that showed interest in me. Cathy often came to our street on her mum's bicycle to play handball with the gang. There came a day where no one showed up for handball or football, and Cathy and I were left without anything to do, so we headed down to the park, which was just down the road from us. We children were urged not to play outside after dark or in green areas due to the high increase in crime in South Africa, things like kidnapping, robbery, shootings, stabbings, hijacking and drug sales were on the rise, and Secunda seemed like a safe haven for criminals. I walked beside Cathy; who was on the bicycle; as my bicycles were normally broken, because I always tried performing tricks I saw on TV, hoping that once I mastered it I would be cooler, but the parts broke off and I'd be injured. We reached the park, and chose to swing for a bit. The park, like everything in South Africa, was covered in long, dry, yellow grass, accompanied by dusty sand paths which formed a circle around the park. After a few minutes on the swings, we decided to race one another on the bicycle. We took out our old, monotone phones, and timed one another's laps around the park. She went first; I was always taught the ladies first rule, and set a rather quick time, but I knew I'd beat her, I was an animal. She handed me her mother's bicycle.

"On your marks, get set, go!" she cried out as she pressed the button to start the timer. The back tyre spun a bit in the sand; I stepped hard, I needed to win. As I cycled through the 'course' I counted my seconds, thinking she would cheat me to try and win; at this point in life I already showed problems trusting people. I realised about 30 metres away from the end that I was at least eight seconds in front of her, so I raised my hands, letting go of the handlebars, trying to impersonate someone winning the Tour De France. The start line was the bridge, that had no railings, and I was coming in fast, to claim my victory. In a flash, the bicycles front wheel rode over a big stone in the path, and the wheel was set off course, heading in another direction. In almost no time I found myself unable to rectify the mistake and I cycled straight off the bridge, falling 2 metres, into big rocks and shards of broken glass…face first. I stood up; the taste of blood filled my mouth, all I could smell was blood.

"I'm okay!" I cried out to Cathy, who stood there in shock for me.

"You're bleeding, Mikki," she hesitantly mentioned. I slowly lowered my head to see what she was talking about, and the yellow shirt I had on, was red. I was covered in blood, and lots of it. I walked up the slope to get back to the path, dripping DNA everywhere. Cathy had no idea how to help, as being a South African, you're warned against going near someone else's blood, due to the volumes of HIV positive people walking the streets. I started walking back home, expeditiously losing blood, but I stopped at the local tuck shop and rang the doorbell.

"One second!" a lady shouted back at me in Afrikaans. I stood there patiently as she approached.

"Oh my soul! Are you okay? Do you want me to take you to the hospital?" she worryingly bawled out, but I refused and asked for a face cloth instead, as I started feeling light headed and needed to stop any more blood loss. She handed me an ice-cold cloth and I continued walking towards my house. I tried finding the wound, it was under my chin, on the left side, deep and long. My dad was hard at work in the front garden as I approached, Cathy wasn't far behind me. Sylvain was kneeled in the bed, shirtless, with a strange blue hat on his head to block out the sun. He looked up to see who was walking up the street and saw me, at first he wasn't sure why I was holding a cloth to my chin, but as I got closer he saw all the blood and sprang into action. He ran to me, asking me who did what, but I admitted to him that I had fallen. He rushed inside, quickly grabbing a shirt and his car keys, and within seconds we were speeding down the road, hazards flickering like Christmas lights, headed for the hospital I was born in. Upon arrival I was seen to immediately, treated as a casualty. I lay on a bed while they injected – what I assume was lidocaine – near the wounds, numbing the pains I was about to feel. The one thing us Nowak lads feared most were injections, and Sylvain knew this all too well from previous encounters with doctors and dentists, so he stood next to me, letting me squeeze his hand. They stitched me up; 12 stiches, and sent me on my way, with the suggestion that I avoid letting go of the handlebars in the future. Whenever people ask me how I got this scar, I normally answer with 'I was attacked by a lion' or something along the lines where I would seem just as malicious as the beast that attacked me. I arrived home to see Cathy disappointingly seated outside of our property, her mother's bike had been damaged badly, along with her favourite friend. I couldn't offer to pay for repairs, nor replace the bicycle, as I was ten years old and had no source of income. The year went on, and my loud, annoying personality became dormant, I wasn't nagging people for things anymore, the transition from needy boy to who gives a fuck man started, a process we normally face in our late teenage years, just I was ahead of the crowd in this sense. Brennan and I found ourselves very intrigued with women and their bits...and to our satisfaction, along came Stella, a tall, awkward girl, covered in pimples, skew teeth and magnifying glasses for eyeglasses, the girl America would classify a geek. We always found ourselves in her company at break time, talking about sexual things, and one day she mentioned where she lived, which happened to be close to us. Secunda wasn't a large town, but it wasn't small either, and what made visiting friends so much handier was the fact that all of the people I decided to associate myself with were in a 500-metre radius of my pumpkin coloured house. Saturday came, and I ran over to Brennan's house, only to see him already waiting for me, both excited for the day ahead of us. We walked over to Stella's house, rang her doorbell and waited for her. She opened the door, dressed in provocative apparel; tight shirt, no bra, her hard nipples visible, extremely short pink shorts, no shoes, hair up in a ponytail. After seeing her open the door and saying.

"Good morning, boys," in her seductive voice, my dick shot up like the Sputnik in 1957. We walked in and she offered us cola, the way she bent over when she handed us the glasses proved our theories of her being keen. She was in seventh grade, and everything seemed more developed than the girls in our 5th grade class. We chatted for a bit before she got enthusiastic about showing us her room. Like Sean, she also lived with her mother, but her mother worked two jobs and was always out, according to my knowledge, her father had passed away several years prior. We followed her to the room, spuriously looking at the photos on the walls before she kissed me on the lips, swiftly moving over to my comrade Brennan a few seconds later. She touched both our private parts simultaneously, rubbing and lightly squeezing them. We began experimenting too, starting off innocently, I knocked her body spray off of the counter, encouraging her to bend over. To our astonishment she did, but her shorts pulled tight as she went down, flaunting her perfect curves. She was talented for a nerd. Stella pressed her tight ass against my penis, pushing into it, hinting at what I'd now understand as, I want it deep inside me. She slowly came back up, seductively mentioning she acquired the item from the ground, sending sexual shivers down my spine. Brennan; a little slow, knocked it over too, and she did the same for him, but he was a step-ahead of me and grabbed her ass while she was angled towards his crotch. Raging, why didn't I think of that? Before we could make any more clumsy mistakes, she asked us to take our shirts off, a proper businesswoman move; give the customer a taste and demand payments. There wasn't much to see, I was slightly chubby and Brennan was skin, bone and asshole alone, but we did as she requested.

"Our turn," we mentioned, and her smile turned naughty with our words.

"You take your shirt off," Brennan blurted out, no sense of foreplay or seduction, but I wasn't complaining. She slowly lifted her shirt, stomach consistently flat, not what we had expected at all, but she stopped lifting it as soon as the bottom seam reached her nipples. OH MY FUCKING GOD! I had no idea what sex was but there was an animal in me that wanted something.

"How badly do you want to see?" she asked in a sweet, innocent voice.

"Badly!" Brennan loudly stated, taking the lead of 'Operation: Undress Stella'.

Her shirt seemed to fly off and her firm, zero-sag boobs stood in front of us, nipples staring us dead in the eyes.

"Do you want to feel them?" she asked, knowing she had us by the balls. My brain went haywire and I forgot about friendship, this became a free for all. I walked up and touched them softly, caressing and squeezing gently. My curiosity drove each movement; I gripped them, circling the shape of her boob.

"Kiss the nipple," she suggested. A vision of a five-year old me, in a similar situation flashed in front of my eyes, déjà vu, but this was consensual... She asked me to stop a few moments later and asked Brennan to try. She asked us to take our pants off, she wanted to see what we were packing, so I nervously looked at Brennan, hoping that he would chicken out so I didn't have to do it, but his pants hit the floor faster than a hooker about to get paid. I followed his example and took mine off too. We stood there, butt naked, in front of Stella, both with flag staff's where our penises once were. She slowly and seductively walked up to us, and stood in between the two erect dicks. She held on to the shafts, and mildly stroked them, rubbing her thumbs over the tips.

"Do you like that?" she asked.

"Mmm," we let out simultaneously.

"Do you want to see mine?" she continued to provoke two ravenous lads. Stella turned around and slowly pulled her shorts down, bending more the further they came off. We saw her black thong and a snow-white bum. She asked us to touch her, and we did, giving each other turns to rub where we had assumed we should. Things got wet and she suggested taking her knickers off, so I stepped in and managed the task. She was shaved in a landing strip fashion, which seemed pretty cool. She got into her bed, under the covers and told us to go to the bathroom while she got herself ready. For what exactly I wasn't sure. Brennan and I stood in the bathroom in total awe, Brennan was more familiar with what to do than I was, I had no idea what I was doing, and I just loved the expose I was at. Five odd minutes of hiding our penises away from one another passed before she called us into the room, her face was red and she told us we had to leave; her mother was coming home soon. We panicked as we knew we would be in big trouble if anyone found out. She got dressed, flashing final sights of her boobs and vagina, as we scraped together our belongings. Stella let us out and we ran as far away from the house as possible, and no one ever found out.

We got back to school, and Stella seemed to avoid us, probably ashamed of her actions, but at least my and Brennan's friendship took shape. Sean overheard Brennan talking to me about the happenings, and decided to blackmail me, for money, to buy him things at break time. I was unable to forfeit any earnings as my father hardly ever gave us money, Jerome, however, was often snuck a R2 or R5 coin by Mom, which at that time could buy a lot. Sean decided to write a note to a group of girls in 7th grade. He handed it to them, with the message.

"Malcolm wanted to give this to you, but he was to shy, so he asked me too." They too were familiar with my work, and found me extremely annoying. 2nd break came and I was approached by a mob of girls, at first, I thought this was my lucky day as they were going to let me pick one of them, ha-ha, that wasn't the case at all. Eight girls, mostly mixed race, walked up to me and asked me about the note, I had no idea what they were talking about and mentioned it to them, but according to everyone I was a pathological liar, and they didn't believe me. It turned into a game *of pin the hand on the Malcolm, and everyone blindly walked towards me, slapping me in the face. Half the school stood around us, watching it, betting on me snapping. No matter how painful it was, or how angry I got, I squeezed the sides of my pants with my index fingers and thumbs, avoiding any possibility of me hitting a woman. A teacher intervened before my face was reconstructed and asked the girls why they were doing what they were doing. They showed her the letter, and I found myself on another one-way trip to the principal's office. Sean–2 Malcolm–0. The principal called my mother once again, and I was suspended for a week. The note stated how I wanted to sleep with them, and touch them in all their places. Threatening that if they didn't submit to me, I would climb through the windows of their houses while they were asleep and do bad things to them. My father asked me about the note, and I denied it being my work, but my words couldn't induce him. Sylvain slapped me in the face, which hurt more than all 8 girls together, and I landed on the floor. He proceeded to kick and punch down on me. I was in tears, screaming for him to stop, but he didn't. Audrey and Jerome stood there, watching it, no one conciliated him. The beating was over and I ran to my room, crying into a pillow. No one liked me, no one wanted to be my friend, no one believed me, and it hurt real bad. Despite all of it, Jerome was always there for me, he would normally sit on my bed, whilst I cried from beatings and say nothing, just being there if I needed him. I never saw it like that until I was older; it was something I should have held on to, instead of fighting with him and making him feel like the worst person in the world. I couldn't see past my hatred, and used him as my emotional punching bag. Things were often fine between us and we would play games in the yard for hours, but I wish I started appreciating the things in front of my eyes, instead of looking for popularity elsewhere.*

With the knowledge of my mistakes and the ability to learn from them, I walked over to Sarah's house, trying to right my wrongs. She sat on their caravan, with the boy from next-door, eating sweets. I called her closer, to speak to her in private, and she walked over to me. With a big black Rottweiler barking at me, and a fence separating us, I asked her; in the most desperate way possible, if she wanted to be my friend. Sarah smiled at me and said yes, but on the condition that I enter her yard, to sit with her and Will; her neighbour. I was in a childish relationship with Cathy still, but Sarah was beautiful and so passionate. She had a bag of sweets, and offered me a few if I overcame my fear of her dog. All of these factors came in to play and I entered her yard, sat beside them and ate sweets. Weeks flew by and I grew closer with Sarah, she was an amazing individual, and it could only be a positive influence in my life. I started re-building my circle of friends, people that I could trust, people that I could rely on, not that I had many to pick from. I had Sarah, which was almost the centre of my circle; the only thing that prevented it was the universal statement that the circle forms around me. Then there was Pule, an ambitious, hard working person, Unathi, the sporty, confident and humble guy, and Brennan, the socially gifted, funny guy. They would brush off on me and I was going to reshape myself, well this was the idea anyway. Sarah and I stood at her gate every day, for hours, talking, getting to know one another, throwing a basketball back and forth during our conversations. I made the biggest mistake of my life and fell for her, which meant I had to leave Cathy, so I went to school and did the harshest thing possible. Cathy and I stood beside the tennis courts during break, in total isolation from the rest of the school; I mentioned that I had written a poem for her, which she looked forward to. "Roses are red, violets are blue, boo hoo-hoo, I'm dumping you." She was disgusted in me, but we were kids and quickly got over it. A few weeks passed and I asked Sarah to be my girlfriend, despite her already dating a guy called Mark. She accepted the proposal and we started dating. The notion of being cheated on while she was at school never crossed my mind, I was just happy that I had her. Things were significantly calm around the house, and Sylvain could finally enjoy this utopia of peace and quiet he tried imprinting in our minds. The year slowly came to an end and I did rather well. Despite the hiccups, I was moved to the 6th grade.

    A new teacher joined our school, but she taught maths for the 7th graders, so she meant nothing to me at the time. I found myself in a male teacher's class, the one that kindly escorted me out of the class in grade 4 for the rape incident. The incident seemed to have blown over with most people in the school, but not with him. His eyes judged everything I did, making silent remarks at each mistake. He was however, an amazing tutor, and treated everyone with respect. I liked him, he was a prick to me in our previous encounter, but this time round he seemed like he wanted to put me on the right path. I didn't need him though; I had my circle, which was doing a great job at the time. The only thing that sucked in this tall, grey-haired man's class was that Sean managed to once again get away with his mischievous behaviour, this time because his mother and this male teacher were too close for comfort. We theorised that they were seeing one another, but nothing could be confirmed as Sean was extremely secretive when it came to matters of the heart. Life went on nonetheless and Jerome and I were trusted to walk home after school, which was the first form of responsibility my parents gave me, it felt good; all I had to do was walk two kilometres and ensure that Jerome was safe. We often walked in groups, but Jerome and I decided one day that we needed some bonding time, so we walked home on our own, through the back streets we normally took. We took the 6th last corner from our house and noticed a huge dog on the loose, standing in the street barking at passing cars. Jerome and I froze, tried not to make a sound, and backed away slowly; we were both scared of dogs. The mutt turned its head and looked our way, let out a few barks and charged at us. Jerome climbed the nearest tree as if he had rehearsed it his entire life and I got up onto an electric box in a single jump. The fear drove Jerome to wet himself, which wasn't funny at the time, but a few good laughs came of it later on. We stood there for about 30 minutes, swearing at the dog, shouting for it to leave, using the common South African term 'voetsek' to deter it from the vicinity. It grew bored of us and chased after another passing car. We climbed down from our hiding spots and cautiously continued our journey home. Most days we would forget the house keys at home, and with Audrey always out with Gabriel or at friends, we resorted to climbing through windows. The only problem with this was the fact that most houses in South Africa had burglar bars welded to the frames of the windows, making it next to impossible to enter the house that way. It was easier for Jerome as he was skinnier. So, we devised a strategy for this: Jerome would climb through the window, acquire the back-door keys, and unlock both the gate and door for me. He would often gain entry to the house, close the window, make breakfast; which we always had for lunch, switch on the TV and leave me outside. It annoyed me and I would scream for him to open up, but he would only turn up the volume of the TV. Just before my snapping point he would open for me and we would laugh about it over a warm bowl of flakes. The brotherhood between us grew stronger, despite the times I beat him up for the dumbest things, something I've come to regret greatly.

Life started getting better all round, and our little group of soccer players headed north, into the dusty, open, makeshift shanty town between Secunda and Trichardt, somewhere white people weren't really welcome. The occupants of these light green and light blue dome shaped houses were actually amazing footballers and had a regular Sunday game against other squatter turfs. Unathi had the pleasure of introducing us to the team, hoping that we could train with them and eventually play for them. It was dangerous, so we never told our parents, as it would be stopped at once, and the passion for soccer could not be stopped. I always ensured Jerome's safety before my own when it came to things like this; this is where I learnt trait number 5; Protectiveness. We trained and played till our legs became numb and toes grew blisters. I loved soccer. I knew I would never be good enough to play for a team or anything in that line, but that feeling of accomplishment after every goal or successful dribble was all I needed. The men we played with were well in their 20s and 30s, all of us were around 11 or 12. On one occasion I was asked to ref a game, to which I failed miserably as I favoured the home team. The year was rather quiet as I was urged to focus on studying for the big exams ahead of us. This year would serve as a preview for the high school we would apply for, to exhibit what we were capable of and why we needed to be accepted, something very general in most schools. I had no option but to study and try get into the school my parents chose for me. A memorable day came when our arts teacher called in sick, and we were sent to another teacher for the 35-minute long period. It was the new teacher, which up until now had no impact in my life whatsoever, Ms Chantal Swanepoel. She was probably made aware of my actions and would probably treat me the same as the other teachers. Boy was I wrong. She was a very perceptive woman, and noticed me alone most break times, eating my cut down the middle cheese sandwiches, whenever I had sandwiches. She noticed how the children grouped up in her class this day, and totally avoided me. I was used to it by now, and took out a notepad to draw tanks and war planes, but before my works of art commenced, she seated Justin next to me, understanding he was probably the most influential person in our class. She probably realised that I was just another misunderstood child, and needed some guidance, something I only got from Christo Van Zyl, but our sessions were reduced to 4 times a year. She taught us both how to play Sudoku, a game that I thought was intended only for the Einsteins of the society, people like Nicole. She spent the remaining 30-minutes teaching me and Justin this game. The looks Jenny and her gang gave, burnt holes into my face, but I didn't care, suckers. The bell rang for us to go to our next lesson and my heart broke, the way this teacher spoke to me, how she approached me, was something I never before experienced, this ensured her first place in my heart, above all other teachers at this somewhat fine academy.

Despite the constant loner persona I formed at school, Sean's shite and the atmosphere around girls, I was content. I had something to work for, to get into Ms Swanepoel's class the next year. I sat down and attempted to study hard to get there. My dad's beatings continued, with my mother chipping in sometimes too, beating me with conveyor-belt strips, hosepipes, kettle cords, sturdy vines, wooden spoons and even on one occasion with the wire attached to my gaming console, but I was able to handle each hiding, despite the laps ran around the dining room table trying to avoid them. Audrey enlisted Jerome and I into a kayaking club that year, to keep us busy after school, away from trouble, and once again didn't take every aspect into consideration. Jerome and I couldn't swim, we were never taught, even though I had been learning how in our P.E (Physical Education) classes. With Titanic being Audrey's favourite movie, one would think she saw it coming, but it never seemed to cross her mind. I was a very aggressive rower when it came to the sport, seeing the thick water as an opportunity to get rid of frustrations, Jerome, however, was more concerned on manipulating the boats movements to resemble that of a car. One afternoon at Lake Umuzi, located near the casino, we were briefed on our goal for the day by the instructor and hopped into our kayaks. This time I was put into a two-seater, along with an Indian guy, Jerome was placed in a single one, lucky fish. This Indian guy and I communicated and we strategized that with my aggressive rowing, that I would sit in the back and give speed and he would steer from the front, nothing complicated. As we set about putting our plan to action Jerome shouted out.

"Look, Malcolm, I can spin my kayak like those cars," trying to re-enact something he saw on TV the night prior, but it seemed that he was creating a whirlpool under his kayak from his constant steering in circles. His boat was sucked down in front of my deranged eyes, the orange life jacket slipped off of his torso as he went down into the water. He was about 50 metres in front of me, head slowly submerging under the waves he was creating, kicking and fighting to stay alive. I jumped out of my boat, tipping the Indian lad with me, I couldn't swim either but I splashed, kicked and paddled towards him as if there was a crocodile behind me. Seconds were running out for him, and you could hear him choking on water already. Each haunting sound of gasping for air fuelled me to try save him. Audrey stood there screaming.

"My boy! Someone help my boy!" doing nothing, I don't think she knew how to swim either. Samantha's big brother paddled fast from nearly the other side of the lake, rushing to his aide, Mila's big brother dove into the water and swam towards him. As Samantha's big brother pulled him out with one hand, he coughed a few times, he was okay. I felt disappointed that I couldn't save him, but I would have drowned alongside him. Needless to say, it was the last day we attended kayaking club.

Elliot lays the pen down on the notepad, noticing the indent the plastic shaft has made on his middle finger. The hours of seated penmanship leave his arm and back strained, and the thoughts of a relaxing walk through the forest fill his mind. It would be healthy to reduce the tensions in his body. Elliot gets up and heads to his room, in search of his white trainers. He finds the semi soiled shoes at the bottom of his wardrobe, placed on a shoebox to prevent the mud from dirtying the white MDF panel at the bottom. Elliot walks out of the house, briefly admiring the nearly purple dusk sky, while doing a few second standing foot grabs on each leg. Dressed in a dark-grey hoodie and light grey tracksuit pants, with no underwear underneath, Elliot prepares himself for the stride, in the same direction he always walks. He confidently inhales the fresh Dutch air, chest expanding harmoniously with the breath, and exhales rapidly through his mouth, before setting out on his walk. The tyre tracks of Katrien's car situated in the subjugated soil drew his attention and he ponders whether she closed the gate behind her. Elliot's path is altered as he wants to confirm his thoughts. While visualising her car conquering the mud, he thinks of the San people of Southern Africa and how they tracked their prey, and pretends to understand what her car did. Mumbling his findings to himself, "The four-wheeled beast had to stick left on this particular stretch as the right was deeper. Here we can see that the rear right wheel was stuck, so the driver had to over rev in first gear, causing slight spin, but once over 3000 RPM, it uplifted itself."

His game progresses to the point where he realises that he's being childish and decides to walk the rest of the path as an adult; in silence. Elliot is pleased to see that there is no litter on his property, something he has been very conscious of ever since acquiring an £80 fine in Glasgow for stumping out a cigarette on the pavement. Through the nearly-dark green tree line, Elliot sees the wooden gate closed, delighted that she respected his property and how he wishes to maintain it. He realises that she must have been in a messy situation with the barrier, because the muddy residue is thick, and appreciates her efforts a bit more. Elliot starts climbing the gate, placing his right leg on the 2nd horizontal bar of the gate, followed by his left leg on the 4th, allowing his body to swing the right leg over the top so that he can be seated at the top of the gate. Elliot remains seated on the almost dry, mouldy scented gate, staring into the almost dark tree line across the 2-lane road in front of him. A few cars speed by with their headlights on, forcing Elliot to raise his hands to block out the blinding beams, disturbing his peaceful seating. Mentally it seems like he is looking for something, confused and focused at the same time, trying to map his somewhat broken life together to finish his confessions. He really hates leaving things half done, having being taught by his father as a wee lad, "If you start something, you finish it." Another imprint left in his mind forever by his biggest hero. The resonance of owls hooting in the surrounding, fill the cliché atmosphere, adding significance to the mood, an eerie sound to match the eerie thoughts. Elliot hops off of the gate, landing in a small puddle that the sun forgot to dry up when it was still out, splashing muddy water everywhere, dirtying his shoes further. He follows his heart through the darkness, trusting his instinct to guide him home due to the lack of lights he has threatened several times to place around the yard. He is unable to identify the tiny ridges in the dry mud, and loses his stability several times, almost falling on his face like he did when he was a mere child. The lights from the house are finally visible and his certitude of the path is clear. Elliot runs up the stairs in an attempt to divorce the darkness behind him. The trainers get removed upon entry, as is protocol in this home, and are carried back to their cardboard pedestal at the bottom of his cupboard. Traipsing in his black socks across the wooden flooring towards the room, he concludes that the empty feeling permeating in his belly is the longing for Katrien. He swiftly slides into the room, places the shoes down and reaches for his phone, hoping that a simple endearing text would be enough to summon her to his bed tonight.

'Hey, how has your day been? I think I've started missing you.' Elliot locks the slim, smart phone and stows it back in the right pocket of his grey pants, anxious to grab some food. Elliot opens the fridge and the freezer, only to witness that the only in-date meal he has left to cook is a frozen, nine-inch pepperoni pizza. Dispirited with the variety of cuisine available, he takes the circular dish out of its box, placing it on the counter as he turns the knobs on the oven, fixed on pre-heating first; Elliot isn't exactly a fan of pizza. While Elliot hovers over the slow heating oven, the message tone sounds. He lowers his head to see a text from Katrien.

'Hey, it was all right thanks and yours? My dad is doing a bit better, I wish it wouldn't be such a back and forth thing, but nothing I can do. Aww that's sweet of you, I think I miss you too x'.

Elliot's smooth lips stretch with an uncontrollable smile.

"Any chance of you heading back here later?" he desperately replies. Elliot takes out a plate for his meal, along with a knife and a half empty bottle of ketchup while he awaits the definite yes from Katrien. Seconds turn into minutes, disheartened with her response time, he turns to the pizza, watching it cook through the glass of the oven door. Elliot recalls the box saying ten minutes at 200°C, and looks at his watch, realising it's been eight minutes so far. He grabs a glass of water to accompany his food, trying to kill time, the pizza anxiety a college student regularly feels is gnawing at him. His internal timer tells him it's time to eat, he opens the oven, and without mittens he removes the pizza from the digital inferno, burning his fingertips slightly. The pizza is placed on the plate and sliced into four large pieces, augmented with small squirts of ketchup on the melted cheese. Elliot proceeds to fold the pizza in half and devours it mouthful at a time, sipping water from the glass beside him to extinguish the heat. While standing in front of the counter eating his sad excuse of a meal his phone sounds, but his hands are too greasy to touch the device, so he ignores it until his stomach is satisfied. After devouring the small pizza, Elliot heads to the basin, places the plate inside and washes his hands with lukewarm water, stealing a bit of dish washing liquid to abolish the oil left on his hands. He dries is hands and takes his phone out.

'I think I'm going to stay here a little bit longer and then go home, I need a good night's sleep tonight,' she replied.

Elliot understands, he too needs a decent sleep and texts her back.

'I understand, well I'll be here whenever you need me.'

Elliot places the phone on the counter and walks over to his manuscript, taking note of his exact position in his writings, understanding that 2006 was the last uneventful year of his life. He wants to continue writing but his hand is still strained, and it would be better to start a new year on a new wind, so Elliot decides to call it a night, switches the lights off and heads to his bedroom.

Chapter 10
Sailing Smoother Seas

Elliot is fast asleep, tossing and turning with a distraught look on his face, sweat dripping from his forehead. The covers were violently discarded a while ago, trying to fight something sinister. Elliot is very aware of the nightmares that seem to occur most nights, flustering reminders of the past, and brief flashes of mistakes made, of people lost. On a scale from 1 to death row inmate with hepatitis C, he understands that he had a better life than most, but the troubles soon to be penned down seem to still display his sensitivity to certain topics and inability to forget the hurtful memories. With a strong lunge forward, Elliot is awoken by the nightmares, panting like a puppy after a run around the block. The final glimpses of moonlight, before the certain sunrise, shine brightly on his face, creating the shadow of his head on the built-in wardrobes. Drenched in sweat, Elliot makes his way to the kitchen, with the disturbing memories playing clearly in front of his eyes. He reaches the bottle of whiskey, trying to drown his demons, even though they've learnt how to swim. Elliot plants himself in the couch, in the pitch-black room, and opens the bottle. The sound of the metal cap spinning anti-clockwise whispers something in his ear, reassuring him that he will sleep this night. The first sip is small and quick, burning everything in its path. The second follows a few coughs later, this time a bit larger. Elliot stands up after the 3rd sip, and heads to the head of the table, chained to his notepad like a slave with a pickaxe.

Jerome and I ensured that we attended each swimming class from that point forward. In a class of 40 somewhat children, I was among the four who couldn't swim, who couldn't grasp the concept of staying alive in water via means of floating and movement. It took a few months before we were confident in the water; Jerome however was more focused on a 7th grade girl called Liz. It was strange seeing Jerome's heart claimed by a tall, fair-haired girl, especially with him being half her size. They always seemed to disappear when we got out of the swimming pool. I was slightly jealous of him as she was gorgeous, and of how this loser that had constant nose bleeds from migraines, due to strained eyes, straight hair that formed an out of style fringe, could pull such a fine young woman. 2006 finally came to an end, and I passed 6th grade, meaning I would finally be in Ms Swanepoel's class, possibly the first goal I ever set for myself and reached. I started getting along with Sarah's parents, well her dad anyways, her mother didn't like me as I reminded her of her first husband; Sarah's real father, he was a soccer player too. Sarah's stepfather, Jake, was a motorcycle enthusiast, who constantly had a new bike in the drive-way. Jake would normally invite friends over to drink with him, and then spin his bikes' back tyre until it burst, which inspired all the lads from the neighbourhood to leave their homes to witness. He invited me and Jerome over for the New Year's party this year, which consisted of a dozen adults drinking and barbecuing to loud Afrikaans music, with some rave here and there, a typical South African get together. Will and his big brother Peter were invited too, as they were every year. What started off as an innocent game of hide and seek in the dark, turned into one of my fondest memories. Will counted to 50, while the rest of us ran to find hiding spots in Sarah's huge yard. Sarah and I hid together in the wash room, closing the door behind us. She sat on the washing machine and I stood in front of her. We already shared our first kiss under a tree on the side of her yard one summer day, but this was our first ever shift. I was a total amateur as this was my first tongue kiss experience; Sarah on the other hand had practiced a lot with Mark at school. It started off strange and ended with her teaching me what to do, until I perfected the act and got caught by Will. After being the first one's caught, one of us had to count, but Sarah and I both made up excuses as to why we weren't allowed to count, in an attempt to get more throat hockey in. Once again, I mentally bullied Jerome into counting, even though he was the last person caught. Jerome had climbed her back wall and hid behind the thick leaves of a tree. Fireworks were let off as Jerome counted, like they are each year, and we kissed under the colourful explosions in the sky. Each time her lips approached mine, my stomach went haywire with emotions, which got me addicted to her. Jerome caught us as soon as he came around the corner, whether he witnessed us making out or not, I'm unsure.

    Just before school started in the New Year, Sarah and I had a fall out, over her kissing Mark and that I saved myself for her but she wouldn't do the same for me. So, we broke up for a bit, while she rethought her priorities. Besides, she was in her first year of high school and needed to focus on the goals she had set for herself. I had my first class with my favourite teacher, mathematics, a subject that puzzled me for the past six years. I had no concept of what they were talking about, and scored the bare minimum to pass grades. Algebra and fractions were my biggest fears, I couldn't grasp the idea of pieces of a number, I liked whole things; don't give me a third of a girlfriend, I want the whole thing. Even at home I disliked maths, as Jerome thrived in it, another subject close to my father, but he succeeded at everything he tried. It took Ms Swanepoel nearly no time at all to convince me that maths was a great subject, and in three classes everything just clicked. I was so grateful to God up above for sending me this angel. Whenever we sat in her class with no work to do, she would tell us stories, ask us tons of questions and create such a warm atmosphere in the class. She mentioned her reason for getting into teaching was so that she could be there to help shape future lawyers, doctors, presidents and sportsman, to teach them right from wrong so that when they got a job, that they would do the right thing for the next person. Which to me was a most inspiring reason to get into the profession, opposed to my train of thought that 'he who can't do, will teach, and he can't teach, would teach gym'. Her favourite student was Nicole, as Nicole was the school smartest student for the 7th year running, she was friendly, pleasant, and a tough competitor on the chess board. I tried year after year to beat her in the strategic game, but only Jerome ever came close. I was so jealous of her, I knew I had the brain power to compete with her, and eventually succeed, just not at that moment. Valentine's Day drew near and I set out asking girls if I could be their dates, ha-ha, out of the 12 girls I asked, including Sarah, I got a grand total of 0 yesses, even my mother rejected me for Sylvain. I took the small amounts of money that I had saved up from working in the garden, washing cars and cleaning the house to buy Ms Swanepoel a rose for Valentine's Day. She accepted it and told me that I was sweet, but it wasn't a proper Valentine to me, despite my childish crush on her. I watched Sarah spend Valentine's Day with Peter, which tore me apart, but there was nothing I could do about it, I was eager to fight for what was mine, but he was twice my size. I angrily sat in my room for the rest of the day, thinking about how alone I was, but it faded from my mind when mother presented me with pork chops for dinner. We were in maths class again, this time learning that Ms Swanepool was soon to be Mrs Opperman, and this broke my heart further, but he was a tall, smart, kind-hearted, calm guy, that I grew to respect after witnessing how he handled the whole breast cancer situation many years later. The pressure my parents had placed on me to succeed this year was huge, and the situation I faced daily at school didn't help. Things seemed dark once again, like I was living under several people's thumbs, but on the annual athletics event our school held, I finally stood up. Jerome became very athletic as he grew up, he had the physique for it, an all-rounder some would say, where as I was more a chubby, couch potato. Jerome participated in the 100 metre and several other field events, winning three medals for his efforts; two gold and one silver, something he was extremely proud of. I watched him perform from the spectator stands, as a proud brother should. Audrey had given him money to buy a lunch at school; I never received anything, as I didn't participate that year. Jerome finished his events and walked over to the school's tuck shop to get some food, which he would share with me as he knew I hadn't received any money. He needed something to eat after exhausting his energy levels on the field. He bought himself a pack of crisps and proceeded to walk over to me; to brag about his accomplishments; this time I would let him gloat, he deserved it. I stood on the hill, overlooking the entire playground, wearing someone's black leather jacket, in clear sight of him walking next to the field, munching away on his crisps. Sean came around a corner with two of his friends, stopping Jerome to talk to him. The world became silent as I stood there trying to listen to what he was telling Jerome, my tunnel vision kicked in and I watched each movement around my brother like a hawk. I was about 150 metre away from them. My friends noticed the focused look on my face, and faced the same way to watch. Sean had asked Jerome if he could see his medals, I already knew that no good could come of it, and I knew that Sean would beat me hands down in a fight if I even tried to intervene. Jerome handed his medals over and watched Sean toss them into the air. The metallic rewards landed on the roof of the three-storey building, and there was no way of getting them down ever again, Jerome understood that too. Sean and his friends laughed as Jerome walked over to me in tears. The watery eyes broke my thresholds, and I lifted my middle finger up at Sean, ready for whatever. He noticed it and felt offended, so he made his way towards me. Jerome kept saying, "No, don't fight," trying to protect me as I wanted to protect him. I took off the jacket as my legs started shaking, and handed it to Jerome to hold on to. I could apologise and let him bully me for a bit and lay there in defeat with Jerome, but I wasn't going to let anyone bully my brother…that was my job, he was my blood, who the fuck was this pomy bastard to take that from me? Sean walked up to me and with no words being said, pushed me backwards. I opened my mouth.

"Who the fuck are you to throw my brother's medals away?" stuttering nearly every word, fearing the inevitable hiding.

He laughed at me, asking what I was going to do about it. At this point it wasn't about the condom, about the two-faced actions, about the letter, about the bullying, about the injustices, it was about Jerome. The shaking throughout my body stopped and I pushed back, the look on his face was priceless, it was something he never expected. As he tried going for a second push, I held nothing back, and swung the hardest right hook of my life, crashing my fist into his face. He tried fighting back, but I grabbed him by the buttons of his polo shirt with my left hand, and continued to punch with my right. He landed one punch on my leg before grabbing a javelin, trying to stab me, but the teacher overlooking the event jumped in before it got bloody and separated us. A feeling of pride surged through me; I did something good this day. Sean's nose was bleeding and the side of his face was red. The teacher suggested that we both leave the area. As we walked away, I placed my arm around Jerome, rubbing his hair with my hand, I said.

"I got you, bro," he never said anything back, the medals meant nothing to him anymore, despite the altercations in the past, he understood that I was there for him, ready to risk my wellbeing.

My parents were never notified about it, as I wanted no more trouble. The next day was filled with people who disliked Sean, congratulating me on what I had accomplished.

Time went on and the school had its annual fund-raising idea; the big walk. Ideally, we would go door to door and ask for sponsors and money donations; in return we would walk 40 laps around the school's soccer field. Where the money had gone I wasn't sure, but people stood a chance of winning some amazing goodies. Also, the child who brought in the most money won something. So, I set about trying to reach this goal, which so happened to be a new bicycle. Pule came with me one evening, just before it got dark, to help me carry the money and papers. We already milked our streets, so Pule suggested going across the bridge to the untapped neighbourhoods, which made sense, so we set out. As we headed to the park, and the bridge I had fallen from, we spotted Doug, walking towards us with a girl, what she found attractive in him is beyond me. We tried to avoid him for the past two years, running back inside our houses when he came out, ducking down in our parents' cars if we drove past him, but this time it was too late. He handed the girl his phone, and I got scared.

"Hey Doug, how are you." I said, cowardly trying to get out of any misunderstanding, but I was greeted by a variety of punches.

He knocked me into the dusty sand, and continued his barrage of punches, landing everywhere. Pule stood by and watched, never once jumped in to help me, which, if the tables were turned, would never happen. Doug got tired and walked away, and I got up, dusted myself off, and marched back home, informing my parents about the incident. Sylvain got in his car, along with me, and we headed to Doug's house, where my dad confronted his dad. Doug's father mentioned that Doug had gone off the rails with weed and he had no control over his son anymore. We then drove to the police station, where my mother laid charges against him, but nothing could be done to him as he was underage. It did however add to his record, which eventually saw him getting expelled again, and again, and again, before he was sent to a juvenile school in Bethal.

Sarah and I got back together, on the condition that Mark was removed from the picture, to which she agreed, apparently, I meant a bit more than him. I was allowed *in her house again, and her parents always made the mistake of leaving us in their house alone while they went shopping. What was once a stolen kiss here and there...turned into shirts being taken off, boobs being shown and privates being touched. I was more mature around this topic now, but still uncomfortable with sex. We took every opportunity we had to feel each other up. Amelia was always suspicious of us being alone in a room, but we were always too quick to remove hands and I was very good at acting at this stage.*

Elliot puts the pen down, and with tears in his eyes, he places his hands on the table, letting out a sorrow filled sigh and proceeds to push himself up. The whiskey hasn't hit him as hard as he'd like, but it will do. Elliot heads over the couch and lays down, in an attempt to close his eyes and forget his brother's face.

Chapter 11
The Quiet Before the Storm

A few hours pass before he wakes again, the slumber a bit better this time round. Elliot slowly makes his way to the back of the house, eager to shower and get dressed, eager to leave the house for a bit; the writing is making him go through emotions he never before worked through. He stands under the sprinkling hot water; head leaned against the tiled wall, in thought. The drops of water calmly run along his skin, wetting every inch of his withered exterior. After rubbing himself down with shower gel, he turns the taps clockwise, putting a halt to the water escaping from the boiler. With wet feet, Elliot heads to the room, ready to dry himself and get dressed in his grey jumper and blue jeans. Elliot dresses fast, returns to the bathroom to brush his teeth and wax his hair, before leaving the house. This time he brings the notepad and two pens with him. Elliot drives toward the city centre, in the middle lane, not in a rush to be anywhere in specific. He ends up taking a turning into Aalst, in order to get on a road that leads to a familiar parking spot. Upon parking and locking his car next to a building that has a security guard, he proceeds to walk through the building and shrubs to get onto the Tongelreeppad. Elliot takes in the scenery, hearing the fast-paced city in the distance. Elliot walks for about 40 minutes in the warm sun, before finding a bench in the Ton Smits Park, overlooking De Vleut Lake. There's not much noise, other than the sounds of fast-moving cars on the Boutenslaan and a few kids screaming at ducks at the other side of the body of water. He decides to neglect the sounds and continue where he left off.

As one grows up, one realises the importance of money, and my father's idea of less than minimum wage payments for hours of suffering in a huge garden weren't beneficial to us, so I tried earning a profit at school and came up with my own business idea. I noticed the price per lollipop at the school's tuck-shop was R2, which was highway robbery at the time. So, I simply bought myself a bag of lollipops, the bag contained 100 suckers and cost me R.50, meaning that I needed to sell 100 of them for 50 cents a pop to break even. I used the outrageous school's prices to my advantage and sold mine for R1. First thing on my business agenda was advertising, so I told the fattest girl in the school about it, as she had loads of friends and loved her sweets dearly. I devilishly mentioned.

"Instead of paying R2 for one lollipop, you could pay R2 for two, meaning you get more for your money," Toying with her cravings.

Having convinced her, I sat back and watched her tell everyone and advertise for me. I would walk around the school with my bag on my back, which contained my store, and people would run up to me with money. I was very sneaky on sales, as I knew if you took business away from an adult that there would be serious repercussions. Business was good nonetheless and after selling the entire bag I reinvested the R100 profit into two bags, being more goal-orientated on this occasion. The third load saw me take a R100 profit as I stuck to the two-bag method.

Near the end of the year, we sat in arts class, with nothing left to do or study, but there was however, a shortage of seats in the room. I was polite and grabbed a seat from the other side of the class room for our new Indian class mate, Devendren. He had bulgy eyes, and was a giant amongst us, but a cool guy, who went on to be a successful rapper in Durban. I missed the name at the top of the seat, Tsepho, and handed it to Devendren to sit on. Tsepho walked into the class and noticed that his chair wasn't where it should have been. So, he swiftly walked through the class looking for it, and found it under our friend's backside. Without any hesitation, he grabbed the seat from under my friend, and proceeded to his desk. Devendren stood up and asked him what his problem was, but Tsepho, having probably grown up in a very fast paced squatter environment, had no patience, and grabbed my Indian friend by the shirt, attempting to slap him. I jumped in and pushed Tsepho away, so he started fighting with me instead. It wasn't a serious fight, a few flat hands landed before we were broken up by other students. The teacher wasn't happy with the confrontation and sent us both to Mr Van Dyk; my grade 2 teachers' husband, for discipline. The only problem was this was corporal punishment, which was still tolerated in South Africa at the time. Everyone feared getting sent to him, and I was soon to find out why.

"Why are you two here?" he asked, Tsepho was too afraid to speak, so I explained, trying to justify my actions, but he didn't want pitiful excuses.

"Into my store room," he mentioned. The class collectively wooed as they knew what was coming. We walked through the aisles of the class toward the room, where he closed the door behind us, and asked who wanted to go first. First, for fucking what now? How did I do anything wrong here?

"Me, sir," I bravely stated.

"All right, bend over and hold the chair in front of you," he suggested.

'Ahh a simple smack to the bottom, not so bad, my dad beats me on a weekly basis, I'll be fine,' I thought to myself. Mr Van Dyk let out a little grunt as he let rip a cracker of a smack, the only thing that I seemed to miss was the ping pong paddle in his hand. It stung my ass as it landed, but I've experienced worse. Tsepho took the spot light this time, and got one too, but he couldn't take it like I did, coward, and started crying, begging for Mr Van Dyk to stop. We both received a grand total of three shots each and were sent back to our class. It was hard for us to sit on our chairs after the shots, so we stood for the entirety of the lesson.

My parents sat me down with admission papers for the high school of my choice. This high school lead in sports, education and cultural diversity, opposed to the two neighbouring High schools; one which was notorious for criminal activity, and the other was for the more Afrikaans community; the school Sarah was in. We had to fill in the achievements I received in this primary school, but my parents weren't exactly on the same page as me so they left me to fill it in. I had to lie, I knew I was a sad loser, having accomplished nothing but play soccer for the school twice, swam for an iron man competition we had, along with a gala event where my shorts came off on the dive and everyone saw my white ass, tried out cricket and was a scholar patrol. So, I wrote down that I had won competitions for BMX events, won a graffiti contest, played Rugby privately; without the schools' knowledge. Ms Swanepoel noticed the Highschool's emblem in the top right of the paper I was filling in and went over my application one day at school. I could see in her eyes that she knew I was lying, but my back was against the wall, what else would I do if I didn't get in, but Ms Swanepoel had secretly been working on other plans for me and my future. My parents were already losing hope with me, having over heard several of their nightly conversations about me being a problem child, that I wouldn't succeed, hearing my dad refuse looking after me till I was 30. There was no faith in me, and I couldn't blame them, I was stupid, an idiot, tunnel-visioned in this idea of fun and foolishness. The papers were submitted and we had to wait, with many other parents, for a response. We tried a high school in Evander, which was a good distance from us, but I would have quit school if they put me there, it was a druggy infested place, with loose girls all over the place, and territorial guys running the show. I would never fit in and I'd be bullied left, right and centre.

Elliot places the pen down, after hearing a message notification. He grabs the mobile and checks the message, it's from Katrien.

'Hey, my dad is doing well, he's got his speech back, and doctors are saying that he needs to be observed for a week before they can allow him to go. I'll probably head up to the hospital tonight to check up on him xx'. Elliot smiles, and texts her back.

'That's great news, I hope all goes smoothly and that he can return home soon, let me know if there is anything that I can do for you x'.

He doesn't seem too eager for a response and returns to the book.

I anxiously awaited the confirmation from the high school, along with my parents. Nicole, Samantha, Sean, Shaun and most of the class already received letters welcoming them with open arms. It became awkward as they asked me where I had applied, to which I lied and said that I was looking at going overseas. I was tired of being the laughing stock, and it would have saved me the embarrassment if I was rejected. The days seemed to drag by, while we awaited the response, but it eventually came, and I was accepted; possibly, the last student to get accepted. One weekend Pule had come over with his cousin, and we had such great fun on the trampoline Santa brought us for Christmas. Jerome and I bounced happily, until I got jealous at Jerome for being able to perform backflips. I went inside, furious, but my so-called friends never followed me in, they were more interested in how Jerome accomplished it so that they could try it. Annoyed at the lack of attention they gave me, I grabbed the closest thing to me, which was an AA battery, and proceeded outside, where I threw the object at Jerome as hard as I could. It hit him in the face, and he started crying, the look in his eyes as the tears flooded his face hurt me till this day, I once stood up for him against people hurting him, but there I was, hurting him. Pule was familiar with how I treated Jerome, and decided to stand up to me, and pinched me under my arm, how most black people seemed to discipline their young.

"Ow! You're hurting me!" I cried out, but Pule never let go, and responded.

"You hurt Jerome worse." It became evident that he wasn't going to let go, so my open hand formed a fist, and I swung at his face. After the shot landed, his cousin suggested leaving, to go back home. Precious, who witnessed the entire thing, told

me that I was wrong, and that I should apologise to everyone. Trying to teach me a very important life lesson of owning up to my mistakes. I acknowledged her words and followed them up the road. I caught up with them at Pule's house, which was two houses away from the scruffy abode of JonJon. I apologised and we shook hands, but they wanted to do something else and I was asked to go back home. I didn't apologise to Jerome, he deserved what he got, I felt, but he deserved so much more than a sorry.

The year seemed to progress rapidly, and we were enjoying the perks of being the big fish in the small pond. Most of the students in my class were elected prefects of the school, sworn to serve the rule book, and report any injustices. I on the other hand cried on the night I wasn't picked, I really wanted that feat, but I wasn't yet ready for that level of power, and would have abused it. Luckily Sean wasn't elected either, that would have ruined my life, like giving guns to bullied teens; there was no possible way of knowing who would die first. Gabriel was getting older now, his blonde hair started coming out, along with his blue eyes, which seemed strange to Jerome and I, as all of us had brown hair and brown eyes, Sylvain being the only exception with his green eyes. We thought that maybe Audrey had cheated on him, but photos of Sylvain as a baby proved us wrong, as Gabriel was a spitting image of him. Us kids each had a nickname, given to us by Audrey, which was used by everyone who knew us, except Sylvain, I had been called Mikki, Jerome had Romeo; due to his good looks and charming smile, and Gabriel finally acquired one too, his was Lala, after a character in a child's cartoon. Gabriel was now able to distinguish between good and bad, along with the consequences when he got them mixed up. On one occasion, Jerome and I failed to eat our vegetables, and as was nearly religion in this house, we were punished. Punishments in this house depended on the time of day; before school meant no music in the car, after school meant beatings or garden work and when night hit it would be corner or no TV. So, we were put into corners, forced to stare at a wall, subjected to listening to my mother's law programme on TV, until we decided that we could stomach the vegetables. Gabriel finished his greens but wanted to be by his brother's sides, and chose a wall next to Jerome, ready to undergo the punishment. My favourite part was where he turned around and asked Audrey.

"Am I doing it right, Mommy?" to which the only response was laughter. His funny question got us out of punishment, and we were allowed to watch the TV series with Audrey. Gabriel was also of age to assist us in chores around the house, not the garden work of course, but with simple day to day tasks. Jobs were split by our parents, if it was Jerome's turn to set the dinner table, and help the chef carry plates to and from the table, it would be my turn to make my parents tea for their bed time, along with patty sandwiches for Sylvain's lunch the next day. It was good that we had another set of hands to help us out, but Gabriel was a push over, and wanted so much to please his brother's, something I devilishly used to my advantage, something Jerome was completely against. Whenever I tried manipulating Lala into doing my chores, or doing a bit more, Jerome would intervene, putting himself at risk of getting beaten up, standing up for what was right. Jerome slowly became unstoppable, having already owned me in school; the various amounts of trophies he acquired each year, sports, cooking for the family, making friends, and there were several times where he would over power me, and was able to calm me down from beating him up. I think his confidence grew the day he floored me, got on top of me and held me down until my energy was drained.

As the year continued, Jerome and Gabriel's bond became stronger. Jerome would sit with him for hours after school, teaching Gabriel everything he had learnt in life already, mentally preparing him for big boy school and eventually how to approach life. Something I take my hat off to. I was jealous of the happenings, I was slowly becoming an evil brat, getting mad that this humble little boy that I use to torment for hours on end, he was killing me with a smile. Destroying the slave hierarchy I had tried establishing in this house. I wanted to teach Gabriel, raise him in my fire.

It was on my 13th birthday where I could feel the magnitude of how much my brothers despised me. I had invited my entire friends from school, to which 75% of them showed up. We had a barbecue, which Sylvain managed before I got my presents. We queued for the hotdogs; Jerome and Gabriel were first in the line, followed by my friends, and then me somewhere in the middle, talking to Brennan. Things were going well, but my stupid, evil mentality saw me complain and push Jerome and Gabriel out of the line, so that my friends could be served first. They didn't take to well to it, and walked inside, despite Sylvain's commands of just waiting for the food. They didn't want to have food anymore, probably already filled with the feeling of disgust. Sylvain got annoyed at it too, but served everyone first, and then retired to the house, to give my brothers their food. I really wish I could go back in time and kick my own teeth in. Sylvain came out half an hour later, and unwillingly presented me with the gift he had bought me, something Jerome helped pick out, keeping in mind what I wanted. It was a silver BMX, with pegs. I ditched everyone at the party to ride my new bicycle in the street. I was too obsessed with material possessions and was too blind to the mistakes I was making.

The year was coming to an end, and Audrey was rushing everywhere to get me prepared for what she anticipated would be my final stretch of school. She was working at a local pharmacy at the time, and where she found time to help me, I have no idea, but I didn't think of those things back then. In an instant it hit, I was going to be a small fish in a huge pond once again, and what do I have to show for it? My childhood was coming to an end, and all I had experienced were these horrible emotions that I couldn't, along with the belief that I was indeed sick. I didn't want to grow up yet; I didn't want to face being a teenager without having first enjoyed my childhood. I still wanted to hear my father say those words, "I'm proud of you, Son," something he told Jerome every so often. There were too many mistakes I needed to rectify, and time was running out. I didn't want to be the person I was anymore. Audrey on the other hand seemed to have lost all faith in me, and decided to pursue her own goals. She tried finding her real father, but all she had was a nickname and the fact that he was Greek. This was going to be an impossible task, but she started tracking down dates, people that he could have associated with, phoned Frankie's sister to find out as much as she could. While she was on various phone calls retrieving information, her motherly figure in the house faded, and we were subjected to Sylvain's way of life, which was the old fashion you don't work, you don't eat mentality. Jerome didn't mind who was leading the family, he got on well with both parents, Gabriel was still too young to understand, and just did what his brothers did.

 The days flew by, and I found myself attending my last day of primary school; the teachers most probably threw a secret party in the staff lounge. I was soon to be one of those kids that came back to visit teachers a few months after leaving, awkwardly standing in the front of the class, looking for public recognition. The kids were collectively excited, saying their goodbyes, getting their shirts signed by fellow school mates, my shirt however was signed with penis figures, loser remarks, hope you dies, and a few decent good lucks. The kids played it smart and signed on the back where I couldn't see it. As the final 30-minute count down in this primary institution begun, so did the tears, mostly girls, having to say goodbye to their favourite, life changing teachers. The depressing atmosphere had me in a spin, as I knew I would never see Mrs Opperman again, which hurt, as she was one of two people who actually seemed to care, despite being paid for it. I must say from a 3rd person point of view, that the teachers in this school seemed to have passion, you could see it even on their bad days, they put the kids first, they may have turned a blind eye here and there, but they always made sure students were generally content within the premises. The school even offered free lunches for those who couldn't afford it and had problems at home, and made sure everybody had something to eat; this was initially an initiative taken by the South African Government, but I feel as if it would have happened regardless of higher up pressure. I wish I had grasped the opportunities school provided a bit better, I should have strived to be more than a bottom of the list, lower than average student, should have gotten more involved in sports and used my straight forward personality to build up some foundation for leadership qualities, but life is a trial and error thing, where we learn as we go along I suppose.

 Back at home, Sarah and I were still hitting it off, being as hopelessly romantic as ever, taking photos of one another and sharing kisses wherever we could. She would often sneak out of her house; which was run like a military camp with fixed times for everything, to jump over a wall and meet me under the cover of darkness. We would stand under our tree and kiss for minutes before her mother came out, yelling her name. Since Sarah stayed in the corner house of two streets, I had no other option but to avoid going towards my house, meaning that I had to run and hide in Mpho's open concept yard. Mpho however was a very annoying kid, that was always sucking on his thumb and laughing at the smallest of jokes, but he meant well. I always heard Amelia give out to Sarah, but due to them being Afrikaans, I wouldn't understand a word, and just prayed for her, as her mother also gave her hidings. When we weren't jumping fences to shift each other, we stood in our kitchens, which faced one another, staring at each other from a distance, sending please call ME's; 1 meant 'Hi', 2 meant 'I love you', and 3 meant 'I have to go to sleep now, have a good night'. These coded messages were cute and fun, something I really held on to for a long time. A new girl moved in next door to us earlier in the year, we never really took notice of her; she was shy and timid, always alone in the sun, spectating the things going on in our yard. Thank God she moved in and the previous family moved out, they were a strange group. The mother was a tall, busty woman, who was somewhat attractive, the father was a tow truck driver, then there was an 18-year old daughter, which was fine and way too sexual, along with her two strange brothers that on separate occasions had sex with a puppy, and shoved the tip of a broom stick up their asses. The house was an asset purchased by a local tow trucking company, and due to tax reasons, someone had to inhabit the building at all times, meaning whoever worked as a chaser; the person that would chase to an accident to retrieve insurance first, would acquire the house. The stepdad of this shy girl drove an Audi A3, which was the fastest chase car in the town, according to our knowledge, and eventually led to my fascination of the Audi brand. Her mother seemed to just be outside all day, in the sun, puffing away on cigarettes with friends. I didn't really care too much about her, or her family, excluding the loud car sounds, but Jerome however, did. Jerome was awkward when it came to girls, and just left things to slowly work themselves out, a lesson I could have used all these years. It was holiday time, and all the kids were playing soccer in the street, experiencing the summer heat. I normally played without a shirt, I didn't have abs, nor was I fat anymore, but I did it to draw the attention of Sarah; who played with us more now than previous years, and of the new girl; Elaine, who just awkwardly stood in her yard, watching us. There were the awkward moments where the ball landed in Elaine's yard, and due to her being Afrikaans, we always nudged Sarah on to ask for it back, which eventually led to their friendship.

The year ended, and we were up and down between Sarah's and Elaine's houses, trying to mingle between the two barbecues going on. Sarah's house was more motorbike, rugby friendly, with beer and loud Afrikaans music and Elaine's was car-enthusiast, fighter type people, who drank hard liquor and listened to rave more than anything else. Jerome preferred Elaine's house, as he was more comfortable with their music choice and style of partying, where as I preferred to go wherever Sarah was. Gabriel was subjected to watching us through the chain link fence, yelling and whining for him to be allowed to join us, to which Audrey never gave in, she didn't want her precious Lala to be seated around intoxicated people. Audrey eventually found; what the information suggested, her father, confirming our Greek roots. I was extremely happy at this, as my military mind set broadened, and I always noticed how most military groups strived to achieve what the famous Greeks did, especially the Spartans.

The countdown brought the New Year in, and I embraced it with my idea of change, my new found identity, my ancient Greek religious affiliation and a girlfriend I desired to marry one day. We all knew that this year would bring something new to the table, but none of us were prepared for what was coming...

The sun starts setting, making it harder for Elliot to continue writing. Elliot decides to pause the where he is, places the pen in his front, right pocket, clipping it to the side of the seam and walks back towards where he parked his car. The city seems to get louder as the night lowers its black blanket, the constant masquerade of hooters in the distance signify everyone's impatience to get home. Elliot, however, is in no rush to get anywhere, and paces himself calmly through the post sunset field. As he gets to the corner of the road, he takes out his car key, and unlocks his car, witnessing the orange flashes on the trees in front of the vehicle. He hops into the car, and pulls out his phone, eager to contact Katrien. He scrolls through the list in his phone book, and taps on her name, calling her immediately. The phone rings and rings, but no answer. '*Maybe she's busy or doesn't have her phone near her,*' he thinks to himself, but Elliot is persistent, and rings again. After he is met with the sound of the operators recording notifying him that the number can't be reached at this time, he turns the key in the ignition, and starts making his way to the hospital where her dad is. Elliot doesn't let his depressive paranoia get the best of him, and proceeds like normal down the streets, until he gets to the hospital. Upon arriving he asks for a patient by the name of Jens De Jong, but to his misfortune they cannot give him any information as hospital policy suggests. Elliot attempts to talk his way through it; as he does most things in life, he mentions that he is the son of this elderly man, who has driven down from Utrecht after his sister Katrien notified him. The nurse at the desk seems tired from what appears to be a long shift, but lowers her head to notice Katrien's name in the next of kin section. Elliot's claims check out, and the nurse gives in to his persuasive ways by mentioning where he can find his father. Elliot proceeds down the cold, ammonia-stenched, sickly infested hallway, tracking the numbers on top of the doors, hoping that everything is still okay. The stench of lurking death riddles the air, a foul smell that is all too familiar to Elliot's nostrils. He walks into the room, only to find the man he was looking for fast asleep, or dead, in the bed the hospital provided. Elliot looks around the room for a seat, but before he can sit down on the single, dark blue, cushioned chair, he notices the abundance of nurses passing by the room; probably attending to other patients, or keeping an eye on him. With this observation, he decides to hover over the bed, pretentiously looking at the sickly stranger in front of him. A nurse, suspicious of Elliot or hungry for his presence walks in.

"Alles goed?" she asks in Dutch.

"Yeah, everything is okay, thanks," he mentions as he does his 'ever so famous' four-step check; nose, eyes, ring finger and shoulders. Elliot has done this his entire life, nose as he likes one specific type, eyes to see whether she continuously stares into his or rushes to look away, this shows her confidence; vulnerable girls from broken situations are easier to persuade, ring finger, for obvious reasons, and her shoulder's posture tells a lot; when shoulders are risen it shows passion or a level or seriousness towards the situation at hand, when they are down or slouched, it shows boredom, or a care free attitude. She seems to pass his test, but he is too focused on Katrien to worry about another; a tale similar to when he was 23-years old.

"I came to visit him, but he's sleeping, so I'll just read a book or something until he wakes up," Elliot continues. She smiles at him and walks away. Elliot finally sits down on the chair beside the bed, grabs the empty notepad on the table, along with a black pen, and tries to pass the time by writing.

Chapter 12
The Double-Edged Sword

Elliot sits there, flicking the pen, clicking the head anxiously as he doesn't remember where he left off, and only draws a few stick figures, trying to pass the time. A loud clopping sound approaches his side of the ward, it sounds a lot like a lady in heels; a sound this bachelor is all too familiar with. Elliot raises his head, eager to see what beautiful creature would pass by the room, but the time between the clops grew longer, signalling that this woman; whoever she was, was slowing down. The odds of her entering that exact room rose with every step she took, until she finally stood in the door way, wearing black heels, tight blue jeans, and a black top and glossy red lipstick.

"Katrien!" Elliot exclaims as he shoots out of the chair like a bullet.

"What are you doing here Elliot?" she hesitantly asks, her facial expression, somewhere between shocked at his stalking capabilities and nervous that he is actually there.

"You mentioned that you were coming to visit your father, so I came to support you," Elliot states as he starts getting suspicious of her awkwardness.

"Uhm, thanks, it means a lot to me," Katrien stutteringly replies. She seems very off, scared one could say. Elliot notices her withdrawn body language, it's obvious that she isn't confident or comfortable with the situation at hand, sure he's seen her naked and has spent enough time with her to know that this isn't her normal self.

Elliot's mind is populated with questions at this point, '*Is it something I've done, or said? Is it creepy that I'm here? Should I give her space after this?*' but just as Elliot is about to open his mouth, to ask her whether he has done something wrong, in walks Henrick, drunk or high on something.

"Oh…I see," Elliot murmurs out in disbelief.

"Wait, Elliot," Katrien anxiously says as Elliot turns to tear the pages he has marked from the notepad, luckily Henrick didn't comprehend her words, assuming she just greeted the male figure in the room.

"Who are you?" Henrick asks, adding his two cents to the already flammable atmosphere.

"I'm just a nurse, sir," Elliot says, playing his way out of a serious confrontation. It's not that Elliot is scared, but he knows that there is a time and a place for everything, besides there's no point fighting for a woman that has her mind made up.

"Well, Mr De Jong's vitals seem to be stable, I'll check up on him again in an hour or so," Elliot states, continuing with this medical professional persona. Elliot leaves the room, and proceeds down the hallway, jaws and fists clenched in anger. Katrien watches him leave, not because she has chosen Henrick over him, but because she knows it's all she can do, if Henrick finds out about them, it could be costly to her well-being; the torment he has caused her with abuse over the years outweighs the feelings she has for Elliot. Elliot slams the car door behind him, and speeds off with the crumpled paper still in his hand. The heavy metal music on the stereo comforts him, as it always has. The loud screams and heavy guitars have been a background tune to all his heartbreaks, something he always went back to when he was upset. Elliot returns home, where he pours himself a glass of whiskey and sits down in his seat, placing the pages and notepad in front of him, hoping that the writing will take his mind away from this fallacious image of her.

"I snapped a photo of myself and Sarah on the flip phone father had bought me for Christmas, hoping to set it as my wallpaper, a tactic to repel the smart remarks of me being a virgin and having no girlfriend. I was still a virgin, yes, but no one would detest my lies if I had photo proof. One thinks that these plans would work, but Sarah's suggestion of us sticking to friends hurt so much, that I changed the wallpaper to some dragon breathing fire."

The night creeps up to Elliot's strained shoulders, caressing them, whispering sweet lullabies into his ears; promises of an uninterrupted slumber. He is too angry to write decently and stands up from the seat, takes his sweater and shirt off, leaving his almost defined torso polychromatic toned under the single ceiling light he had left on. Elliot is aware that he hasn't written as much as he planned, but the emotional strain of Katrien got to him. He slouches towards the couch, where he crashes into the apparatus he made love to Katrien on, the memory of the moment lingers in his mind like the smell of freshly cut grass in the country side. He places his hands behind his head, and stares at the ceiling with sad eyes. Elliot compares the pain to that one time in Ireland when he was 23-years young, but the pain can't be compared, he felt something deeper then. He couldn't see himself with anyone else, not in a loving way anyway, so he committed to a bachelor life of meaningless sex and deeper loneliness. Her face still dwells in his depressive mind, and he wonders how her life turned out; whether she got married, had kids, moved to that place she always wanted to move too, but he passes out with that being his final thought for the night.

Elliot awakes to a slow morning, where he gets himself breakfast and a coffee. He polishes the plate, without even sipping the beverage. Elliot places the dish in the dishwasher and heads over to the porch, where he leans against the thick wooden post, sipping his coffee. He stares out over the lake, thinking about how stupid he had been to trust her.

"Elliot, we're supposed to know this already, why the fuck do you keep making the same mistakes?" he asks himself out loud, but there is no response from his timid side. Before the silence threatens his sanity, Elliot hears his phone sound from inside.

Elliot pauses in the middle of self-reflection to read the text on his phone. After swiping to unlock the device, he sees that it's from Katrien, asking if they can talk. It's a good attribute to have when you're straight to the point; Elliot isn't one for pleasantries and fake concerns, but a 'good morning' or a 'hello' could have set a better tone. Elliot plays with the idea in his head, pondering the effects of both his choices, *'If I message her back, it shows that I'm easily walked over, desperate for her, or even ready to be a fool for her, but on the contraire if I ignore her, it means that I'm done, and I lose again, as she can just run back to him for good'*. It's a tough call on his part, he wants her, it's the first time in a long time that he felt something like this, and maybe she is the one that can help him stop thinking about the past and start living in the present.

'Yeah sure', he texts her back...leaving room for her to figure out what he's playing at. Not even a minute passes before his phone starts ringing. Elliot answers the phone, letting out a sigh before putting the device next to his right ear.

"Hey, Elliot, I'm sorry that I was with him, he forced himself into my place again, and I didn't want to leave him there by himself, and was too scared to tell him to leave, so I took him with me, please don't be mad," Katrien blurts out before Elliot can even greet her back.

"Look, Katrien, I'm a simple person, if you want to be with him, let me know, and I'll walk away. I don't want to compete with anyone, especially not a junkie," Elliot firmly states.

"You aren't competing with anyone, Elliot, I swear, I really like you, we have something special, and I cherish it. It's just that I am scared of him and don't know how to get away from this," she fearfully admits.

Elliot grinds his teeth, noticing that there's always an excuse associated with this woman, but he buys it, mentally promising himself that this is the last time he'll do so. "Katrien, it's fine, we'll get through this. Firstly, let's focus on getting your father home safely, and then we can talk about getting rid of Henrick for good, and once that's done, we can enjoy this, does that sound fine?" Elliot suggests. "Sounds perfect to me, thank you for not walking away," she gratefully replies. Elliot hangs up the phone, leans forward and picks up where he left off.

High school started, and as was tradition, a six-week phase called 'initiation' had to commence before we could be recognised by the rest of the school. Initiation was a fun way to bring some life and laughter to the boring, academic atmosphere the school had lingering above it. During this unclear phase, we as 'freshmen' had to collect the signatures of the Grade 12 prefects, which sounds simple when put on paper, but in reality, we had to do something to get that signature. Little challenges or dares were given to us by each prefect, and once you completed it to their liking, you would receive the signature. The female prefects gave challenges that were much easier compared to the male prefects, things such as finding a certain flower, or coming up with a cute poem on the spot, or even saying something cute to a passing teacher. Whereas the male prefects pushed it to the limits, challenging kids to kiss other kids on the lips, sometimes of the same sex, dry hump dustbins, climb trees and yell profane language, and even the most common challenge, the push up challenge, where they put two lads seeking the same signature beside one another, forcing them to do push ups, until there was a victor who was worthy of the signature. I didn't excel in this as well as I had hoped, but I got my signatures after weeks of sheepish behaviour. Many things went on in the first three months of my high school career, I met a cute girl called Chanal, who was extremely emo, I made a few more 'friends', Sean and I had become closer, not as friends, but more as culprits, I found myself part of a group of boys, which seemed to be managed by Jarod; a part British lad that moved to our town and school, and then, sadly, I found myself jocularly bullying Shaun, who had no one on his side, except his chubby sister in grade 11. Among the 'prizes' behind these doors that had been opened for me, I found myself really disliking one of the awards on the other side of these hardwood path openers, a guy called Armand. A 5 foot nothing, spikey haired, son of a teacher, that was roistering in 12th grade. He must have noticed how much abuse I could take from the initiation, and decided to put me through some of his own trials, but I was aware of his non-prefect status. He would make me pick up litter and talk to girls for him, which was all right, I mean I got attention from it and was helping a brother out. However, he started bullying me, throwing me into bins, wiping the wet, insides of banana peels on my face, in front of people, punching me on the arms and chest, strangling me in front of the girls he tried impressing, and on one occasion lifting me off the ground with his bare hands. He was remarkably strong for such a short guy, or maybe it was just because I was shorter than him and rarely ate more than a meal a day. I avoided him like the black plague; better safe than sorry. My lollipop business started declining, as most of my clients had gone to to an opposing school, and the only other markets that students showed interest in, were cigarettes and weed. Even good old Brennan started smoking, and I often had to steal smokes from my parents to rent out Brennan's PlayStation 2; as my parents couldn't afford to buy me one. I quickly noticed the need for single cigarettes in this school, opposed to the expensive, hard to store packets, which cost around R20 at the time. This meant that if I had a pack of 20, I would have to sell a single smoke at R1 to break even. However, I inquired about other vendors in the school before going forth with my plan, comparing brands and prices. With my research done, I realised that each vendor sold at over R2 per unit, meaning I had lots room to compete, so I set my fixed price at R1.50. I felt accomplished and placed my hands behind my head, posing like a real business man with a clever strategy, until it hit me... I was 12 years old, how was I going to acquire stock legally? No shop would serve me, my parents wouldn't be keen on the idea, even if I was to share the profits with them, and I'd, more than likely, get beaten for such an unconventional way of making money. I had no other choice; I had to steal from under my parent's noses, and stole two cartons from their stash. In fairness, I did leave the money in the same cupboard, on top of their stash, to somewhat compensate for their loss, but reclaimed it two hours later, as I needed the money. Sales went well, and in the first week, I offered everyone who had brought a friend, a free fag – a great upselling technique, which seemed to be very effective. Like a mob boss, or a catchy salesman, I slowly started building my popularity, forcing other vendors to reduce their prices. Whenever stock started running low, I would head to the nearby shops, where there would always be some needy person outside, who would buy a 12-year old smokes or booze, for some profit. Other than the small business I was running rather deftly, I found myself in and out of various women's lives, Chanal was meant to be my valentine this year, my first valentine at that. However, when I went to her house after school one day, which was just up the road from my house, and across from JonJon's, I found Doug and JonJon in her living room. She was panting like a puppy, and red in the face, I wasn't too experienced in sexual things, but I knew something happened. I made a poor excuse and walked away, I couldn't defend what was mine, I knew better than walking into two-way traffic. Revenge was and is a huge component of my cleverly twisted mind, and I started seeing Chanal's friend, Abigail. She was taller than me, and we would always end up in some stairwell, making out, away from prying eyes, but she soon shifted her attention towards another Afrikaans guy, who I presumed was gay. Then there was Kylie, who I remembered from my kindergarten years. She took a shine in my pathetic face, but she was too chubby for me, and I acted like a real dick around her. It may have just been my emotionless self-pushing every form of love away, *preventing the chance of getting hurt. I wanted Sarah, with all my heart and soul, but I had to wait, like father tried teaching me. I felt so bad for Shaun however, he was clearly misunderstood, and the group I was part of, would constantly bully him. I knew we had our differences in the past, but I felt for him as they tripped him, smacked the back of his head and looked away before he could figure out who did it. We were at an athletics event at the Secunda Sports Stadium, and I noticed Shaun talking to Kylie, why is it always a sporting event? It's not that I cared greatly for her, I was more focused on another girl in grade 12 that I had no shot with, but boys will be boys. We left the shot-put event and headed to the moist, green patch of grass behind the hill, with an audience of 11 kids. I shook a bit from anxiety or fear as we started swearing at one another. I knew that my friends were all watching, and if I lost this, they would more than likely disband me and bully me too. I really didn't need any more bullying. Shaun swung the first punch, but my reflexes were on point and I leaned backwards, avoiding what seemed to be a hospitalising shot. I threw a few punches that landed, and the next thing you know, Shaun storms towards me, and has me in a head lock, pounding my face with a collection of welts. I was able to avoid a few hits by keeping my elbows in front of my nose. It's funny how fast one can think and react when faced with certainty, and I certainly didn't want to lose. I put a cheap shot into his baby maker, and broke free as his hands fell towards his groin area. The fight continued for a few more minutes before it was evident that I had won, and we were broken up by the audience.*

The fight gave me a malicious kind of 'confidence', and I found myself becoming more and more aggressive, towards family, friends, strangers, fellow students and teachers. I had bumped people that walked past me, on purpose, injudiciously begging for a scrap. However, no matter how copious my pugnacious spirit grew, whenever I saw Doug, JonJon or Armand, I would walk the other way. I wasn't yet ready to face those demons. A teacher noticed how violent and provocative I was becoming, and suggested trying out for the school's rugby team. I thought about it, and it ticked all the boxes in my mind. I was given a number 2 jersey, the good 'ol Hooker position, and thought that this was a piece of cake, until they put me in my first scrum. I quickly asked for another position, somewhere my neck wasn't at danger of getting snapped in two. Other than the rugby, I had been playing soccer during break times, along with Chess after school on Wednesdays. I was invited to represent my school, in this year's first, annual chess tournament, which would take place in the school's hall. The tournament progressed as planned; I had one victory and an official stale mate, after our kings danced around the chequered board for more than 50 moves. After the nerdy chess official ruled the game a draw, I found myself in dire need of urinating, having held it in throughout the lengthy game. Unfortunately, the school had locked the bathrooms of the hall we were in, smart fucking move, and I had to find a lavatory elsewhere. Our school had some 'rules' regarding restrooms, which made no sense to me; the 3rd floor bathroom was for grade 8 and 9 students, the 2nd floor was for grade 10 and 11 students, and bottom floor was for 12th graders. I tried my luck on my floor, being an 8th grader, but it too was locked, so having no other option, I took a chance at my luck in the 10th grader bathrooms... which were open. I walked into a clouded bathroom and saw three boys smoking, one of which was a regular customer. I tried to mind my own business and walked up to the urinal, ready to do my business and leave. The big guy, who seemed to be the leader of the pack, grabbed me by the back of my pullover and sarcastically told his friends that I was going to squeal on them, but I would never do such a thing, especially with my sales on the line. He didn't believe my plea and told me that I had to have a smoke, to prove my claims, and if I refused, he would beat me up and flush my head down the toilet. I faced people scarier than this clown, I never shook over size, but what made me submit, was the fact that he was black, and I was afraid of these untested waters. I had never fought a person of another colour before, as that was commonly viewed as a racial dispute, something you really want to avoid in South Africa. I did as I was told, took a smoke out of the packet he had open in front of my face, lit it with his lighter, and inhaled. With the smoke in my mouth, I went about the business I originally intended on doing. I was five puffs in, feeling extremely light headed, with a tingly cough creeping up my throat, but I had to keep my cool. Not long after the light headedness faded, I returned to the chess tournament on the other side of the school, but my next opponent inquired about the heavy tobacco smell lingering around me, and asked whether I smoked, to which I replied.

"No." I played chess on a psychological level compared to the kids around me, I noticed how people's eyes switched from piece to piece while they thought of their moves, and when watching their eyes, one could more or less see what they were planning two or three steps ahead, revealing crucial information that would ultimately lead to their defeat, but most kids were familiar with this trick. I however, used this common trick, devilishly to my advantage, I would normally position my queen; my favourite attacking piece, in a cluster of pawns and other pieces early on in the game, hiding it well from their direct thoughts. I would then make a few regular moves, sometimes opening my queen's path, but whenever I did this, I dragged my eyes across the board, slow enough for them to follow, fixating my eyes on a random piece exactly opposite my queen, sometimes mumbling to myself, manipulating them into believing that I was really interested in playing that piece. Eight out of ten times this strategy worked, the other two games were usually against Unathi or Nicole, who were harder to manipulate, as they never raised their heads from the board. I added another victory to my tally, and walked out the huge, wooden double doors on the side of the hall, in search of those smokers. Something about the attention drew me to them. After finding them on the pavilion, overlooking the dry grass covering the rugby pitch, with their school bags between their legs, they handed me another smoke. I wish I could go back to that exact moment in time and slap the cigarette out of my hand, what a waste of money, time and good health.

Days go by, and all Elliot is focused on is getting things off his chest. There something deep about the writing, its drawing him in and pushing him away at the same time. The bags under his eyes, the depressed look on his face, the state of him, they all suggest that he is struggling to cope with something, but it doesn't stop him from writing.

Smoking at home was a bit of a mission at first, I knew that had I been caught, severe beatings would follow. I did, however, have some leverage regarding the situation, as both my parents were chain smokers, and the house always smelt like the smoking section of an airport. Having moved into my own room years prior, and being allowed to keep my door closed, I found it rather simple to feed the addiction. I'd be leaned over, between my blue wall and the blue military pattern curtains;

mother had fabricated for me, puffing out the window. So that in case my parents walked in, they wouldn't think they were in Snoop Dogg's tour bus. With no clouds lingering in the room, there was no way they would catch me, perfect, right? Wrong! Mother had been busy with something in the back yard, and took note of the cigarette buds outside my window; silly me forgot to remove them in the mornings. At first, I denied it, and she gave me the benefit of the doubt, until one day I was puffing away, still in my school uniform. She walked in to find me bent over in front of the window, with the curtains covering my upper body.

"Are you smoking?" she firmly inquired. I threw the cigarette out of the window, and kept whatever smoke I had inhaled, in my lungs, as I stood up to face her. "Were you smoking?" she asked once again. My eyes were tearing up, as I needed to breathe, but I wasn't risking the chance of smoke leaving my mouth. Before the colour of my skin turned to match that of my walls, I exhaled, letting some smoke out. I figured the jig was up, and I may as well come clean.

"Yes, I was, I'm sorry, please don't hit me," I fearfully answered.

"When I was a little girl, my mother caught me smoking, and do you know what she did?" she continued. I remembered that my grandmother was hard on Sonja and Audrey, because she tried raising them into decent, respectable young women.

"No," I mumbled out, awaiting something dark.

"She made me eat a packet of cigarettes, and I vomited from it," she told me. It didn't sound tasty, and I wasn't eager to try either.

"Please just hit me, I don't want to eat it," I answered, knowing that it was probably very unconventional for my stomach. To my surprise, she handed me her packet of smokes, which had about seven cigarettes in, and told me not to tell my father. I never expected her or anyone from my family, to help feed my addiction, but then again, I may have reminded her of Sonja and herself, when they were younger, stealing smokes and puffing away in places Frankie couldn't find them.

As the days in this high school went by, I started noticing trends, especially how certain people wore their clothes. Smart kids would wear their ties, with unfolded sleeves, freshly polished school shoes, and neatly combed hair. The more intimidating, bad boy/bad girl personas never wore ties, had their sleeves rolled up to their elbows, and a pull over covering their torsos. The guys would have their hair waxed or gelled in these spikey, Mohawks. While the girls would make sure they looked as cute and provocative as possible. I knew I wanted to be classified as a smart person and not this imbecilic bad boy. So, I wore a tie, and neatly polished shoes, but at the same time I hated rules, so I had my pullover on, with the sleeves of my school shirt rolled up. The more I continued going to school, the friendlier I became with Sean the snake, and the more compromised my somewhat innocent mind became. The heavy influence from the 10th and 11th grade lads didn't help either. When I finally realised what I had become, it was too late; I had started bunking school, drinking during school hours, smoked in the bathrooms, never handed in homework, and on some occasions fought with other pupils over petty things. I came home one day, and sat on the door step after having a smoke. I sat there thinking about life and where I was going, until Sarah came home. I waved and indicated with my hands that I wanted to chat, but she hesitantly ran inside. At first, I thought she wanted to get changed, and then she'd come out, as was the case many times before, but she reappeared a few moments later, with her mother trailing her.

"Shit," I angrily mumbled under my breath, as I knew no good would come of this.

I stood up and ran away like a coward, scared to face her mother. As I made my way around the back, I heard the loud yell, "Audrey," coming from Amelia's throat. The next 45 seconds, the time it took for them to come around back, to where I was attempting to hide, and confront me, felt like an eternity, an eternity that saw its end. This short, Afrikaans lady grabbed me by my shirt, told me that I was bad news, and threatened that if I went near her house or daughter again, that she would get her husband Jake to sort me out. Humiliated in front of my parents, Sarah and Jerome; who was peeking around the corner, I broke free from her clutches and stormed off. Sylvain grabbed me by the arm, trying to teach me to see my mess through, but I was already in a very dark place, and knew this would make things even darker, so I pulled away. Everyone stood there, shocked at the resistance that I had put up, I felt ashamed for how I was acting, but the wrestling continued, until my father put me on the floor and held me down, trying to calm me. The demons inside me wouldn't go that easy, and I put up a fight, like an animal trying to escape trap. I screamed.

"Fucking leave me alone! Let me die!" with tears rolling down my face. I lost the one person I had, all the time that I had invested meant nothing now, the hours of throwing a ball over a fence at one another, would just be an eerie memory of something that I could have had. As the tears fell from my dirty face, onto the almost green grass below me, my father's grip on my arms lightened and he tried to calm me down by hushing near my ear. I had sensed that he could feel my pain and anger, so I stopped fighting back. He let me stand up, and dust myself of, before telling me to go to my room. The days that followed were the darkest I had ever experienced, the thoughts in my mind were somewhere between suicidal and mass murdering the entire fucking town, and luckily, they were never acted upon, despite my talents. The school had, at this point, already served me several warnings; even going as far as notifying my parents that if my behaviour didn't change that I would be expelled. It didn't matter anymore to me, and I made it extremely obvious. So, one afternoon, at around 15:30; after my father came home from work and opened a beer; a ritual of his, my parents sent Jerome and Gabriel for a walk to the park. With no eavesdroppers nearby, they sat me down on the single sofa in the lounge. It was evident that they had planned this approach, being the most assertive approach yet, better than the beatings and garden work punishments anyway. It wouldn't help me, I kept thinking to myself, I just wanted to disappear, anywhere was fine with me. They laid out their forecast of where I was headed if I didn't pull up my socks and get my shit together, they also mentioned that they were losing patience with me and that boarding school was swiftly becoming an option. After witnessing Sonja selling her children to the highest bidder, it hurt immensely that my supposed 'loving parents' would cast me away too, I mean how much more do you want to put a 13-year old through? I was too hurt to say anything back, and let them ramble on, and once they had finished, I stood up and depressingly walked back to my room, head hanging low. As I left the vicinity of our living room, I heard the couch my father was sitting on creek as he stood up, he would normally stand on the porch, having a smoke when he was stressed or faced with a tough situation. I understand now the frustrations he felt, but I walked away and didn't take the hand that had been trying to get me out of the hole I was in. I fell onto my bed, lit a smoke, and stared at the ceiling with tears in my eyes. I knew I was wrong and where I was headed if this didn't change, but I just couldn't change, it was hard, shit didn't make sense, I felt lost and there was an overwhelming urge to serve the dark, something I couldn't easily break free from. The more I saw Sarah, the more aggressive I became, because now I was alone, with no one except Sean, who never really cared about my feelings, it was all about the laughter and the attention we could get. I found myself in fathers dirty, white-walled garage a lot, sharpening anything I could get my hands on, subliminally hoping Sarah would see from her kitchen window, and maybe re-think her decisions, but nothing good ever came from sharpening knives and axes. On a warm, sunny, Wednesday afternoon, after yet another day of getting thrown into dustbins for a girls amusement, after more lectures from teachers and authorities that I should pay more attention to school because I was failing, and the constant arguments with fellow learners, I sat down on the couch beside Jerome, hoping to bury the pissed-off mood I was in. We would always watch some cartoons, but Jerome intended on watching some science programme instead.

"What the fuck is this?" I angrily questioned him as he put the remote down beside him. He looked at me with scared eyes.

"I really wanted to watch this. Let's see how it is and we can change if we don't like it," he said, finding a solution to both our needs.

"Fuck that," I loudly exclaimed as I leaned over Jerome to get the remote on his far side, but he held onto it, fair play to him for always standing his ground and trying to show no fear.

"You always get to choose! Why can't I pick?" he tried arguing, but my only response was the suggestion to let go of the remote before he regretted it. Audrey over heard the argument from the kitchen and came in, guns blazing, swear words at the ready. She always found more confidence in confronting me when she had a weapon in her hands. The words and insults kept coming, Jerome was hiding behind her at this stage, and I was on the verge of snapping. I walked away after a few minutes of Audrey swinging a hosepipe in my face and calling me the most useless son on the face of planet Earth. I really wanted to avoid the worst, because I could feel the pressure building, and we were now venturing into unchartered waters. As I walked away, she started whipping me with the one meter in length synthetic rubber, hitting legs, back, head, ass, arms; anywhere she could. As the shots from behind kept coming, I kept moving forward, towards the garage, like an American on D-Day. I could no longer feel the pains from her lashing at me, and only registered the sound of the pipe crashing into my skin. I walked into the cold, somewhat dusty car port, where my father had kept his tools and equipment in precise order; every spanner hanging from a nail, every grinding or cutting disk neatly packed on a table, metal shelves holding paint and paint accessories meticulously, like a hardware merchant with OCD. She stopped at the entrance, fearing what my intentions were in such a confided space, Jerome hovering 15 metres or so behind her. I picked up the axe that I had spent the last month and a half sharpening, from the bucket I had left it in, and turned to look her in the eyes. The blank expression on my face along with the hatred in my eyes petrified her to the marrow. She put her weapon down and slowly started backing away; I suppose hoping to avoid the dangers that could follow.

"Jerome run!" she screamed, as she turned to gap it, but I wasn't slow at all, and was right on their tail, chasing them around the house.

Luckily the yard was easily accessible, with no obstructions in the way. They both kept turning their heads, trying to see how far I was from getting them, but as they turned around, I noticed the tears rolling down my brother's cheeks and the fear in both their eyes. Jerome's cries of.

"Run, Mommy, run!" reached my ears.

Who am I? What am I doing? I asked myself, as I slowed down and allowed them to run to safety. This isn't who I wanted to be, or who I saw myself becoming, but I couldn't prevent it for some reason. They got inside the house and locked me out. Audrey jumped on the phone and phoned my father, as well as the police. I walked into the garage and put the old, wooden handle axe on the table, and walked back out. I sat down beside the garage, with my back against the terracotta-coloured wall, regaining my breath. Sarah had been standing by her window, and had witnessed the entire thing. I felt so ashamed and guilty, not only because of how her perception of me altered, but also due to being trapped in this monstrous emotion that I had no control over. A few minutes passed, and my father's car loudly skid on the tar road as he pulled up to the house, he opened the latch on the gate, leaving it to swing wide open, and rushed inside the yard. He passed the garage where I was seated and briefly looked at me in disgust, as he continued to the main entrance of the house to see if everyone was okay. The police van pulled up a few seconds later, and two officers got out, one walked towards me with his hand on his gun, the second walked up to the front gate and pressed the doorbell. My parents, along with Jerome, came out, bombarding the second officer with the details of what had happened, and all that scared victim shit. I sat against the wall of the garage, depressed and dead inside, ready for the consequences that were to follow. My mother spoke loud, and I could hear each word clearly, but never once was it mentioned how she had hit or beat me, and the officer didn't ask what provoked the attack, but I was beyond justification. The second officer came towards me, and tried to get the other side of the story, but one side was sufficient to make a decision. Sylvain stood beside the cops, trying to finding a solution for the day, because according to law, I was supposed to be removed from the property, and due to the lack of family, the only other place left to go was jail. I was scared, I admit, but I also didn't care anymore, as suicide had once again become a priority. Sylvain had told the cops that I could stay in my room, and that they would phone, should there be any further problems. Thank you, Papa, for risking your life to see me not go through that again. I was locked in my room from that point forward, with a bucket, just in case I needed to go. The only time that they had opened my door, was to give me food, which my father handed me, with my mother right behind him, 10111; South African Police Services, already dialled in and Jerome at the front gate, ready to run to Amelia with Gabriel. The disturbing feeling that one feels when your family takes such precautionary measures to secure themselves from you, is something so difficult to explain, but even harder to work through. Sitting here now, I'm ashamed of who I was, and should have given them happier memories opposed to the piece of shit I was. There is nothing I can say to justify these actions, I was a troubled kid.

The pages of the calendar tore away, like the time passing cliché used in most films, stopping on the 25th of August 2008. Another bleak and boring Monday upon us, but my parents urged me not to put on my school uniform. I asked them why, but they just mentioned that we were going to see someone. I didn't think much of it, and assumed it would be another doctor or psychologist. Little did I know that on the

22nd I had been expelled from Hoerskool Secunda, for constant failure to comply with school rules. Apparently, according to various letters my parents received, I had been a danger to myself and everyone around me, which all my psychiatrists seemed to agree with, and that I was going to see a social worker that could fast track me into boarding school. A week prior to my expulsion, the school had assigned a teacher, who accompanied me to a bathroom, to check if drugs were the cause of my behaviour. I urinated in the cup this male teacher gave me, and awaited the results patiently in the corner of the bathroom. Sadly, they were left with their dicks in their hands as it came back negative, I wasn't the one you should have tested, Sean, and all those 10th and 11th graders would have rendered you more success, dumbasses. We arrived at the social workers offices at around 9:30 that Monday, a woman introduced herself, I forget her name, and told us that she would be responsible for handling my 'case'. After the pleasantries, this lady explained what would happen from this day forward and stated that I ran out of chances. She took no shit, and asked whether I wanted to drive to Standerton; 60 kilometres south of Secunda, with her or with my parents, as both parties needed to be present on the day of enrolment at this new school. My parents preferred me with them, probably so that I wouldn't annoy her with childish fairy tales of child abuse. We passed the sign saying 'Welcome to Secunda' and I knew that this was the real deal; all that I had feared was now upon me. The drive took about an hour, and I kept my eyes thoughtfully gazed on the African landscape outside the window; the tall, dry grass, whimpering from the slight wind blowing in from the west, old Zulu ladies walking beside the road with baskets of fruits on their heads, acres of farmland that seemed to stretch over the horizon, cows, majestically grazing in the warm fields, and silos in the distance, I assume were used to store corn or maize. While this unforgivable trip commenced, the only three thoughts that continuously crossed my mind were: I was going to get raped by some guy called Dirk, leaning over to the driver's side and pulling the steering wheel left as hard as I could, so that the car could flip, killing us all, and that one way or another, I would get my revenge. The more I kept wanting to pull the steering wheel, the more I thought of leaving Jerome and Gabriel as orphans, I loved them dearly, but I struggled to express or show it, however, that thought died out as did the road. We entered the dusty farming town of Standerton, which had one main road, filled with potholes. 50 metres after the entrance of this dull place, on the right-hand side of the road, read a sign 'Vaalrivier Skool en Juegsorg Sentrum': Vaalriver School and Youth Care Centre. On the left-hand side, directly across Vaalrivier, was another school, which didn't interest me much. About another 400 metres on the right, was a sandy cemetery, which seemed to house over a thousand different graves. Behind the school, a chicken processing plant…which set the smell for the next five years of my life. My father indicated to the right, and as he turned at the sign, I took note of the 10ft cement pillars that circled the school, obviously to keep children in. There was a 150 m drive to the boom gate, where a security guard, dressed in dark blue, asked us to sign in. The social worker signed us in and we followed her to the main office, which was another 500-metre drive on the tarred road. There was a soothing, calm atmosphere associated with this place, but I refused to admit or accept it. I wanted hate to be my only emotion, and revenge my only aspiration. As we drove along the road, where huge pine trees, planted some 50 years ago, blocked out the sun light, I noticed the little houses on the right, which belonged to the teachers. Beyond that, there were four hostels; two on the right, approximately 100 metre away from the road and from each other, with a huge grass patch in between them and two on the left, which were closer to the road, but bared some Old Dutch architectural design. We continued on the road, which housed even more teachers on the left, and across from these houses were three old, worn-down tennis courts, with metal cricket wickets on each side of the first one. It seemed that this had been where they played action cricket. Finally, the school, just a tad further on the right-hand side. We parked outside the main office, on a bricked surface, under an aluminium canopy. The school yard was cleaner than any other place I'd seen before, birds chirped in the surrounding trees and the air was clearer than Secunda's, but the stench of chicken feathers burning, smacked you in between the eyes. We walked in through the reception, and were seated at an eight-seater conference table, where the social worker of the school and the social worker whom my parents had dragged along, sat beside one another, opposite me. My parents sat on the far-right, away from the situation; – talk about facing the world alone. The two professionals spoke Afrikaans at first, highlighting as to why I was there, and why enrolling me on this exact day was crucial. I didn't understand Afrikaans, but the facial expressions of the lady learning about me hinted at what they were talking about. They switched to English and my parents got involved, then I got involved when I was asked to speak. The lady explained that this school had once been a military camp, which then converted into a military school, which then changed into a normal high school, but it still more or less followed the same protocol and structure as before. She continued to mention that the school aimed at rehabilitating angry, violent children, kids with broken homes and orphans who needed an education; they strived to teach young men discipline, manners, respect, as well as give them the first-class education that they needed, in order to compete outside school walls.

"Young men?" I asked hastily.

"Yes, this is a boys boarding school, other than mothers that visit and female members of staff, there are no women on this campus," the kind lady explained.

"I see," I gently responded as my self-esteem dropped another level.

"Due to your age and size, we will put you in the baby hostel, hostel 4," she mentioned as the meeting ended. My parents signed a few papers, with me silently contemplating my suicide beside them. We then drove down to the first hostel on the left; the one we had passed on our way up to the office. This hostel had four huge cement blocks, placed next to one another in a square formation, forming a parking space. Attached to the hostel, was a nurse's office, apparently the school had its own qualified medical practitioner, something not yet introduced to South African schools at the time. They handed me over to the hostel mother, Mrs Pieterse, who gave my parents and me a tour of the facility. Upon entrance, through a double glass door with wooden frames, we stood in a magnolia tiled hall way. There was a huge mess hall, which had an old colour TV mounted to the wall, on the right. To the left, the rest of the initial hallway, where we stopped next to two rooms, the room on the left, she considered her office, even though it was just a linen lock up, the room on the right was what I came to know as the medicine room, it was locked tight. Directly after that, another hallway, left housed rooms 1 to 6, along with a bathroom and shared showers, right housed a youth worker office, rooms 7 to 11, along with the same amnesties. Finally, directly in front of us was a hallway leading up to the nurse, I was surprised to have not found the floor filled with blood, as I knew Afrikaans kids were immensely violent, especially farmer kids with shitty circumstances. She walked over to room 8, which apparently had an opening, and allocated a bed and locker to me, I didn't like the locker as it stood a mere six-feet tall and three-feet wide. While taking in my surroundings, she mentioned that I should always lock my belongings away in the locker, as some kids were prone to stealing.

"I have no belongings," I worryingly admitted to her. She seemed distraught by my statement and accompanied me back to my parents, who were now having a smoke with the social workers outside. She inquired about the lack of utilities and clothing. My parents had forgotten to pack stuff for me, and failed to even advise me to do so, so my father told her that he would drive back later that day, with all my belongings. Everyone shook hands and I stood there, heartbroken, a little 13-year old boy, beside a big lady dressed in a long flower dress. I knew it was time to say goodbye to my parents, because I'd probably never see them again, and even if I was allowed to, I didn't want to. My mother got in the car, after a brief, fake hug and my father just looked at me, and headed to the car, where he reached into the cubby hole for his spare packet of Benson & Hedges. He handed them to me, along with his personal lighter that he took out of his pocket. He said nothing, but actions spoke louder than words, it was evident in his eyes that he had not lost all hope in me, unlike everyone else. His eyes remained in my mind the remainder of my time in Vaalrivier, they spoke to me, I could almost imagine his voice saying 'don't fuck up, you can still be great', maybe it was just hopeful thinking in the face of abandonment. They got in the car and left, I stood outside and heard my dad changing from first gear to second, and then to third before the 1.6 litre engine sound faded. I was told to make myself familiar with the place, so I walked around a bit, lit a smoke next to some bushes on the back side of the hostel, and just stared at the 10 feet tall pillars. I wandered back after about an hour and noticed that all the other kids were back from school. Mrs Pieterse called me into her little room and assigned another student to be my friend, to show me the ropes; his name was Andrew, one of the two twins. His brother, Jeffrey, was a more vicious-looking child, with a brutal sense of humour and a massive scar beside his right eye. I introduced myself and he seemed happy to take me under his wing, all I could think was 'yeah this is the guy who's going to rape me', but he walked back to the room with me, and explained that no one rapes anyone here. He also mentioned that he was in 8th grade, supposed to be in 9th, and that he too was from the boring town of Secunda. It was lunch time and the kids lined up on a quad, forming six lines of five, there were four kids in the front of the lines, who faced the lined-up ones, commanding things in Afrikaans, and then allowing the lads in to eat. It was obvious that they were leaders and were to be respected, or feared, as they were taller and built bigger compared than the rest. They all walked in and I was given to the youth worker on duty, Mr Shabangu, who led me inside the mess hall, where I saw six long tables, seating six kids per table. I was asked to sit on table 2, beside Andrew. There was a strong lingering stench of a common Afrikaans stew in the air, something I recall smelling in Sarah's house most weekends. I didn't like the smell, nor the taste, but before we could dig in, someone had to pray, leaders would normally pick someone out to pray if there were no volunteers. After the prayers, the table leader on table 2 told me to dish first, so Andrew handed me the metal dish, which contained dry rice. I kind of understood that this was a test, to see how greedy I was, so I put two spoonfuls in my plate, and passed it back to Andrew on my left. I received the other metal bowl from the right, which housed the stew. I quickly passed that on to my new friend without dishing a thing.

"Are you sure?" Andrew asked before taking the bowl.

"Yeah, I'm really not hungry," I quickly replied. I proceeded to eat the dry rice, something I was criticised for during my tenure at this school. Lunch finished and an 'x-group' was called to clean the food hall, it was clear that these kids had messed up somewhere and this so called 'x-group' was a form of punishment. The rest of us headed to the designated smoking area, where everyone asked for smokes; along with the regular questions they seemed to ask all newcomers. There was a massively built Afrikaans guy, called Ryan, who walked into the smoking section ever so proudly. It was clear that he was someone important, and I learnt that he was the head boy of this hostel, a first team rugby player, a first team cricketer, that had received provincial colours for both sports, and that he was only in the 10th grade. He stood inside the unmaintained side building we smoked in, and asked me for a cigarette in this deep, intimidating voice. I was so scared, I almost offered him the entire packet, but he took one out, lit it, and said something in Afrikaans, before walking over towards a bench, where he put his blaring earphones in, and blew smoke circles in the air. The questions stopped coming, and I was allowed to enjoy my cigarette with the twins. Jeffrey had mentioned that he and his brother had only been in the school for 2 months, but because their parents recently got divorced, and due to their father being in the accident recovery sector; forced to be out till the early hours of the morning, there wasn't anyone to raise them. My dad returned to the school, a few minutes to 18:00, and dropped off a huge duffle bag with all the clothes I didn't like, along with a carton of smokes, and some soda. The gesture of giving me so many smokes indicated that I wouldn't be seeing them for a long time... Night fell and we kids were ordered to bed at 9 P.M.

As the snores slowly became the melody of the dark hallways, I lay awake, somewhere between depressed and determined. I remembered the looks of utter disgust on the faces of the people I had disappointed, remembered the words of those who didn't believe in me, all the injustices, and it got to me. I think this is where I made a life changing decision; I had always imagined it being me versus the world, and now? Now it was a reality. "Fuck them all, I'll show everyone," I whispered to myself in this dark room, as the youth worker walked up and down the hallways with a torch, making sure everyone was asleep. I'm glad it came to this, I feel as if life would have been very different had I not taken this opportunity to look at things differently.

Before the sun even had the chance of bringing in the new day, an alarm sounded, and we were all up, forced to stand on parade, wearing nothing but what we slept in. We were told to make our beds, clean our rooms, and get ready for school. It seemed simple, but this wasn't the regular bed making that occurred in your parents' house, oh no. There were to be no creases on the sheets, blankets had to be folded properly, and placed at the bottom of your bed, and the single pillow you were given, had to be centred exactly. Any infringement of this bedding code would result in your bed being overthrown and you would be rushed to get it right before breakfast. Breakfast was served by the African ladies that worked in the kitchen, and once it was served, we were called via the loud siren to line up on the parade ground. Ryan stood in front of us all, I looked up at him from the second line left of the wall, and promised myself that one day I would stand there. After a hearty breakfast, we left for school, and I was now, more than ever before, determined to turn my life around, to change who I was, and steer my ship into the direction of success. I got to meet most of the teachers, and attended all the classes scheduled for that day; not like I had a choice. It seemed as if the teachers knew that I was going to fail, that I would have to repeat the 8th grade, and decided to go easy on me, but they didn't yet know the fight in me. Weeks went by and I got more familiar with the school, how it operated, who was who, and in some sick, twisted way, I fell in love with it, there was room to grow, room to learn, and room to be me. Here I'd be able to establish myself, with no negative remarks, reminding me of who I'll never be, and I put a lot of effort into turning things around. My friendship with Andrew took a negative turn, as he was a smart cookie in the classroom, and as we've established already, I hate competition, so my after-school friendship turned towards Jeffrey instead. The year finally came to an end, and despite the odds stacked against me, I had passed grade 8, with 60% on my report card. I wasn't exactly happy, but it was way better than my previous report card of like 15%; which was probably the highest I had ever obtained. I was finally allowed home, after three or four months of isolation from the outside world; no one was allowed to leave the school without written consent. I didn't know how I felt about going home, sure I'd be back in the room I never wanted to leave, but at the same time, I wanted to stay at school, with the kids that had no families, or homes to return too, and learn more for the next year, but sadly I was urged to go home. My parents picked me up from the bus stop in Secunda, and cautiously welcomed me back home, but in my time away I grew distant, still unable to forgive them. All I really needed was someone to listen to me when shit was rough and I needed a break, but beating me and calling the police when I stood up for myself was handier, I suppose. How the fuck do you call the police for your 13-year old son four times in a week? How? I arrived at my orange coloured family home, where Jerome and Gabriel kept their distance and treated me as a stranger, but who could blame them? School holidays were about four weeks long, and the first three days were wasted in my room, hiding in shame for what I did to these people I would call 'family' for the rest of my life. I was now somewhat able to comprehend how bad I really was, which made looking them in the eyes at the dinner table extremely difficult; much needed humiliation. I don't know whether Gabriel had felt sorry for me living like a gardener in my four-walled prison, isolated until the bosses needed work done, or if he had missed having that full family feeling, but he approached my room, knocked on the wooden door, as hard as a four-year old can, and asked me to play outside with him. A sense of gratitude and relief surged through me; it was one of those cute moments in life that you just can't explain. I followed him outside while he told me about the ball that Papa had bought him. As soon as we got outside, he ran towards the left-hand side of the house; wearing his cute blue shorts and grey short sleeve shirt, to where he had left the ball. I lifted my head, to catch a glimpse of Sarah's home. I looked at her house, starting with the dark green gutters, which seemed to blend so well with the light green walls, before switching to watch their Jack Russell running around the place. As my eyes wandered through her property, I noticed her standing in the kitchen, looking back at me, but none of us waved, and in a deep atmosphere, I realised that I had to accept that it would never be the same again. Those years of friendship and puppy love, stolen kisses and curious feelings, all had to be forgotten. Gabriel kicked the ball towards me, and asked me to show him some soccer tricks, such as tapping the ball in the air, like he had seen on TV. Being somewhat experienced in soccer, I performed the tricks with ease, while he stood in awe, clapping his hands and laughing so happily. It was nice to see someone, outside of school, delighted with my existence. Jerome came out to see what the commotion was, and stood on the door step with his arms folded, watching us play. Jerome was way more mature than me back then, he was quiet, extremely smart, and if any of us stood a chance of succeeding in life, it would most definitely be him. He later joined in for a few kicks, and we were kind of united as brothers again, with a few cautious stances. Christmas was around the corner, but it had a different feeling associated with it this time round, I didn't ask for anything, I felt more like the adopted kid that had no right to ask for anything, and should be grateful for the roof I had over my head. The fireworks lit up the New Year sky a few days later, but it too felt very different, the family walk was now something of a myth. Sarah's place housed the same faces, the same booze and the same music, the only difference this year, was her boyfriend, who came over on his dark blue, 400cc four-wheeler. All the memories of us celebrating this date years prior, were thrown back in my face as she snogged him after the count down. 2009 set the tone for the rest of my high school career, but it was based on some smart strategic plays on my end, along with many dark emotions. Due to my good behaviour, I was now allowed to go home every 2nd weekend, if my parents saw fit, but Audrey didn't want me home that regularly, so I'd see them maybe once a month if I was lucky. Sylvain still felt sorry for me, and would normally take me shopping for crisps, soda and sweets before dropping me off at the hostel. In the six months or so of my tenure in this school, I paid close attention to Ryan's likes and dislikes, his walk, talk, actions and the motives behind them. Whenever I came back from a weekend or holiday, I would offer him some soda, crisps, smokes, basically anything that I had acquired from home, which eventually led to our friendship. At first this was a strategic measure, covering several areas I needed to focus on to ensure success here; Afrikaans speech and understanding, rugby basics and mentoring, someone big that had my back, reputation building, and finally to gain the trust of teachers and youth workers alike. The exchange of knowledge and presence for a father funded friendship seemed like a win-win situation, and it went well for the first month or so, yes I was using him for my own benefits, but I then grew to admire him as a friend, and we became best friends not too long after that. Ryan was a decent person, with good morals and values, that knew never to abuse the power that had been bestowed upon him, a proper leader, but due to his size, people thought he was some kind of bully, that had no emotions; human nature I suppose. Ryan enjoyed the rap and R&B genres when it came to music, Chris Brown being his favourite artist, he was obsessed with rugby, with the Golden lions being his team, which at the time weren't doing so hot, it would be no surprise if I told you that it became my team too. I then discovered something deeper; his father had been struck by a car and passed away a few years prior, when he was only 12...turning 13, leaving him and his brother; who was the head boy of hostel 3, in a dire situation. He saw his mother maybe once a year, I guess it was a financial situation too, but I never dared going deeper, as it was his business. It became complicated being friends with Andrew and Jeffrey, as well as Ryan, because I not only saw Ryan as my best friend, but also, I viewed our friendship as an asset, that could not fall into the hands of my competitors. So, I never mixed the two groups, meaning that in school I hung out with the twins, and at the hostel, with Ryan. School was going well, and I was maintaining a consistent growth, working towards the long-term goals I had laid out for myself, but also smashing the short-term ones in the process. Near the middle of the year, father booked a holiday for the family, and we flew to France. It would be the first time that the French side met Jerome and Gabriel. I remembered nothing of them, and had hoped that they would be classier than Audrey's side of the family, but to my disappointment they were too classy, and extremely snobbish towards us. They said that we had dressed poorly, and that we kids were too loud, ill-mannered and very unpleasant. Audrey didn't take too kindly to the words, but kept quiet around them, as she was still seen as a black sheep, an outcast, someone who would never be good enough for my father. My father on the other hand, didn't let it get to him and allowed them air their opinions, because at the end of the day they were just words. I can't say that I was disgusted with it because I had no room to talk, no normal 13-year old boy could say that he had been thrown into jail, expelled, attempted to murder his family, tried to light his house on fire, smoked, drank, violently fought with fellow students, got abused on a daily basis, or had illegal business experience. However, one of my fondest memories are attached to the small town of Henriville. The smell of fresh cut grass blended ever so delightfully with the smell of freshly baked croissants, the sight of light grey clouds hovering above the village, torn here and there, allowing the sun to shine its perfection on small patches of French soil, and the sound of a loud church bell, meshed euphonically with the multitude of chirping birds, making it memorable. As Nowak lads, we always considered ourselves French, but this new found experience gave us a different sense of patriotism, it was an uncommon feeling at the time. Even the great city of Paris, that sees millions of tourists each year, could not compare to the beauty I found in the country side. What made the feeling of patriotism even stronger was the fact that I had been in South Africa my entire life, and never once considered it home, and now I finally had a place I wanted to call home. We returned to South Africa after a two-week long break, where I continued my schooling. With every passing day away from home, I felt more like a freelance and less like a member of a somewhat functioning family, which ultimately led to another trait I found, independency. My sports abilities got better thanks to Ryan, and now that I was confident in rugby, I was given the number 15 jersey, where I fell in love with the sport. Other than rugby, we had daily sports meetings, where we played softball, action cricket and something called 'jukskei', which involved knocking over a stick that had been placed in a rectangular sand pit with a plastic, bottle shaped object. On the flip side, I never let the academic sector slip. I was continuously improving in the 90s, out-doing everyone in my grade, and staying humble about it. My parents were invited to my boarding school's annual prize-giving, and to their amazement I had finished 1st in my grade. I picked up around 8 different certificates for my achievements, along with my 2nd consecutive chess player of the year trophy. For the first time in my life, I was proud of where I was, what I was doing and where I was headed, but I didn't want it to end there, I had loads of fight left, and a lot left to prove. After the ceremony, we were sent home for the December holidays, but my holidays from that point forward changed drastically. I spent most of my much-needed relaxation time strategizing key areas on the path to excellence. I was getting older, and closer to being a candidate in the next vote for leaders, yes, I was somewhat respected for my bravery in tough situations, and for how I treated my fellow students, but I needed another approach, something with bigger impact, that *would ensure a few more votes. I also realised that school was getting harder, and competition was on my tail, so subjects I didn't perform so hot in needed to become a priority. I also had to become more creative in the way I played sports, because the other kids were getting bigger and faster, while I remained five-foot short. My only choice in such a rapidly evolving environment was to add a different dynamic to the game...*

Smoking was no longer prohibited by my parents, it was a 'my life, my choice' kind of thing, but with the condition that I didn't smoke in front of them, which I respected, well, until my mother asked me to light smokes for her. Hostel life became the norm for me, and felt more like a home than my own home, the lads around me, I saw as brothers, the teachers and youth workers as parents, uncles and aunts, and within this yard I was making my family proud. I slowly started executing my plans, and became a bit crazier, bolder, more daring, doing things to make others laugh; it was easier to lead as a friend than a stranger. Key subjects in the academic world were noted and worked on greatly, I also put more time and effort into sports after school. The big school across the road, that meant nothing to me on my first day, now became a place of importance as my hormones kicked in. The school was exactly the same as our school, just for girls, and a bit darker in terms of discipline, but was always viewed as our sister school. Interactions with the opposite sex were crucial in the teen years, as we had already experienced a few homosexual outbreaks in the dorms late at night; when people were supposed to be asleep. Not that any of us were homophobic, it was just unfair that we straight lads weren't getting any. Luckily a system, with several interactions were put in place years prior to allow for such social necessities, firstly there were the Sunday visits, and only kids with a certain amount of credits or points were legible to visit; points were given based on good work, attendance, politeness and various proactive activities at school, secondly there were the sending and receiving of letters; one could write a letter to a girl and place it in a basket in front of the youth workers desk, which would then be delivered the next day, and after two days, if the girl was interested in you, or the way you worded things, you would receive a letter back. Receiving a letter was an interesting thing, as you had to do a minimum of ten push ups for each letter, but the amount of push ups were adjusted based on the weight of the letter, the colour of pens the girl used, the amount of hearts she drew on it, as well as how much perfume she sprayed on the letter. Then thirdly, there was a Saturday evening dance, where either we walked to their main hall, or they walked to ours, music was put on for about three hours, while we awkwardly sat on opposite sides of the hall, looking at one another for an hour, until youth workers from both school's put couples together, forcing the interactions. I had my share of these interactions the previous year; two visits and one dance, where I took a girl called Joan and her seductive ways too literal and ended up losing my virginity to her in the town of Morgenzon one long weekend. I laughed at these fools doing push ups for letters, as Joan and I had used our phones as a mean of keeping in contact, but then we broke up...and then the letters swarmed in. I had gone to one fucking dance, where I danced with one girl, after awkwardly sitting next to a guy called Ben for an hour and a half, only one dance, and 6 girls decide to send me story books confessing their feelings and emotions towards my European looks, which was another humorous thing as I was short, skinny, had pink braces on my teeth, Elvis Presley styled hair and pimples everywhere, I was one ugly son of a bitch, but hey look not everyone has good taste in men I suppose. I remember on one occasion I had received about 11 letters from girls in a single day, and ended up having to do over 300 push-ups, which were obviously broken down into sections of 50. My smartass would always write back, out of either desperation for female attention or out of politeness; I found none of these girls attractive. As time went on Cathy, Sarah, Nicole, all of the girls I have either crushed on or invested in, faded from my first level of consciousness. During one of our school's friendly rugby games, between the first and second teams, I somehow got Ryan and Jeffrey talking, they're personalities and passion for rugby complimented one another, and they just clicked. It was good until I realised how I had fucked myself over, because Andrew's presence would soon follow behind Jeffrey, meaning I put a huge obstacle in my path to leadership. Andrew was already two up on me as he was elected both table and room leader a few weeks earlier, but later on joined the crew. Cigarettes were hard to come by for four teenagers trapped in these walls, so we established a 'joint account' where each person would contribute a few packets to the cause, and these packets were held in Ryan's locker, as no one would dare steal from him... or so we thought. John Hudson, an English-speaking pupil, who was rather smart in school, a tad taller than me and quite respectable of the hostel rules, must have taken some magic juice or something, as he stole two packets of smokes from Ryan's open cupboard, while Ryan was in the shower. It was hard to find out who took them, as there was a hostel population of thirty-five kids that weekend, but we needed answers, so we entered the smoking section, ready to interrogate everyone, but how would we approach people? We bought one brand of cigarettes, which not many people in this hostel smoked, making it a bit easier to identify, as it bared the blue mark of the company above the filter. Other means of investigation were looked at too, such as kids with theft history, kids who never had smokes and all of a sudden had some, and also kids avoiding the smoking area whilst our squad occupied it. We noticed the blue mark on one kid's smoke, called him into the attached room beside the main smoking section, and asked him where he had gotten the fag, to which he hesitantly replied.

"John gave it to me for my macaroni and cheese dinner." Smokes were used as currency here, everything from food, clothes and chores, to beverages and toiletries could be traded with cigarettes. I already had a run in with John months earlier, due to a similar situation where he had poached someone from my food giving herd.

"Interesting," Ryan said as he told him he could leave the room, we looked around the smoking room for John but he was in front of the TV, watching some cartoons. John had a history of stealing prior to his arrival at this school, but we never suspected that he would try it again.

"Call John there," Ryan told someone nearby, who nipped his smoke half way to do Ryan's bidding. I secretly hoped that it was him, as I still didn't get my full revenge for him poaching a Sunday custard dessert from my flock, but I also felt sorry for him as I knew if it was him, that it was going to hurt, a lot. John walked in on very shaky legs, scared as he noticed Ryan's face leaning out of the entrance of the attached smoking room. "Walk into my office, Mr Hudson," Ryan commanded, as he double clutched his smoke and followed the poor lad in. "Everyone else out," Ryan continued, trying to get everyone else out of the room, no witnesses meant no trouble. "Sit down, relax, take a smoke buddy," Ryan told him as he offered him a cigarette from our freshly opened packet.

At this point I could see the intimidating point Ryan was playing from, but he left the questions to Jeffrey, as he was able to catch a liar in record time; his street smarts always came handy in these kinds of situations. The questions commenced and went on for about ten-minutes before Andrew took note of where the situation was headed and jumped in to play good cop, harmonising with his bad cop brother. He offered John a peaceful way out, but only if he came clean to the theft, swearing that we would do nothing to him if he chose the path of honesty. John was scared, and for good reason; liars, thieves and kids that disrespected female teachers were beaten in this school, and it's not that the authority or administration of the school turned a blind eye, but more so the kids in the wrong were made to understand where they had messed up after the beating, and refused to snitch on the leader who chose to rehabilitate them. This was the perfect system for me, because the only way you learn in life is through pain and humility, well that's my opinion anyway. The good cop approach failed, but before we could give up on him, Jeffrey had asked an extremely smart question, which John answered incorrectly, as it conflicted with two previous questions Jeffrey had asked earlier on. After being made aware of it, he admitted to stealing the smokes, and gave the excuse that he was hungry that evening and needed the smokes. Ryan stood up and told him that the chance of coming clean was offered but he refused to take the deal.

"Malcolm, you know what to do," he said, as he looked at me with those deep, blue eyes. I slowly walked up to John with my sleeves rolled up and a lit cigarette in the side of my mouth. I asked him why he did it, but as the final word left my mouth and before he could answer, a huge right-hand slap hit him on the left cheek. A few seconds after he regained his balance, and tried standing upright, a quick left slap followed, but this one stung as I was left-handed. Props to him for still trying to stand after the shots landed. His eyes started tearing up, but I felt no remorse and punched him in the face, half on his cheek and half on his mouth, but this time he didn't get back up. I grabbed him by the shirt, and with all my power pulled him up to my level, his tears fell on my wrists. I then proceeded to ask him whether he would do it again, but he seemed to be in another world, zoned out or blank from the wallop. At first, I thought he was faking it, so I half killed a cigarette on his arm, but there was no reaction. He had gone into shock, and I got scared. I got a hose and sprayed him with cold water, but nothing, gave him sugar water, still nothing. Ryan suggested putting him in a warm shower, so we did, but I feared the worst and confessed what I had done to the youth worker on duty; a youth worker that had admired me, but that all came to an end with the knowledge of my violence. We dressed him and put him in bed as the youth worker suggested, and monitored him throughout the night. I think it's safe to say that it was a long, sleepless night for me. I went on my knees, beside his bed, and prayed for him to be okay. During my pleas, I had promised that I would never, ever raise my hands to another person again, unless I really had too. At around 4:30 A.M., he seemed to regain consciousness and started asking me questions, he couldn't remember anything, so I told him everything, and mentioned that I was extremely sorry, but I also tried justifying myself, by arguing that he shouldn't have stolen in the first place. I knew that the incident had been jotted down in the 'Journal', which was passed onto the deputy principal every Monday. The journal was a collection of events or incidents that took place in the hostels that were reported to the highest authorities of the school, preventive or corrective actions were taken based on the situation. I sat in mathematics, beside Jeffrey and behind Andrew.

"Malcolm Nowak to Mr Van der Westhuizen's office please, Malcolm Nowak," the lady on the intercom announced. Yep...where were my friends now? I bowed my head in shame as I left the class and headed to reception. I walked into his office after he called me in, and saw John standing there with a blue eye and a swollen face, with the same distraught look he bared the previous day.

"Did you hit this boy?" the huge, scary authority figure started; he was a massive guy, standing at least six-feet tall, weighing easily over 100 kg. I wasn't always an honest person in life, but I did start cherishing it in this school.

"Yes, sir, I did," my response came.

"Why did you hit him?" he continued.

"He stole something from me, sir," I responded, no longer trying to justify my actions.

"Do you think this is an appropriate measure to take when someone steals from you? Or are there other systems in place to deal with this?" he asked me, but this time in Afrikaans.

"Sir, it could have been handled better, and I should have controlled my emotions differently when dealing with the situation, I am sorry for what I did," I nervously replied. I was ready to accept my punishment of x-group for two months, but things took a turn I did not anticipate.

"Would you like to press assault charges against Malcolm?" he asked as he turned to face John. John was nervous, he knew that he would mess up any chance of me having a decent future; as people with a criminal record were never hired, and I would more than likely be expelled and put into a juvenile centre. He took his time thinking about it, and it was the longest 20 seconds of my life.

"No, sir, I don't want too, he is a good guy and means well, but sometimes we make mistakes," he said as he looked into my eyes, wow talk about guilt.

"Very well, two months of x-group for you, Mr Nowak" Mr Van Der Westhuizen said as he dismissed me from the office. I ended up buying John a pack of smokes, a coke and a fudge to say thanks to him for not ruining my life, but I also intended on keeping my promise from that day forward. I can still say that I have never lifted my hands to another person, other than in a situation where I was forced too.

Grade 10 wasn't exactly a difficult year, and I found myself doing crazy things most of the time, things such as spraying my entire body with body spray and then setting myself on fire, whilst head-banging to my favourite metal band. I would burn for about 10 to 15 seconds before rolling around like a pig in mud to avoid 3rd degree burns. The other kids, who were spectating this atrocity, found it severely hilarious and filmed it on their camera phones. During this time, Audrey had finished writing her biography; A Cry of the Heart, which wasn't a great seller, but definitely a good read, however, instead of being a decent mother, from what I saw on the weekends I was home, she was on the phone for hours to a guy called Ger, talking about her book and life in Secunda. Ger was what one could consider a family friend, who the family never met. He lived in Cyprus, and had been good friends with John; my step grandfather, during school and army in the old Rhodesia. He knew Audrey through John and Frankie, and had to look after her as a child when John was on one of his drinking sprees. I had never met the guy at the time, but he sounded like a prick when I picked up the phone in the bedroom to listen in on their calls. Ger use to be Rhodesia's number 1 heavy weight boxer, who then moved to South Africa that in turn moved to Cyprus, after acquiring a fortune. She would only ring Ger when father was at work, and would hide her conversations from us behind a closed kitchen door. I found it a bit suspicious, but I had my own shit to worry about, between running from a dark past and trying to rectify the mistakes I made by working hard at school, playing sport and trying to secure a place for myself in heaven by running a bible/prayer group in the hostel; which attracted over 15 kids who had similar pasts. I was determined to change their lives, get them off the drugs they would run back to whenever they went home, and give them a sense of hope. Audrey would regularly fly to the Greek island of Crete, to catch up with the father she never had over a few coffees. Money was an issue for her, as she quit her job at the local pharmacy, had no extraordinary savings, and had no other form of income. Sylvain was understanding to her situation and paid for her flights, hotels; whenever she needed it, and gave her some spending money while he stayed at home and manned the fort. Audrey flew out one day, as was discussed with my father, to the airport in Heraklion, Crete, and returned when I was at school. Friday arrived and my mother drove down to Standerton, to pick me up for the weekend as planned, and when I got home there was a heavy atmosphere, something didn't feel right, Jerome acted a bit strange, and since we bonded more in the past year, it was easier to tell when something was up. I left it as just a bad feeling and went on with my studies on the dining room table, like I did every weekend. 15:30 arrived, and like an unbroken tradition, dad's car parked outside, he came in, and got a beer, but this time there was an unusual expression on his face. We had grown accustomed to his grumpy face and slowly developing 'get of my lawn' personality, but there was something more sinister going on; I think after my years of pain, hate, anger and depression, I could see through people well enough to know. He opened his beer, took a sip while he stared out the kitchen window, and proceeded to call us children to the lounge. This was bad; we never had family meetings or anything that remotely seemed like equality-based discussion/s. Jerome, Gabriel and I sat on the two seater couch, against the window; Lala in the middle of course, Father sat on the three-seater couch by himself, in front of a TV that had been switched off for this chat, and Audrey sat with her legs folded on the single seater beside the computer, close to the front door.

"So, we have something very important to talk about, and we want you guys to be very mature about this, and to understand that you have to put yourselves in our shoes from time to time," Sylvain began, here was I thinking that someone had died, or contracted something serious, but I wasn't going to jump to conclusions too quick. I had already learnt to keep my mouth shut and see the entire picture before making any judgements.

"Your mother, not me, has asked for a divorce, and as much as I don't want this, there is nothing I can do to prevent it from happening," he continued before Audrey hastily jumped in.

"It's not that I want this, but people change over time, and Papa and I have been married for 20 years. We are no longer the same people we once were, and I feel it would be best to go our separate ways."

"How do you feel about this?" Sylvain asked after she finished. Jerome looked at me, but something told me he already knew about it, as he was a favourite, and he and Audrey shared a different kind of bond. I looked at Gabriel, who was six-and-a-

half; as he liked to call it, and saw that he had no idea what the fuck was going on. To him 'Die Wors' was an Afrikaans sausage made from beef, which tasted good with mash. Not to say I was over dramatic about the situation, but I stood up and pointed at my mother and said.

"Fuck you," and then looked at my dad, pointed once again and said, "Fuck you too," before storming off to my room. *My entire life, I was beaten, condemned and criticised for going against the bible, our religion and this code of ethics that was battered into me, and now, after all the teaching me to be a proper man, and all the values we, as a family, built on the foundations of a religion I questioned many times, meant nothing? All of it in vein? Saying that I was furious at the injustice was a huge understatement. Sunday arrived and father took me back to school, where we had a nice long chat, about what would happen to us kids.*

"Well, because you and Jerome are old enough to decide, the court will ask who you want to be with, and because Gabriel is still a baby, the court will rule in favour of the mother as the constitution states," he explained. *I thought long and hard for the next two weeks about whom I would pick, and to be honest neither were good candidates. Audrey would just fail to lead as a parent, and would resort to ringing the cops, and Sylvain on the other hand would take his stresses out on me and my face, so I chose school. Audrey had bribed Jerome to go with her, promising him things such as quad bikes, motorbikes, a huge ass television, a fast computer, making it tough on him, because even though he was smart and had a sense of right and wrong, he was also just a kid who liked material things. What made it extremely tough on him, was the fact that he loved being around Sylvain too. It got to a point where I had to make a decision, and because Sylvain was alone in South Africa, with no family, and everyone planning on leaving him, I chose with my heart, and decided to stay with him. I would rather take a beating over a fake lifestyle with a pretentious mother that has the police on speed dial any day. The house soon after became as segregated as South Africa prior to 1994, with me taking the equivalent to the Soweto deal. Everyone stayed in their rooms, but Audrey didn't want to be beside Sylvain anymore, so she occupied my room just as quick as it took the Nazi party to occupy Northern France. I had nowhere to sleep, so I spent a good six months either in school to avoid the situation or sleeping on the couch with wooden arm rests; which hurt my neck greatly. Audrey had mentioned that she would be moving to Cyprus, meaning that Jerome and Gabriel would be far away from me, something I didn't want. I knew I couldn't change the Gabriel outcome, as that involved challenging the constitution via the social welfare on how unsuitable Audrey was as a parent, but I could change Jerome's mind however.* "Learning Greek, and basically having to start school all over again isn't what you want," *I would often argue, I wanted him to succeed, not repeat his entire life. Audrey found out of my manipulative ways against her, and along with the video of me burning myself on purpose that I had accidentally showed her, she approached a renowned psychiatrist in the capital, Pretoria, who was convinced by Audrey that I had some mental issues. They worked closely together to get me admitted into a well-known mental home, for twenty days, from May 5th to May 25th. Why this specific date? What else was happening in this time? The divorce was going through of course, and Audrey didn't want me near her or Gabriel; according to her, I wasn't her son. This meant that I wouldn't be able communicate with Jerome, putting an end to my persuasive ways, and also so that I wouldn't stand in front of the judge telling the him/her of how bad a mother she* actually was. I learnt after the divorce, after it had become public knowledge, that Audrey had caught a flight to Cyprus, instead of Crete, to see Ger, where she committed adultery on Valentine's Day; something Jerome was aware of since the beginning. She noticed us getting too close, and feared that he would spill the beans on her, leaving room for me to work a perfect revenge and save my father. My parents were married in community of property, which meant 50/50 on everything, which is a fair trade, the only problem was that 99% of the assets on our property, including our property, were purchased by my fathers' blood, sweat and tears, while mother sat in front of a TV, drinking eight cups of tea a day, hiring a maid to clean up and cook dinner. If Jerome had told me, I would have raised it up with Father, who would have told his lawyer, and had she been found guilty of the indecent act, she would walk away with nothing. Due to her quick play of getting rid of me in time, and Jerome's loyalty, she ended up taking something like 3 million Rand in the settlement, leaving everything my dad had worked his entire life for in vein. During my stay in this mental institute, I met many interesting people, especially a girl called Melonie; a model for some guys magazine. She took my mind away from the entire divorce, and in return I saved her life; one late night, I was out for a smoke and noticed her slashing her wrists on the barbed wire on the walls of this 'sanatorium'. I saw that she was losing blood, and took my belt off, and tightened it around her arm as we walked to find help. I wasn't fond of the wrist cutting culture that was sweeping South Africa at the time, as Jerome had attempted it twice before, once with broken shards of a beer bottle, and the second time was whilst Jerome was in the bath with a razor blade. Sylvain and Audrey rushed to help him, as there was more blood in the bath than water. I wasn't always sure on how to approach victims of self-mutilation, but with the fad becoming popular in the hostels, I had gained some experience on dealing with it, and approached it in the same way. It was evident that she had some kind of depression; the scars on her wrists told a story she didn't need to explain. I felt a sense of duty, and befriended her in an attempt to keep her away from that lifestyle. We would mostly sit next to a tree, or near a bush, under the cover of darkness, getting to know one another. She mentioned her feelings towards life and I told her how all hope was gone, and that I would probably never see my brothers again. She felt sorry for me, to a point where she let me play with her boobs behind a building...they were nice. There was great sexual chemistry between us, the only issues was that I was 15 and she was 21. My attraction to her short, curly brown hair and deep blue eyes, slightly pale-white skin and perfect ass became stronger and we eventually exchanged numbers, hoping for more than a few kisses and hidden touches. I left a few days later, with 10 different tests completed and all the sleeping pills and anti-depressants in the world prescribed to me. I honestly needed no professional help, and always refused to share anything, waste of money mom and dad. Audrey picked me up, with Sonja in the front passenger seat; as she felt safer with her. It was an awkward two-and-a-half-hour drive home. I got home and started devising plans to keep Jerome in South Africa, and it took hours; but that's why I wanted to be a lawyer, I always managed to find solutions and ways around tough situations. I went to my father, who had become the biggest Christian in Secunda; he quit swearing, being violent, went to church every Sunday, and went on his knees every morning and every night to pray, sat next to him in the garden and told him that I had figured out a plan to keep Jerome with us. He was interested, of course he was, we were talking about his prized bull here.

"If we get Jerome expelled, we can approach the social worker with the same story you did with me, he would be put in my school, and would be under the government, making it harder for Audrey to get custody of him," I mentioned. Father sat quiet for a while, thinking about it, but said nothing. I felt that this was a great idea, and proceeded to tell Jerome about it, but in such a manipulative manner that he believed that it was the best move for him too, as he disliked being in Evander. He started messing up at school, getting into fights and in with the wrong crowds; becoming a younger me. After several warnings from the school, Jerome was then moved to my school, where I was already established as a potential leader. I knew that he would have tough times in this school, but I was going to have his back now, more than ever, and prove to him and my father that I could be a member of a functioning family, pulling my own weight as a big brother, something I could only ever dream of up until now. Jerome fit right in and hung out with my crew a lot, but also went his own way to establish his own name in the academic sense, and boy did he...the school thought I was special scoring over 80% in most subjects, but Jerome pushed their opinions of me aside as he scored over 90% in everything. The teachers always spoke highly of him whenever I inquired, and I was so proud of who he was becoming, I wanted him to excel in everything he did, to be better than what I was. Audrey bounced back and forth between Antoinette's house and our house. Sylvain was very generous in letting her live there after what she did to him. My mother took her final flight to Cyprus, along with Gabriel, and the day she left, I gave my little brother the biggest hug that I could, because I knew that when we met again, it wouldn't be the same thing. I gave Audrey (I refused to call her Mommy as I usually did), the exact same fake hug she gave me when she dumped me in that school, with only one arm. Jerome was saddened by it, it was obvious, and one could see him questioning his decision to stay with us. Time passed and father felt that he needed to mend the relationships with his sons, especially with me, the child that he had taken for granted all those years. He bought me an Xbox, the Halo Reach themed one, the one I stared at through the window of a gaming store whenever we went shopping, the one that was too expensive for our household. Jerome fell in love with the world of motorsports, especially off-road biking, so Sylvain bought him a 150cc Pit bike. Melonie and I dated for a while, about 3 months. She would normally pick me up on a Friday afternoon from Secunda in her aqua green Opel Corsa, and then take me to her house in Cullinan, a small town near Pretoria. It was a good arrangement, until her mother found out that we were having sex under her roof, and strongly pushed for us to break up. It's not that I was a bad kid, or had bad tendencies, but more because the legal sex age in South Africa was 16, and she didn't want her daughter being done for statutory rape. I really didn't care about those kinds of things; I was more worried about making a mark in people's lives. Distance became an issue for us and we broke up, she took to the clubs to drown her regrets in booze and find another guy, and I took to the Xbox, where my gaming lifestyle began. I was aware of the life that I had lived, and knew that I was working extremely hard to change the outcomes, but I too wanted to be lost in a magical world of make belief, where I would have complete control over a character, and would be able to express my weird side with no repercussions. It was an amazing way to get away from reality. On Sundays, when we were taken back to school, I'd lock my console away, put my huge duffle bag with fresh clothes in the boot, beside Jerome's, and sit in the passenger seat of Dad's Chevy, thinking about how he lived after dropping us *off at school. I always imagined him returning to the empty house he had spent his entire life trying to turn into a home, visualised him sitting in the sound of sweet silence, in front of his computer, passing time on the games that social media applications provided, saw him making himself dinner and going to bed alone, only to wake the same way. I felt really sad for him, but I was too proud to cry or mention that I was proud of him for standing his ground even though Audrey had slandered his name by everyone he knew. Sylvain wasn't one to make friends, and kept to himself and his garden a lot. He never showed interest in other women, and no matter what we said, he understood that he was raising men, and how he spoke about our mother or approached the situation after the divorce would set the tone for how we treated women when we were old enough to do so, which I admired greatly about him. You would never see him put himself before anyone else, he was a great man, and would give you the shirt off his back if you needed it. On weekends when Jerome and I came home, he would book the entire weekend off to spend time with us. He'd normally get us pizzas, bottles of soda for me, and cans of energy drink for Jerome's, let us do our own things in peace, like play games or do wheelies in the road with the bike. Between it all, we would always head down to this old man pub across from the police station, a place which holds one of my fondest memories. Once at the bar, Sylvain would order the same bottle of Castle lager that he always ordered whenever we had gone out, and Jerome and I would get Coke, or Fanta; something fizzy. The bar had two, pristine, red surfaced pool tables. A game of pool cost R5 back then, so my dad would lay out about 15 R5 coins on the side of the table, indicating to other potential players that these many games were already booked. He would always let Jerome and I play the first round against one another, which was tough, because at first, we had no idea what we were doing, and don't even get me started on the understanding of solid and stripes, but we had fun. Sylvain always challenged the winner, and then challenged the loser, which was pretty fair. Sylvain played very intelligently, thinking about where he was leaving the cue ball, Jerome played cautiously, and tried hiding the cue ball behind one of his balls, making it harder for his opponent to have a clear shot, and I, well I was reckless and thought of different strategies but just smacked the ball hard to see what would happen. Even though I should have savoured the moment more, I was competitive and tried adapting to their play style, which ultimately allowed me to beat most people I played against. When the games were done, we would get food, and head back home, where Father retired to his newly built green house, and we would do our own things.*

Chapter 13
Surprise Mon Amour

The ordeal of writing has Elliot depressed and down in the dumps, so he decides to pick himself up and head over to the bar Katrien works in, to surprise her, it's been days without any human contact, and the need for beer is taking over. Elliot heads to the bathroom to freshen up, but he realises that his beard has grown significantly messy and decides to shave before meeting Katrien. A while passes before Elliot looks and feels as fresh as a daisy, dressed neatly in a polo, dark-blue slim fit jeans, and a head of hair waxed in a comb over style. With his appearance attended too, Elliot gets into the driver seat of his SUV and heads to a florist on the outskirts of Aalst. While driving down what seems to be the typical main road of a small town, where everything you need or that's on offer is all collectively placed in the same street, Elliot notices a little store that resembles that of a florist. Elliot pulls over, beside the green framed, big windowed; all plants on little shelves, store on the left-hand side of the road and he gets out of his car in a peaceful manner. He clenches onto the golden door knob, attached to the mossy green painted door of the store, turns it anti-clock wise and pushes forward with a little thrust. The bell on top of the door is triggered and the owner immediately turns around from dead heading a few flowers in the back of the shop.

"Hi, how can I help you today," the little old lady running the store mentions as she walks up to this sharply-dressed man.

"Hi, I'm trying to surprise a girl, and I'm not quite sure what to get her," Elliot replies to the general vendor-customer question.

"Well, what kind of a girl is she? What does she like? Does she have a favourite flower?" the lady asks, trying to narrow down an exact flower from the 100 plus different plants on show. Elliot is aware that he should know these kinds of things, especially before jumping in the sack with someone, but the way modern society chose to overlook this kind of gesture over the past few decades has really impacted most men out there, so much, that a mediocre dinner and wine would get you where you wanted to be. Is it women that lowered their standards and gave in at the first hint of something? Or is it men that found a way around the pleasantries? Elliot believes it's got a lot to do with women trying to be men, not that there was ever an issue with gender equality and same pay for the same job, but more so when women decided to do everything men do, to point where most women lost their identities completely. On the contraire Elliot also believes that men have gotten soft, sensitive and irrational with the lack of war and increase of political correctness, which saw many women having to rise up to the occasion and pamper their husbands. The world changed a great deal since Elliot was a child, but c'est la vie.

"Well, she is sweet, kind, beautiful, smart, and going through a rough patch at the moment," Elliot replies to the lady, who has her hands on her hip, being attentive to her customers' needs. Judgementally she stares at Elliot, it's clear to her that he doesn't know a thing about her, and how society changed chivalry bothers her too, but she remains quiet, bills need to be paid and all she can do is make a sale.

"Well, roses are always a winner, especially if you are serious about her," the lady mentions as she starts walking over to the rose section.

It's clear to Elliot that she is trying to make a sale, as roses seem to be more expensive than anything else in store, but Elliot doesn't seem to mind too much, *'Old lady still got game,'* he thinks to himself. A few awkward questions later and Elliot walks out with a bouquet of roses, priced at €55. Elliot puts the flowers in the back seat and confidently drives down to the bar where Katrien's shift is about to start. Katrien is well settled into her shift by the time Elliot arrives, and it appears to be one of those 'high roller' weekends, where the pay enters and exits a person's bank account the same day. Elliot walks in the bar, towards Katrien, who is standing with her back facing the busy front of house. Some people pause from their beer and sports, to witness a true gentleman approach a woman with a bunch of flowers in his hands. They stare, as if it was something they had only heard of in children's books. Katrien appears to be sweeping something, but Elliot only notices the ceramic shards lying all over the place once he reaches the wooden bar. He thinks about greeting her, but he stops himself, long enough to watch her posterior jiggle as she thrusts the broom back and forward. *'I'd tap that,'* he thinks to himself before lifting his eyes from sin.

"Guess who?" he warmly asks, like a soldier surprising his wife after a tour in a foreign country. The flowers are hidden, pressed up against the bar, concealed from her view.

"Hi!" she somewhat yells out as she turns around to see who's trying to surprise her.

"What are you doing here?" she asks the sharply-dressed man in front of her.

"I just came to check up on you. I started forgetting what beautiful looked like, so I had to refresh my memory," Elliot tells her in a cheesy manner; as if he practiced that line the entire drive down. Her blushing face and shy smile indicate the lines effectiveness.

"Thank you, Elliot," she mentions as the conversation starts opening to awkward silences. Elliot is ahead of it however, and lifts the flowers up, handing them to her in the process.

"These are for you," he says, as his arm stretches out.

"Aww, thank you so much," she replies to the gesture, "How did you know that red roses were my favourite?" she questions the man in front of her. As happy a coincidence as it may seem, Elliot decides to ride the wave, and says.

"I wasn't too sure what your favourite was, but I assumed that a wonderful woman like you deserves nothing short of wonderful." The atmosphere is almost enough to make an emo sick to his stomach. Katrien's manager leans his head in from the kitchen, and notices the flowers in her hands and the warm smile on her face. He wants to give out, but as his face lifts to vocalize the thoughts in his mind, he stops himself; he knows that she deserves some form of love.

"I'll get these into a vase," Katrien states, "Here's the menu if you want to grab something different this time," she continues as she hands Elliot their menu and walks off to the kitchen. Elliot browses through the list, a very fussy eater, even when he was a child. During the search for an adequate meal, Elliot notices the dishwasher walk by him, wearing a dark blue shirt; riddled with water stains, typical pizza chef pants and those horrible rubber shoes they are forced to wear. She's in her 40s, maybe 50s, dripping soap and water all over the place, smiling ferociously at Elliot. Obviously Katrien mentioned that the guy at the bar got her the flowers, what colleagues wouldn't ask? The lady paces herself back, and Katrien returns shortly after.

"So…Mr Elliot, what can I get you to drink?" Katrien playfully asks the man she is slowly falling in love with.

"Uhm…can I get a glass of house wine please…Miss Bartender?" he replies, playing along with her flirtatious initiative.

"Certainly, sir, coming right up," she tells him as she turns to grab a wine glass hanging from the ceiling by its foot. While she gets to work on pouring the wine, Elliot turns around, to face the rest of the restaurant. A few people look back at him, but the others are concerned with their meals and drinks. Elliot notices an old couple in the corner, looking back at him, somewhat judging his previous actions. The elderly lady is smiling ever so joyfully, as she witnessed something beautiful, but the expression on the gentleman's face screams 'Run kid'. Elliot jokingly plays with it in his mind for a few seconds before Katrien places the glass down on the oak top.

"Elliot, I have to work, so forgive me if I'm not very responsive," she states, letting him know that he may need to keep himself occupied on such a busy evening. *'Not a problem,'* Elliot thinks to himself, there's some hockey game on the television, there's other lonely males seated down at the bar that he can chat with, but what he really wants to do is write. Elliot hates procrastinating, especially after that one lesson a Buddhist monk shared; "The problem with people, is that they think they have time." Those words are extremely difficult to shake from your mind after hearing them.

"Hey, Katrien," Elliot loudly says, trying to get her attention before she heads off to other patrons, "Can I lend a notepad, or even some paper?" he politely asks. It seems desperate that he'll sit there while she works, and entertain himself, but we all face such situations in life, and Elliot really doesn't mind what people think anymore. Katrien passes him some old, ragged, A4-sized notepad that had been laying in a drawer for some time. Elliot starts going through the first few pages of the notepad while he tries remembering where he left off. "Ah, pool!" Elliot tells himself as he starts writing again.

"At school, Jerome befriended the new guy, Koos. Koos was a shy introvert, who had a persistent pissed-off facial expression and terrible table manners. I was wary of him, because I knew how…"

Elliot pauses, takes a sip of his wine, and calls Katrien over.

"Do you spell snakey, S-N-A-K-E-Y or S-N-A-K-Y?" She thinks to herself for a second, and replies.

"The one with the 'E'." Elliot puts his head down again and continues writing.

"Snakey people could be, and I didn't want Jerome to feel betrayed or hurt ever again in his life. There were some dodgy people in this school, people you just knew would rat you out for a chocolate bar, especially that 'wannabe' cool, first team cricket player Desmond; fucking idiot he was, but he was in Jerome's class, so communication was inevitable. One had to commend him on his cricket skills, he was a darn good batsman, and reached nationals at a young age, but his drinking problem, constant drug use and how he treated the people around him, especially women, made him the scumbag we all perceived him to be. Fortunately, Koos never smoked, didn't drink, and thought drugs were just as stupid as the people who used them, and so I eased up on him. Ryan got too big for hostel 4, and was sent to Hostel 3, along with Andrew, who had been in trouble a few times for stupid things, like fighting. With the main leader relocated and my biggest competitor gone, it was only a matter of time till I was asked to stand in front of hostel 4's parade ground, as a leader. I didn't have to wait too long, Mr Scheffer asked me to be a leader just before the weekend started. I said yes, obviously."

The night progresses well and the bar starts clearing out, it seems like the patrons are eager to head home, some even mentioning the name of a local night club on their way out. Katrien anticipates less work as the minutes go by, and heads over to where Elliot is seated; he stopped writing a while ago and switched his attention to the hockey game on TV.

"Elliot," she calls out as she walks towards him, "I meant to ask you," she continues, "When I stayed over, I noticed a photo of a girl stuck to the inside of your cupboard. Who is she?" she finally gets out, using her calm voice and word selection very cautiously; she doesn't want to come off as jealous or possessive.

"Ah," Elliot utters; clearly saddened by the memories now playing in his mind, allowing some few seconds to pass before continuing, "I moved to Ireland when I was 21, I fell in love with this girl, she was cool and all I ever wanted at the time. We dated for a while, but eventually realised that no matter how great the chemistry, we just weren't compatible and treated each other very badly, so we broke up. I kept the picture because I cared greatly for her, she was and I assume still is an amazing person," Elliot lays out as he reaches for his wine; eager to sip it, trying to hide much more. Katrien looks at Elliot; deep inside she has a respect for him, because he still speaks highly of an ex. It shows maturity and understanding, something a lot of women supposedly look for in a man.

"When last did you see her?" Katrien asks, hiding her real investigative intentions behind the common curiosity.

"I haven't seen her in years to be honest, the last time I saw her was the day I left Ireland for the Netherlands," Elliot honestly tells her.

"Do you still love her?" Katrien asks, finally, getting to the point.

Elliot doesn't like the question, but doesn't want to leave it on an awkward note, so he decides to answer, "I do, I always have and always will, but not in the intimate way you love someone you sleep with or have been with for a while. It's more that I appreciate the time that I had with her, and the lessons learnt. I don't know if it makes sense, but I am grateful that she crossed my path, as without her, who knows where I would have ended up. She played a role in changing me into the man I am today, so I have to cherish the memory, who knows where I would have been without her." Katrien is flabbergasted at the answer, it's not something out of the ordinary, just she's never heard of something like that from the small towns she's lived in, perhaps it has a lot to do with her little exposure to decent men, perhaps she was too busy looking after her father and her own life to pay attention to things like that happening in other people's lives, regardless of the past, she is still amazed, and it warms her even more that a man can feel like that.

"Would you ever take her back? I mean, if she was here and you had the chance?" Katrien asks, trying to find out whether she has competition. "What kind of question is that?" Elliot retaliates, hoping to not answer her; deep down he doesn't even know the answer.

"Do you want another glass of wine, Mr Elliot?" she politely asks, trying to change the subject, understanding that he is not keen on this line of questioning.

"Only if you'll have one with me," he smartly replies. The bar has two customers left, and both appear to be too drunk to comprehend anything around them, so the offer starts weighing in her mind. Out of the blue, the manager walks up to Katrien, places the keys in her hands, and mentions that he has to leave for the night, so lock up is her responsibility. The manager heads out the door, and leaves it up to Katrien and the dish washer to man the fort. The chat continues for about another 30 minutes, before the dishwasher heads out the door too, trying to get away from this forsaken job, and to be with her family.

The bar is empty, with the exception of these two love birds. Katrien's apron is off; they're seated at a random table near the middle of the bar, both sipping on a newly opened bottle of red wine. The chit chat simmers down, and Elliot looks deep into Katrien's eyes.

"What? Why are you looking at me like that?" she shyly asks, curious at his actions. Elliot lets out a little smile, his eyes narrow, fixated on her.

"You're beautiful," he proudly let's out in a scratchy, flamed-up voice. Katrien finds it amusing, arguing back between small breaks of laughter.

"I have no makeup on, I've just finished work, my hair is a mess," but before she can go on listing everything she feels imperfect for, Elliot somewhat squats up awards, leans in and kisses her. Katrien almost drowns in her words; the passionate smooch silences the excuses. The kiss is brief, but meaningful, both of them feel the lust take over, and understand that it can lead to something else, but it's pointless, especially with the cameras in the bar.

"Would you like to dance?" Elliot confidently asks the shy woman in front of him.

"I can't exactly dance well," she tries to argue, but Elliot learnt a long time ago to never take no for an answer.

"Who's going to judge you? Besides I can't dance either," he admits to her. The bar's laptop is still silently blaring some local music, but Elliot quickly finds himself in front of the device, switching to something a bit more intimate. Patsy Cline's Crazy comes on; Elliot likes the oldies, 'they really knew how to describe a feeling back then' would be his answer whenever someone questioned his music choice, but Katrien doesn't ask a thing. Elliot looks up from the laptop's screen and starts swaying towards her in sync with the beat, hands out in front of him, shoulders bobbing back and forth. Katrien lets out a little giggle at the site.

"*Crazy... I'm crazy for feeling...so lonely,*" Elliot sings along in his scratchy, tone-deaf voice, but it makes her giggle even more. Elliot's 'smooth' approach slows down as he gets to her; he raises his right hand, leaving it about 30 cm in front of her. Katrien gently reaches out and grabs onto his hand, her smile shining brighter than any other time before. Elliot takes a few steps back, to get them away from the tables; the bar is packed with empty seats, but there is just enough space in the centre for the pirouette. Once in place, Elliot places his right hand on Katrien's lower back, gently bringing her closer to him, the left hand is risen half way, awaiting Katrien's hand as confirmation to start the dance. Katrien grabs on to his shoulder with her left hand and places her right tightly into his open palm. The dance commences, there are no words shared between the two, only slow paces to the left and right. A few moments pass before Katrien gets comfortable with the situation; once the pace has settled and the awkward tension flees, her head lowers, finding a resting spot on Elliot's right shoulder. Elliot isn't a dancer, never was, but he is trying his best not to step on her feet, something his mother tried teaching him when he was six years old. Before the song fades to the sound of crackling, as most oldies do, Elliot kisses Katrien's neck. The goose bumps conquering her skin depicts how surreal it feels to her. She lifts her head from his shoulder and with big eyes stares at his lips. She creeps closer to his freshly shaved face and promiscuous lips, and kisses him. Her soft lips land on his, but he doesn't kiss back, a little tease to their playful relationship. Her stomach fills with butterflies, similar to a woman's first love, but this feels more real to her, something she can grasp on to and trust. The kiss turns into a short session of passionate kissing that only the French would be proud of. Mid-smooch, Elliot opens his eyes, trying to observe where the cameras are and in which direction they're pointed. As his eyes scan through the building, he notices her eyes are still shut, embracing the moment, savouring the feeling and taste. Like a 14-year old, he feels guilty for opening his eyes, but he quickly realises that the world isn't perfect, and that a man with an answer to the sexual question she's dying to ask is more attractive than a man who wants to take unsecure risks. It seems like there are only two cameras in the bar; one facing the bar itself; obviously protecting the cash register, and the second above the bar facing the entrance, catching a small bit of the sides. Elliot thinks to himself, *It's an older model camera; it wouldn't have a wide capture, so the left-hand side of the bar should be a safe zone.* Elliot is just guessing it would be much easier if they had access to the manager's office, but sadly he locks it whenever he isn't in, poor management or untrustworthy staff?

"Do you trust me, Katrien?" Elliot asks as he pulls away from the tongue lock.

"Yes," Katrien answers. A short, silent pause passes before she continues questioning him, "Why? What are you thinking about?" Elliot doesn't say a thing, and starts dancing once again, taking lead, as the man should, and leading her towards the desired spot. Katrien might not have several degrees and be a successful investor/business woman, but she isn't stupid and realises where it's heading. "Elliot, they'll catch us on the cameras," she firmly exclaims. Her authoritative voice doesn't seem too convincing for Elliot, there are hints of interest and curiosity in her stance. He doesn't want to spoil the mood with words, so he hushes her and presses on in the form of ballroom entertainment. They get to the booth Elliot has in mind, on the far left, against the white wall with paintings of trees, in the middle of four other booths. The four chairs are on the width of the table, two each side, leaving the breadth open for Katrien's Dutch bosom. Elliot lifts her up by the waist with his strong arms, places her on the table, and leans in to continue the kissing. Katrien knows where it's heading, and she opens her legs to allow him in, despite their clothing. His hands are plastered to her cheeks, he refuses to let go of this moment, the passion, the memory, the taste. Katrien notices that Elliot is taking his time in getting this started, the thought of *'perhaps he wants me to lead it this time'* crosses her mind, so her hormones force her to initiate it. She unbuckles his belt, unzips his zipper and takes his shirt off before he eventually jumps in to undress her. Her T-shirt is lifted from her warm body; her black jeans are unzipped and dropped all the way down to her ankles. Elliot finds her un-matching undies rather cute, he can't judge as she didn't intend on this. Elliot slides the bra strap on her right shoulder off, pausing before going to the second strap, allowing the anticipation to simmer down and the craving to rise. She grows impatient with his lack of motive and slides it down herself, but sadly the bra sticks to her firm breasts, ultimately leaving the decision in Elliot's hands, literally. Katrien rushes a bit and pulls Elliot's penis out of the underwear it receded in. She strokes it firmly, trying to persuade him into doing the same for her. Elliot catches the hints and pulls the bra off with his left hand, allowing his right to creep up her inside thigh. She starts trembling at the tickle his fingers cause as they caress her thin skin. Elliot's hand goes off course, and heads straight for her lacy white undies. He rubs gently, applying pressure, moving in a clock wise motion until that infamous wet feeling can be felt. Katrien's arm gets a bit weak after long strokes, so she decides to lie back, leaving the rest in Elliot's hands, literally. Elliot doesn't quite understand that her arm went numb, he takes it more of a hint that she wants to be pleased, orally. He leans in, unhooks the pants from her ankles, pulls the now, wet undies to the side, only to see the moist patch intended for him. He leans in and wildly does what every man should, further turning her on. Not even seven minutes of pleasuring pass before she asks him to put it in. Elliot, all of a sudden, a people pleaser, does as he's told, and gently rubs the head against her extremely moist pasture. Somehow, the wine has made the skin on skin feeling more of a memorable feel compared to when one is sober. Katrien bites her bottom lip and seductively looks into his eyes in anticipation of the dirty deed. The entry is gentle, as all gentlemen aim for, and Elliot leans in to kiss her as his back and forth movements begin. 45 minutes of passionate love making passes before both parties finish. Katrien seems worried about the camera footage, but Elliot reassures her that there is nothing to worry about, he is certain that nothing was caught on film.

After getting dressed, Katrien pours another glass of wine for herself and Elliot, trying to end the evening on a relaxed note. Elliot leaves the bar for a second while Katrien fills their glasses, headed for his vehicle, to get cigarettes from his glove box. Elliot lights the stereotypical post sex smoke, and proceeds to puff away on the bricked paving outside the establishment. Katrien opens the door, hoping to chat with Elliot while he has his smoke, but Elliot turns his back to her, hesitantly killing the smoke in the process; he tries to follow that typical 1940s mafia gentleman code, where men never smoked, nor committed acts of violence or aggression in front of female company.

The two head back inside, and chat for another half-an-hour before Katrien mentions that she's tired, suggesting that they go home.

"Do you want to come back to my place?" Elliot rhetorically asks…the deed is done and there's no need, but he wants something to hold onto tonight.

"I'm a bit tired tonight, Elliot, and have another long shift tomorrow," Katrien replies, hoping that he understands.

"Not a problem at all, I understand," Elliot says, "I didn't want you to think I'm just here for sex," he continues.

"No, I know you're not here for sex, don't think that of me either please," Katrien retaliates. The two come to the agreement that sex is not the underlying incentive between them, and continue finishing their glasses of wine. They both take the last sip from the red-stained glasses, and decide to call it a night.

"Please, don't drive home," Katrien commands Elliot; he has had a few and she doesn't want to see him go to jail or worse, end up in a collision with someone or something. Elliot knows that a taxi will be costly, possibly over €200, but he respects her wish, especially with it being something close to her and books one. Katrien turns off the lights, sets the alarms and locks the front door. The two stand on the paving…leaned against the wall of the bar, laughing and chatting as they await the arrival of the taxi. Passers-by give them something to talk about, especially a group of young lads singing and chanting some Dutch patriotic phrases or lyrics, allowing them to reminisce about when they were younger. The taxi arrives a few minutes later, and Elliot opens the door, ready to leave, but they both feel the need to engage in one final embrace, so Elliot walks back to Katrien, and leans in for a goodnight kiss. Surprisingly, Katrien leans in and kisses him first. In the distance, about 50 meters in front of the taxi, lurking in a dark alley, wearing a dark grey hoodie, is Henrick. He was on his way to try and patch things up with Katrien, but stopped as soon as he saw the two chatting. Elliot jumps into the taxi and proceeds to go home, passing Henrick by, who is trying ever so hard to see the face of the man that took his woman. Elliot is very aware of his surroundings, but misses Henrick, taking him for a drug dealer waiting to sell some stuff to kids on their night out.

Elliot arrives home, and heads straight to his empty bed, eager to wake up and continue his writings the next day.

Chapter 14
Turned Around

Morning arrives like a package from a speedy courier service, and Elliot heads straight for the notepad in the underwear he slept in. The table is riddled with paper at this point, there are the original sheets he started with, smaller sheets he had scribbled on, the dirty pages from the notepad Katrien handed him earlier, and even a serviette with a few words jotted on. Elliot brushes the unneeded papers aside and continues…

On another note, away from hostel life, I was the school's reigning chess champion for two consecutive years, but I knew it would be a tough position to hold with Jerome here now; he was better than me, by far. Luckily, we worked on a point system, and it was too late for him to accumulate enough points to outdo me this year, he did however give me a tough game when the kids asked us for the 100th time to face off. Reputation as the school's best aside, it was an event I really enjoyed, and the atmosphere of 15 or so kids standing around us in total silence, 'oohing' and 'ahhing' after moves were made, added a sense of pride to the memory. The school also started noticing the influx of African students being admitted, and that this was slowly becoming a very diverse school, which at the time was unavoidable. The principal, a very fair, modest and smart man, had to cater to the needs of everyone, and this meant that rugby could no longer be our only prioritised sport, and therefore a soccer team was established. I was excited about the change, because out of all the white kids, I stood the best chance at making the team, but that year was spent practicing and structuring a possible team, rather than looking for opponents.

The annual prize giving evening was upon us once again; I swear it was my favourite event of the year, and at 18:00 my father parked his 1.6 litre Chevy in a designated parking spot, and walked up to the school, wearing his regular plaid shirt mother always told him looked like a table cloth, along with his light blue jeans. He didn't wear suits or dress shirts like the other fathers. He made his way towards the main hall, trying to get a good place to sit before the other parents went in; somewhere near the back, where he could go for a smoke, but also somewhere he could see the entire stage. As he was walking in, the principal of the school shook his hand, and mentioned how proud he was to have Jerome and me in his school, they stood there for a while, talking about the future of his sons, that he anticipated would be very bright.

"Come men, line up for parade," Ryan loudly called out, getting the attention of the students. We stood in a parade formation, a bit more unique compared to how we stood at the hostels, which then progressed into our ceremonial military styled

drill, followed by a chant of the school's creed, and then finally being allowed to walk into the hall in single file. "Heads down," Ryan continued as the parents became silent to see what separated us from other schools. With our feet spaced exactly a metre apart and our hands behind our backs, we awaited the call of our newly elected head boy. "Parade!" Ryan shouted, and our heads lifted, chin up to show the confidence we had built. "Attention!" he continued, as our hands transitioned from behind our backs to our sides, and our feet slid in, from the 1m gap to right beside one another. "Right turn 1," he proceeded, we turned right, in a synchronised fashion, "2,3,1," he shouted the infamous number mix that we would never change, signalling us to stomp our feet, and not as several different people at different times creating a machine gun effect, but as one unit, making one single loud stomping sound. Shivers raced up my spine, and I felt the goose bumps under my white formal shirt and black blazer, as they always did whenever we did this. It was ours, no one else did this, and we were so proud of it.

"Hoist the flag," Ryan mentioned, signalling the leader at the flag pole to raise the South African flag. We stood in silence as the leader elevated the colourful fabric, the only sound that could be heard was the squeaky sound the pulley had made when the rope was tugged on. Once completed, the leader turned back to face us, showing that the job had been done, and that we could commence with the next phase. Ryan commanded his second last command, "Begin," this is where we chanted the school creed, a creed drilled into us by the leaders, something aimed at giving us meaning, and awareness of what we stood for. My father never understood the creed, as it was chanted in Afrikaans, but I translated it the best I could for him:

*'I want to make a success of my life and to be a winner
Therefore, I will use every opportunity to develop my talents.
I will strive towards honesty, dependability and duty
I promise to be loyal towards my school
In honour of my Creator.'*

The collection of broken voices, firmly chanting these binding words was inspirational. Whether you were mad, sad, happy, broke, a virgin or hated life and all it stood for, this creed meant something to you, and you proudly roared each word.

"Walk in," Ryan said; his last line, telling us to walk into the hall in an organised fashion.

The award ceremony commenced, and as tradition, Jerome and I cleared the stage of trophies and certificates, awards we deserved for an entire years' worth of hard work. Jerome was still new to the school, but he got way more than what I did when I had started. Whenever I was on the stage, receiving an abnormal amount of certificates, I'd see my father sitting in the back, with his black polyester jacket on the empty chair beside him, smiling back at me with pride. In a weird way, when you looked at what the children of the parents in suits were capable of compared to our under dressed father's children, it kind of kept people humble. I once again received my award for chess champion, third year in a row, but I knew that the next year Jerome would take it from me, so I savoured the last time holding it.

We went home after the ceremony had ended, but this time Koos came with us, as he was an orphan, with nowhere to go, and he'd be subjected to staying at school, but because he started growing on us, we begged our father. We would play Xbox and drink fizzy drinks all day long, or we'd be outside taking turns on Jerome's bike; I must say I could not ride at first, despite my cocky attitude beforehand. After a few falls I found my feet, well the handle bars anyways, and Jerome trusted me more on it.

2010 finished and once again New Year was upon us, but this time we didn't care anymore, we had each other and we were humble, we didn't need the fancy BBQ, drinks, music or spinning of motorcycles like Jake across the road. Sarah left her quad bike loser and started dating a tall, blond guy, who I didn't think was attractive at all, but hey he had his own car, enough to get any woman in the small-minded town of Secunda. They stood in front of the green gate we had used as our leaning post during our hour-long conversations, and kissed so heavily, leaving traces of saliva everywhere. It was a sad thing to see, and I knew Sarah was aware of my presence, but at the time I didn't believe that humans could be inconsiderate. I took it as best as my emotions let me, but if I had learnt anything during my time in Vaalrivier, it was how to identify my emotions, and approach my feelings, and most situations in a logical, rational fashion. I was surprised that almost three years had passed and I still couldn't get over what I had felt for her. Jerome was in a relationship with a girl called Bethany she was a strange girl, very quiet, shy, with these seductive almost evil eyes, and somewhat emo behaviour. I didn't quite understand why he chose her, but she made him happy, and that was all that mattered. She was out celebrating new years with her own family, but Jerome was constantly on his phone, texting her throughout the night. Jerome became a bit of a loner during this time, and I may have played a big role in his 'Emo kid' phase, as I listened to metal more now than ever before, and I somewhat influenced him into listening to it with me. He took his bed, along with most of his belongings, and single-handedly moved into the attached room behind the garage; this was the room we often gave to hired help, and it was strange that Jerome would choose such a small, sometimes cold space as his living quarters. We understood that we were getting older and needed some privacy, but Jerome took it to an extreme. Jerome and I became closer as time went on, the hostel life was mostly to thank for it, but it was also due to the time we spent at home, because I had taken Audrey's old hi-fi system and placed it on the dresser in my room, where we religiously listened to the Bullet for my valentine CD Melonie had purchased for me the previous year. Whenever father was at work, and we got a lift from one of the kids that lived in Secunda's parents, we would stand in front of the loud speakers, screaming the lyrics and head-banging together. To me it was a great bonding experience, to the neighbours that could hear us it was a collection of concerns. I cannot, in words, describe the amount of stress I put on fixing the relations between my remaining family and me, but I can express that I understood greatly my father's words.

"You have to work hard for what you want in life."

Sadly, after a longish, somewhat enjoyable holiday, we returned to school; most students hated going back, but I on the other hand loved it. We once again left Sylvain behind, for a new year, with new challenges. Mr Scheffer; our hostel father, was on duty that evening, and came down to the hostel to give kids their medication. He welcomed us back, and took me into the medicine room, where he mentioned how crucial this year would be for me in my pursuit of a greater leadership role, the voting would commence in either September or October, and that if I was serious about it, that it would be better to make an impression earlier on in the year. I understood that many leaders in our school faked their friendships and smiles to get to where they wanted to be; I came to realise it works this way outside of school too, but I didn't want to be that guy, I lead by example and wanted to earn it, and if I didn't reach my goal of being head boy, I was still going to be the same person I always was; life is too short to be someone else. Besides I knew that my actions and reputation would precede itself; kids even witnessed me save another boys life when he was almost hit by a car going 80 km/h. Despite my feats in this school, I was still going to work hard for what I wanted, it's who I became, something that never left me. It was especially hard saying goodbye to Ryan the previous year, he did well in school and found a job with his brother; who left a year prior to him, in some engineering line, not really sure what they did exactly, but it paid the bills. Ryan was someone I looked up to dearly, I mean I ended up walking the way he walked; in this slow, somewhat wild lion that demanded respect and feared nothing fashion, spoke the way he spoke, played sports the way he played sports, and remained humble after every achievement, something he taught me early on; quoting that many men have succeeded before me and many more will succeed after I am gone. We tried to stay in contact, but he was always busy, and I was trying to leave behind a legacy at this school, so I didn't mope about it for too long.

  Athletics season started, and as always I'd be picked for my mid to long distant running abilities, I was also picked for my shot-put talents, Jerome on the other hand was quicker than me when it came to running and was picked for short to mid-range races, which I assumed would happen before we even went for the try-outs. Jerome wasn't a sporty kind of person, but you didn't really have a choice in this school, you had to do sports, unless you had a physical deficiency that prevented you from participating. Jerome and Koos were very close at this point, I mean I was close to him too but they shared a better relationship, because instead of spending time with him, or anyone else for that matter, I would be studying, sorting out childish fights in the hostel or working on making history. Jerome won a few medals from the races, like he did in primary school, but this time no one would strip him of his winnings, because I was confident in myself and I would beat a person within an inch of his life to protect my little brother. Whilst we were at school, Sylvain met a lady, whom he knew from his earlier years in South Africa; before Audrey, and starting dating her it seemed. It was good to have someone there in the house with him, because at the rate things were going, I would finish school, go to university to follow my dream of becoming a lawyer, and move out, and Jerome would still be in school, and once he was done, he too would seek out tertiary education to become an architect as he had planned; he was creative and meticulous when it came to things. Father would print off the basic outline of a shoe or shirt, and we would design a ton of things with various themes, from nature and sport, to industry and bettering famous brands. We would often ask our parents who was better, and eight out ten times he would win as he could draw really well, and had a better sense of creativity. One weekend Sylvain introduced us to Marylin; his new bird, and at first, we were happy for him, it wasn't fair that Audrey was getting it elsewhere and father had become the regular church going hermit, but I honestly thought he could do much better. Yeah, he'd been out of the game for 22 years, being faithful to Audrey, but Marylin wasn't attractive at all, had a very dull personality, and had some drinking problem that we could never prove, no matter how hard we tried. I know my father meant his words of only ever loving my mother, but I know that primitive human necessities and the hormones behind them became too strong and he settled for this, one could see that he didn't love her, and she was there for the company.

It was disturbingly awkward when father worked night shifts on the weekends we were home, because we would be stuck in a house with this lady we didn't really know. She would quietly sit at the dinner table and play online poker with her laptop while we did our own things. I was too focused on the rugby season around the corner, as well as the creation of the school's first ever soccer team shortly after that to worry about her or her relationship with my father. The divorce and new partners affected us greatly, Jerome and I handled things very differently here, I loved my family, greatly, I still cared a lot for my mother, but I was mad at her for what she'd done. I hated the fact that no matter what, it would never go back to how it was, but I didn't care about who dated who and who felt sad over what, internally we could have differences, but if someone from the outside came in and hurt my family, then I would intervene, this is where I watched Ger and Marlyin like a hawk. Jerome, I feel silently sat there, hating the divorce, I know he stood with Audrey in the beginning, being a little spy for her before switching to Sylvain's side and sticking with us. He was torn between both parents. Audrey was still messaging him over social media, asking him how he was, how school was treating him, that she missed him and so on, but she never spoke to me, which upset me greatly, what really got to me was the fact that she never wanted to be associated with me on a normal day, but whenever I did something great, that defied the odds stacked against me, she would claim parenthood, and want to be involved in my life, saying things like, "My big boy," but where the fuck was she when I was going through the struggle to get there? Jerome would never express his feelings, you would see happy or sad, but he wouldn't elaborate on it, unless you had about three hours for a deep heart to heart where he still withheld information from you.

Rugby season came, and I was delighted, because I had found my feet in the sport, and I was confident in running into groups of four people with all my speed and power, not to blow my own trumpet, but it was hard to take me down, I played with all the hate I had in me. Jerome replaced me in the backline and took the number 15 jersey, and I was moved and took the number 7 jersey. Jeffrey was our captain and 8th man that year; and he was a big lad anyways. We played the regular league and did fairly well, we lost to our toughest rivals W. H. De Klerk, but beat the Jim Van Tonder school; the school Doug had been in years earlier. My favourite game was always against the Platorand School, they were a school of big guys with cocky attitudes. Big people moved slow, couldn't run quick, and they were only big on the outside, deep down they would shit themselves when one of us came charging. As a forward, I stuck to my job of cleaning rucks, scrumming and putting tons of pressure on the scrum half, but I always kept an eye on Jerome; full back was a scary position to play. As a number 15, you understood that you were the teams last line of defence; enormous pressure, you needed to be able to catch, kick, run and play well under the pressure of six or seven guys running towards you, and I always kept myself in a position where I could fall back to save him, and several times I had too as he would hesitate a lot. I could never play full back again after that, in my mind, that's where my brother belonged. As the rugby season progressed I was asked to act as a substitute for the 1st team, just in case someone got hurt, I could play nearly any position on the field, except frontline positions like Hooker or Props, sadly the first team never needed me, and I sat on the side lines cheering them on. Rugby season ended and finally, the moment we were all waiting for, soccer season. The kids in the mechanical engineering classes built the soccer posts for us, the janitors placed them on the huge open space between hostel 1 and the main road, and three youth workers were appointed as our coaches. With all the small things ready, we set out, training most days, doing fitness, practicing ball control, team building exercises and once we were ready, we had some friendly games between ourselves. The Afrikaans kids sucked at playing soccer, one or two exceptions but generally the African kids ran circles around them, it was a bit harder with me and Jerome, who had been taught soccer in the streets by other African kids, so we knew what to expect, what moves to look for and how to play against them. We formed a team, which I really wasn't happy with; we could have put a few less-fat people in and used a few more athletically capable people instead. We received our fixtures, and set out to get a captain, I honestly didn't want to captain the soccer team, like I had the ability to motivate a team into winning, but I knew no amount of words could change the huge losses I had forecasted for this team. We did a quick vote on the side of the pitch at our first game against Jim Van Tonder school, between Wallace and myself, it came down to a 50/50 vote where Wallace said I should be captain and I said he should be, the youth worker/coach looked at us, and I stated to just put Wallace in charge, as I already had leadership opportunities, it was only fair that he was given some too. During this time, I had started texting a girl called Danielle, she was friends with some of my friends in my previous school, she was really cute and shy. I met her through Facebook, and we started chatting, it was all fun and cute, but it was hard to see her as I was always 60 kilometres south. She wished me good luck for our first game, and we went forward with the fixture. We had a boy three times my size in goals, and a very inexperienced team in front of him; our substitutes couldn't even save us. After the first 10 minutes of Wallace and I trying our best to out pressure attackers, 1–0 for Jimmies, then 2–0, and 3–0, 4, 5, 6, 7, 8. It started turning into a slaughter. Wallace was good at soccer but no matter what him, I or Jerome brought to the pitch, nothing could change the outcome, we tried hard, but they identified us as okay-ish players, and started avoiding playing on our lines. It got so frustrating that Wallace had purposely scored an own goal just to prove to the coach how awake our goal keeper was. The final whistle sounded, and we shook hands with our opponents who were still laughing at us. We walked back to our bus, which was parked under a huge, shady tree in utter shame after a 34–0 defeat. Saying that there was room to improve was an understatement.

    The weeks went by and we got word of the provincial try-outs; this is where all the schools came together, with a few talent scouts from the soccer world, and picked out kids that had great potential in the game, formed a team with them under the flag of the province they belonged too, in my case Mpumalanga, and went fourth with a league. I trained hard, worked on my fitness and game plays, passes and strikes, forgot a bit about Danielle as I wanted to succeed, and let my school work slip a slight bit. My coach, Mr Shwonga, had sat down with myself and Wallace about a month before try-outs, and mentioned that if anyone in our school had a shot at making the provincial team, it would be us. In our chat, he highlighted a key move, which ultimately led to my success and also added to my new and improved way of thinking. He did some research and found that with the amount of kids that had attended try-outs years prior, only a few kids were left footed, and because majority of kids wanted the striker positions, where they could claim the fame, spots like left back, and left wing were left uncontested. I played striker at school, I was confident enough up there, and during our matches against other schools I played left winger, like Beckham did, because I had some level of vision, could always fall into the midfielder spots and control the play, and was able to make decent attacking runs. He mentioned that the odds of me making the cut would be greater if I took the undesired left back position, opposed to my regular spots. I trusted him, and he started training me on the role. I didn't like it much, as I preferred my winger spot, but I also knew that this was for the bigger picture, so I went with it. We removed ourselves from the league and focused on bettering ourselves before going back into one, and this gave me more time to focus on things left backs need to focus on.

After weeks of training, our school allowed a few boys to go to the provincial try-outs. I went with like six other boys and two youth workers, sadly Jerome wasn't allowed to go, but I don't think he wanted too either. Upon arrival, they placed us in random teams, and we played against each other with about eight judges judging us. I played three games, where I did better in the left back spot than I had hoped for, and on a few occasions, I had made runs like a left winger would. After about 6 hours, they sat us down on the field, some 300 boys I'd say, and started calling out the names of the kids that had made the provincial squad. They started with goalkeepers; they needed 3, and then went on to right and centre backs before getting to the left backs. I knew that I had worked hard enough to succeed, but I also knew that the chances of a white kid playing soccer for a province were slim to none as it wasn't normal in South Africa, but I accepted my fate and I was ready to get back into the school bus and head back, ready to try again next year.

"Malcolm. No—Wha—" the announcer struggled to pronounce, "Malcolm from Vaalrivier," he continued as he gave up on the surname. I stood up; weak at the legs, noticing everyone staring at me, asking how a white kid succeeded, walked over to the bench the others went too, introduced myself, congratulated them and sat down. The ceremony ended, and they gave me a paper highlighting training dates, locations and contact numbers of everyone, which I passed onto my head coach as he would be able to sort this out with the school. I phoned my dad, to let him know of my achievement, and told Danielle too. A party was in order, and we organised one for the upcoming Friday. My friend Jackson had a free house that weekend as his parents were going out, and decided to throw it there. I invited Danielle. The party started and we barbecued and drank a few drinks, the only problem was that Jackson had invited several girls, none of which showed up, and we were four guys and one girl, talk about a sausage fest. They weren't too worried about it as they played guitars and chilled while Danielle and I sat against an old fridge and made out. The night progressed to a point where I was wasted, along with everyone else, so I called my dad to collect us. He wasn't too happy to be driving his drunk son and his sons squeeze around town but also didn't want us to get hurt trying to get home on our own. Once I got home, to Koos and Jerome playing on my Xbox, I told Koos that we had made out, and he was happy for me. I went to bed, and as soon as my head hit the pillow, like a spring that had been held down for a few seconds, my head shot back up and I vomited all over my wall and blankets. I passed out immediately afterwards. Sylvain wasn't too happy but he closed the door to keep the smell in my room and called it a night himself.

The days passed and I was training hard for the upcoming provincial league, I knew that I had to prove myself once again, as there would be talent scouts scouting for the national team; chances were I would never get it, but hey no harm in trying I thought to myself. School was getting back on track, and the chess was going even better, Jerome and I were fighting hard for the trophy, he would win the first game, then I would win the second, making it hard for the teacher in charge to pick a winner. At this point Danielle and I were properly dating, it seemed serious at the time, and I liked her a lot, but looking at it now gosh I was such a child with no standards. The time eventually came to head out the infamous school gates for the trip to Pietermaritzburg, where the five-day long league would be held. Audrey had returned to South Africa, to visit a few friends and sort out some stuff. She had heard of my accomplishments in soccer and knew that I was travelling down the country to play soccer for my province. She felt obliged to give me some spending money whilst down there and gave me R2000. My father's new 'lady friend' was already trying her best to make an impact in our lives, and when she heard of Audrey giving me money, she outbid my mother, handing me R2500. Audrey then moved to a R3000 bid, placing Marylin in a difficult position. It was a messy display of jealousy and attempted parenting rights, but the R8000 I had received compensated for the trauma.

I found myself on a bus with about forty other kids that had been chosen for the squad, and set out making friends and singing Zulu songs with everyone. It was a strange memory, but I enjoyed being able to diversify my cultural exposure without any racist comments flying around.

We arrived at the renowned Protea Hotel, where we signed ourselves in and set out admiring the facility. We were informed that we had a game later that evening, so we headed down to the pitch where we would be facing Gauteng, and warmed up a bit. I didn't play the first game, but sat in the stands and supported my team. We lost 3-2, but the referee played in their favour as he didn't give the penalty we deserved after a Gauteng defender slid tackled our striker in the penalty box. With our defeat we made our way back to the hotel, where we all wandered our separate ways in search of decent food. I went to a fish restaurant on my own, as I was mostly on the phone to Danielle, and mentally prepared myself for the next game against the Northern Cape. On the second day of this five-day long venture, we practiced for our next game the following day, and once training was done, we walked around a local mall, where I had bought gifts for everyone with the hefty pocket money I had received. We played our game on the 3rd day, which we won, I forget the score, and got ready for our final game against Kwa-Zulu Natal on the last day. I think it was around this time that I fully comprehended how much of a risk taker I was, I mean I was having fags before warm ups, during half time breaks, and even after the games, and coaches weren't happy with me never being where I was supposed to be; if I had a dollar for every time I was in that situation, I'd be...right here actually. Mr Shwonga was the only person who knew where I was, as I kept my smoking habit quiet, soccer players shouldn't smoke. After the final whistle of my last game for my province blew, we were told that the Free State beat the Northern Cape, and this meant that we had finished 3rd out of all the provinces. Third isn't bad at all, but first place is where I like being. That night we were all invited to the town hall where we had dinner with the mayor of Pietermaritzburg, surprisingly an award ceremony followed. I thought nothing of it, and was more focused on texting Danielle before she called it a night, but then they started calling the names of players they had chosen for the South African squad. It interested me as I wanted to know what they categorised as 'talent'. The goal keepers were the first to be called onto the stage, and as good sportsmanship 'rules' dictate, we all clapped hands in an orderly fashion after each name. Well, except for the kids from the nominees' team; they whistled and shouted in excitement for their fellow team mates who were one step closer to living everyone else's dream. The constant flow of African names started boring me, and my thoughts slowly started drifting away from the ceremony and more towards the buildings architectural design. "Malcolm Nowak from Mpumalanga as our left back," the announcer said into the microphone.

'Deja vu is this real?' I thought to myself. I stood up, once again on legs made from jelly, and made my way through the collection of round tables placed in this big hall, all while my team yelled, clapped, whistled and chanted out.

"Mlungu! Mlungu! Mlungu!" which translates to white person or white guy. I walked up onto the stage, where I shook the Mayor's hand, received my medal and a small trophy, and walked to where the previously called players stood, facing the 200 or so other players there. What the actual fuck was going on? I didn't expect to make the provincial team, let alone the U/19 national squad, I didn't feel that I deserved it, I mean I was good back then, very good, was always on my man, never hesitated, had insane ball control when I needed to dribble, but there were many other kids that were better than me. The ceremony ended, I was still in awe with everything, I never expected to go this far, but I walked up to my school coach; the one who suggested the left back position, who trained me for hours in the rain, who gave me more fitness training than anyone else; I hated him for it at the time, and thanked him for everything he did. I wouldn't have made it without him. We went back to the hotel, and I ended up phoning everyone I knew, my father was sleeping, so I called Audrey; I was too proud to care about our differences, Danielle; who didn't seem all too happy about being woken up, and Jerome, who was proud of me, but the ruins of the wall that use to be between us still acted as a border when it came to feelings. Audrey was ecstatic for her son that had pushed beyond everyone's expectations, and succeeded despite all the numbers against him. The next day the bus took me back to another school, where Audrey picked me up and took me back to Secunda. We went to Antoinette's house, where she was staying until her flight back to Cyprus. I walked into their house, through the side door, where they'd prepared a little surprise party for me, there was a huge 'congratulations' banner hanging from the ceiling, a few balloons here and there, and a bottle of champagne waiting for me on the table. We ate, danced and drank to our hearts content. Audrey got to meet Danielle that night for the first time, Jerome was there; how he got home that Friday I can't remember, but he was there, and Gabriel, don't even get me started on how excited he was.

Elliot stops after hours of writing, grabs a glass of water and decides to text Katrien, to see how she's doing.

'Hey, Katrien, how are you today?' he sends over the messaging app.

Elliot switches on the television as he waits for a text back, hoping to find something interesting on to take his mind away from things; the pain of re-living the childhood he was raped of, the eerie emotions associated with the struggles and challenges are a bit too much. He knows that the worst is still to come. Writing really helps him cope with the demons inside, but some demons can't be conquered with a pen. The sights and memories haunt him daily, the regret of not standing up when he should have, as well as the moments he stood up when he should have been quiet play back and forth in his mind. At the age of 31, a normal man should be fully trained in dealing with such emotions, should understand that the past can't be changed and that there's no point beating yourself up over things you have no control over, but Elliot is not a normal man, never had normal experiences, never thought the way normal men think. The news comes on as Elliot falls into the sofa, something about North Korea again; they've been on and off the news like a light switch since late 2017. Elliot sees the presenter talking, and sees the images but can't make sense of the words. His mind is somewhere else, riddled with *what ifs*? The black smart phone beside him vibrates, its Katrien.

'Hey Elliot, I'm fine thanks, I asked my manager to check the cameras, I told him that some guy was hanging around the bar after he had left and that I felt threatened, so I wanted to show him, but he told me that the cameras don't work, they're just there for show.'

Elliot doesn't feel an ounce of relief as he reads the message, he wasn't concerned about it, it wasn't his job on the line, and even if they let her go for such an act, he could always reach out to his contacts to get her something better.

'See? I told you not to worry about it,' he texts back. The news doesn't make sense, and Elliot feels in the zone, so he returns to the table, to try get to the part that haunts him the most.

Audrey dropped us off at school on Sunday, in her aqua-coloured rental, where she managed to snap a photo of Jerome and I sitting on the hood of the car, laughing at some joke Jerome had made.

I started making friends with this one troubled kid called Jack, he went to school with us and lived in Secunda too, it started with our parents sorting out some kind of lift arrangement; my dad would fetch us along with Jack and his father would drop us off or something like that. This Jack fella was in a world of bad, not because he couldn't get out of it, but because he kept himself there, and as a leader and a human being trying to get into heaven, I felt it was my duty to help him out. From the meaningless sexual relations with girls he was involved in, to the heavy drinking and substance abuse most weekends, all the way down to fights and beating up homeless people, he was involved in it all. I understood his feelings when he mentioned that he had an abusive father; and his father was huge, but it was also clear with the amount of women that he chose to surround himself with, that he was crying out for some female attention as his mother had passed many years prior. With Ryan gone, I was open to new friendships, but Jack somewhat faked what we had, and I found it extremely hard to trust him.

At prize giving, Jerome and I had cleared the trophy table up; as most people expected. This time Danielle and Bethany accompanied us on our award ceremony; Danielle drove up with her father, who I became relatively close with, having fixed old cars together. Bethany drove up with her family, as her brother, Ian, was in school with us. We took a few photos together before the ceremony commenced. Jerome was the best student in grade 9, and picked up around twenty something certificates, and about three trophies, he did very well, and the pride in Sylvain's face shone brighter than the spot lights above the stage we received our rewards on.

I had once again stood on the stairs beside the stage, the last in a formal line of kids receiving awards; the last was always the best, staring into the crowd at Danielle, who seemed disinterested in everything. I felt this urge to tell her that I loved her, and that I felt greatly for her, but there was something holding me back, a feeling of insecurity, as if I didn't belong there. I ignored the thoughts when my name was called.

"Ladies and gentleman, let me tell you something about this kid," Mr Barnard continued after reading my name, hinting for me to stand in front of the podium while he told the crowd a little story. "He came to us in 2008, as a quiet, troubled kid, I've never seen this boy slack on any given day. Earlier in the year we introduced our first ever soccer team, and not only did he participate in it, but he reached the provincial and South African levels for it, a first for our school. We as staff are immensely proud to have him in our school." He finished and my ears went red, after hearing such a great acknowledgement on the amount of effort I had put into turning the shit in my life around, especially in front of every student in the school. The night went on, and one of the happiest memories of my life came, something that still brings me to tears whenever I think of it. It was time for group 40 something to come up and receive their awards. I knew that around this time it was time for cultural awards, and chess was one of them. Jerome and I stood together on the stairs beside the stage, while we waited for our names to be called. Again, he mentioned something to the audience of family and friends in the hall, starting with a joke, "Malcolm can you please relax next year?" the crowd laughed but he went on, "Malcolm has won the trophy for Best Chess Player consecutively for three years, and now he wins it for the 4th, but this time he has the honour of sharing it with his brother, Jerome. Malcolm and Jerome Nowak, chess champions of Vaalrivier for 2011." It was such a privilege to share this with him, they handed me the trophy, along with the certificate, but I passed the trophy to Jerome, I had held it many times before, it was his turn.

The part of the ceremony that I waited four years for finally came, the part where the next leaders of the school were announced. Everyone had cast their votes, all the kids were bribed with smokes, there was nothing else we could do other than sit in anxiety and hope for the best. The leaders and prefects were announced, about 20 of us, but from the 20, only four had been chosen as the 'leerlingraad', something like the student governing body, here we had a head boy, deputy head boy and two associates that out ranked the other leaders. These four students called the shots on how things should be dealt with and would act as ambassadors when going to events where the schools name had to be upheld.

"The four students are…" the announcer started, creating suspense with his constant pauses, the hall went quiet, the lights seemed to dim, the faces of the people staring at me blurred, I wanted this, I had worked hard for it, it was time to reap the fruits. "Jeffrey…" the announcer called, giving him time to take a step forward from the line of leaders before continuing to the next leader, "Andrew…" There was a round of applause for each leader, but we all knew Andrew's brown nosing would get him here. "Malcolm…" the claps came, one could feel the sense of happiness from everyone in the hall, but I didn't get my hopes up yet, we still needed to be assigned a role, and I wanted head boy. "Chris…" he finished off with. Mr Scheffer walked up to the four boys who proudly had their hands behind their backs, and handed us the famous material scroll that we stitched onto our blazers after a warm

handshake. Now was the time, from these four lads, only two would be called out as head boy and deputy head boy... There we were, shaking from anxiety, standing tall and proud, chests out, and poker faces on. "The deputy head boy of Vaalriver for 2012 is," the announcer started off, continuing his game of suspense with a long pause.

"Andrew," some kid yelled from the audience.

"Chris," another shouted in retaliation.

"Quiet please," the announcer commanded, like this was an intense Wimbledon game. The world went quiet, and I watched Mr Barnard's lips call "Malcolm Nowak" in slow motion. I was upset that I wasn't head boy, I really wanted it, but my face remained the same, I couldn't let anyone know how it destroyed me to lose. The students clapped and whistled as good old Mr Scheffer walked up to me and shook my hand, pinning the black and gold badge that stated 'Deputy Head Boy' on my blazer's lapel. He looked me deep in my eyes and said.

"Really well done, Malcolm, I am really proud of you." I realised at that moment in time that there was no point in being greedy anymore, I had come a long way, from being a bullied loner that fantasised about murdering everyone, to being one of the most respected students this school has ever seen, it was time to be grateful for what I had. The moment flashed by and Mr Barnard was ready with the next name.

"The Head Boy of Vaalrivier, for the year 2012 is..." he repeated his pause, "Jeffrey." Well, fair play to him, kind of guessed it would be him, he was a teachers' favourite, because of his charisma, and also did very good at sports, better than me anyways, but I owned him in the academic sector.

The ceremony ended, we all walked outside in our groups, only to disband to be with our families. Anyone with an ounce of emotional intelligence could tell that I was upset, I kept my head low, but fellow students kept walking up to me, to shake my hand on yet another outstanding performance; it was rare for someone to walk away with 10 plus trophies and close to forty certificates. I was modest about it and made my way to my father, who was standing beside Danielle's dad, puffing away on a smoke. Danielle's father shook my hand, and mentioned what a pleasure it had been for him to witness such an event; he had no idea how serious I was about school. Jerome walked up to us, where Sylvain gave him a hug, and mentioned how proud he was of him. It broke my heart as Sylvain still hadn't ever told me that he was proud of me. We walked down to the hostels under the cover of darkness, to collect our bags, so that we could go home for the weekend. I packed hours earlier so I came out first, put my bag in the trunk of father's freshly washed Chevy, and proceeded to listen to him as he puffed away on another smoke.

"Malcolm, I am very proud of you, I was always proud of you. You are my first-born son, and I want you to understand why I was so hard on you, look at what you've done." He told me before I could open my mouth to say anything. Sitting here now I get that the world is moving into an anti-bullying 'age', and that it's more focused on making the relationship between children and their parents friendlier, but in all honesty, without those two main factors playing against me my entire life, I would never have made it. It takes a whole lot of guts to notice the world firmly standing against you and everything you stand for, but it takes even more guts to comprehend the odds and continue fighting for what you believe in. Something I feel kids these days are deprived of, everyone is raped of their passion early on, and taught how to react and feel, instead of adapt with basic instincts. We went home, ready for some relaxation before the big exams just around the corner; these exams along with the second quarter and final exams in grade 12 were important for admittance to any university in South Africa. For kids like Nicole that I hadn't seen for years, and Unathi who seemed to have his life figured out, these exams weren't so important, they would get accepted immediately, unfortunately I didn't have the universe on my side, and needed to work extremely hard for it. I cannot stress how serious I was about succeeding in life. I spent every fallen eye lash, birthday candle blowing, shooting star opportunity wishing for success and a spot in this world, but if the hard times taught me anything, it would be that you have to go and make it happen. The universe won't give you shit.

The exams crept on us like the Japs during Pearl Harbour, but I was more prepared than the Americans, locked onto my target, honed in on victory, never blinking, no hesitation, only flipping through pages to score the highest in my grade. We sat in this huge hall next to the sports pavilion, writing three-hour long papers most days. I was normally done within an hour, I couldn't dwell on the same question for too long, if I didn't know the answer, I wouldn't fish for it, but I never scored less than 80%.

Exams finished and school holidays were upon us, Sylvain had booked a holiday for us, but only Jerome, himself and the lady friend wanted to go. I didn't want to have a 'family' holiday with someone who wasn't family, secretly I missed Audrey and Lala, and couldn't replace their presence by laughing with someone else. I decided to be with Danielle and her family, and bailed on my father's holiday plans. It would have been a very forward move for any other guy, but Danielle's dad worked with my dad, and they knew each other years before her and I were ever an item, which made things easier for me. We ended up going to Alberton, where we camped out in a swamp-like, wetland setting. It was all fun and games, until the sun set and you could hear over a hundred different species of frogs filling the night with their music; I felt isolated and away from civilisation; something I strive on now. Danielle and I had tried exploring each other's bodies when no one was looking, but it was difficult as her brother took a shine in me and wanted to be around me most of the time. Danielle's father took us fishing during this trip, and I finally caught my first fish; after years of practice with Sylvain at the Evander dam, little bastard of a fish put up a big fight. I went on a social media application I had, and saw that my father had uploaded photos of Jerome on the beach: he looked happy. Jerome had broken up with Bethany at this point, and started dating Elaine from next door, he had publicly announced it on the photos by writing her name in the sands of Durban's' beaches. It was cute, and as always, I was happy for him.

We arrived back home, and I think Danielle and I spent too much time together, because we started getting pissed-off at one another. I had developed some serious trust issues, due to my mother's adultery, Sarah moving on so quick and even Melonie texting other guys during our relationship, and it made it extremely difficult for me to rationalise whenever her gay friend messaged her.

Jerome and I headed back to school, I was ready for my final year, a year where I can keep to my word of being the best leader that I could be and not slack now that I got what I wanted, a year where the sky was the limit and nothing was going to stop me. Jerome was ready to do more with his grades, and push himself further, and I'd be behind him, pushing him to where he wanted to be, getting his name in the teacher's good books, securing leadership for him and a better school life than what I had. I patiently waited for the athletics season to pass, so that I could play my final year of rugby. Jerome and I became so close that we made a pact, that no disease or person would take us from this world, that we would take ourselves when we were ready, a very serious pact I would never urge anyone to make.

I can't exactly remember what happened, but during this time Jerome and I had stood up against Father's lady friend, forcing her to leave. We shared a few words in the lounge one weekend, she cried and we never saw her again. It was harsh, but Father agreed that he couldn't force a step mother upon us, it was something that we had to agree on first, but Jerome and I never took into consideration the male 'needs' father was experiencing. The fact remained that we didn't like her, she didn't like us, and one should always pick their children over sex.

We hardly ever saw Jerome on weekends, he was either on his bike, or next door with Elaine; with her stepfather being in the accident recovery industry, and Jerome in love with speed and dangerous hobbies, it was pretty clear why he didn't stay home. He would regularly be in the passenger seat of a small car moving at 200 km/h, reporting to fatal accidents, where he would see the victims of serious crashes spread all over the place; something a 15-year old should not see, ever! Having hung around this crowd of people, Jerome slowly became a risk taker, and started stealing Fathers car at night while father was asleep. One Saturday night, at around 1 A.M, Jerome drove up to Danielle's house, where I planned on sleeping over, and insisted on driving around Secunda with me. I liked the idea, I took risks too, I mean Danielle and I had already finished a bottle of vodka that night, and I was wasted, but I kept it quiet until I started the car; Jerome panicked after I mentioned it. We drove around the town, doing handbrake turns on slipways, going over 180 km/h in 60 zones, hooting at people walking around late at night, and all this as a drunk 17-year-old, with no licence and a semi stolen vehicle, what could go wrong? We did this almost every weekend, until father noticed that his petrol was going much faster than usual. One night he caught us sneaking into his room, to take the car keys from his jacket pocket, and told us that if we ever took the car again that he would phone the police. The damage we caused went a bit further than that though, as whenever we went back to school, we would tell the kids in the hostel about what we had done. We thought nothing of it, as it was just teenage stupidity, but one kid, Jack; who had already started looking up to me, as some kind of role model, paid attention to everything I said and then came one night...

Jack had fallen in love with one of Danielle's friends, which was not okay with me, as Danielle and I broke up a few weeks earlier. She couldn't do the every-second-weekend thing, I never had money to take her anywhere and my insecurities were becoming too much for her. From the breakup came a very special moment in my life. We were driving back to school one Sunday, directly after the breakup, and I was seated in the passenger seat beside my father and Jerome sat behind father, as he always did, always on the right-hand side of the car. While we drove back in the heat, the radio kept playing depressing breakup music, which really started getting to me. The thoughts of her kissing someone else, or sleeping with someone else tore me apart, but I kept quiet about my thoughts. We got to the school, neatly packed our things into our cupboards, locked the padlocks securing our belongings and walked into the smoking section as brothers; Jerome had become my smoke buddy, as Ryan was gone, Andrew and Jeffrey were sent to another hostel and the only person I could willingly share my stuff with was my brother. We lit up our smokes and kind of went our own way, I had earphones in; I guess I wanted to get away from all the shit and find peace in the metal I was obsessed with. Jerome was telling kids about his weekend and engaging in random chatter. The artist I was listening to was screaming about a girl that broke his heart and betrayed him, and it finally got to me. Tears fell from my cheeks, and kids started noticing it. Jerome noticed it too, and tried to protect my reputation as a strong kid that feared nothing, so he shouted at everyone to get out of the smoking section. At first people just looked at him, like what the fuck bro, but he raised his voice a second time and they kind of got the hint. He put his arm around me and suggested going to the other section of the smoking room, where kids wouldn't be able to see me. He lit me another smoke, and asked me what was wrong, and I told him.

"I don't know how I'm going to get through this, why can't I be loved? Why can't things just work for me?" but he said nothing. He came closer and gave me the tightest hug I have ever received in this lifetime. I can still feel his embrace haunt my skin most days. Once his arms consolidated behind my upper back, I started crying, not because I was a clingy little shit, but because I couldn't comprehend why I couldn't have what others had. Jerome had the white and grey Monster shirt I had bought for him for Christmas on; he was truly obsessed with motocross and off road sports, and even though I had little money for the holidays, I spent R400 out of my R600 to buy him this shirt as a surprise, it was to thank him for being my brother, to say sorry that I was never there for him as I should have been; it was the first and last thing I had ever bought for him. Jerome stopped hugging me, and took his favourite shirt off; it meant a lot that he called it his favourite shirt, and started wiping the tears from my face, and gave it to me to blow my nose on. I can explain this story 100 times to anyone, but I cannot describe how admirable this act was, he would wear that shirt for days on end, sleep in it, no one was allowed to ever touch it, he really loved it.

Jack came to my house one Saturday, for a beer and a chat, but he invited Danielle's friend too. I didn't like that he was making such moves without my consent, but I understood that he was trying to pull, and the bro code dictates help a brother out. We all sat in my kitchen chatting about things, but he was making sexual remarks and jokes, as we guys do to understand how comfortable a woman is with the people around her. The only issue was that Danielle's friend was also seeing one of my other friends, a guy that use to be in school with me, but this guy was twice Jack's size, and I've seen Jack with too many blue eyes to know that he couldn't defend himself. Having been caught in a conflict of interest, as well as a recent heart break, I kept steering the conversation towards Danielle, how she was doing, finding out whether she had met anyone yet, things like that. Danielle stopped outside my house about an hour later to collect her friend; she had passed her learners test and could finally drive her dad's old Nissan legally. We watched them go home, but Jack didn't want it to end there, so we did what most hormone raging teenage boys do, we pursued with the wrong heads. We walked towards Jack's house, where he suggested getting his dad's car, which he insisted he was allowed to drive and that he drove very well. I on the other hand tried suggesting that we just walk to the other side of town, to where Danielle and her friend were; it would only take an hour, but he persuaded me to go to his house.

We arrived at his house, he grabbed his dad's keys, and started pushing the car out of the yard, he used the excuse that the battery had some issue, and needed to be pushed to start, but we both knew the engine was loud and would wake his father. A bystander noticed him pushing the car out, and warned him against it, but he made up some excuse and continued. With the car a few houses away, he started her up, and told me to get in. He kept mentioning how good a driver he was, but let's be honest, no matter how much you tell yourself something, sometimes it doesn't become a reality. We drove off, with me in the passenger seat, scared as hell. He took the first turn abruptly, almost driving on the sidewalk, and drove too fast for my liking. We drove for about two minutes before we stopped at a gas station, where he filled her up with R20. I took note of the jeep behind us, but he didn't. We continued driving towards Danielle's house; something that should have taken us 10 minutes at max, was now taking longer, as he kept taking the wrong turns, kept driving on the wrong side of the road, and stopping in the middle of the road to light a cigarette. The jeep behind us flashed us at every error incurred, but he put his middle finger out the window at the jeep. After handbrake turning a slipway just outside the town centre, the jeep over took our car, got in front of us and tried performing a rolling stop, but he tried out manoeuvring them. I kept telling him to stop so that I can walk, I didn't want to be a part of it, but he persisted on trying to race this jeep. They switched on their blue lights after we over took them, and started trying to pit-manoeuvre us; fucking unmarked police. They hit the back of the car; we lost control going about 100 km/h, slid over the paving, almost rolled, and came to a shocking stop. I didn't want any part of this, so I tried to get out of the car and run for it, but my leg and my neck were in pain, and as soon as I got out of the car we were surrounded by like 14 police chaser units, pointing guns at us. There was no way we were getting out of this, so I just laid in the field, holding my neck hoping that nothing serious was wrong with me. News of the accident came over the radio Jerome was listening too, but they decided to report to another accident in Bethel. I was put on a stretcher, and taken to hospital, where my father was notified of the accident; he was on night shift but got out and raced to the hospital to see if I was okay. Jack's dad was there too, asking my father for compensation, but my father pushed for legal proceedings, where we were in the clear after camera footage at the station showed me in the passenger seat and police reports highlighting that he was driving under the influence. We remained friends after the incident, but his father stopped giving Jerome and me lifts to and from school.

 Once rugby season arrived, I was approached by the coaches of both the 1st and 2nd teams, asking me whether I wanted to captain the 2nd team, or play in the 1st team, it was a tough decision; either lead in hell or serve in heaven. My thoughts always traced back to Jerome's wellbeing, I didn't want to leave him in a spot where I couldn't save or protect him, so I decided to captain the 2nd team. The first friendly game we played, to get some kind of understanding of where we stood as a team and what should be worked on, was against HS Standerton; a school renown for having vast amounts of sporting talent that always failed against HS Secunda. The event, on this occasion was covered by the media; a photo of me tackling their number 12 appeared in the local newspaper the following week. The title read Vaalrivier lads are once again ready to take on the league or something along those lines; Father has it snipped out and stuck somewhere.

The first quarter exams had already passed and we were in the second quarter's exams, the ones students feared most...the record exams. These exams would decide your future for you, if you failed, you were gone, and you'd be somewhere small, going nowhere, just waiting for life to end. In this mash up of rugby and exams, I found myself really focused on succeeding, and nothing would stop me, well so I thought...

On the 26th of April 2012, we got on the bus as usual, ready for our game against the big lads from Platorand, this time it was an away game. We sat on the bus, chanting what we at the time called patriotic songs, songs we as students created through the years of being in Vaalrivier. The songs would often be sung in a mellow, deep, southern blues kind of tone, to match the dark words that accompanied the pitch and rhythm. We sang about how we were forsaken by this world, by our loved ones, how we really felt under the disciplined surface, and how we viewed the world outside the school walls. We arrived at the host school, started warming up as usual, and because I was captain I got to toss the coin with the ref. After winning the toss, I chose to play with the wind; it would aid our kicks, and if I knew anything about my team's performance, it would be that we scored majority of our points in the first half from kicks, besides the sun was in the opponent's eyes too. I had a small chat with our coach Mr. Scheffer about the game, and then proceeded to chat with my team. We grouped tightly in huddle formation, we always gripped the person beside us by the waist, as a symbol of 'I got you bud'. I laid out the plan, to win of course, but also highlighted key areas we could focus on; they had big lads in the front, bigger than ours, so our objective was to let the ball fly to the back row; that was a bit quicker than theirs, another strategy I mentioned was that with the sun in their eyes, and the wind going with us, we should definitely play high balls from the backline, it would be hard for them to catch, giving us either certain knock-ons or great hit tackles. A few suggestions from fellow team mates later and we closed our eyes in prayer, to ask God above to lead us to the victory we worked hard for, and if we didn't deserve victory, to give us the strength to make them earn it. There would always be a volunteer to pray, but this time I wanted too. We ran through the tunnel and took our spot on the southern side of the pitch, left of the stands. Never have I ever seen a team so ready to give themselves to a win, they kicked off as I chose sides, and as predicted the ball flew against to the wind, forcing it to land just after the 10 metre line it had to pass, where my team was ready to collect and perform. The game went well and Jerome was doing good too, I was playing 8th man this game, following in Ryan's footsteps, I was actually too small for the position, but the size of my heart for the game was bigger than anyone else's. I scored two tries in the first half; one was an easy run over the line, but the second one I scored by diving over a loose ruck and planting the ball behind the line. I played very unconventional rugby, my front-line players knew that if you were getting taken down, to pull at least two opponents with you, especially back-liners, so that when I joined the backline that we would have an overlap every time. Jeffrey pulled in both their centres as he went down near the half way line, and once the ball left the ruck, it switched hands very quick; like a game of hot potato. I was between the outside centre and winger, selfishly running for the line, I wanted my first hat trick. Their winger and fullback were quick enough to catch up to me, and they were trying, but I realised that even if they tackled me, that the momentum would still push me over the line, besides, the offload pass to the winger option was still there. The winger ankle tapped me, *causing me to trip and fall, but I slid over the line, and scored another five points for Vaalrivier, but the full back didn't stop and ran into me, kicking me in the face. He left a mark below my bottom lip, just above my chin, but I was a tank and brushed it off and went on with the game. Our kicker sustained an injury and I had to cover for him, ever see an 8th man kick to poles? We wiped the floor with these bulky boys, and the final score of 54-0 proved it. I had scored 19 points; from three tries and two conversions, Jeffrey and some other lad scored a few tries and our kicker took I think two or three penalties. Overall performance of the team was amazing, and it was an honour to have led them.*

The next day, at school, the teachers and learners; that didn't make the team, learnt of my performance and outstanding leadership. I was that jock, that nerd, that leader, that one person that would act outside of the conventional norm set out by American television. Popularity wasn't what I strived for, but I wasn't saying no to it. The principal awarded me with a 'Man of the Match', in front of the school.

Somewhere during the middle of the night, Elliot stopped writing and went to bed. He didn't check to see if Katrien messaged back, it was too late and she was probably fast asleep by now.

Chapter 15
An Abyss of Anguish

The sun has been burning brightly in the sky for several hours before Elliot's eyes open. He knows it's a late start to the day, but he also knows that the next part of his writings will tear him apart. He reaches for the phone, to see what she had said, but there is no text back.

"Strange," he tells himself.

He doesn't let it get to him, and walks towards the kitchen, where he grabs a coffee and hovers over the last piece he wrote. One can tell by the look in his eye that something is bothering him deeply, that it's something very close to his heart. Elliot lets out a little sigh and goes outside, to get some fresh air. Barefoot he walks around the side of the house, to the garage. He removes the padlock from the metal piece holding the two doors unlocked. The doors swing open without his intervention, his body fills with anxiety as he looks at the khaki-coloured sheet covering something big. Elliot takes a sip of coffee from the white cup in his right hand, and places it down on the ground beside him. He walks into the garage, grabs the sheet tightly, and tugs at it once, revealing the car underneath it. Elliot lets out a small, painful smile as he looks at the green, black and white coloured race car in front of him.

"My greatest achievement," he mumbles out, as if there was someone with him, listening to his words.

He bends over, filing through a red tool box, trying to find the key; he always hid things in obvious places. The battery was removed a while ago, but Elliot manages to unlock it manually. He jumps into the passenger seat, and rests his head against the head rest, once again having to come to terms with the reality. The car is astonishingly clean for a car that has been sitting in a garage for years, there's not an ounce of dirt anywhere inside, the glove box is empty, and the only atrocity is the stale smell of old lavender.

Elliot gets out of the car with watery eyes.

"I miss you," he mumbles once again, closing the door as he gets out.

He knows that this will be the hardest part; it's something he has held on to for years, something he has put aside and avoided for a long time now. Elliot gets back inside, grabs the bottle of whiskey and determinedly walks towards the papers. He takes a swig from the bottle, pulls a face, and gets to work...

After school, we lined up on the parade ground, for a small assembly before the long weekend, and as always, there was some mention of school rules outside of the premises, things like behaving and returning to school on time, what time the buses would collect us and so on. Normally at the end of the month, the school would give us a closed, brown envelope, which contained money, as we didn't get pocket money from our parents and kids needed to also have some sort of 'reward' to work towards. The school divided money equally according to behaviour and status; a good kid that had no offenses against him in that month would get a grand total of R60, which was useless at the time; maybe three packets of smokes worth. Depending on your offenses, and scalability of seriousness, you would receive only a portion of the R60, some kids skipped a class and walked away with R43.50, others who had fought with other students received R11.23, how it was calculated I hadn't a clue. Kids like me, Andrew, Jeffery and Chris; who hated the fact that I was Dep. Head Boy instead of him, received around R120 but our behaviour was included too. I never cared too much about money, it complicates things, memories and relationships with fellow human beings mattered more at the time.

Most students relied on that money for smokes, others who didn't smoke needed it for sweets and cheap body sprays, others that had families and received money from their parents would buy useless things like shoes or speakers that pulsated neon lights in accordance to the bass of the song. Then there were the different kids, like Jerome, that bought alcohol or petrol with the money... The school got word of the happenings, and in this specific assembly, the principal announced that there would be no more 'Govi pay'; as we called it, from that point forward, subliminally pointing a finger at Jerome. Oh... the scandal, the kids looked at him in anger, but I could on several different occasions point the finger back at those accusing him for doing the exact same thing almost every month. We were dismissed and started heading back to the hostels, and all you could hear were threats, left, right, and centre. They wanted to beat Jerome up, I knew that he was pretty strong and could defend himself in any situation, and normally I'd let him, but he was smaller than me, and they were about 50 attackers, so this time I would have to intervene. I stayed on his six, sleeves rolled up, lighter firmly held in my curled-up fist, ready to fight, ain't no one touching my brother but me. I ordered Koos to walk beside him, to make it look like we had numbers on our side, but in reality, we were three, against whoever came. Most of the kids respected me, and would never go against me in any way, shape or form, which I appreciated, but it's always tricky when money is involved. We walked into the smoking section of the hostel, which was secluded, away from the eyes of any youth workers, and lit our smokes. Normally I would be on my phone or talking to someone about rugby, but I kept my wits about me this time round. Kids started flooding the smoking section, looking for Jerome, threatening him.

"Jerome, get behind me," I told my brother who was taking a puff of his smoke.

"I'll be fine, don't worry," he replied, but I didn't have time for games of modesty, I never liked my back or sides exposed to an opponent.

"Get fucking behind me now!" I shouted at him as I turned to face the twenty-five kids in front of me. Some of the kids were in my rugby team, and some were bigger than me, but I played it calmly and told them to have their smokes and leave.

"No! We want an answer, we want our money," one of the taller guys stated to my face.

"You're not getting money, I'm not getting money, so have your smoke and leave," I responded, ready to drop my smoke at any time to fight.

"Nah, this is bullshit, he has to pay!" this persistent boy continued.

"Look, I'll lay it out for you, your chances of going near Jerome are between zero and fuck all, so please listen before it gets bad," I firmly stated as I stood my ground.

"This is bullshit, Malcolm, I needed to buy smokes," he said as they started getting jumpy and started pushing me. I pushed back, luckily they were grouped together so the domino effect came into play, they stumbled back and I confronted them for the last time.

"I'm not fucking asking you, I'm telling you, you aren't going near my brother, end of story." They backed off after seeing that I was dead serious and no longer smiling; I was a great guy, and wouldn't just stand my ground for nothing. Like I always warned new kids that started in the school.

"I'm a great friend, but an even worse enemy."

Things died down and we headed to the buses after our smoke.

We arrived at home, I was still heated from the confrontation earlier, but I was taking my frustrations out on my Xbox that was hooked up to the TV in the lounge. My dad was on the computer with his back turned towards the living room, with Jerome seated on the two-seater couch across from him, texting someone. Sylvain saw something interesting on the computer and called Jerome over to see it. He walked by and accidentally kicked my Xbox over, cancelling my game progress without saving. I walked to him with a fist raised; so close to hitting him, he was already ducking, scared of the shot coming, but he knew that he was wrong and said sorry while his hands covered his head, but something strange happened, I lowered my fist and patted him on the back.

"It's just a material possession, I love you, bud," I mentioned as I smiled at him.

"That is beautiful to see," Sylvain said. I couldn't hit him, it wasn't the promise I made two years prior, or the fact that I worked hard to build this that stopped me, it was something else, something special, it felt like love, I still can't explain it. An hour or so passed before Jerome got on his bike, with money he had stolen from Sylvain's money jar, which was 'locked' in the cupboards of the TV unit. He set out to buy a bottle of his favourite Brandy from the illegal alcohol salesmen in Secunda. We worked together to get that money; we dislodged the back board of the TV unit, and also manipulated the latch system with a credit card; true South African's. I didn't need the money, I just liked challenging things.

After hours of gameplay, and Jerome's booze cruise, Father ordered us pizza; something that started happening more now than ever before. We sat down to eat, but Sylvain didn't like pizza, so he left it for Jerome and me to devour, while he grabbed some tinned-fish from the cupboard. I always felt sorry for him, but I had already gotten use to his weird way of thinking; the more simple life, the better. We sat down after dinner, as a family and watched some comedy that was showing on TV at the time, it was funny, but also brought the acceptance of no matter what shit we go through, at the end of the day at least we have each other, and great television. The movie finished and Sylvain called it a night, it was around 8 pm, he was an early sleeper. As soon as he closed the passage door to avoid the disturbance of his slumber, Jerome turned on this horror movie that we had planned to watch for some time. Before we started, he poured a glass of brandy for us both, mixing it with coke and never adding ice; ice is shit. We sat down to watch the movie and drank peacefully in the comfort of the two-seater couch we had dragged closer to the screen. We often tried scaring one another when the ambience started, and made *comments here and there as to why we felt the movie was unreal. The movie finished and I was bored, I didn't want to watch another, nor did I want to play Xbox, the drink did work on me, but I wasn't drunk, so I told Jerome that I was going to go lie down for a bit.*

Jerome said good night to me as I made my way to the passage door, I replied with a simple "good night", and proceeded to my bedroom without closing the passage door behind me. From my room I could see the dining area, and noticed Jerome got back up, probably to pour another drink for himself. There was a long pause in what was happening. Jerome stood in the dining room, which had no light turned on, but instead the light from the kitchen next to the dining area shone over him. He stood there and looked at me; all tucked in and comfy under my blankets, looking back at him.

"Love you, bud," I loudly whispered to him, trying to let him know without waking father, but he stayed quiet and smiled back at me. I didn't think anything of it, he was a quiet kid, and you would never get him to share his emotions, I was use to this already, so I proceeded to count sheep.

Elliot puts the pen down, the *'Love you bud'*, is playing viciously on his mind, it brings the waterworks back, but he swallows the tears, takes a huge sip of whiskey and presses on.

I woke to a scream; it was a girl, I wasn't sure who it was, but I saw red lights flashing through the see-through curtains of my room. Sylvain woke up as well, and asked me if I had heard it too. After I had answered him, we rushed towards the kitchen window, which was a perfect vantage point to find out what was going on. We saw Sarah's lights on, but before I could assume that Jake had gotten drunk and might have started beating Amelia and Sarah, we noticed an ambulance outside our yard. Ah man my stomach is in knots from this. A cold chill made its way through my body, and we rushed to the front gate, unlocked it and saw the garage open... At first, I thought that Jerome may have gotten his hand stuck in the chain of his bike, or that the bike fell on him and he was calling for help, but as we continued towards the brightly lit garage surrounded in darkness, the paramedic jumped our eight-foot gate. As my left foot touched the bricked paving we had leading up to the garage, I saw the most disturbing image I have ever seen. Jerome was hanging about a foot from the ground, from a chain, which was wrapped around the support beams of the garage, and secured by a padlock that I never found the key too. Saying that time stood still in that moment is an understatement. Behind me, Sylvain fell to his knees in what seemed like slow motion, he raised his hands towards his face, to hide the tears coming from his eyes; seeing him cry was a rare sight, and it added depth to the bottomless abyss that I had started feeling. I couldn't fall to my knees, I couldn't cry, time was of the essence I thought to myself, I needed to save him, I had saved so many people before, this time won't be different. I ran towards Jerome, and noticed the urine that had stained his light blue skinny jeans, the mucus dripping from his nose, his closed eyes, his head tilted to the left, his body swinging left to right, left to right, left to right. The paramedic tried to hold me back, but I broke free, grabbed Jerome around his legs, and lifted him up, hoping that some air would pass into his lungs, giving him life again, but it wasn't enough, so with one arm I was holding him up, and with the other I was struggling to get his head out if the noose. The paramedic felt sorry for me, and proceeded to help me, he took the chain off his neck, and I gently placed him on the cold, dusty cement floor. I tried CPR; something I was forced to learn in scouts back in 3rd grade, surely it would save him I thought, but after two or three presses on his chest the paramedic started pulling me away from him.

"What the fuck?" I yelled as I pushed him away, and tried again, but he started pulling me back once again, I got really mad and this time I pushed him away and told him to, "Fuck off," as I tried again, at least allow me to try, but he got persistent. I know he meant well, but we could have saved him, well so I thought anyway. At this point the police had already arrived on the scene, and jumped over the gate too; father was too broken to think about opening the gate for them. The stench of death lingered in my nostrils, I leaned in over his mouth, tasting my failures, but the paramedic pulled me off again before I could try, this time with all his power.

"He's gone," he told me in my ear as he held me tightly from behind, trying to get me away from hurting myself any further.

"He's not gone, we can save him!" I screamed in a teary, crazed voice. I broke free and pushed him hard, I didn't even take the time to watch him fall and trip on the lawnmower on the side of the garage, but before I could kneel down a police officer grabbed me, and told me that assaulting a paramedic was a criminal offence.

"Lock me up then!" I shouted as I kept fighting for his life. The captain of the police force intervened and told me to go inside, but I didn't want too, I couldn't just leave my brother there on the cold floor. As I relive this moment almost every day, I realised that even though there is a will, there's not always a way, and the faster we learn to accept that everyone around us will die, the faster we learn to cherish those moments we often take for granted with them. I went back inside, in utter shock, and stood in the lounging area, shaking; looking down at my hands that had failed to save him, my shirt, stained with his urine, my hair, upper lip and nose was covered in his mucus. I wiped my face clean with my forearm and walked to his room, sat on his bed, angry with myself for failing him, especially now when he needed me the most. I went outside, lit a smoke and sat on the grass far away from the garage. I watched as they put him in a body bag, and loaded him into the back of a van. I didn't want him in that black bag, he wasn't rubbish, he was worth more than that, he was my fucking brother and we should have saved him, but before I could stand up to fight for his life again my father came towards me, and gave me a long hug, but I know he needed it more than I did. One of Jerome's friends, Dan; a strange guy that was always inviting us to sleep overs and giving us sleeping drugs, showed up, but I didn't want to talk to him, I didn't want to talk to anyone. He gave his condolences and left. They closed the back of the van and left, along with a few police officers. Sylvain was left on his own outside, broken, seeing the other officers off. I got onto the phone, and phoned Audrey who was in Cyprus at the time, and told her that Jerome had killed himself, but she was mad and told me that it was three in the morning, that I needed to stop with my bullshit and go to bed, but I told her.

"Ask Papa then, I just felt you should know." Sylvain had walked in and had seen me on the phone, so I handed it to him and he spoke to her. It was funny how whenever my parents were on the phone I'd try listen in, but this time I didn't want to know about it. Father hung up the phone, and silently sat down on his chair, in front of the computer, the same way he did every day, and lit a smoke. I sat on the first seat of the three-seater couch, facing the TV; that served as a platform for me

to share my last memory with my brother only a few hours prior. We both stared at blank screens, not taking note of our reflections or the cold air coming into the house through the front door we had left open, just deep in thought. After about an hour of silence, the strength I had, the hard person I became over the years of pain, the rock I had moulded around my emotions after the shit I had faced, all of it fell apart and I burst into tears. It was the first and last time in my life that I cried like that, chunking, howling like a little girl. Sylvain walked over to me and held me, he knew that I was young and I had no idea how to handle such a situation. I could feel his tears fall on my head... on my hands, but he never made a sound, he was too proud to cry in front of people, but I know that no amount of strength could block out the water works. I don't know how long I sat there crying for, but I went to take a bath afterwards. I contemplated drowning myself, I didn't want to live with this feeling, I had felt a lot of it in my life already, but this was different, this was too much, this was real pain. I laid in the bath, for about an hour before I realised my fingers had pruned and the water had gone ice cold. I was so deep in thought, trying to imagine what Jerome's final moments were, what he was thinking, why he did it, where he had gone. I got dressed as a red sun rose in the early morning sky. I walked through to the lounging area to see how my dad was doing, but he wasn't where I had left him.

"Papa?" I called out.

"Ja?" he answered from the door step. He was sitting on the door step, like we both had done whenever we were troubled. I saw the beer beside him, and the smoke rise in the air from the cigarette he had lit. The ashtray beside him had three butts in it, hinting that he was chain smoking. Sarah stood in her kitchen window, watching us through the white curtain they had up. She probably thought we couldn't see her, but we could.

"Why are you sitting here alone, Papa?" I asked my father, but I received an answer that broke my heart even further.

"He can't be gone, I know that any minute now, the police van will come around the corner and drop Jerome home." It was obvious that he was in the first stage of the grieving process, denial. A tear fell behind him, from my watery eyes, I had witnessed my father get cheated on and divorced after twenty years of marriage, I had heard of the arrest on suspected rape, I had watched him not only lose his father, but also skip out on the funeral because it was expensive and he had to look after his family first. I knew that he had no friends, that times were lonely for him and how my dysfunctional behaviour tore the family he so desperately wanted to keep together apart, but this? To lose his favourite son, the one that resembled him, the one he had mentored and cherished so dearly. Favouritism was no longer a topic in my mind anymore; I couldn't even imagine how he felt. Hours passed of me sitting on the couch, deep in thought before I phoned Danielle.

"Can I come see you please?" I asked, nearly begging her to accept me into her house and away from mine.

"Why? We broke up, you need to move on," she harshly stated.

"Jerome did something really bad and I don't want to be here," I tried to explain, keeping some details out.

"What did he do?" she asked in this frustrated voice.

"He committed suicide," I mentioned as I gave into honesty and desperation for less depressing company.

"Go away with your bullshit, that's not even funny, stop looking for attention from me and move on," she shouted out at me before hanging up the phone in my ear. She lived on the other side of town, about five kilometres away from my house, beside one of Jerome's friends. I didn't know what to do, sure it was weekend but how do you play Xbox, or computer, or study or do anything peacefully with such a raw image lingering in your mind? I put Jerome's grey helmet on my head; kick started his bike and proceeded to the front of the yard. Sylvain would have stopped me normally, but I guess he knew the pain I was feeling, along with all the guilt I had accumulated over the years of being a shit brother, and let me go, telling me to be careful. I wasn't scared on a bike, I was however very cautious, but this time was different. I drove fast and hard, gearing up on sharp turns, and gearing down on straight roads in order to hit the power band and wheelie straight into a fucking truck, I had lost my sense of caution and care. God must have followed me on the bike that day because I didn't fall, never got hurt, despite my intentions. I drove to some dusty road between the main Secunda area and the casino, where the cemetery laid on my left-hand side, got off the bike and lit a smoke. It was dangerous to stop around here as this is where the quick criminals would operate, due to Embalenhle being a five-minute drive away. My phone vibrated, I took it out and read the message from Danielle, and she apologised after her father informed her about the incident. I didn't text back; she wasn't there when I needed her, despite my childish undying love for her.

I rode back home after my smoke, in the same reckless manner as before, but I saw people at my house; the neighbours, chatting to my father, asking if he was okay and being there for him. Sarah was there with her mother, but they didn't know how it would affect me, so they kept their distance just in case I snapped once again.

The tears fall from Elliot's eyes, dripping in sync with the writing, he doesn't stop, he lets the pain from the pen, and the pain from his eyes stain the virgin paper. It's a painful site to see, his hands are shaking, teeth grinding with regret, he doesn't take his eyes off the empty lines in front of him, and it's a good thing, it's the first time he gets to express it the way he wanted too. For years people told him to go see someone about this, people always wanted to know what happened, but he couldn't express it clearly, he hated the 'feel –sorry-for-me' feeling people were giving him.

"Relax, we all have our own battles," he would say when people started trying to be there for him. Relentlessly, Elliot pulls some courage together and goes on.

One of the hardest parts came when I had to inform Gabriel, but in honesty each passing moment after Jerome was a fucking hard part. We were on the phone to Audrey, talking, trying to comfort her; I put my hatred and pride in my pocket and tried being there for another human being. She cried hard, we couldn't comprehend her English at all, and the bastard of a husband she had, really didn't care, apparently, he called it, he didn't like Jerome at all. Audrey wanted to be transparent with Gabriel about the matter, I didn't understand why, he was like seven years old, he wouldn't understand it, nor would he be able to control the emotions once it clicked, but there I was, tasked by my mother to inform little Gabriel. Sylvain probably would have done it, but the idea of going back to the image in your mind is hard, and I didn't want him hurt anymore.

"Hey, Lala, how are you?" I started out, trying to lighten the mood.

"I'm fine," he answered in his cute voice.

"How is school going buddy?" I continued, this time swallowing the saliva in the back of my throat, preparing my voice to be as sweet as it could be.

"It's good thank you, I made so many friends, and I was playing soccer and this boy tripped me, and..." he went on, oblivious to the hint at what seemed to be a serious family talk, but I listened to him none the less, it was good hearing my brothers voice. I knew that I had to cherish him and not make the same mistakes again, I didn't want him in the same place Jerome was.

"Look, Lala, I have something I need to tell you," I laid out as my hands started shaking, "I want you to be a big boy about this okay?" highlighting the behavioural requirements for this information.

"Okay," he said as he prepared himself for possibly the harshest news he had ever experienced in this life.

"You know Jerome? Jerome went to the angels today, to be with Granny and Grandpa, and he told me to send you all his love." I swear it was one of the toughest tasks I had to do in my life, I sat there, with tears in my eyes, trying to understand what the fuck ever happened in this life for me to tell my little brother about Jerome passing away.

"What do you mean, Mikki?" he asked in his curious voice.

"Jerome was an angel from God, and God needed him back," I continued, there was nothing else I could say, how can one remain so calm and patient with a little kid with such a serious event? I tried my fucking best. Audrey took the phone by him and started speaking to me, looking for answers, but I had none, no one knew why he did it, there were no notes left behind, no one was sent a message, and his phone had a password on it, so we couldn't see his last messages and to whom they were sent to. Audrey mentioned to me that she had taken the cordless phone with her to check up on Gabriel, and upon arriving in his room she saw him sitting on his bed, with his head in his hands, crying. I guess he understood what I tried saying, I wish it wasn't like this little brother, and if I could have had it my way, I would have sacrificed myself to keep him here with all of you, I swear. We drove down to Mila's mother, to organise the memorial arrangements in the church we use to go to, and once again people seemed to avoid me regarding this situation, was it me that caused it? Why are you treating me like murderer? Once we spoke about it, we headed down to the pub, to where we all played in harmony the day before. The bar had two regulars in it, the pool tables were clear of people; just the way Jerome and I liked it. Father ordered a beer, and I'm guessing he would have let me have one too, but we'd been waiting for my 18th birthday to share one together, so I ordered a coke instead, to respect his wishes, even though I really needed one. Father bought an extra coke, lit a second cigarette and left it in the black ashtray on the table beside the pool table.

"Papa...are you okay?" I asked, I didn't understand what he was doing, but he answered me, establishing his motive for such a strange scene.

"One for Jerome." Sylvain wasn't usually sentimental when it came to things, so this was strange. We played about ten games, all in Jerome's name. During our fourth game, I sunk an unbelievable shot, where the cue ball curved and knocked the ball I aimed at, like in the professional games you see on TV, I turned to my right, to tell Jerome, but as soon as I turned, I remembered everything. I just kept quiet and continued my last shots in silence. We bought food, but none of us ate, and we both struggled to sleep that night. Sunday morning came, and father headed to church and I stayed home. I stood in front of the mirror, with the memory unwillingly replaying in my mind. I looked at myself, and started advising myself on what to do.

Look, Malcolm, I'll make it simple for you, Jerome passed away, yes it hurts, it hurts a shit load, but you're in the middle of the most important exams of your life and your last rugby season. Your parents can't handle this, no matter how badly they're trying to pretend. You've worked so hard to get to this point in your life, you need to take that strength you've found, and take all the courage inside you and fight hard bud. Don't shed a tear in front of anyone, no one may ever see you cry again, stay strong for your family, carry them through this, go sit down and start studying, use it to fuel you, be there for Gabriel more than what you were for Jerome. Succeed first, we can cry later, I told myself. It was a strange situation, but the first time I ever spoke to myself so seriously, especially in the mirror, but I listened to myself and took my own advice, it seemed like the reflection was well capable of handling these types of things. Monday arrived, I phoned the school, with my father beside me, and explained the situation to Mr Scheffer, who had answered, he didn't need to speak to an adult, he trusted me, he believed in me.

"It would be best if you didn't come to school for a few days," he mentioned, I kind of hinted at it too. Me, in a school filled with vulnerable children, who have the tendencies to annoy a person? God alone knows what would have happened.

Audrey's flight was to arrive on the Wednesday, and we went down to Johannesburg's OR Tambo airport to collect her. There was some time to kill, so we did what most guys with time on their hands do, went to the nearest bar. It was a rather expensive bar at the end of the terminal, but it had a smoking section inside it, so we entered. We walked up to the bar, and father ordered his usual, the waiter then turned to me after padding down the order and asked.

"What about you, sir?" It must have been the fact that I had some stubble from not shaving for nearly a week that made me look of age, but I turned to my dad, and looked at him in his eyes, kind of telepathically telling him that I was sorry that I wouldn't wait for my birthday five months away, I too had been experiencing a hard time.

"Can I have the same, please?" I firmly said, standing my ground in front of all authority. My father rolled his eyes and took out a R50 note, paying for us both.

"To Jerome," he said as he lifted his bottle, toasting to his name and the memory he left behind. We took the first sip together at the same time, and placed the bottles down on the table. As the idiot I always believed I was, I started testing Sylvain, taking more than the finger given to me, and lit a smoke in front of him. It was hugely disrespectful, but I could see he didn't care anymore, after about three puffs I felt remorse and walked over to the other side of the bar area, looking away from him as I smoked my cigarette.

We collected Audrey and Gabriel about an hour later, greeted them, and as much as I hated myself at the time for giving Audrey a hug, it was important to stay emotionally intelligent about the situation, she needed comfort and love to help her get through this too.

We drove the long drive home, and I must give my dad props for keeping his cool, especially after everything. Family from the Gauteng province, Botswana, Evander and Secunda started pitching up at our house, and as always, I hated the crowds, I liked being aware of my surroundings, meaning the more people the less aware I can be to everything. It's something I worked on bettering my entire life. I was in a real dark place, but I didn't want to talk to anyone, especially not about Jerome, the only person who was able to scratch about 5% from the surface was Sylvain, he was the only person I trusted. I found myself most of the time getting on Jerome's bike, wearing his helmet; trying to soak up the final essence of him the world had to offer. My phone was filled with messages of people all around town, saying sorry for my loss, but I ignored most of them, except three girls. It seemed like whenever something bad was happening in life I would try to find something to fill the gap, and it would always be sex, so I drove down to this Afrikaans girls house, near Hoerskool Oosterland, to get my emotional fix, but she was a skank, and didn't really care about me, it was a pity thing I suppose, I didn't really care either, I got what I wanted. Back at home my parents were trying to plan the funeral with the relevant people, but my parents were lost, despite their experience from burying Frankie 11 years earlier, and both the church and funeral home were frustrated because they needed to approach them in a comforting manner.

"Right, we will hold the service on Saturday in our regular church, we will use the hall besides it for the memorial service, and then bury Jerome after that in the cemetery where Frankie was buried. Catering will be organised by the Greek guy who owned the supermarket near Oranjagloed Laerskool," I burst out, laying out the plan, frustrated from the circles everyone was going in. All the parties agreed to it, and it went forth as so. I hated the whole burial idea, I personally always wanted a Viking burial where I was placed on a boat, and an archer would set me alight from some 100 metre away. I would have preferred if we cremated Jerome, as I think it's what he would have wanted, but Audrey and Sylvain preferred the traditional method, so we went with that.

Sonja or one of Audrey's family members gave me money; I can't remember who, for some or other reason and took me to a liquor store, where I picked up my first bottle of whiskey. I drank, and drank clean, ending up drunk and in tears, but in the safety of my own room, where no one would see. I often snuck out to Jerome's room when no one was looking, to comfort myself with his possessions; wearing his shirts, going through his school work, and then I stumbled upon something that changed my life. He was a very talented artist, and had a rough sketch of his favourite car, a VW Scirocco, among his school papers. He didn't draw the car to represent the standard one we would see in the streets, it was clear that he added a spoiler, changed the body kits, and even went as far as styling it to match that of the renowned rally king Ken Block's Ford Fiesta, it was styled to the tee. I recall him telling me that it was his favourite car and that his dream was to buy the car and style it exactly, but I thought it was just chatter, and that he would change his mind as soon as the new Lamborghini came out. I sat there, amazed at how serious he was about it, but returned to my room before anyone could find me there. I stayed in my room, drinking whiskey and falling asleep in a wet pillow most of the time, until the day came where we had to bury Jerome. I dressed in my school uniform, opposed to the black suits everyone wore, I felt stronger in this uniform; besides I didn't own a suit. Before we headed to the church for the ceremony, we went to the funeral parlour, to see his face for the last time... There were a few people there, all in tears; lost, confused, but grouped together, acting as pillars for one another. There was a cold, 5 m x 6 m room where Jerome lay in his dark-coloured casket. I stood quietly in the corner of the reception, watching everyone walk in to say their final goodbyes to him. Once everyone had finished, I walked in, alone, and closed the door behind me. With the heavy atmosphere and tears in my eyes, I spoke to him for the last time. I remember each word clearly, as if it was yesterday, and as my tears fell on his cold, dead body, I made a promise. That no matter how hard I had to suffer in this life time, no matter where God led me, and no matter what it took, I would make his last dream of buying and building that car, a reality. The hurse pulled up to the church, and there were many people there, even Vaalrivier's Principal, along with one teacher, Andrew and Jeffrey. Koos was with me at this point, standing in the middle of the church grounds, waiting for this morbid ceremony to begin.

Everyone headed inside, and there I was, along with Koos, who was still more Jerome's friend than mine, along with my parents, Elaine's stepfather and some other guys, bearers of the brown box. I took point, front left to be exact, leading us into the church along with Koos on the right. We placed it on some wheeled apparatus, and gently pushed it to the front of the altar, where we left it to find our seats. The preacher began, and then we sung sad songs, which I fought hard to keep out of my ears, as they started messing with my plans. I walked out of the church, in tears, I couldn't take this anymore. I lit a smoke and sat behind the building of God, trying to man up. I returned to where the pastor asked if someone from the family would like to say something. Everyone looked at me, like I was some kind of saviour or scapegoat from the big things, so I stood up, walked up the three stairs in front of the altar, stood behind a little podium and a microphone, shaking.

"Firstly, I would like to thank everyone who came out today to pay their final respects to Jerome, we, the family really appreciate all the condolences and shoulders during this tough time. Jerome was a great kid, better than anyone I knew, and we will miss him dearly." I said, holding back my emotions, fighting away the tears, but each word that left my mouth made it harder, I shook uncontrollably in front of the 150-200 people there. I could see in their faces that they weren't judging me, and felt some sort of sorrow, but despite the few encouraging faces, I couldn't go on and thanked everyone a final time and sat back down. The ceremony ended and we drove slowly, with our headlights on, behind the hurse, on the dusty rode Jerome use to love riding his bike on, towards the cemetery. The tears of my parents fell almost in sync with the coffin lowering, mother almost fell in as she stood too close to the edge of the hole, but I held onto her, protecting her as she should have protected us. Everyone threw flowers, rose petals and letters down in the hole, saying a final goodbye. I stood in front of the six-foot hole, broken, and unpinned my black and gold Deputy Head Boy badge, my greatest achievement in life thus far, something I worked extremely hard to get, in with him. It's not that my leadership status died with him, it was more of me sharing something important, that I cherished, with him for the last time, something I know he would have acquired and had been working on achieving too. We got in our cars and left as they covered the wooden box with soil stained by our tears. Sunday was quiet as I returned to school. Boys from all hostels came to pay some respect, to say their sorries and to try and comfort me with heartfelt words. It was nice to see people care, but in all honesty...sorries do absolutely fuck all to change things, and I didn't raise myself from where I was to be treated differently for shit. Chris got annoyed with me, for some or other reason, but he was a dickhead towards me because he would never be able to become the Head Boy or deputy, as he too was in his final year; jealousy is a nasty thing. He walked past me and said in Afrikaans.

"I hope that your brother is burning in hell." He was bigger than me, but I went for him, luckily Koos held me back, because he would have smashed my face in. That night, as the kids fell asleep, I contemplated putting a padlock in my knee-high school sock, tying it into a knot to ensure it wouldn't get lose, and while Chris slept, smack him over the head a few times. As tempted as I was, I let it slide; I'll kill him with kindness. I didn't work so hard and suffer so much in my life to celebrate my graduation day in prison. Thursday came...and once again we were playing a game of rugby against what was supposed to be an easy opponent, Jim Van Tonder School, but this time we were playing without our original fullback, Jerome. Before the game, both coaches from the 1st team and 2nd team approached me, and mentioned that the 1st team was short a player, even with reserves and I need to play there instead of with the second team. 1st team games were played after the second and third team games, which was good, perfect for me actually as I told them I'd play both.

"You're crazy, you can't play both games, you're a smoker, you won't last," the first team coach told me.

"Watch me," I replied as I turned to see my 2nd team into battle. We kneeled down in our circle, with the coach amongst us, and said a little prayer before the game commenced, the same way we always did. Some kid jumped up after the prayer session and dedicated the game to Jerome, some kids supported the idea with praise, but it was a stupid idea. I get the sentiment behind the notion and respect their intentions, but they didn't yet understand that the game mostly relied on me, where I wanted to play the ball, what I was seeing on the field, what gaps I saw, and this time I wasn't thinking clearly; I wanted to run, full speed, into the biggest guy I could find, and hopefully break my neck, and there were some big guys on the field. We kicked off and played as best we could; size was always against us, both my parents sat in the stands; first game of mine they ever watched, with my teachers around them, comforting them after the tragedy. Sadly, after both halves of intense physicality, we lost the game, by a small margin, but I wasn't done yet. In front of the other guys, girls, parents, teachers, I took my second team jersey off, and put the first team number 15 on. It's not that I was ripped or anything at the time, it was that I would never, under any circumstances take my shirt off in front of anyone, unless the room was half lit and she just cared about dick. I had/have scars all over my back, some from acne, a crazy spread of pimples over my shoulders and upper back, but I also wore scars of the abusive parents and fights I chose to get into. We played, and as always, I gave everything I could, but this time I offered more, I smashed into guys twice my size, cleaned rucks as if the coach of the Springboks was watching, pushing lads who were once covering the ball from a turnover, onto their asses, securing possession for my team. I can't remember the outcome of the game, but the coaches were shocked at what they witnessed, yeah I wasn't the best they'd ever seen, but I'm sure they never saw passion like that before.

Elliot doesn't want to write anymore and gets up. He takes another big sip of whiskey, puts the bottle down, and walks to the wooden shelf above the fire place, and reaches for the photo of Jerome. The tears silently fall, landing on his brother's face. He turns his head to his right wrist, where he had Jerome's name tattooed into his flesh, a reminder of his promise to his brother. Elliot lets out a smile, he knows he kept to his word, and got that car for Jerome, it took him years of fighting and financial struggle to get, but he never gave up, despite what everyone said. He spent two years after buying it, building it up the way Jerome had wanted, and spent a good bit of money getting it transported to the Netherlands from Ireland; getting insurance on a 600bhp car is a bit tricky in Europe, so it had to be towed and shipped around. With the thoughts of the car on his mind now, he puts the photo frame back down on the shelf, after kissing his brothers' forehead, and heads outside, towards the garage. Elliot bends over, acquiring the battery required to start the Scirocco under a shelf in the back. He pops the hood, inserts the battery, attaches the cables and heads to the driver seat to start her up. Five minutes of constant turning the key in the ignition pass before one can hear the loud, roaring engine of his brothers modified car. He once again gets into the passenger seat, leaving it to idle while he looks at the roof of the car; he doesn't like driving it, he feels that it isn't his, that it's Jerome's, that he has no business driving it. Elliot closes his eyes, trying to picture something less disturbing than his brother's face. Deep down he knows that he faced a lot of unpleasant moments, but this has haunted him for a long time, something that still feels somewhat raw, an image always playing on a loop in the back of his mind, it keeps him fuelled, keeps him fighting, keeps him up at night, grinding his teeth. Elliot still feels as if he could have saved Jerome's life, and it hurts deeply knowing that he could never attend Jerome's graduation, nor his prom night, will never be able to hug his brother again, won't be there to witness his brother become a husband or a father. Elliot can barely feel pride when he accomplishes something anymore, because it doesn't feel the same, that "Well done, Bro, I'm proud of you," will never be heard again, even the simple "I love you" sounds different without his presence in this world.

Elliot gets out of the car and heads back to his lonely home, back to the four walls that mock him for his failures, to the seat that doesn't fully support the weight on his shoulders. Elliot's cheekbones are still stained from the tears, but he doesn't wipe it off, he wants both heaven and hell to witness the pain, as if they were to blame. Lost and confused as to what to do now, Elliot heads to his phone, hoping that Katrien is up for a call, because the voices in his head, ridiculing him, grow boring. As he unlocks the phone, he notices four missed calls from Katrien. Elliot feels a strange feeling in the bottom of his stomach, fear? He doesn't take the time to identify it, and phones her back immediately. The phone rings four times before Katrien answers.

"Hey, Elliot! I need help," she blurts out, breathing heavily over the mic.

"Katrien, what's wrong?" Elliot quickly responds, but he knows that if anything, time is of the essence, and starts heading outside, in an attempt to get to her.

"Henrick is here, threatening to kill me. He saw us kissing and I'm trying my best to keep him out, please help me!" she loudly mentions, it's clear that she is scared.

"On my way!" Elliot tells her, reassuring her that she will be fine. "Send me your location, and keep your phone on," he commands her as he turns around and runs towards his bedroom, to get the 9mm from his safe. He doesn't know where she stays, and that if Henrick tries to kidnap her that the location will reveal where he has taken her. Elliot tucks the gun into his waist band, covering it with the shirt he had just put on, and runs outside, to his vehicle. In a rushed mindset, Elliot forgets that he had left his car at the bar the previous evening, and has no other way of getting to her. The world becomes silent as he asks himself how he'll get there, but the silence is answered by the purring inside the garage. He feels guilty doing this, but has no other choice; Jerome would understand. Elliot slams-close the bonnet of the Scirocco, and hastily sets off; following the directions his phone is giving him. The car roars and moans in his control, hand brake turns like a track master on race day. Elliot knows that he is over the legal limit, and if caught he will get a DUI, but it doesn't stop him, he puts the vehicle in 5th gear, and proceeds speeding with his hazards on. The phone application suggests that he will be there in twenty-five minutes, but it's not good enough, a lot can happen in twenty-five minutes. Elliot minimises the phone screen while driving and phones the police, notifying them of the situation. They dispatch a unit to the location provided, and ask Elliot to remain calm. Elliot knows that he needs to get there before them, so that there is no proof of him driving whilst under the influence.

Elliot arrives on the scene, a worn-down block of apartments in Aalst, more than likely housing for those living on social welfare. Elliot jumps out of the car, locks it, and quickly places the keys in his pockets. Elliot hears a man shouting in Dutch, and decides to follow the voice. Little children, victims of lower-class society, wearing dirty, torn clothing are kicking a plastic ball around the dusty parking lot. They stop to watch Elliot run up the first flight of stairs, but it seems as if they're familiar with these kinds of situations. A few seconds later, the police arrive, and hastily proceed to follow the voices too, but this time the handful of kids follow them up, all but one girl, aged between 4 or 5, wearing a light blue dress, playing with her doll and chewing on her finger. Elliot notices the police on his trail, but doesn't stop to wait for them. He gets to the 3rd floor, where he believes the shouting is coming from, and sees Henrick kicking and punching the door in front of him.

"3rd Floor!" Elliot shouts back at the police as he sprints towards Katrien's assailant. Henrick is oblivious to the flopping sounds of someone running on the corridor, and continues shouting for her to come out. The police are just behind Elliot, watching him charge for the man in front of him.

"Stop Police!" one officer shouts out, hoping to prevent any further disorderly conduct. Henrick turns to see the person shouting, and notices Elliot rushing for him, but it's too late to avoid the impact. Elliot bends down, places his arms out, leans his head to the left and tackles Henrick away from her door. All those years of rugby paid off it seems. The two of them land on the floor about 2 metres away from the tackle point.

"What the fuck dude?" Henrick shouts out at Elliot, but Elliot isn't concerned with answering him, he knows that he has a few seconds before the cops take him into custody and pat him down.

"Katrien! It's Elliot," he shouts, as the out of breath officers make their way down the hall way. Luckily, she unlocks the door, and he pushes himself into her house in the form of a hug, taking the gun out from under his shirt, commanding her to hide it. Katrien is in shock, she didn't think that such a nice guy would own such a thing, but she hides it in the cupboard under her kitchen sink. Elliot leaves the apartment to confront Henrick, somewhat acting so that the police don't suspect anything inside the house.

"You stay the fuck away from my woman!" Elliot shouts out at the guy lying on the floor. The police finally get to the two, and as anticipated they handcuff both Elliot and Henrick, patting them both down for weapons and drugs. The smart play on Elliot's side gets him in the clear, but cocaine is found by the other officer patting

Henrick down. Elliot is told to sit against the wall while the police get the story from Katrien. After about ten minutes of chatting to Katrien, the police understand that Elliot came to help her, and that Henrick has been harassing her for months. One officer takes Henrick down to the squad car, while the other stays with Katrien, to find a solution to the situation.

"She can stay by me for a bit if she needs to," Elliot mumbles out at the two in front of him. The officer says that it seems like a reasonable, band aid solution.

After the situation and adrenaline dies down, the second officer leaves, leaving Elliot and Katrien standing on the corridor.

"Why did you bring a gun?" Katrien angrily whispers to Elliot.

"I wasn't sure how it was going to end, so I needed to be safe," he regretfully answers her. She invites him back inside, and gives him the gun back, but as she walks in to place it in his hands, she notices blood dripping from his elbow.

"You're hurt Elliot," she tells him, pointing at the blood dripping on her floor.

"Ah, it's just a scratch," Elliot mentions as he turns his arm to see the wound. He scraped the floor pretty badly whilst tackling Henrick. Katrien heads to her bathroom, where she gets some alcohol wipes, and proceeds to attend to his wound for him. "Really it's nothing," Elliot says, trying to stop her from worrying so much, but she is persistent in cleaning it, it's the only way she can really say thank you for being there for her.

After half an hour, Elliot suggests that she comes back to his place, just for a while, to make sure that she's safe. Internally she has said no a hundred times, she doesn't want to give a man the satisfaction of protecting her, but she knows that if Henrick is not locked up for a long time, that he will act quicker next time, especially with confirmed knowledge of someone else in her life now. She grabs a bag, and packs a few clothing pieces, female necessities, as well as her work uniform. The two walk down the stairs together, towards the car, all the kids silently watch them, assuming that Elliot is some kind of hero, especially after such a hard tackle they only get to see on wrestling programmes. Elliot walks Katrien to her car, returns to his vehicle and the two of them drive towards Elliot's home, Katrien following Elliot with her own car.

Back at the house, Elliot makes a cup of tea for Katrien, who is sitting on the couch, deep in thought.

"Are you okay?" Elliot asks as he hands the cup of tea over to her.

"I'm fine," she tells him, but it's clear that she isn't, it's obvious that the entire thing is bothering her.

"Look, you don't need to be scared, I'm here for you, and he won't go near you ever again," Elliot says, trying to comfort her, but it goes beyond that.

"Thanks, Elliot," she says, clearly trying to avoid the conversation.

"Well look, I'm tired, and a bit dirty, so I'm going to call it a night," he mentions, frustrated at her lack of interest in talking. "Make yourself at home and goodnight," he continues before heading to the shower, where he cleans himself up.

Katrien looks at the time, it is a bit late, but she is too shaken to even consider sleeping. She picks herself up from the couch, and walks over to the shelf, to look at the photos. Whilst in front of Jerome's photo, she turns to see all the papers on his dinner table. Katrien curiously walks over to the papers under the half-dimmed ceiling lights. She isn't one to snoop, but after three sessions of coitus, she has the right to know things, well so she feels.

Katrien starts reading through the notes, noticing blood on some of the papers, the scribbles and things he had scratched out. She spends hours reading through the writings, understanding more about Elliot, where he came from, what shaped him.

She feels disgusted when she reads about the beatings, she smiles at the times he wrote about his brothers, she sheds a few tears when she reads about Jerome and how he had to break it to Gabriel. It's a messy feeling, she understands that some of it he deserved, but it saddens her that he had to face things like that. It's clear that he misses his brothers, and that he never got a chance to experience a normal childhood with them, that he never got to experience a normal childhood at all.

Chapter 16
Manhood and Hardships

Elliot wakes up, noticing that she didn't jump in bed with him, so he walks down the hallway to investigate. He silently walks down the passage, trying not to wake her in case she passed out on the couch. He notices her reading his story, and leans against the door frame, watching her. She sniffles as she gets emotional, but she continues turning the pages, trying to understand what man he is. Elliot can't watch her torturing herself anymore, so he lets out a little grunt, trying to clear his throat; she gets a fright and wipes her tears away.

"Sorry, Elliot, I didn't mean to read it," she apologetically states.

"It's okay, Katrien, if I didn't want it read, I wouldn't have written it," he responds to her.

"Do you want to talk about it?" she asks him, it's clear that she has more questions than he has complaints.

"Is there something you want to know?" Elliot replies, trying to figure out what she's trying to understand.

"How did you end up in the position you are in now? I mean coming from such a background," she starts off. Elliot lets out a little chuckle before he answers.

"Well, there's nothing in life really stopping you from achieving what you want, and when you're in such a situation, forced to feel all those feelings, forced to see everyone you know in this world against you, you learn to have your own back. I knew I wanted to win, I didn't know how I was going to do it though, but I wasn't going to allow myself to lose, I owed it to myself. So, I took my shit, and walked away to start again." Elliot openly admits to her.

"Ah, so you came to the Netherlands to start a new life?" Katrien asks, trying to figure out where Netherlands comes in.

"No, so like I said a few days ago, I was 21 years old, I was busy welding some round bar onto a gate for my father, and while the sparks were flying, while the blue light damaged my eyes, I had a deep conversation with myself. I wanted to live my dream; I wanted to protect my pride and all I had fought so hard to become. So, I sold my car, sold my Xbox and games, golf clubs, everything I owned, and booked a one-way ticket to Ireland, the country I had dreamt of living in. I got onto that plane, without a plan, I felt that I was never going to succeed in life, and that eventually I'd be homeless again, forced to eat out of bins, beg for money, and I was too proud to admit defeat in South Africa, I was better than that, subsequently I felt that I'd rather suffer 9500 kilometres away from anyone who knew me. I arrived in Ireland, stayed with this lady, ended up working 2 jobs, but she got mad and kicked me out one night. I left the house with my luggage, and was having a smoke in the cold Irish winter wind, pondering where I was going to sleep that night. I recalled seeing a generator outside a fast food joint near work, and thought that it was probably the warmest place to stay for the night. Before I set out on my way, my newly found friend Glenn, told his parents of my predicament, and they took me in, allowed me to stay on their couch until I could find my feet. I was so grateful for his parents; I don't know where I would have gotten without them. I found a room to rent, and moved in a week later with my friend that had accompanied me to the country. I got a 3rd job, painting houses with the landlord, but my friend still didn't have a job, and wasn't keen on painting houses with us. I understood that finding a job was difficult, but he wasn't even trying, he was out drinking, getting with women, smoking weed, taking real advantage of me. I gave him an ultimatum, I had no choice, I had €500 to my name, rent was €420, and we were going to suffer if he didn't pick up his socks," Elliot passionately lays out for Katrien.

"Did he find a job?" Katrien inquires.

"No, he worked at a diner for like two days and got fired, I couldn't take it anymore, so I told him I can't do this anymore, he had incurred over €1500 worth of debt by me. With nowhere to go he returned back to South Africa and I stayed in Ireland. Once I found a pace, I quit my other jobs and stayed at the DIY Store I was working for." Elliot lies out, before walking over to the tap to get a glass of water.

"I guess switching between parents over the years was tricky," Katrien mentions, assuming they stayed apart. Elliot once again lets out a subtle laugh, understanding how weird his life seems for others.

"Well, shortly after I left for Ireland, they got back together, and then re-married after my first promotion," Elliot mentions.

"Oh, that's strange, at least you didn't have to travel between them then," Katrien continues, not fully understanding the situation yet.

"It's a funny thing actually, I always felt that had they stayed together, my brother would have had a better chance of avoiding suicide, I just feel that if the divorce was his main reason for what he did, then his death was in vein," Elliot says before Katrien jumps in.

"Well you can't say for sure that it was the reason he did that, so you can't blame your parents."

"True, but even if there was another reason, we could have monitored the situation better, my mother would have seen the red flags." Elliot says before letting out a little sigh of frustration, it's clear that he doesn't want to go through this anymore, "Regardless of his motives, it wasn't easier to see them, as I chose to not go back to South Africa for a while. The anger I felt over those years out-weighed how much I missed them," Elliot firmly lays out. Katrien wants to ask about his little brother, but the look of anger in Elliot's eyes scare her, she feels as if he still has some demons he needs to face.

"I'm getting a bit tired actually, would it be rude if I went to sleep?" Katrien politely asks Elliot.

"No, not at all, go ahead," Elliot kindly tells her as he finishes the last sip of water from his glass.

With Katrien all snuggled up in his blankets, Elliot feels the fire inside him again, he wants to write more, so he sits down on the seat, trying to find where he left off.

I missed most of my record exams due to the funeral, and all that was happening, but at least I could still write my mathematics paper, which at the time was probably my favourite subject. I loved all my subjects, but this teacher, Mrs Brown, had a different approach towards the students, she didn't sugar coat shit, and treated you how you treated her. She was real, and that's what made her unique. We sat down and wrote the exam and a week later it was handed back to us; apparently, I was in the top 100 students in South Africa for that paper, scoring 98%. Normally I browsed through the paper to see what I got wrong, I didn't like bragging, and I was so humble at this point, especially with Jerome no longer there... It's funny what lessons loss can teach. Mrs Brown did something awkward, that I still can't say how I feel about. She used me as an example to better the other kids' performance.

"That boy there, lost his brother, missed most of his exams, and had very little time to study, but ends up scoring 98%, how can you guys barely touch 70?" she blurted out. The days of sleeping pills and tears went by slowly; I mostly kept to myself, having earphones in most of the time so people couldn't bother me with 'how are you'. Our life orientation teacher pointed out how black my eyes were, as if I was possessed by a demon, and tried getting me back to God, but what God? What God would take away such a great person? I lost all my faith, which I regretted, because in the end we all go back to him. I didn't care much for things, I wanted to finish school, go to university; hoping that my marks were still good enough to meet the requirements to study law, and run away from everything. With all my papers submitted to university of Pretoria, University of Witwatersrand and University of Bloemfontein in A4-sized, brown envelopes, I waited for the final exams and to see what life was going to hand me next.

My matric farewell, or South African term for 'prom night' was just around the corner.

"I'm not going to it," I told my Life Orientation teacher; who was organising it, there was no point, I wasn't exactly interested in girls at the time, I didn't want to fake-smile through an event where everyone is flashing white teeth, I didn't want the rent-a-car parade, but I was talked into going. Finding a date was difficult, as I didn't want any girl from our sister school, I didn't want those five message sluts on my phone, I wanted it to be something meaningful, something that wouldn't haunt me when I looked at the photo's ten years from then. I decided to ask Elaine, somewhere I shouldn't tread, but she was like a sister to me at this point, and I knew that she was locked in her room crying, regretting the fight they had the night it happened, so I asked her. She accepted and I sorted out her dress, sorted out my suit and big Hummer H3 to arrive in. The prom went well, other than Jackson who went on his knee with a microphone and decided to propose to his girlfriend in front of everyone, only to break up with her six months later. Father picked us up after the event had ended, dropped her off at home in Bethel, and drove back to Secunda where I went to bed shortly after arriving home.

Father switched pubs, to a lonely one in Trichardt's industrial sector, not because they had better pool tables or better music, but because the bartender was a single mom that seemed interested. She was an independent, hard working woman, with a can-do attitude. I liked her over the previous lass my dad went for, because she was Ray's mom, who was one of my best friends from school. We were in her bar a lot; beers came at discounts, we were allowed to alter the music as we saw fit, and due to the lack of patrons the bar saw, we could practically do anything we wanted. Ray, myself and Duke; another cool, prospective IT engineer from school, *partied almost every weekend, I was only using the alcohol induced meetings to avoid my feelings.*

The final exams came a few months later, and I studied really hard, trying to score high marks to compensate for my shortages in the record exams, hoping that the universities would overlook it as a minor fluke. The last official school day of the year was upon us, and kids were eager to go home for the holidays; bags packed, best clothes on, hair gelled, strongest body sprays lingering, but we 12th-graders had our final exam in two days' time, so we weren't allowed to go home yet. It was the last day that I saw everyone I had come to appreciate as family; kids I cared for and helped get out of tough situations, teachers that shaped my life and mentality, grounds I roamed and ruled with Jerome, fields where I gave my all to ensure victory for our school, the end of an era, a sad day. More than fifty kids came to me, personally, before the buses set off on their routes, and thanked me for my thought leadership, my fairness in every situation, for being the helping hand whenever they were struggling, being a role model to every kid on campus, even after losing someone so close to me, and they wished me luck for the future, saying things like 'if anyone deserves greatness in this life, it's you Malcolm'. Sadly, they didn't grab my first lesson of 'The world doesn't owe you shit, you go out and work for what you want.' In all honesty, this school was all I knew, and I knew it very well, everything within those grey, ten-foot columns was home to me, I knew every nook and cranny. After everyone had left, we were a mere handful of students, down in hostel 4, wanting to do something different, something memorable. We all sat around the yellow metal table in the smoking section, brainstorming ideas to make the next two days unforgettable, and that's where ideas clashed. I wanted to focus on school, get my shit done, and go, but everyone else wanted to smoke weed and drink, which I didn't have a problem with anymore, just don't include me. It wasn't the first time that I had encountered students smuggling booze and drugs into the school, just this time I didn't reprimand them for it, I let it slide. Jeffery, along with Xolani and two others stepped and went to an illegal booze store, run from someone's backyard in the township on the far side of the cemetery. It was a long, hot walk for them, some four or five kilometres away from the wall they jumped over, through yellow, waist high grass, definitely festered with snakes. During this time, the rest of us kind of studied in our rooms, covering for the lads that left. Afrikaans was the final exam, and I was proud of where I was with the language, from walking into the school, knowing only the word 'cow', to being completely fluent with an Afrikaans accent. The lads returned and we smuggled the bottles of beer, brandy and a box of white wine under our shirts and in bags past the youth worker on duty. Our systematic approach of someone keeping him busy, while the rest made it to the rooms, so we could lock it up worked like a charm. As soon as darkness lingered in, we smuggled the goods back out, to the smoking section, where we drank, chatted and smoked for hours. We even had a spotter sitting near the entrance of the smoking section, informing us on the youth workers movements, and whenever he came near us, our books would be out, bottles back in bags and headphones in. We would have gotten away with it too, but a few loud mouths couldn't handle their liquor and vomited everywhere, raising the suspicions of the youth worker who had already been asking why kids who never got on with one another were hanging out all of a sudden. He began asking us one by one, but Andrew came clean, telling him that someone gave us drinks, saving the steppers in the process; he relayed the information back to us, and we all followed the same story. We were sent to bed and our 'fun' was limited the next day, but because it was a hot day, we were told we could go swim in the 25-metre-long swimming pool the school had. We barbecued some meat that the hostel father had given us, drank our sodas and when we were completely alone, we pulled out the left-over drink we had.

We sat down in the hall to write the Afrikaans exam the following day, and it was the first time I couldn't complete a three-hour paper in less than an hour, I struggled with simple things, I guess my mind was too fascinated with what happens after the examiner takes our papers, what will I do with my life after I leave that boom gate for the last time.

The papers were collected after the timer hit zero, and we broke our rulers and pens; as was tradition, and headed to the hostel to collect our stuff in order to get the bus home. Before we left the hostel with duffel bags on shoulders, backpacks on backs, and wheeled luggage at the ready, we had a final smoke in the smoking section. After we had finished, everyone made their way up to the bus, I was behind like twelve guys, who didn't look back. I paused for a second, looked at the high trees, birds flying from branch to branch, squirrels running in the tree line, the buildings and their colours.

A final, deep inhale of this heaven on Earth before I continued my walk to the bus brought me to tears, I knew I'd miss this place, this truly was home for me, and that life outside of here would most likely suck. I got onto the bus, not dwelling on the sentiment anymore, but looking forward to hearing of my acceptance into university.

Getting home, cracking open a cold beer and lighting a cigarette on the door step was first on my agenda, the world could wait till tomorrow, I finished school, despite all those comments people made years back.

I realised the next morning that there was literally nothing I could do until the universities got back to me, which was bad, as with nothing to do, my mind wandered, and the further it wandered, the harder the cold memory of Jerome was to deal with, and the harder it was to deal with, the more I drank. With drinking and gambling at the Graceland casino slowly becoming my daily routine, I found myself taking unnecessary chances on the bike; driving while drunk, driving with one hand so I that could hold the beer in the other. I found myself a lot of the times next to Jerome's grave, drinking beside him, having long chats, trying to ease the pain but unlocking the door to so much more.

As we approached the end of the year, father came home to me playing Xbox; he had finished work and went to collect post from our post box on his way back home. He handed me the brown envelope, addressed to me from the University of Pretoria, I was excited.

"Finally!" I yelled out.

I paused my game of Halo to open it. All the years of self-rehabilitation, hard work in school, effort into extra mural activities, all led to this moment. I got a butter knife from the utensil stand we had beside the microwave, and proceeded to open the letter. Heart pounding with joy, who could deny me my well-deserved chance at this life? Sylvain sat down on the couch and opened a beer, but held back on taking a sip; he wanted to cheers on the good news. I was kneeled down on the other side of the glass coffee table, with the papers in my hand. "Mr Nowak, we regret to inform you that you have not been successful in your application to the University of

Pretoria..." my heart sank, my somewhat remnants of a smile faded, and Sylvain knew immediately; I didn't bother reading the rest. I mean c'mon, I lost my mother, but I was trying to adapt to the situation without putting any pressure on anyone, I lost my brother to suicide during my important exams, cut me some slack, I was a hard working individual and I felt that I deserved this more than anything else, but I never used it as an excuse.

"It's fine, Malcolm," Father told me, "You will get into Wits, which is better than Pretoria." Thanks for the optimism, but if you can't get into this basic university, then a university that specialised in law, that failed even the great Nelson Mandela, would definitely not accept you. I went to my room to think, what was I going to do now? I don't have a problem working in the mine with my father, but how I will reach my goals as an individual? How would I keep my promise to Jerome's on R5000 a month before tax?

The weeks that followed were rather dark, all I could think of is taking Jerome's way out, and I wasn't scared to do it either, but I knew how it felt to lose someone, and I honestly could not do that to my father again, he would probably die of a heart attack or find himself sinking into a world of depression had I acted on my thoughts. All I could do was grind my teeth and see what I could do to change where I was, motivation isn't hard to find when your back is against the ropes. I typed out a resume' and proceeded to put it everywhere I could; sport shops, clothing stores, post offices, gaming shops, you name it. I handed a CV into a graphics design studio, who asked me a few questions regarding graphics designing on the spot, which I was familiar and confident with, but after three weeks I found that they had given the spot to a 45-year old black woman that typed with her index fingers, fucking BEE bias. The sad thing was that was life was repeating itself, sure I was becoming popular around the bars and clubs, lads by the dozens shook my hand at the first sight of me, but I was still in this depressive state, going nowhere with my life, just like before. The thing that played to my advantage was that I had already been here before, so getting out wouldn't be an issue, well so I thought. It was easier as a child as I didn't make the decisions, but now I had to, but what do I choose? The fight and fire inside me was worth more than a minimum wage mining job, but I had nothing else to choose from. Luckily the universe once again came through for me, and provided answers as it always has... but the answers didn't come cheap.

I was at some car rally event being hosted on the casino grounds, chasing tail to fill the void and drinking beer with Ray and some biker friends I had made. Some guy started talking a lot of shit because his girlfriend took a shine to my Greek looks and accent, so I stood up and confronted him, telling him that he should go talk to his bird about it instead, but in a very harsh way, I wasn't one to hold back. He didn't appreciate the tone, and wanted to fight, so I got myself ready, but when he saw I meant business he phoned someone, but not just anyone, he phoned Doug. Doug at this point had been kicked out of his house, been on drugs for a while, and was living the hard street life South Africa had to offer. Deep inside I was ready to face this bully, and get my revenge for those years of torment, but the phone was turned on loud speaker, so that I could hear each word. Doug mentioned bringing a 9mm pistol to take care of the situation; meaning kill me. Living on the streets of South Africa, especially as a druggy, was a dangerous lifestyle, so it made sense to always carry a firearm or even a knife with you, should things go differently to what you had expected. It was always evident that he was jealous of me; I had a better shot at education than he did, I had some money, more friends, and he definitely hated me over dating Sarah, he had some kind of evil lust for her, but he would never score with that personality. I stood my ground, and called my friends too, but I didn't ask anyone to fight for me, I asked my friends who owned guns to lend me their piece; I had played enough video games, watched enough TV, seen enough war documentary's to aide my chance of survival in a gun fight. None of my friends answered their phones, and his friends were on their way up, so I did what any rational person with logic did, I slipped away from the venue, got home, and laid low for a few days. I recall getting on the bike and heading down to one of my friends on the other side of town, where we sat in a park talking about all the shit I was feeling. One of his friends walked up to us; to lend a smoke, but overheard me saying that I wanted to kill myself. He walked away after that sentence and came back about fifteen minutes later with a 9mm pistol. I didn't know this guy at all, but he changed the way I valued my own life. He stated that it was a bold statement to make, and that I as a man should never say something I can't follow up on. He handed me the 9mm and told me to be a man, to follow up on my claim. "It's already loaded," he mentioned as I took the handgun from him, all I needed to do was pull the trigger, so I put the 9mm against my right temple, and squeezed the trigger. The gun let out a click and it became obvious that he had rid it of ammunition before handing it to me, which was probably a good idea. Two things came from that encounter; (i) always be a man of your word, people won't take you seriously if you just talk, and (ii) you are here for a reason, there could have been bullets in the chamber, but something made him take them out, so there has to be a purpose for us all.

 Sylvain heard of the situation with Doug, and understood how frustrated I was; getting nowhere with interviews or with life in general, so he and Audrey had a long chat, and bought me a ticket to Cyprus, for a two-month break away from everything, to clear my head. It was sad, because it seemed like he was giving up on me, and didn't want me free loading off of him until I was thirty-five, which made sense, but he had to understand I tried hard, and it was extremely difficult for white people to get a job in South Africa without knowing anyone. I said goodbye to Brennan, who seemed like my only friend at the time, got my bags packed and set out to OR Tambo international airport, a place that I started getting all too familiar with.

 I walked to customs where Sylvain gave me a hug, said goodbye and left immediately afterwards, he said it was due to him feeling uncomfortable driving in the dark, but personally I think I was on his last nerv. With no plan in mind, and no sense of direction as to where I was going in this world, I walked through customs, border control and the duty free, and awaited the Arabic wings of hope. Being a nervous flier, I blared music from the complementary headphones the hostess handed us and listened to nothing but Linkin Park, hoping that if we went down that I'd go down listening to the band that started it all. After nine hours of being in the air, we arrived in Abu Dhabi, which was hotter than South Africa by a long shot. I got off the plane, followed the signs and asked relevant people as to where I should go, and found myself outside another platform, this time waiting two hours for the connecting flight. I got myself a fizzy drink and tried staying awake, as I was extremely tired; sleeping on a plane is not an option, and had a few smokes in the designated smoking room, which was like half a kilometre walk away from my gate. I got on the flight, and once again feared for my life, but my fatigue outweighed the fear, and I passed out almost instantly. Four or five hours passed before we landed in Larnaka. With morning breath and messy hair, I made my way through the airport, to a section where many people were standing, waiting for their loved ones. I walked through the sliding doors, and saw Audrey and Gabriel waiting for me. I still hated her for not being there for us, had she stayed Jerome would have lived, but if I blamed anyone for the loss of Jerome, I blamed myself and no one else. My hair had grown out of control, it was a thick, curly, afro at the time, but it didn't stop Audrey from taking me to the airport coffee shop, where she probably introduced me to the world's greatest beverage, the Frappe; a cold, coffee-flavoured beverage, best served with ice, especially during a 40 °C heat wave. We drove home in Mother's maroon Nissan, all the way down to Paphos, which was about an hour and a half long drive. We chatted about things we never got to chat about all those years. She was proud of me for standing tall during such a tough time, for finishing school despite what people had said. She told me that I should be proud of myself too, because not many kids in the world have had the misfortunes I had had in this life, and it should be what made me unique, but I didn't know how I felt about it, so I let that conversation die out. We drove up a mountain, which had a radio tower on the summit, to where Audrey lived. It was a big piece of land; dry grass and sand covering the property, along with a house that definitely wasn't built by professionals. "Ger built most of this house himself," Audrey proceeded to tell me, as she knew I was very fussy when it came to things, and for good reason. The shitty craftsmanship burnt my eyes, but I went with it, not like I had much choice. We parked the car, got the bags, and proceeded to go inside. Ger must not have heard us open the loud squeaky gate, as the porn channel he left on was blaring some blonde bimbos moaning. 'Great start,' I thought to myself. I shook his hand, unfortunately, and mother proceeded to make my favourite dish, spaghetti bolognaise. There was literally nothing to do on this lonely mountain, nothing, other than catch up with Gabriel, and play computer games with him, which I really enjoyed. We went down to a pub beside the beach, where Audrey treated me and gave me my first shot of Uzo, the Greek spirit from hell. Father gave me a call a couple days into this new adventure I had taken on, to check up on me, and also to inform me that another letter came in the post, this time from Wits. He hadn't opened it yet; he believed in privacy. I asked Sylvain to open it while I was on the phone, but he just repeated the same line Pretoria had used, I wasn't surprised by it. I felt slightly angry at Jerome for what he did, because it cost me admission into fine universities, but I didn't want to be selfish and blame him for anything, he was in a better place and I had to face what life put in front of me, besides he had his own, unknown reasons for the act, despite Audrey's 'speculation'. I inquired about Universities in Cyprus, and Audrey told me about one, that was close enough to where we were, Neapolis University. Coincidentally, Audrey had introduced me to one of Ger's cousins or nephews, a family member anyway, her name was Chrissie, and she was the nicest lady I had ever met. We mentioned the university and our plans to Chrissie. She told us that her husband Valentine; what a great name, had been doing his master's degree in real estate there and would be able to help me get in. Between Chrissie, Valentine and Audrey, they had formalised a plan, and gotten me an interview with some higher up of the university. We phoned Sylvain that night, but I wanted to speak to him privately, so there was no loud speaker this time.

"Papa, I am going to apply for this university, but I don't have money to pay for it, and Mommy won't help, so if I get in could you please pay for the first year? I will work extremely hard to get a bursary or a grant to finish the other three years, or I'll get a job on the side and save up some money to pay for it." I started off after he asked why I was calling him. It angered me so how all my friends, and even people I met later on in life had education thrown upon them and there I was begging for a chance.

"Malcolm, I want you to succeed and make your life, I will pay for this year, but first let's see if they accept you, and if they do, send me a quote of how much it will cost and I'll pay for it," he thoughtfully answered.

"Thank you so much, Papa, I won't let you down, thank you!" I exclaimed, excited that I may just get another shot at this law degree.

"But I want you to understand also, that if you get accepted, mama took half of my savings, pension, house, cars, shares, and I also had to pay for the funeral and tombstone," – which in fairness is expensive in South Africa – "so please, don't waste my money or your time. Also ask Mama if she can maybe put some euros aside for the next year for you," he told me. I don't recall ever asking Audrey for the money, as she mentioned that she had converted her Euros to Sterling, and placed it in a long-term fixed account, that could only be accessed in tough times, or when Gabriel turned 18, so that she could pay for his university. It didn't make sense that she would let him have his dreams, and keep me from mine, but I was under her roof, and her messed up husband already disliked me, so I had to keep my mouth shut. A few days went by, I got my messy afro cut; my small beard shaved, and got neat clothes on, ready for the interview with this director. We sat there, he asked about primary and secondary education, and I provided the documents I had with me; I took my final reports with me just in case of anything. He asked me several questions, from simple things like was I willing to take an English test; bitch please, to complex things where I had to use my brain, but he found the answers he was looking for. The director then asked me what I wanted to study, and I told him law, thinking there is no way anyone will deny me now.

"Unfortunately, law is out of the question, as all of our law courses from first year till fourth year are given in Greek," he stated. Fuck! Another milestone. I sat there; quiet for like twenty seconds, quickly thinking whether I had it within myself to learn a new language, with characters I couldn't yet comprehend.

"I see, what other courses are available here?" I asked, hoping I could pick something that had some law in it, which would aide me if I ever got to study it. He listed out several courses the university had offered, and I struggled to pick, not because I feared that I'd fail, but because I didn't want to pick something I didn't want to learn. So, I chose to do a BSc in Real Estate Development and Valuation, which covered basic engineering, geography, finance, statistics, accounting, economics, law, and of course, real estate. We went home to inform Sylvain, who didn't seem very happy with my choice, but it's what I signed for, so we went with it. I mentioned the cost of the studies to father as Audrey emailed him the quote, €12 000, 12 000 fucking euros, that's twice the price Pretoria and Wits asked for. Sylvain didn't seem too happy with it, but he asked for the university's banking details, and he would wire the money to them once off when university started.

I hadn't even been in Cyprus for two months yet and I was making more progress there than in dead-beat South Africa. I tried to stay outdoors as much as possible, not only because I was lonely in my little, warm, dusty outside room, but because I wanted to be there for Gabriel in the way I wasn't there for Jerome, however I also wanted to monitor the situation between my mother and Ger. I honestly didn't like him, and there was something about him that just screamed out dickhead. I always loved my mother, and respected her as she tried to bring me up in the best possible way, but we all make mistakes, and I was extremely angry with her mistakes, an anger that I don't think passed for a long time. Ger worked in one of the five-star hotels beside the beach, and didn't really earn a lot of money, but it was still enough to sustain basic needs. Then came one evening, which showed me his true colours; Mother had made dinner, but there wasn't enough to fill us as usual, and we had to make do with what we had until Ger's pay check came through. Audrey mentioned the food shortage to Ger, trying to be secretive about it, but when you grow up being a leader in a boys boarding school, you learn to hear everything. Ger stood up, walked over to the counter where the plastic plates had been laid out, and dished himself a handsome plate full. There wasn't enough food for Audrey, Gabriel and me, so Audrey dished up for Lala and me, gave us the plates along with cutlery, and headed to the make shift porch; that bore more wind chimes than a wind chime shop, to fill her belly with smoke. I looked at Gabriel's plate, and it was a relatively good portion of food, enough to fill him. I looked at my plate, and it wasn't as much as Gabriel's, but it would suffice. I stood up, looked Ger dead in the eyes, in total disgust and walked past him and placed the plate on the counter top. I followed the smell of a fresh lit cigarette outside, where I found Audrey in tears, puffing away on a smoke. She tried hiding the tears and the situation, but I was well aware of her secretive ways.

"Mommy, go eat," I told her.

"I had a big lunch today, I'm really not hungry," she replied, trying to justify why she wasn't eating with everyone else.

"Mommy, we both know that even if you weren't eating that you would still sit there with us," I told her, having observed my family well over the weekends I spent with them.

"There's nothing to eat, Mikki Mou, he didn't buy bread, there's only a little cereal left for Gabriel in the morning, I can't make anything because we haven't bought anything to make," she openly admitted.

"Go and eat my food!" I commanded her, trying to be the man my father raised.

"Mikki, I can't eat your food, you need to grow and be strong, I will be okay till tomorrow," she said, trying to avoid the situation. I can't remember what exactly happened, but I don't think either of us ate the food, and starved together. After Ger went to work the next day, Audrey took us to Chrissie, who I presume lent her money, but on the way there she mentioned that she had used a lot of my father's money to renovate Ger's house, she had bought him a car, and she even purchased him new clothes and had started backing him financially.

It explained why Audrey wouldn't even offer to cover the expense of her child reaching his dreams. I was fuming, not as bad as the axe situation years earlier, but I really wanted to fight with him, but I knew that Audrey and Gabriel were in a very bad situation, and if I reacted in any way, that it could land them in big trouble, so I kept quiet, subliminally hinting at her to divorce Ger. I'd say not even a week passed before we were faced with a similar situation, but this time Audrey put her boys first and dished for us first and then put an equal amount between her and Ger.

"What bullshit is this?" he blurted out, "I work hard, long hours to pay for this food, and your deadbeat son takes all the food!" I understood his point, I should have contributed a bit too, but I didn't have any money, other than the R6000 father gave me before leaving South Africa, which was used to buy food too. It seemed that he forgot that most of the appliances in the house had been purchased by Audrey, and only saw me taking his food.

"If you want to switch plates I don't mind, Ger," I suggested, but he didn't want any of it.

"You need to leave; I don't want you in my house anymore," he said firmly, trying to back his authority with a deep voice. Audrey jumped in at this point.

"Hey, guys, let's just eat and go to bed, it's been a long day," she tried resolving it as she knew I didn't have anywhere else to go, other than the streets.

"No, I want him out, now!" Ger shouted at Mom. I didn't know if Audrey had this protocol laid out for Gabriel, because he put his plate down on the table and retreated to his room, where he closed the door behind him. "Audrey, I want him out, I pay for this food and he does nothing but enjoy his life, now I'm putting my foot down, if he isn't out immediately, then I will get the police to escort you and Gabriel out with him," Ger shouted out.

What a fucking prick, I thought to myself, he sweet-talked her into cheating on my dad, suggested divorcing Sylvain because he could love her better, and told her that if she married him, he would gladly raise Gabriel as his own, all those lies to get laid. You could see Audrey was shocked, but didn't want to say the wrong thing, so as always, I stood up, and made the decisions.

"Mommy, it will be fine, I will just go," I said to her, before turning to Ger, telling him.

"Ger, look the food was made, and it will be a waste if we don't eat it, so can we eat in peace and then I'll go to sleep in my room. Tomorrow, I'll gather my things and leave you all in peace." Gabriel overheard the argument through his closed door and barged into the room, in tears, yelling.

"That's my brother, how can you do this to my brother?" But he ran away before he could get an answer. It was sad to see a nine-year old fight against an injustice, but he wasn't old enough to have the emotional intelligence to understand Ger's side too. Ger fought a bit longer but then ultimately agreed to my suggestion. Audrey didn't eat the rest of her food, I didn't touch my plate either, and I think Gabriel cried himself to sleep that night. I really felt bad for Gabriel, he lived alone with them on this mountain, with no neighbours, no friends, and the one person he could confide in, laugh with and spend time with was getting kicked out, other than that he use to play online games with Jerome sometimes, and Jerome wasn't there anymore. He was so precious to me, and I didn't want to break his little heart by going, but I didn't want to see him on the streets or witness Audrey wheeling and dealing for a room to sleep in. Knowing Audrey, she probably had a plan B in place when it came to this, but it more than likely involved her sleeping on the ground so her sons could share a bed. This is where a man puts his hatred and anger aside, and looks after his family first, making the decision that's best for the ones you love and not for yourself. Ger sat alone in front of his TV, where he watched some horse racing event, and Audrey and I retreated to the porch, where we lit smokes and spoke. I told her that I wanted her and Gabriel to be in a warm bed and have food in their tummy's, and not to try fight him to save me, I would be fine, I had been through a lot, and nothing this world put on my path could hurt as much as losing Jerome. She didn't like how modest I was being, but she ended up agreeing with me and letting me go.

We went to bed and I laid there, fearing being homeless, asking God why he had put me through very tough things other kids don't ever get to experience, but I fell asleep before I could get any answer.

Elliot feels the sleep deprivation kick in, and unclicks the pen, picks his broken, anxiety filled self-up and heads to the bed where Katrien is sleeping in. He jumps in beside her, turns over on his side to hold her, to feel something real before closing his eyes.

Somewhere in the earlier hours of the morning, Katrien wakes to shouting and screaming, it's dark, she can't see Elliot, but she can feel him constantly moving, tossing and turning, fighting something. She places her hand on Elliot's forehead, trying to hush him as you would a baby, but she feels the sweat dripping. She doesn't know what to do; she holds his hand, hoping that he'll calm down. It works, but now she's awake, and can't exactly leave Elliot alone to face these demons. She lies there, thinking about her situation, about her father, about how she fell in love with a broken man, that seems to still be stuck on an ex. She thinks about Henrick, somewhat feeling sorry for him, she knows that his world revolves around her, he may have chosen drugs and booze over her, but it's because he doesn't know how to cope with the pressures of life. Between guilt and confusion she gets up, runs to the bathroom, and ends up vomiting in the toilet. She feels stressed, all of it, playing on her nerves, causing her to feel sick. She can't do this anymore, she wants Elliot, but she is only twenty-seven years old, she doesn't know how to handle this stress. Katrien is too quick to judge, assuming that Elliot is giving all now to be a prick later on; she doesn't take into consideration how he'd feel if she just abandoned him. In a swoop of selfishness, Katrien grabs her possessions, her car keys, and heads out the door, leaving a note for Elliot to read when he defeats his nightmares.

Chapter 17
All Grown Up

Morning breaks, Elliot wakes up.

"Good morning, beautiful," he quietly says as he turns around to face Katrien. His eyes catch the indented pillow her head had rested in. Shocked, he jumps into a seated position, trying to hear any movement in the house, only to hear a sizzling sound. *'She's making breakfast,'* he thinks to himself, allowing the anxiety and paranoia to settle. Elliot puts on his slippers, and makes his way to the kitchen where he can't wait to have a homemade breakfast. Elliot walks through the door, and looks over to the left, into the kitchen but notices that there's no one there, the stove is off. Elliot turns to the right, and sees the front door wide open, he walks up to it, trying to see if her car is still there. There is no car, his heart sinks, she ditched him, he notices that the sizzling sound was actually the rustling of leaves caused by the windy breeze. Elliot lowers his head, in emotional agony, and closes the door on his dreams. He walks over to the table, to escape the pain of her leaving by delving in the pain of his life, a horrible choice. Elliot notices a piece of paper, lying on top of where he left off, signed by Katrien:

"Elliot, I'm sorry that you had to wake up to an empty home. Things are just too much for me at the moment, I can't deal with everything... I need a break. I hope you understand.
Katrien"

Elliot reads the words with no emotions, crumples the paper up with one hand and throws it against the wall, yelling, "Fuck you!" He is hurt; he tried so hard, he doesn't understand what he did wrong. He doesn't care anymore, and reaches for his pen, ready to write until his arm goes numb.

Morning not only brought the sun and birds out, but also brought my fears into play, and as always I started my day with a cigarette. As I puffed away, I stared out into the little forest behind the house, wandering what I was going to do. I was about five months away from starting university, and only then could I get the accommodation that Sylvain had paid for. I didn't tell Sylvain about the situation, I didn't want him to worry, but I also had no way of contacting him as I wasn't allowed inside the main house anymore. I got in Audrey's car about an hour later and headed down the mountain with her, and once I left that main gate I was homeless. We set out, looking for an apartment or room to rent, something cheap to last me at least a month. After about I'd say 3 hours of searching, I realised it was time to submit to the streets, but luckily, we came across this block of apartments that had a banner hanging on the side of it, with a contact number. Audrey called the number, explained the situation, and this guy was there within an hour. Once this Cypriot landlord arrived, we shook hands, and he showed us the place. It was clean, big enough for one person, close to places where I could find work, but the price was important at this point. I hesitated asking for the price, as I only had €350 in my pocket.

"€250 for the month, then €50 to register you on the electricity," he mentioned after Audrey had asked. There's so much I can do with the remaining 50, but it wasn't enough to survive with. Ger was gracious enough to get me an interview with the Food and Beverage manager of the hotel he worked in later on that day. We took the apartment, got registered on the electricity and headed down to the hotel for the interview. We met the six-foot tall, suit-wearing manager, who resembled the stereotypical business-type man and walked into his office ready for the interview. It was sad that Mommy had to hold my hand during the interview, but it went well and he told me to buy suit pants and white shirts for the job, as I was starting on the coming Monday. I can't say that I was excited, because this isn't where I pictured myself when I laid on the grass late at night, staring up at the stars, fighting with myself to keep my promise to Jerome, but I needed to survive first. We headed to some Russian store that sold cheap clothing, trying to make the most of the €50 note in my pocket. I laugh whenever I look back at this memory, because now I only wear slim fit pants, designer shirts and blazers, but in that shop, my God, if it covered me the way they wanted me covered then I bought it. The final price came to like €53 something, but mother spotted me the difference, luckily. With that we headed back to my new 'home', where Audrey's phone kept ringing, it was more than likely Ger, wanting her home immediately, or wanting to know where she had been for the past seven hours. My guess was always good and she mentioned that Ger wanted her home, immediately, it was time to make dinner, but told me that she felt bad leaving me there on my own.

"It is what it is," I replied, implying that she should go home and leave life to unveil itself. With that she left, more than likely in tears; she wasn't as strong as she tried appearing in front of company. I closed the door behind her, sat at the head of this big, brown four-seater table, with nothing but an empty cup I had used as an ashtray and about seven smokes in a crumpled packet in front of me. I lit a smoke and reached for my phone in the centre of the table. I needed music to kill the silence, so I switched on some metal band I was listening to at the time, and kind of mumbled the lyrics as the smoke left my throat. About 20 minutes passed, I was in the same seat, same position, but only now the smoke was long dead and I was practicing my air guitar skills to a different band. Mid guitar solo there was a knock on my door, I paused the song, held my lighter tight in a clenched fist; as I always do when I feel threatened, ready to fight anyone.

"Who's there?" I loudly asked, knowing that I knew no one in this country and no one knew where I lived.

"It's Mommy," I heard, recognising Audrey's voice through the thin PVC door. I unlocked the door with the single brass key, and let her in, questioning why she had come back. She had bought me some ham slices, a loaf of bread and a six-pack of beer. I couldn't cook, so it was pointless buying me anything to make. Despite her financial predicament, she had scraped together a few euros to help me get by. Before she left, she handed me like eight smokes, and mentioned that she would visit *me the next day while Ger was at work. She left again, for real this time, so I decided to have a beer, and sat in the same place, listening to the song I had paused, mostly in thought as I held the beer tilted in front of me. The days went by quick, and finally I was at the hotel, dressed in my two sizes too big uniform and taken to the restaurant where I'd be a waiter for the next 3 months. At first it was weird to be serving people, cleaning tables and carrying drinks around, but I got used to it pretty quick, thanks to the half South African manager I was given too. I made friends with most of the guys, but I struggled with the Romanians, they would always be in the bar after service, drinking, talking about fights and betting on sports. It's not that I wasn't use to it by then, I was just in that frame of mind where I understood that I could no longer surround myself with these kinds of people. I wasn't sure whether I was naturally lucky or if God had my back despite my insults, but there was always a beneficial factor to every bad thing I had ever faced, and in this sense, especially regarding my food situation, there was an answer. The hotel had served free food to its employees down in the staff canteen. The ham and bread Audrey had bought me was finished within three days, but I was too proud to submit to the canteen food, so I starved for about three days, pouring myself nothing but water whenever we headed down on breaks. I was logged onto the hotels Wi-Fi and would regularly sit in the canteen texting Audrey, telling her how I was doing and so on. I had mistakenly mentioned my food situation to her, but tried reassuring her that I was fine, that worrying about me was pointless; she knew I was suffering, but also understood that I was too proud to admit anything. She eventually called my manager on the fourth day and explained the situation to him. I was already weak, starving, nearly passing out every time I stood up, so when break came, my manager followed me to the canteen and noticed that I went for the regular glass of water, and sat down at the same table, waiting for my peers to return with their food. Before my colleagues returned, he sat beside me, and inquired about my eating habits. At first, I was a rock, and told him that I had had a big breakfast, that I was still full from it, but he was a great manager, and started relating to my way of thinking. He eventually convinced me to walk over to the food stand with him to grab some grub. I packed my plate with everything on offer, even with veggies; I hated vegetables; but starvation has no dislikes. From that day on, I walked into the canteen like I owned the place and ate till I couldn't move, and why not? Take what the world offers you, always.*

I didn't enjoy this way of life, but I fought hard, waking up to 30° of heat, wearing long sleeved shirts in such humidity, walking about 2 kilometres every day in the blistering sun, trying to earn my place in this world. My new shoes had cut into the cartilage of both my feet, my toes were full of blisters, and don't even get me started on the buckets of sweat I was leaking. I still never looked it as suffering to survive; it was more an internal struggle to prove myself and everyone else wrong. I wanted to push myself beyond what I knew, to learn more about how much I can take and keep moving forward. The worst part of my first employment experience was boredom, because I; by law, had to be off at least twice a week. It seems like a dream to most, but being stuck in a house with no TV, no internet, no washing machine, no friends, nothing, is utter shit. I'd buy a six-pack of beer on each pay day, to congratulate myself on surviving another month. It seemed like a great idea at the time, but it wasn't, especially with so much time to myself, and the raw memories of Jerome...still haunting my woke mind. I'd start my first beer in sync with cool club music, the second, third and fourth beer was accompanied by my metal preferences. The fifth beer would be accompanied by old songs that I use to sing with Jerome and Sylvain whenever we drove back to school, and on the sixth beer I'd be knee high deep in tears, listening to Jerome's favourite songs, drowning in mucus as I sang along. It's not that I enjoyed torturing myself, it was more the matter of I could release emotions without anyone seeing or knowing about it. After my second month of work I found myself considering taking Jerome's way out once again, I didn't see the point of working so hard for €600 a month, how was I going to save for an education? How would I save to support a family? Sure, I still had university to go through, but I had 0 confidence in myself, and in my mind, I had failed university long before I even attended the first lecture. I sat by my table one evening, with the pocket knife I had bought, in tears, feeling alone, as if everyone had abandoned me because I was a problem. I had not spoken to my father in almost two months; Audrey came maybe once a week to see if I was still alive, women didn't take notice of me, so finding a companion was a mission, I was lonely as hell. With all that pain I started cutting my left wrist, firstly horizontally, across the veins, but after the fifth cut I started enjoying the pain, like an addiction, so I went vertically, but I cut myself only once before I snapped out of it. I had spilt a good few drops of blood on the notebook I had opened on the table in front of me. I would regularly jot down some poem, or short story, to help me cope with what I was feeling towards life, but my most recent poetry was more or less ruined by the red confessions leaking from my wrist. After my 3rd month of employment, my manager approached me and asked me whether I wanted to move to the dispenser bar, something most of the Romanian guys wanted badly. I knew that this was a serious move as whoever worked there needed to cater to the beverage needs of 1200 people at each sitting, and he/she needed to move quickly. I was happy that he considered me for the spot, but I was mostly happy at the fact that I'd be working in my own space, the fridge. The 'fridge' that I had been placed in had a set temperature of 4 °C, which was perfect for me. Whenever I started feeling cold, I would just walk out into the scorching heat of Cyprus. I had my drinks laid out perfectly, along with a notepad beside me where I kept tally of the drinks going out; I'm not sure whether it was required or not, but I felt it was important to do, to get an understanding of what was being sold most, so that I could prep better. I worked opposite the kitchen, where I took a shine to this Ukrainian girl, Yuliana. She was beautiful, and her smile lit a fire inside me. I had mentioned to her how much I loved strawberry yoghurt, having noticed her handling all the yoghurts, so she started preparing a bowl for me every morning. While I worked away, getting my bar in order and serving drinks, she would regularly walk past me, giving me the 'eyes' and warm smiles. My hormones were hard to control around her, and I could only think of one thing, but sadly it never came to that...

Right when I started falling in love with her and being at the hotel every day, they cut my hours, as it was no longer tourist season. I wasn't too worried as university was in about a weeks' time, and I was ready for it all, but I was sad that I'd never see her again. One night, another waiter and I headed to a local bar, for a beer, it's always one beer isn't it? As we were seated, watching the live music on stage and drinking a pint, we noticed two girls behind us. One had brown hair, wore blue jeans and some cleavage-friendly shirt, the other had blonde hair and a red dress on. I got a paper from the barman, who had this point was my closest friend, along with a pen, and proceeded to write down my name and number; I was always too shy to speak to girls, and this was very unconventional, but I didn't expect anything from it. I walked over to their table on my way out, and whispered.

"I think you're beautiful," in the girl wearing the red dress's ear, and handed the paper over. I took about twenty-five steps away from the bar before my phone sounded my message tone. What? This actually worked? It was her, and she had asked me to get back to the bar, followed by that not so innocent 'x' at the end of the text. I spoke to my friend, and told him that he could have the other one, but he wanted the Blondie, which I wasn't going to settle for, like we were friends and that's it, not more, me first, then you was my approach to this. We got back to them, introduced ourselves, and waited for them to introduce themselves, but they had the thickest Scottish accents I had ever come across. It was clear that they were speaking English, but what they were saying was beyond me. We suggested heading up town to the club, to which they agreed. We drank, sang songs, danced; I suck at dancing so I just bopped my head to the beat. About three hours in, this blonde girl started getting tipsy, flirty and very touchy. I wasn't complaining…I hadn't experienced this kind of feeling in a while, so I was all in baby. We walked down to the Coral Bay Beach after several minutes of wet smooches. It was dark, the moonlight shone so innocently on the calm Mediterranean Sea. There were several hundred beach loungers laying everywhere, which people rented out for €2 a day, but there was no money collector this late at night. She pushed me on the lounger, got on top of me, started kissing and feeling me up. After a few minutes of play, she proceeded down, unzipped my regular fit slacks; I still hadn't changed my work clothes. She proceeded to give me a painful blowjob, to which I kind of complained, but defused the situation by wanting to kiss her. Before we could go any further someone with a torch walked up the beach from the northern side, so we got dressed and acted like a couple who wanted to play in the water. We headed back to the club, which stayed open until 5 A.M., to find my friend; who we had left with Blondie's friend, on his phone, drinking a pint on his own. I kind of had the idea that she would ditch him, but when we inquired about where she had gone, he pointed towards the dance floor, where we saw her making out with a six-foot tall Brit. It was about 4 A.M. when she called a taxi, eager to get back to the apartment she was renting for the next three days. I started walking away, trying to imagine how I was going to function at work in three hours' time. She pulled me by the arm, telling me that I was going with her. We got into the taxi; she sat in front and left me at the back with these two lovers that couldn't leave each other's goods alone. Once we got to the apartment, both the girls took off their clothes, and proceeded to the back of the complex, where they jumped into a huge swimming pool. The Brit jumped in with them, but I still had an issue taking my shirt off in public, so I sat with my legs in the water, joking with them. My Scot got out of the water, and put her dress back on without drying herself off, drenching the dress in the process. She grabbed my hand, and took me up several flights of stairs, to the roof of the apartments. We looked over the ledge to see her friend getting fucked by the side of the pool; she was on her back, with no clothes on, and the lights shone brightly on her jiggling white titties. Blondie placed her hand on my appendix area, and proceeded down, where she unbuckled my belt and unzipped the trousers. We started kissing, and I slid the straps of her dress down her shoulders, letting them hang by her elbows. Her black bra came off pretty quick, despite my inexperience, and even though she was petite in stature, her boobs followed a different code. She took her arms out of the straps and let the bra slide down. My body shook with a devilish lust as we continued. The sun was in its early stages of rising, and the red beam crept over the horizon, but it didn't stop us. We sat down, and touched one another. She couldn't control herself anymore and stood up, only to sit down on me a few seconds later. As she lowered herself, she moaned almost in sync with her friends several stories down. We finished up and got dressed. I told her that I needed to get ready for work, and invited her on a social media platform before leaving. I got a taxi back to my place, but it was already 6:10, and there was no point sleeping. I jumped into my cold shower; it was expensive to switch on the boiler, but every day was around 38°C, so cold water was the norm. I got dressed in a cleaner, un-ironed uniform, and preceded down the road, towards the hotel. I was so tired, and had booked myself in for a 14-hour shift. The day went by, and even though I was sleepy through most of it, I did what needed to be done.

During breakfast service I would be prepping my bar, during lunch and dinner I was serving all that I had prepped, and as soon as the last customer left the dining area, I would close up and go for my smoke. After my cigarette I helped out as a waiter, catering for a few hundred people invited to celebrate a wedding in one of the huge event rooms the hotel had.

A few days later, Mother picked me up and took me to the university to enrol myself. I found myself in a queue of mostly Greek speaking learners, eyeing out the cute girls... There was one girl who took my attention by storm, she had short hair, like a boy, and wore tracksuit pants with a white t-shirt. I always liked the odd things in life, things that stood out from the rest, and in this crowd of girls obviously trying to get attention from the guys here, with their tight clothing, and make-up to the 9's, it was clear that she was completely different. She had headphones on, had been bopping her head to the beat of whatever she was listening too, and smiled at me when she noticed me staring at each detail of her. She had such a cute face, with big eyes, like one of those Japanese Anime girls come to life, but with a Greek twist; Surprisingly arousing.

I successfully enrolled myself into the university, got back into Mom's maroon car and called up the landlord that had rented me this warm apartment, to give him notice of my departure. He understood, and promised to give me back the €50 deposit on the electricity; sadly, I never saw a cent of it. Audrey snuck away from Ger, and came down to the apartment to help me pack and move into the university. Blankets, pillows and the very few clothing items I had, all fit perfectly into two black bags. We got to the university, where I was allocated room 249. This room was possibly the best room in the university, in my opinion anyway. It overlooked the long, circular shaped swimming pool, and from the balcony I could see the cafeteria and the seating area beside the pool; the perfect vantage point in my sick military mind. The room itself had an attached bathroom, a desk with two chairs, and two single beds side by side, which I covered with a double bed sheet; as it was all I had, but I always slept on the side closest to the door; my first double bed, kinda. I moved one of the chairs onto the balcony, so that I had a place to sit when I wanted to enjoy my early morning smoke. The fresh morning smell, that you could smell anywhere in the world, blended so well with the salty smell of the Mediterranean Sea; which was about 500 meters away from the university. Classes began, and the first lecturer asked if there was anyone in the class that was not from Greece or Cyprus, in a class of about a hundred and fifty students I raised my hand, along with five or six other kids. There was one guy from Russia, who quickly became my friend, a girl from

Ukraine, another girl from England, a lad from China, and a few others from various parts of Europe. As soon as I mentioned South Africa to the lecturer when it was my turn to answer, the entire class turned around, and stared at me. Was I the first white African they had ever seen in their lives?

The days went on, and I ended up introducing myself to that girl with the short hair that I liked. She seemed rather interested in me, something I didn't expect at all, I still had no confidence. We started hanging out regularly, sitting beside one another on lectures, going for frappes on a daily basis, and meeting in my room to make out. The hallways were remarkably similar to most hotels; smoky-grey carpets, white walls, and glossy white MDF doors with gold door handles. Across from my door, was the door of a short, shy girl, who kept to herself a lot, beside me, closest to the elevator was a tall girl, who had a very Irish-structured face, and on my other side was a short, chubby girl that loved to party. Classes went on, and I was fairly content with how quickly I was adapting to this, my back was once again against the ropes, I had no one in my corner believing that I could pull this off. I was scared that I wouldn't be intelligent enough to cope here, and would fail, failing myself and my father in the process. Classes were optional, and many students avoided early morning lessons, something that was completely new to me, having been in a boarding school, where we were forced to wake up at 5:30. I didn't want to slack at all, so every morning I had my shower, got dressed, walked down to the cafeteria, got myself a coffee and a cereal or eggs on toast, and took my classes as I promised myself. I was still mad at the fact that I had invested so much time in learning law prior to leaving school, and now I had to learn all these business things, which I surprisingly picked up fast. My favourite subject had to be Eco 101, which seemed like such a complicated thing on day 1, but after the 3rd class it made so much sense. My gaming history, especially in the field of strategy games, where you had to build and maintain civilisations or empires via means of economic situations really played a huge role in me understanding this better. During my time at this tertiary educational facility, I managed to keep my job as a barman at the hotel, which really took a turn for the worst. I would wake up at 5:30 most mornings, do a few push ups, go on my knees; despite my anger at God for the loss of Jerome, and pray for a good day, and that he would bless the people I knew with a good day too, go to all my lectures, focus on every detail I was being taught, then run back to my room to change into my uniform so that I could work as a barman till 11P.M, get the €1,50 bus back to the university, go through the notes I had taken in the lecture, only to pass out on the papers and books at around 1 am. The cycle continued for a few weeks, until the hotel laid me off, the season ended, and they weren't making enough money to keep us all employed, and with me having my fingers in other pies, it was easier to let me go than the next person. Saving money was awkward, as I had no idea how to cook, something I should have learnt by my father, the only thing I knew how to make was pasta, so that's what I had, with ketchup every evening, which helped me save a good few quid. Some evenings I was sick of eating the same thing, and went to the nearby South African restaurant, to have the South African cider I had missed dearly, along with the foods I longed for, which was pretty expensive. I despised the kids around me, they didn't need to work for shit, drove roadsters, wore designer clothing, even this girl I was seeing was more privileged than what I was. Monday to Friday they'd all be out, drinking coffees and going to the beach, but there I was, putting the effort in. Friday nights they'd be out, drinking and doing drugs, and I'd be in front of the laptop Audrey had bought me for my 19th birthday, out of the money she had put aside for Gabriel's education. Luckily, he had consented to the purchase. Saturday's; well most weekend days were somewhat awkward for me, as I would be in bed, trying to study, but all I could hear was the tall girl next to me, moaning, getting banged by this guy I presumed was her boyfriend. I would move to my desk, which was closer to the short girl, who was also experiencing this university on her back, faking her moans to stimulate her lover's performance. Thank you, Nathaniel Baldwin for inventing the earphones. Despite the sexual ventures of my neighbours, I sat in front of a screen; hoping that my efforts would pay off and that I would succeed. I ended up cheating on the girl I was seeing at the time with one of her friends, scumbag move. I'm not sure how it came to be, she followed me to my room, and we ended up kissing and touching, fortunately it never went further. My short haired fling found out about us, even though it had only been one time. I was seated with my Russian friend Dmitri, on the seats outside the cafeteria, enjoying a soft drink and a smoke before my next lecture. She walked up to us, and asked me if we could speak in private. It's one of those moments, when you just know this won't end well. We walked to the other side of swimming pool, to where none of the 70 plus students seated beside Dmitri could hear us, and told me that she had found out about us from a friend who watched us go into my room together. I'm all for honesty and told her what had happened, with tears in her eyes, she swore at me in Greek, slapped me and walked away; never cheat. The collective awe swooped over the pool, towards my ears as the shot landed on my face. I got over it fast, and went about my business, but I also chose to leave both girls alone. During this time another student entered the university, he was very strange. With the name Artyom, and the body of a young Arnold Schwarzenegger, one could guess that there was more than likely an interesting story behind him. He was from Dagestan, a very rough part of the old Soviet Union. He spoke very little English, and the little he did speak was extremely difficult to comprehend. He didn't want to be in university, as he didn't feel he was smart enough to compete with the other kids. The only passion he had was towards gym and gaming. I felt somewhat sorry for him, his parents had been divorced for a while at the time, and he hated going to lectures, as he didn't understand a thing, having no idea where he was going with life. He attended only two classes in the entire time he was there. Whenever you needed him, he'd either be in the gym, working on putting muscles on his muscles, or in his room playing online games with experienced Russian gamers. We made a deal, that I would take notes for him, and teach the classes to him at his own pace, in exchange for a few of his games, and act as my private trainer in the gym. The European Union had this exchange student programme in place, which saw a few people leave our campus, to go to Lithuania, and in exchange a few Lithuanians would come over to Cyprus. There was one girl, Orelija, (which translated to gold in English), who had caught my eye. She was somewhat busty, and reminded me a lot of a hamster, as she was just as cute and energetic as one, but damn she was smart. Artyom and Dmitri became good friends, expressing mutual views on life in their mother tongue. We formed a little group, which mostly consisted of Russian, Ukrainian and Latvian people, who all spoke Russian by nature, so my level of Russian and understanding of their culture, way of life and mentality improved greatly. Political conversations were avoided at all costs, especially around the time Russian forces started invading Kiev back in 2013. We started introducing this

Orelija girl into our group, as she understood Russian, but it involved allowing her 'know it all', political correct, environmentalist friend in too; not that I had a problem with saving the planet, or being respectful to people of other races or nationalities, I was just in that frame of mind where I questioned who we had to save the world from, from ourselves?

As time away from employment went on, my money quickly ran out, and I had been struggling a bit, but running to Audrey wasn't an option anymore, as she too was running low on the resource I was looking for. So, I manned up, phoned my father, despite our regular conversations on how life was treating me, and asked him to send me money. One could hear the pride leave his body when he asked how much I needed.

"€700, Papa," I told him. I was disgusted in myself, but it is what it is. There was nothing else I could do, I had applied to nearly all the hotels in the vicinity for a job, but the season was against me. I needed to network more, and ended up chatting to a South African who owned a restaurant on the corner of what the locals called 'Bar-Street'. I asked him about jobs, subliminally hinting that I was applying, and he caught my drift, but he mentioned that he had no vacancies as him, his brother and mother worked there, and weren't making enough to take anyone else on, but he did tell me that there were a great number of South Africans in the Paphos region. He mentioned that they normally all met up at the local rugby games. I was sold by the word rugby, and emphasised my enthusiasm in joining the team, so he gave me a number, mentioned practice times and that he would be there to introduce me to the team. I ended up applying for a part time job in the South African restaurant near the university; the one I had previously gone too whenever I missed my favourite cider. The owners; a husband and wife duo, gave me a week-long trial, to which I responded with my best foot forward, but sadly I wasn't what they were looking for. Having failed myself once again, I took to a bottle of wine. I sat on the stairwell behind the cafeteria of the university with a wine glass and a bottle of dry red, hiding from the truth and the other students. In honesty, I was struggling with a few subjects, mostly statistics, had nearly no money left and didn't know how I was going to pull this off, I knew I had fought hard to get to where I was, but I couldn't leave it there and let everyone else be right. I was about three glasses and six smokes in before the cafeteria manager came out for a smoke. He opened the fire exit type door and noticed me somewhat lying on the stairs, listening to metal and staring up at the night sky.

"Is everything okay, Mike?" he asked; everyone seems to call me Mike for some reason, as he walked down the stairs to where I was.

"Uhm...yeah everything is fine, sir," I responded, standing up in the process, trying to be respectful to the imminent conversation. He was an elderly man, always cheerful and glee, the typical grandfather figure, but on top of that, he was very wise. He could tell something was up, and it was obvious that I would never share my pains with anyone, but he somehow worked himself into my thoughts. I had mentioned my fear of failure, my failures at trying to find a job, being in a predicament where I had no choice but to fight, I expressed my anger and jealousy towards the other students and their easy lifestyles. He started simply, saying that every person has their own battles, and just because they aren't fighting theirs now, doesn't mean they will never have too. I emphasised my disappointment in studying real estate, my passion was in fighting injustices and arguing for what I felt was right, the reason I wanted to be a lawyer. He could tell that I was confused, especially after I added military and engineering to the list of things I had been interested in, but what he said after that changed my perception of career completely.

"If money didn't exist, what would you want to do with your life?" Damn, that was fucking deep; I had been so concerned on making the correct choices regarding my financial standpoint in life, that I blindly forgot that happiness and peace were important factors to sustain life. Everyone knows that a competitive mind-set, along with the obsession of money, only leads to greed; something I hated with a passion. I would most definitely keep my promise to Jerome, but once I had reached that goal, what would happen then? I'm happy that this old man intervened when he did, life would have been very different without his input. I always used his line whenever a friend or someone close to me found themselves in the same pickle. He continued speaking to me for another several minutes before his phone rang, but it didn't matter that he left to speak to the Greek person on the other side of the call, the underlying lesson had already been shared.

I lay awake most nights, trying to answer the question he had asked, as I didn't have an answer on the spot. It is extremely difficult to sleep at night leaving something unresolved; something I inherited from Sylvain.

One evening, after a long day of lectures and study, I found myself lying in bed, half asleep, watching my favourite car programme hosted by three British guys. I was about two seconds away from fighting my demons in the dream world when it struck, the answer to the question I had been stuck on for over a week. I realised that I didn't care for money, I didn't care for the status of having an important role in some big firm, nor did I need to be a renowned somebody, all I really wanted was peace. Where I usually found peace was a disturbing realisation, I found peace in the struggle, in the fight, in the strive. I always understood the goal, what the expected outcome was, the lack of support in my corner, that the road may not always be a smooth, flat surface under a clear, blue sky. What made me more confident in myself was the fact that no matter what obstacle was thrown on my path, that I would fight fucking hard to overcome it, and the process of struggling, with the desired outcome in mind, is where I found peace, that's what I wanted to do with my life, to fight against all odds. With that question finally answered, I fell asleep, ready to challenge myself the next day.

The weeks that followed were among the most peaceful moments in my life, I'd be up at 4:30 A.M. every morning, jog down to the harbour which was about three kilometres away, watch the sunrise; there should always be time to admire the beautiful things in the world, jog back, shower, have breakfast, and by 7 A.M., you'd find me in the classroom, ready for my lecture in two hours' time, studying the things I didn't understand. I was always passionate, but this was a whole new level. It was evident in my results that something great was happening. I recall writing an economics test on a warm Wednesday afternoon; I was so used to scoring over 85% on everything, that I wouldn't settle for less, and once I finished the test, I walked up the stairwell beside the class room, where I proceeded to cut my wrists with my bed room key. I felt horrible with my performance in the test, and as the Art of War teaches; 'The goal should be clear, with clarity on rewards and punishments', so, I took to punishing myself for the lousy performance. A week later the test was returned to me, marked and signed by the Professor, I scored 89%; I may have jumped the gun on the punishment part. It's something I don't judge myself for, as *the discipline to follow through on my word was there; but whether it's an actual punishment or not is debatable, as I enjoyed the pain.*

Elliot places the pen down, he doesn't feel any better, and he thought that it would help, but it didn't. He looks at the time, noticing that its 9 P.M. already, the day flew by. He checks his phone before making another meal for himself, but there is no word from Katrien. While the oven pre-heats, he texts her.

'Hey, Katrien, can we please talk about this?' Elliot looks at the previous six messages he's sent, all desperately apologising for anything he did wrong, that he will try be better, but there is no bite from her. Elliot hangs his head in shame, eats his dinner in silence, and calls it a night.

Chapter 18
Happy Endings Are for Fairy Tales

Elliot wakes up to his alarm, gets dressed in a suit and heads to the bathroom to brush his teeth, but refuses to look himself in the eyes. He feels a ton of pressure on his shoulders, between the memories he is forcing himself to go through, losing someone he had opened up to and protected, the feeling of guilt for not visiting his parents when there was time, and for not forgiving them when he should have. A dark depression hits him, he doesn't even need to go to work today, he only starts in another two days, but he doesn't want to be alone, he'd rather do work and get away from this hell. Elliot drives down to work, parks in his spot, and heads up to his office.

Once in the office, Elliot catches up on some emails, and notices that the global head has handed in his resignation. A lucky break? Elliot doesn't smile, as he respects the guy greatly, but is the universe compensating him for his losses? Elliot scrolls through a few more emails, trying to see if someone has replaced the head, but no one has yet. There's hope after all, he has a good feeling about this, he has worked extremely hard for this company, why wouldn't they give it to him? Elliot locks his computer, as per company policy, and heads to the coffee machine to get a cappuccino. Whilst at the machine, Raj, an Indian employee that flew from Bangalore to train staff on a new product, mentions that the CEO of the company is coming in today to announce the new Global head. Elliot is impatient, and counts down the seconds to the announcement.

After lunch, the CEO walks into Elliot's office, along with the current head. "Good afternoon," Elliot firmly says as he stands up to shake their hands.

"How are you, Elliot?" the head asks.

"I'm fine, thanks, and you?" Elliot firmly responds. Normally Elliot would say 'Sir', but he doesn't want it to appear as if he is licking arse to get promoted, so he sticks to a blunt approach, letting his work speak for him; something his quality mentor back in Dublin taught him when he was younger. It would make his mentor so proud if both his prodigies were in chief positions. Jorge, Elliot's best friend, became the COO three years-prior, overlooking the company's European operations, but everyone knew he would get there, and finally Elliot could go back to his mentor and say the same.

"All fine, thanks, Elliot," the head answers, "So Elliot, you know that I have handed in my resignation. I'm getting too old for all of this, and so I decided to retire," he continues, "We need to appoint someone, internally, to take over the role, and this person will be trained in over the next two weeks."

"I just read the email this morning. It saddens me to see you leave after many years of great results," Elliot mentions as he appreciates the work his boss has done.

"Having said that, I just want to let you know that you are one of the candidates we've considered," the man openly tells Elliot.

"Thank you for considering me," Elliot gratefully replies.

"At 3 P.M., we'll have a conference call with all the other candidates and make our choices," the CEO blurts out, informing Elliot. "Everyone has been interviewed, other than you, but it shouldn't be an issue as you worked closely with me," the head tells Elliot.

"Are you sure? I don't mind an interview now, if you have the time," Elliot eagerly responds, he doesn't want to lose this opportunity.

"It should be fine, Elliot," the CEO responds before they greet him and walk off.

3 P.M. arrives, and Elliot is the first person on the conference call. He is riddled with anxiety, but tries relaxing himself. A few people from across the world pop up on the call; Elliot greets them and congratulates them on being considered for the spot. There are a few familiar faces, people he had worked with previously, or seen in other calls. The CEO and Global Head jump onto the call, talk a bit about the role and how they've considered candidates. Performance, results and quick thinking were among the factors they listed. Elliot knows that he hasn't had the best performance compared to this one guy from India, and no one thinks quicker on their feet like that guy from Germany. Elliot can feel himself losing this battle already, but keeps quiet, positively responding to every question.

Forty-five minutes into the call, they finally reveal the person they've chosen, and, it isn't Elliot. It was that guy from Germany. Elliot stays professional, stays on the call and congratulates his new boss. Elliot leaves the call a few minutes later, as do all the other candidates.

Elliot sends an email to his boss, CC-ing his new boss, mentioning that he was going to head home, as he was initially off today. He gets into his car and speeds off, disappointed that once again he wasn't chosen. He knows that the company has a better chance of success with the German than with Elliot, but it's too hard to swallow.

Elliot gets home; kicks his shoes off and decides to once again hit the whiskey.

"Fuck it," he says before taking a sip. It's a dangerous atmosphere, he is severely depressed, angry, and self-harm crosses his mind several times.

In the midst of it all, Katrien is down at the local clinic, getting her 3rd pregnancy test. The first two that she got from the shopping centre both tested positive. Elliot continues writing...

I built up the courage to talk to the Lithuanian girl I was crushing on, and invited her out to a pub for some drinks. We eventually got together a few weeks later and things were looking up for me.

Just as I thought the world was done trying to rape me without lube, mother called... It's never a good sign. Ger had kicked her and Gabriel out of the house in the middle of the night, leaving them to fend for themselves. It's not that I wanted to be there for my mother, she brought this upon herself, it was that I had Gabriel's back no matter what. You can't fucking do that to a nine-year old, who has gone through some of the most uncalled for shit in life, he didn't know who dad was anymore, was confused as to where home was, still had Jerome to cope with, now this homeless factor on top of his own little problems of trying to do good in school? Audrey was in tears, bawling her eyes out over the phone to me, who had this point was putting on his shirt and shoes, to walk over 50 kilometres, all the way up a mountain to kick a former Rhodesian Boxers teeth in. Audrey had tried verbally stopping me several times, but begging me wouldn't work, I prioritised Gabriel's safety and wellbeing first, then hers, then my personal vendetta third. She mentioned that her one friend would take them in until she found a place for herself, so I calmed down and walked back to the university; I was about 750 metres away from the university at that point, following through with my intentions. The next day Audrey and I met up for a coffee, and spoke about what had happened to cause this uproar. I can't recall what exactly the issue was, but what I do remember highlighting in my mind was the fact that Audrey's money was done, and he no longer had a need for her.

 I spoke to Gabriel about the situation too, trying to investigate his feelings and thoughts towards what had happened, but I don't know whether he was completely oblivious to the world around him or if he was extremely good at hiding his feelings, but he didn't come across as the slightest bit worried. Before I set off to have a dinner with Orelija that evening, I offered my mother some money, to help them out a bit, but she was too proud to accept it.

 Weeks went by, and mother seemed to find her feet, managing to feed, clothe and house Gabriel and herself, as well as keeping Gabriel in school. At the time I was practically living with Orelija, what had been simple shag-and-sleep-over, turned into me being there full time, trying to build a true, meaningful relationship, for the first time in my life. Exams were just around the corner. I had hoped that if I did well enough, that the university would have understood my situation and helped me out a bit, so with that wishful thinking in mind, I set out, ready to give it my all.

 Exams were going so well, I was scoring well over 90s for each subject, smoking the other students, but I'm not sure where things went wrong. Orelija and I had had an argument at a beach party one evening, so she broke up with me, I had about two weeks left in my student accommodation and didn't know where I was going after that, and was still struggling to find a job. Caught in the mix was Audrey's situation, I knew she was trying her best, but she needed help; she hadn't really worked in years. After the breakup, I couldn't take the isolative state that I had put myself in, and headed over to Artyoms's room, where he had been playing online games. I knocked on his door, he let me in, and I explained that Orelija had left me after he asked what was wrong in his thick Russian accent. People viewed him very differently compared to how I viewed him, I knew that he was a misunderstood person, trying to work on the pain he had accumulated over the years; he was good at heart and was there for a friend. He didn't really know how to help me regarding the breakup, as he warned me against relationships, "Relationships is shit thing..." he would often say whenever I mentioned Orelija to him. With very few answers to aide me in my situation, he encouraged me to smoke weed with him. I had always been against drugs, but I trusted him when he said it will take the pain away, and honestly, I wanted the pain to go. We went to an undisclosed location, and smoked the devil's lettuce. He was right; it took the physical pain away, eased the thoughts of her, and made my head all fuzzy. I wasn't exactly proud of myself for engaging in the act I had previously considered a scruffy pass time, but I was however happy that I never got addicted to it.

 The two weeks on my student accommodation flew by, and I had no other option but to move in with my mother and little brother. It was dark at first, as I tried starving myself, minimised my shower frequency, and sometimes dehydrated myself, just so that I could see Audrey get by, but she noticed my selfless consideration and told me to just make myself at home, reassuring me that the angels will look after us. Audrey had lost all her faith in the Catholic ways she had spent most of her life teaching her children, and moved towards what most people would consider pagan worship. She started off simple; getting her tea cup read, praying to angels, the non-significant things, but as time went on, she seemed to find some level of satisfaction in it, and started her slow descent into what I was taught was devil worship. I would come home after university, to a house riddled with intense smoke, crystals wherever I looked; on the TV, on the tables, in the fridge, she took to reading her own cups of tea and even acquired a deck of tarot cards; which she eventually made a 'career' from. I contemplated standing up to the hypocrisy; having being condemned for my obsession with metal music and the colour black, but I understood that she was in a tough situation, and that this was probably her body's way of venting the frustrations. While she pursued this scapegoat hobby, I got my job at the hotel back, and started making money again. It wasn't enough to support them the way my father had once supported them, but I contributed to sustaining their lives as best as I could. I never thought that I'd be in a position where I had to look after my mother and little brother, especially not at 19 years old. Between university, work and the rugby I had taken on, I found myself being stretched too thin, demotivated and confused as to where I was headed. I remember sitting on the balcony of Mother's apartment one early morning, with a white coffee cup in my right hand and a fast burning smoke in my left, listening to a motivational video I had found on a video sharing platform online. That woody, musk cigarette stench stained the fresh early morning smell I had fallen in love with, and the warm, milky, coffee taste woke me up. The video was a collection of inspirational people, speaking about the fight, giving advice to those facing up-hill battles, their voices were accompanied by several uplifting background beats, which added to the overall psychological affect. Needless to say, I listened to that specific video nearly every day for the next ten years of my life, sometimes twice a day depending on the situation I was facing.

 A few weeks went by before I acquired the results of my first year in university, and I was proud of myself, I had scored well above the target I had set for each subject, scoring the highest in my year. Work went well too, and things once again started looking up for me, but as the saying goes 'History repeats itself', I anticipated the bad news lurking around the corner. I sat on the red couch Audrey had bought for the apartment, with my report in my hands and hundreds of crystals staring at me; ready to phone my father to share the news of my efforts. The call went well and he was immensely proud of what I had accomplished, despite his disbelief.

 "So...2nd year, Papa...what can we do?" I asked, hinting that I was ready for my 2nd year but that I didn't have enough money to pay for it.

 "Look, Malcolm, I don't have enough money to pay for this year, I did tell you to save. Why don't you ask Mama for money?" he responded. In fairness, he told me to plan for this, and I should have, but how do you save when you're only working a few hours a week on minimum wage? The phone was on loud speaker, and mother heard each word. Audrey looked at me, and awaited the response back to my father, but my head was hung low, with tears in my eyes. I didn't know what to say, I was heartbroken, all I wanted to do was get a degree and make my family proud. My mind raced to find solutions; I always had an answer, but this time I didn't have one.

Bank loans were out of the question, as I didn't make enough money to repay it, I had wealthy family members who definitely didn't like me, so asking them would be pointless, the only other option I had was to directly ask the university if they could sponsor me. I get that during my life, whenever I had mentioned this situation to close friends, the first go to argument would be "Why didn't you get a summer job?" or "Why didn't you just work weekends like we did?" The truth is, South Africa, at the time, had an over 30% unemployment rate, the Black Economic Empowerment law was against me, and being in a boarding school, where I was forbid to leave without permission, all worked against me, but trust me, if I had the opportunity I would have. Hell, I think I even applied to every business in Paphos to no avail.

I approached someone high up in the university; I can't recall what position he held, and asked about bursaries and sponsors.

"Yeah we do offer them to really good students," he mentioned after my enthusiastic question. There was hope after all I thought to myself, I had stressed for nothing, but as life teaches us again and again, never count your chickens... "But the student has to be a Cypriot citizen," he continued after a small pause for air. He had mentioned several other things; which didn't play in my favour, but his words seemed to fade with each passing sentence. Well, shit, what to do now? There was no way in hell that I'd be a barman or waiter for the rest of my life. I laid awake that night, deep in thought, going through my options. It was about 1 A.M., Gabriel was in the bed beside me, snoring loudly; how I missed being that age, before Audrey walked into the apartment. She had finished her third shift as a barmaid at a local pub. I get that I never respected my mother much in life, especially after all the shit, but she did something so inspirational that one has no other option but to respect her. She had taken on two jobs, just so that she could give Gabriel an education and a warm plate of food every night. Some nights she would skip food just so that there was more for us the next day, but I never ate without her. She was a very proud woman, so I know it took a lot out of her when she had to clean toilets in the mornings and get whistled at by men at night. My suggestion to our situation remained the same, returning to South Africa, there we could regroup and re-evaluate our strategy, but she didn't want Sylvain to have the satisfaction of knowing that she needed him, that she was suffering without him. I admire that type of feminism, where the woman will fight hard to prove everyone around her wrong, but the spiteful, vindictive, man-hating philosophy we are subjected to these days is a load of fucking bullshit.

About three weeks went by before the internal battle within was lost, I decided to head back to South Africa, where I would work in the mine, just like my father and all my schoolmates, for the rest of my life, without fail. It was hard, as I didn't want to leave Audrey or Gabriel in a tough spot, I know they needed me more than they had mentioned, but there was nothing here for us, we were going nowhere slowly. Audrey called up the local radio station, and told them that I was headed back to South Africa, they wished me luck over the radio and played an African song mother had dedicated to me. We drove to the airport, walked through the crowds, and just before customs I said a very hard to swallow goodbye. I wished Audrey good luck with everything, and thanked her for taking me in when I had nowhere else to go. I also expressed how much better South Africa would be, but she held on to her pride and I got on the plane.

Elliot is upset...angry...he can't do this anymore, the humiliation is gnawing him, the memories all collide in his mind, and the regrets are just too much. The rain outside is lashing, the whole world seems fucked to him. Elliot reaches for a knife, attempting to cut his wrists, hoping that some level of pain would take the mental and emotional shit away, but it doesn't help. Elliot is already drunk, having finished half a bottle clean whilst writing. Elliot is in a daze, the photos seem to laugh at him, all he can hear is his own voice criticising him for not being good enough, he turns his head to the left, envisioning Katrien running away from him, as if he was some monster, he turns to the right, and he envisions his brother hanging from that chain, with his family all looking at him, condemning him for not saving him.

"Stop!" he shouts out at the apparitions, but they taunt him further. Elliot stumbles towards his bedroom, coughing, nearly choking on his own saliva. He reaches the room, opens the safe and grabs the pistol from above the important papers.

With the 9mm in his hand, he proceeds back to the bottle. The laughter becomes more serious, as if his demons found a way out of his heart and head, and into the real world, where they can torment him constantly.

"Fuck off!" he shouts out at whatever's causing the laughter. He reaches for the bottle of whiskey once again, takes another huge swig, hoping to pass out before he puts the gun to bad use. He doesn't want to go through the thoughts, to script will only get heavier.

Meanwhile, Katrien has her results; she is pregnant with Elliot's child. She is still contemplating how to break the news to Elliot, but she's sure he would be happy; he seems like the kind of guy that wants to be a father.

Elliot takes the safety from the gun off, and places it to his head. In that moment, the laughter and mocking stops and all he can hear is the rain falling outside, the strong wind blowing, creeping through the nooks and crannies of his home. He can feel the pulse of his racing heart against the shaft of the cold weapon, his sweat drips onto the metal, staining it in the process. Elliot lowers the gun, thinking that it's all over, but the voices return a few seconds later, as if they're pushing him to do it. He picks up the pen, and starts writing...

> *A hard roof over my head*
> *A huge empty house*
> *I choose to sit here scared*
> *As silent as a mouse*
> *Hiding from the rain*
> *Falling hard above me*
> *Dripping from the windows*
> *Trying to find my seat*
>
> *My hands clench my ears*
> *I try to out scream the memories*
> *The pain accumulated over the years*
> *This wasn't supposed to be my legacy*

Come home! Please
Anyone, I need you!
But I'm responded by a cold breeze
From under the door it crept through
The photos laugh so loud
Mocking my life long choices
The emotions have me bowed
Forced to listen to the voices

A 9mm in the hand, a perfect fit
It was all a load of shit
I whisper to myself this is it
Here I openly admit
It's time to quit
To the gun I submit

Sincerely signed;
Elliot

Elliot pulls the trigger in sync with the loud sound of the thunder outside, honouring his pact with his brother before the booze can kill him.

Katrien feels the excitement growing in her belly, eager to tell Elliot. She phones him but he doesn't answer. *Not a problem*, she positively thinks to herself, *I'll just drive up and tell him to his face, things like these are better off face-to-face*. Katrien drives in the rain, not regretting her choice, anxious to share this news with the man she now wants to spend forever with. She opens the big gate and continues up the path to the house. Once she arrives at the house, she jumps out of the car and runs up the few stairs leading up to the porch, despite the rain falling on her. She knocks on the door, but he doesn't answer, but luckily the door is unlocked.

"Elliot!" she yells out over the loud creek the door lets out. She doesn't hear a thing, and walks in. Something on the right catches her eye, and there she sees Elliot, in a huge puddle of blood, next to the handgun he had passed her just the other day.

"No!" She screams out as her body starts shaking with fear. In the midst of the madness she calls an ambulance and the police.

She kneels beside his body, drenching her stockings in his blood, crying out.

"You can't be gone, Elliot, you're going to be a daddy. We're going to be a family. Wake up please, I'm Sorry!" but Elliot doesn't respond.

Police and paramedics arrive on the scene, and pronounce Elliot dead on the spot, the cause of death being suicide; a single bullet to the right temple. The officers are concerned for Katrien's mental health, and tell her to go home, to get away from the scene.

"He was supposed to be a father!" she cries out as they try pulling her away, but none of the people on duty understand how she feels. One female officer, that appears to be on standby, walks her out of the house, and tries comforting her on the porch. Katrien's tears drench the officer's shoulders, but the officer knows that words can't help at this point, but she does offer Katrien a lift back home, or somewhere better.

The two of them get into the car, and drive down the path way towards the big gate. The driver indicates left after Katrien mentions where she stays. "Let's listen to some music to lighten the mood," the officer suggests as she turns on the radio, hoping to kill the silence and help Katrien cope a bit better. *'Crazy... I'm crazy for feeling...so lonely,'* the radio lets out as the car disappears into the darkness.